Tuesday Night
AT THE BLUE MOON

Tuesday Night
AT THE BLUE MOON

DEBBIE FULLER THOMAS

MOODY PUBLISHERS
CHICAGO

Editor: LB Norton
Interior Design: Ragont Design
Cover Design: Chris Gilbert, Gearbox (studiogearbox.com)
Cover Image of People: Michele Constantini/Veer

Library of Congress Cataloging-in-Publication Data

Thomas, Debbie Fuller, 1955-
Tuesday night at the Blue Moon / Debbie Fuller Thomas.
p. cm.
ISBN-13: 978-0-8024-8733-9 (alk. paper)
ISBN-10: 0-8024-8733-5 (alk. paper)
1. Mothers and daughters—Fiction. 2. Infants switched at birth—Fiction. 3. Single mothers—Fiction. 4. Birthparents—Fiction. 5. Domestic fiction. I. Title.

PS3620.H6266T84 2008
813'.6—dc22

2008000047

We hope you enjoy this book from Moody Publishers. Our goal is to provide high-quality, thought-provoking books and products that connect truth to your real needs and challenges. For more information on other books and products written and produced from a biblical perspective, go to www.moodypublishers.com or write to:

Moody Publishers
820 N. LaSalle Boulevard
Chicago, IL 60610

1 3 5 7 9 10 8 6 4 2

Printed in the United States of America

CHAPTER 1

Marty

We weren't strangers to this courtroom. The first time we came, it was to petition to have Ginger's hospital birth records opened. When you lose a child to a genetic disease that doesn't haunt your family, you want to know why.

Two female Caucasian babies were born on the night of October 31, 1994, at Interfaith Hospital. DNA samples confirmed that the precious child I'd buried two years ago wasn't mine, and that Andrea Hayley Lockhart was actually my biological child.

Now Andie sat across the courtroom wedged between her grandparents, blonde head tucked, jaw clenched in anger, eyes darting in dread. Avoiding my side of the room. She took my breath away, she was so beautiful. Quicksilver. A perfect amalgam of Deja and Winnie, my other daughters. There was no question that she belonged to us.

We weren't trying to replace the child we'd lost, though the thought clawed my protective grief on sleepless nights. No one could replace Ginger.

I hadn't just lost her physically. The minute the birth records were opened, I lost *possession* of her. Sole ownership. At least I never had to hand her over to strangers.

Dad sat beside me doodling a perfect likeness of Andie on the manila folder stuffed with evidence that argued our right to disrupt her life. I squeezed his arm gently, so my nails wouldn't pinch. Though we wanted Andie desperately, we only wanted the best for her and would accept whatever judgment the court handed down. She wasn't a bone to be fought over by Dobermans.

Was it right to take Andie away from her grandparents? I wasn't sure until I saw her picture in the tabloids. Her face side by side with Ginger's had framed my gut instinct that something had always been slightly out of focus.

I sneaked furtive glances across the courtroom. Andie chewed her nails, one knee pumping and bouncing. The grandmother touched Andie's knee, and her leg stilled. When Andie looked up, the grandmother's eyes lingered on her face. They had no need for words.

People filed in, blocking my view. The odors of stale tobacco and sweat intensified along with the crowd and the heat, aggravating my nerves, adding to the tension in my neck from straining to catch glimpses of Andie.

What a shame, the way the grandmother dressed her. Andie's skirt and blouse could have been sewn from my mother's vintage fabrics tucked away with her treadle sewing machine. There was a talcum-powder look about her, as though in the years since she'd lost her parents she had soared over adolescence, skimmed the surface waters of adulthood, and come to rest with her grandparents in their rocking chairs on the far shore. It couldn't be healthy in a girl of thirteen.

I glimpsed the familiar, unwelcome Mia Cross seated directly behind Andie. Mia was a local reporter who'd covered Ginger's struggle with Niemann-Pick for the paper the year before she died, and hounded us for interviews when she learned about the baby switch. She'd obviously chosen her next victim.

The judge entered from a side door and took his seat. Voices fell to a whisper. The bailiff called case after case, moving us closer to our own. A woman sought a restraining order against her boyfriend. A father requested shared custody with his child's mother. A single mom wanted to garnish her ex-husband's wages for child support.

A uniformed sheriff waited at the door as a reminder to keep things civilized.

A man at the end of our row squeezed past, and when I untangled my legs to let him through, my skirt twisted against the velveteen seat cushions. I wore the navy suit I'd bought for Ginger's funeral. The polyester blend was more suited to that rainy spring morning than this blistering July afternoon. I touched a tissue to my forehead and chin, wishing the humming electric fan faced us instead of the judge.

The bailiff called our case. Dad gave me a nod of encouragement, and I got to my feet, managing to keep my balance in three-inch heels while clutching the folder to my chest and straightening my skirt one-handed.

We sat at the attorney's table before the judge's bench. I took the farthest chair, putting our attorney, Martin Walker, between Andie's grandfather and me. Mr. Walker smoothed his tie into his jacket front and leaned toward me, smelling like the fragrance counter at Nordstrom.

"We're in good shape," he whispered, his breath minty fresh. "The grandfather is diabetic, and his kidneys are failing. Word is he's looking at dialysis before the year is out." He tugged at his jacket sleeves to make them even. "I don't think the uncle will be a problem either. He's got DUIs in California and Oregon. We'll use it if we have to." He winked, like that was a good thing.

What would Andie think of our vilifying her family? I felt an overwhelming urge to bake. Oatmeal cookies. Coconut dandies. Molasses joes with crystallized ginger.

The attorney tapped his notes into a perfect rectangle and cleared his throat. A sweating white carafe tempted me; the paper cups were within my reach, but I knew I'd never keep my hands from shaking.

We were sworn in by the bailiff while Judge Goodman spread out the paperwork before him. As he studied the file his jowls sagged, creasing his face like a bulldog's. He glanced up in Andie's direction and then over to us. "This is quite a difficult case. Unusual."

He flipped through the papers, studying one in particular and rubbing his chin. He looked over the top of his glasses, throwing dark shadows into his eye sockets and brows. He addressed the grandparents.

"Mr. James, you and your wife received guardianship of Andrea as maternal grandparents when your daughter and son-in-law perished in a hotel fire approximately three years ago. Is that correct?"

"Yes, Your Honor."

"And did the paternal grandparents express any interest in shared custody at that time?"

"No, sir, they didn't. It was all just too painful, I guess, and their health was bad. They send Andie cards now and then. Birthdays and such."

"I see," the judge said, referring again to his file. "At the time you resided on Dancing Dog Way. You now live at Whispering Pines Estates. Is that a housing development?"

"Well, no, sir."

The judge looked up, the unanswered question still between them.

"It's a mobile home park, Your Honor."

"Would that be a senior park, by any chance?"

The grandfather tried to clear his phlegmy throat, but it only pitched his voice up an octave. "Uh, you see, Your Honor . . ."

The judge's head dipped down again to pin the grandfather.

"Yessir," he admitted. "Fifty-five and older."

Judge Goodman steepled his fingers. "Has Andrea been residing there with the knowledge and consent of park management?"

I stole a glance at the grandfather. His knobby hands picked at the papers before him.

"No, sir. They don't know about her living with us. Leastways, they didn't until it come out in the paper. We just didn't know what else to do, is all."

"How long has she lived at the mobile home park with you and Mrs. James?"

"We moved in about a year and six months ago, I reckon."

The judge's eyebrows lifted, briefly easing the shadows on his face. "That's a long time to hide a young girl in a senior park."

"She's no trouble, Your Honor, and our—"

The judge held up his hand. "Please don't elaborate, Mr. James. We don't want to create hardship for any neighbors who may or may not have been aware of your arrangement."

"No, sir. We sure don't."

"And now that park management has been alerted to her presence, will they allow Andrea to continue living there?"

"No, sir, they won't." He tried again unsuccessfully to clear his throat.

I heard others in the courtroom do the same.

"We're gonna sell and buy a house so Andie can stay with us. The lady realtor said she already has some folks interested."

My attorney inclined his head to me and whispered, "It'll never happen. It will be a contingency sale, and they'll never have enough for the down payment in that market."

Real estate was booming in the foothills, with retirees from the Bay Area and Sacramento scooping up land for mini-mansions. The grandparents were headed for deep water, and Andie was a passenger.

"How much longer will they allow Andrea to reside at the park?" the judge asked.

"They give us till the end of the month. That's all." He sounded fragile. Heartbroken.

I sat immobile, sensing disapproving eyes on my back.

"Thank you, Mr. James." Judge Goodman sifted through the paperwork again and turned his attention to me.

A bead of sweat trickled down to my collarbone.

"Mrs. Winslow, you are petitioning for custody of Andrea; is that correct?"

"Yes, Your Honor."

"You are her biological mother?"

My attorney spoke up. "She is, Your Honor. My client has submitted a copy of the birth records from the hospital. The DNA results are attached."

The judge flipped through his file and stopped. He tapped his pen as he read. "Andrea was switched at birth with Ginger Celeste Winslow, the biological granddaughter of Mr. and Mrs. James. The child has since passed away due to terminal illness." He glanced at me apologetically. "This was how long ago?"

He'd touched a nerve, referring to Ginger as their granddaughter, and I fought the urge to correct him. The attorney inclined his head to me, silently prodding.

"One year and four months," I managed to say, "next Tuesday."

"Please accept the court's condolences. We know this is difficult. Who else is currently living in the home?"

"My father, Carl McAlister, and my two daughters, Deja and Winnie."

"What are the ages of your daughters?"

"They're fifteen and nine."

He looked through the bottom of his glasses at his paperwork, frowning. "That would place Andrea between them in birth order." He looked up over his glasses at me. "How do they feel about the possibility of adding another family member so soon after their loss?"

"My youngest is happy. Very excited. My oldest is dealing with the usual teenage . . . stuff."

My attorney pressed his fist to his mouth and lightly cleared his throat in warning.

"She'll come around," I added, forcing a smile.

A flicker of doubt crossed the judge's face.

"Is Andrea's father a party to this custody petition?"

"No, sir. I have sole legal custody of my girls. I share joint physical custody with him, but he never sees them."

That can't be good, I realized, introducing an unknown entity like Russell.

"What is the arrangement for child visitation?"

"He has summers and alternate holidays. But he never asks to take them, Your Honor. They haven't seen him in years." I was glad Deja and Winnie weren't in the courtroom to hear that admission. Starr would make sure he never saw the girls again, if it was in her power to do so. "He's remarried. He lives in Elko."

"So there's no restraining order that the court should be aware of?"

"No, sir."

"Your address is Newberry?"

"My father owns a home there. We live with him."

"And it has adequate living space for three siblings?"

I blinked. "Yes, sir. Your Honor, sir."

"Do you anticipate a change in your living arrangements in the near future?"

"No, sir. We operate a business on the property. A drive-in theater. It's my dad's retirement."

"A drive-in." He nodded. "Is there another source of income?"

"I'm a checker at Shop 'n Save. I've been there a little over a year."

He studied the file and flipped pages back and forth. His pen tapped, then stilled. He removed his glasses and rubbed his eyes, repositioning his frames on the bridge of his nose. He made notations, then looked up, briefly making eye contact with each of us.

"As I've said before, this is a very difficult case, and the court must consider all ramifications and decide what action is in Andrea's best interest. I have spoken with her, and I'm aware that she wishes to remain with her grandparents. However, due to the uncertainty of a suitable living environment, I'm temporarily removing her from the James household."

An adult gasped, then a loud whisper, "No way!"

"Andrea will remain in the custody of the biological mother, Matilda Winslow, sharing alternate school holidays with the maternal grandparents, Orville and Evelyn James. A review hearing will be set for six months from now. If in that time the grandparents provide proof of a suitable home, I will then consider her adjustment to the Winslow household and make a final determination."

He looked at me pointedly over his glasses. "Mrs. Winslow, a worker will be in contact with you periodically. If you take Andrea out of the area for any reason, for a week or longer, please leave an itinerary with Family Court Services."

I nodded, not hearing the rest. A rush of elation had left me light-headed. Andie was *ours*. Maybe temporarily, and there were strings attached, but nothing we couldn't overcome. I tried to remain calm and keep the smile off my face.

The future was like an unwritten recipe of the known and the unknown, or a new take on rhubarb pie. If you add in enough of the sweet stuff, and you expect it to be a little tart, it can turn out well.

I leaned over to the attorney. All threats of DUIs and dialysis blissfully erased. "Thank you, Mr. Walker. So much."

"You're welcome," he said, shoving his notes into his briefcase. "But it's not over yet. My office will contact you again before the hearing in six months."

I got to my feet, and he herded me back toward the seating area.

"In the meantime, everything had better be rosy when the worker drops by for visitation. If you decide to keep her."

I turned to find Andie and her grandparents already heading toward the exit, with Mia close behind. Well-rehearsed words stuck in my throat. Things I'd imagined saying at this time. *I'll take good care of her. I want her to be happy. I'm not taking her away from you.*

Mrs. James leaned heavily against her husband with Andie's arm threaded around her waist, struggling to stay linked like a severed chain. Andie glanced over her shoulder, her head bobbing up and down with the grandmother's uneven gait, searching for me. For a moment, my hopes rose. But her eyes focused, narrowed, and pierced me. I raised my hand to the sting on my cheek.

Dad and I followed at a distance while the attorney explained the custody decision in finer detail. I trusted Dad to catch it all.

Several reporters accosted them outside the courtroom. Kids are a sure sell. Mia's nasally voice pitched above the others, shouting questions that no self-respecting person would ask. For that reason and others, we no longer took the *Times*—not even the weekend edition.

We slipped away, heads down, giving the reporters a wide berth. Dad swatted at one hovering reporter, who gave up getting a statement from us and joined the swarm around Andie and her grandparents.

Dad and I spoke little on the way home. It seemed mean-spirited to celebrate someone's loss, even if it meant our gain. Dad said August 19 was the day the grandparents had to hand Andie over to us. I told him I would go alone to get her.

We stopped at the Shop 'n Save to pick up molasses and butter on the way. I slid wordlessly out of the car and went in alone. Practically everyone there knew why I'd taken the day off, and when the automatic doors opened, I hesitated. I considered turning around and heading back to the car, but I needed to use my employee discount. The complications in our case had the attorney fees splitting and multiplying like sourdough starter on steroids.

Jo caught sight of me where I stood at the entrance in my suit and heels. She turned off the light at her checkout stand, came over and grabbed me by the arms, and dragged me to a quiet corner.

"So, spill it. What happened?"

I took a deep breath, licked my lips, and said the words aloud for the first time. "We got Andie." I held my breath, waiting for the dream to burst like a child's bubble on a plastic wand, but it didn't. We screamed and hugged each other as if we were fifteen again.

Jo got on the intercom—honest to goodness—and announced it to everyone in the store before I could stop her. Scattered applause and whistles filtered back. Most of Newberry's population had read in the papers about their local celebrity switched-at-birth kid, and most had their own opinions. Customers in the checkout lines craned their necks to gawk at me, shifting impatiently, their arms overflowing with purchases and squirming kids. Some were clearly annoyed, others openly complaining.

"Oh, whadda they know," Jo said. "Pearls before swine . . ."

At home I got the expected reactions from the girls. Winnie, my little Pollyanna, squealed with delight, pocketed a handful of cookies, and went to work on a welcome sign. Deja, my firstborn rebel-without-a-cause, said, "This is wrong. This is just wrong," and set up a command post in her room with the phone. From there she spread the word to every friend at Gale Langford High School what a dirt clod of a mother she had.

At dusk the girls and I helped Dad with the drive-in just like it was any other evening. Every drippy cheese tray and dirty pizza pan was a joy to me. After the last feature, we shook Winnie awake enough to guide her back toward the house, lumbering along, savoring the coolness of the night, relieved that the hearing was now behind us.

I tucked Win into my bed on Russell's empty side and went out to the kitchen, too wired to sleep. I threw molasses, eggs, flour, and shortening together for molasses joes while listening to oldies on the radio. A balmy breeze ruffled the curtain. As I wondered what the future would hold for us, a big yellow moon, low on the horizon, winked at me through the birch tree, illuminating the backyard. The second full moon in a month—a proverbial blue moon.

Surely a good sign.

Somehow, even then, I sensed that Andie's coming would define the edges of my night and draw me back like a spring tide to the shores of the living.

CHAPTER 2

Andie

If my life was a made-for-TV movie it would start this same way, with the monster truck pulling up in front of Grandma's and this Barbie-wannabe getting out with the blonde hair clipped all messy on the back of her head. Fakey smile plastered on her face, lime-green flip-flops, flowered board shorts that nobody wears anymore, and a screen print of the Eiffel Tower on her tank top.

Like she's ever been to France.

That would be my life—my new life.

She slammed the door of the truck and tugged at her shorts like they were giving her a wedgie, then slipped her wrist through a huge key ring like the one Barney Fife hangs up on the wall so Otis can get out of jail any time he wants. I know because Grandma and Grandpa don't have cable, and we watch a jillion reruns.

The keys jingled when she pulled off her sunglasses. Her long nails, like slices of tangerine, clicked and clawed at the lenses when she wiped them on her shirttail.

I guess she wanted a good look at me. She was my new mom.

My biological mom. She was the reason I had to leave Grandma and Grandpa. I'd sneaked a peek at her at court when she wasn't looking—she looked like a flight attendant in that suit and French braid. Which one was the real her?

She inspected her sunglasses and stuck them on top of her head, which made her even taller. No wonder I was taller than every boy in my class—I was from a tribe of Amazons.

Imagine, you wake up one day and someone tells you your parents were given the wrong bundle at the hospital, like the tags were switched on a gift under the Christmas tree, and this stranger claims you. You wouldn't believe it either.

She tried to smile, but the corners of her mouth just curled up, sort of Grinchy.

"Hello, Andrea," she said.

"AnDRAYa." I hate it when people get my name wrong.

"Oops—sorry." She gave a nervous little shrug, shaking her head.

Grandma and Grandpa didn't say anything to her, but Grandma's hand on my shoulder squeezed like a vise. They just let her stand there. It got . . . awkward.

She looked up at us on the porch with sad eyes like a puppy that's been swatted with the newspaper and doesn't know why. Something told me she wasn't faking it.

Okay, so sometimes I exaggerate.

It wasn't really a monster truck, and maybe she wasn't a low-life or a carny. Even though I wanted her to be. Maybe she was just trying too hard or something.

Grandma says my middle name should be Grace because it's hard for me to be mean to people, although I was really trying and I had a primo reason.

I shifted my feet. "Just 'Andie.' "

She nodded and smiled kind of bashfully. "I'm Marty."

Grandpa shuffled up close beside me, stretching up to his full height. "Little missy," he said with his voice quivering, "this here's a temporary arrangement. Don't you get used to having Andie around."

That's my grandpa, fighting for me already.

He sniffed, like he smelled something bad. "We have an attorney, and he'll be talking to you directly."

She put a hand on her hip and looked down at her bright orange toenails. She might have been counting to ten. I think her lips were moving. Then she cleared her throat and looked me in the eye. "I guess there's no easy way to do this," she said to me, as though Grandma and Grandpa weren't even there. "Is your stuff packed?"

I jerked my thumb at the pile of boxes on the porch behind me, feeling like a traitor.

She dusted imaginary dirt from her hands. "I'll load up the truck."

She came right up the steps, and we shuffled backward on the porch out of her way. She squeezed past without touching, and I got a whiff of cookie dough. When she bent down to pick up my box, the backside of her shorts strained at the seam. Dangerously. I looked away from the imprint of her lacy bikinis. Grandma snorted fire on the back of my neck.

"We're not giving up," Grandma said. "Andie belongs with us. She is *our* granddaughter."

Marty paused with my Procter & Gamble box full of books resting against her knee. She so totally expected this.

"Mrs. James, I'm sorry. But we've been through this on the phone already. The courts decided what was best for Andie, not us."

That's not the way I overheard it. One day Grandma told my Uncle Greg on the phone that Marty was putting up a fight for me for some insurance money and for my part of the settlement. Whatever that was. I figured that Grandma must be confused. I didn't have any money, or they would just buy another house so we could stay together.

Marty hefted the box and headed for the truck.

Grandma wobbled like an unstable rocket on a launchpad. Then she blew. "You're sorry, are you? Girlie, you're not sorry one bit. You got another child for the one you lost."

Marty jerked like she'd been punched. Two points for Grandma. Then she sagged onto the box with her back to us and fumbled with her sunglasses to jab them back on her face.

She loaded my last box and suitcase and slammed the tailgate. Turning to us with her eyes shaded behind reflective lenses, she folded her arms and then unfolded them to hang by her sides. Her lips were just a slash on her face, and her wrist jingled the key ring against her thigh.

It's funny the things you notice at a time like that. The Mickey Mouse dangling from her key ring had a stupid grin. Didn't he know what was going on?

"Andie," she said to me, "you can come back for Thanksgiving and Christmas both, and you can call your grandparents any time you want. Any time. If you want to spend some weekends up here, it's no problem. But we have to go. Please say good-bye." She turned and marched back to the truck.

All the air squeezed out of me like Grandpa's wheezy accordion. This was *it*. How did this day come so fast? I'd used every trick I knew to slow down time, trying to stall till we got a call that it was all a huge mistake or just a bad dream. But the juju didn't work, and suddenly I felt responsible for Grandma and Grandpa's pain. My stomach churned. If I didn't do something I was gonna hurl, or worse.

I turned and hugged their necks, breathing in White Shoulders and tobacco, which Grandpa wasn't supposed to have. Trying to hold it together, for them. They clung to me like they were losing me forever. I knew if I had a meltdown, it would just be harder on them. For their sake, it was best if I left without making a scene. It was only temporary, I chanted in my head.

"Andie," Marty called gently from the truck. "Time to go."

I kept my back to her. "I'll be okay, I promise." I smoothed down Grandma's collar and didn't look them in the eyes. "Don't worry. I'll write you lots of letters, and I'll call you every day. I'll come home soon."

It's a good thing I reached out for the porch railing. My eyes filled up and I couldn't see the steps, so I tripped on a loose board and a splinter jabbed into my hand and I almost landed on my face. What a geek.

I tossed my backpack into the truck cab, climbed in after it, and looked back through the window at Grandma and Grandpa, holding on to every last second. It hurt so bad I couldn't breathe. Why did I have to go? First my parents, and now Grandma and Grandpa. It wasn't fair! Who would take care of them now?

They blurred into a watery puddle, and I wiped my eyes as we pulled away. The Crown Realty sign hung like a red smudge in a corner of the yard between their mobile home and Mrs. DeMarco's. That sign was my only hope. It hung next to Bilbo, the lawn gnome. "There and back again" had worked for Bilbo; I would come back again too.

And then they were out of sight.

Marty sniffed and wiped her eyes under her sunglasses with her knuckle. I saw it out of the corner of my eye. What in the world did she have to cry about? I scrunched as close as I could to my door, putting lots of space between us.

We inched over speed bumps, one big wheel sliding over at a time, until we came to the entrance of the mobile home park. Harve stood up and shouted something as we went by, waving his beer can. I almost waved back, but I stopped when I saw his face. Wow. Grown-ups get really cranky when they're scammed by kids.

"Who's that?" Marty asked.

"That's just Harve," I said, pretending it didn't bother me. I looked back through the window at him. "He's the park manager. His uncle owns it."

She watched Harve in the rearview mirror. "What's with him?" Marty asked. He was standing in the middle of the road shouting and making rude gestures.

"I think he got in a lot of trouble when the reporters found out I was living here."

She snorted. "I'll bet he did." She slowed at the gate, then catapulted the truck into traffic. The little hula dancer suctioned to the dash spasmed. "The reporters really hounded us. How about you?"

"Yeah. Grandma hit one of them with the car."

Marty's head whipped around. "With that Lincoln? Did she kill him?"

"Just his foot. I mean, she broke it. He was hiding in the bushes, and when we got in the car to go to Safeway, he jumped out to take my picture through the window. Grandma got confused and hit the gas by mistake."

I hated that reporter. He made Grandma feel like dirt, yelling at her in front of all the neighbors when it was his own stupid fault. "She was always afraid somebody would jump out in front of the car after that."

"Your sis—" She stopped and cleared her throat. "I mean, Deja was in PE, and the school had to call the police on some of them." Marty shook her head. "As if she'd let them photograph her running laps." She caressed her cheek with her long, fruity nails. "I think I saw that photo, now that you mention it. It was a side view. You were looking down at something."

"I was looking for coupons."

Her head tilted like a little bird's. "Coupons?"

"I always tear them out of the newspaper before we go to Safeway. And then I organize them in this little organizer-pocket-thing." It sounded like a dumb thing for an almost eighth-grader to do. And I wasn't there to do that dumb little thing for Grandma anymore.

Looking out my window, I promised myself that it was okay, 'cause they were gonna get me back. Grandma and Grandpa promised to buy another house so we could move out of the senior park, and we already had an attorney. We couldn't lose.

I didn't feel like talking any more. She might be a nice person and all, but it wasn't fair what was happening to me. The judge could make me go, but he couldn't make me be part of their family. And he couldn't *ever* make me call her *Mom*. I picked at the splinter, ignoring how much it stung, and sucked my palm to stop the bleeding.

"Hey, you feel like cinnamon rolls? Maybe I'll throw some together when we get home. How's that sound?"

I knew it was rude to keep my back to her, but I just couldn't look at her. I shrugged my shoulder, feeling loneliness like a ball of dough already lodged in my throat.

Marty turned the radio to an oldies station and hummed along.

I rolled my window all the way down and rested my chin on the V of my elbow, closing my eyes. Hot wind whipped my hair around my face, making a veil to hide behind.

The truck's tires made a thwapping sound on the twisty, bumpy road down from Pine Run. When I was little I used to think the road was built by the Romans, because I've seen some Roman roads and they're just as bad.

It's funny that I fell asleep, because I've never been able to sleep on road trips. By age eight I believed I could keep us safe by staying awake and alert, just like Mom. It wasn't that she didn't trust my dad's driving; she was just a worrier. We had this great telepathy—like two minds working together could keep the driver from slipping over the edge of sleep.

I don't remember when I first started feeling responsible for controlling things. Dad said it was my defense mechanism when things went bad, my way of staying in charge, but it didn't work where my parents were concerned. Besides, they didn't ask my permission before they took that vacation in Cabo.

Maybe it would have been different if they had let me go to Mexico with them. When they left, I was mad at them for going on a getaway without me. And when they didn't come back, I wondered if "getaway" was code for ditching me. It was easier to think they were jetting around the world having fun and would come back one day, sorry for leaving me behind, instead of facing the truth. That's how kids think. But I finally realized my ability to control things was bogus. A kid has no power at all.

Anyway, I gave in to the tires' thwapping spell. Maybe I fell asleep because I didn't really care if we careened over the edge and I woke up in heaven. The wind left me with severe cotton mouth and drool on my arm, which I secretly wiped on my sleeve so Marty wouldn't see me slobbering like a two-year-old.

When you shake yourself awake, there's this blip in time. A whole stretch of highway is gone, and you have no memory of anything in between. A chunk of your life came up missing when you weren't looking. That's what it felt like when I finally realized my parents weren't coming back.

We were almost down the hill to Sacramento. "Down the hill" is what people in our town called the long drive to the valley. It was Africa hot. Cars cut in front of one another on the freeway like kids in line for the Tilt-a-Whirl. The houses were packed so close together, they didn't even have yards.

We took the exit that said Newberry and passed strip malls, movie theaters, and fast food. The town was crowded and dirty with weeds in the sidewalks and trash in the gutters, just like I expected. Then the truck slowed. The blinker flashed.

"Ever been to a drive-in movie?" Marty asked.

Ahead of us I saw a huge blue-and-yellow crescent-shaped sign with BLUE MOON DRIVE-IN and GODZIL-A – 9 PM, THE WEDDING SINGER – 11:30 pM in mixed-up letters. It was the middle of the afternoon, in broad daylight, but she turned in just like she owned the place. The giant tattered screen was like something out of an old horror movie where the kids are making out in the backseat until the mass murderer sneaks up and knifes them.

"I thought drive-ins were extinct," I said.

"Yeah, it's too bad. It's hard to compete with big cineplexes. All that stadium seating and those high-backed rocking chairs. Here, your seat's only as comfortable as your car." She laughed at her little joke. "But our pizza's better than theirs."

"Why would anybody want to go to a drive-in? I mean, when you can just go inside?" Then I felt mean because it sounded snotty, and that's *so* not me.

She kept her eyes straight ahead and didn't say anything for a minute. Then she said, "Well, you can bring a whole carload of kids and spread blankets on the parking lot, or set up porta-cribs.

Pack a cooler, or stop by the Colonel's for chicken. The kids can run around; they don't have to stay cooped up in their seats if they get bored. I guess you could say we're family friendly."

We drove slowly across the parking lot, which was a gut buster. The cracked asphalt sprouted thick weed-hair and broken speaker poles like toothless combs. At the back of the parking lot sat a small building with SNACK SHACK painted across it in blue.

She passed the building and kept going. "Dad . . . um . . . *my* dad, shows classic Westerns once a month. This month he's got *The Man Who Shot Liberty Valance*. You know that movie, with Jimmy Stewart and John Wayne?"

"Na-uh. But I heard a song on the radio once."

"The song was written for the movie, but it's not in the soundtrack."

We pulled into a hidden driveway in the bushes and parked behind a green Toyota with duct tape over the right taillight. Maybe she did own the place.

"We're open every night during the summer. Sometimes we feature oldies, as you can see from the marquee. The movies change every two weeks. Tuesday night is family bargain night. It's only four dollars a car."

Marty got out and flipped open the truck bed. "Come on in the house."

Baby blue was kind of cheesy for a house color, but at least it didn't look like Freddy Krueger lived there. Islands of flowers floated in old tires around the yard. A million wind chimes hung from the porch and tangled in the breeze.

The screen door opened, and a pudgy blonde girl came out.

"Hi, sweetheart," Marty said, draping an arm around her. "This is AnDRAYa," she said. "But she wants to be called Andie." To me she said, "This is Winnie. She's the baby."

The girl grinned, half hiding behind her mom. Her eyebrows were so white they almost disappeared into her face, making her eyelids look spring-loaded.

Marty held the door open for me to enter, but I looked back at the truck that held everything that was still mine.

"Don't worry about your things. Carl will bring them in," she said.

We stepped into the house. It was decorated with horses and cowboys, with a wagon-wheel light fixture hanging from the ceiling.

A one-eyed black cat sharpened its claws on a corner of the sofa. Of course, there would be a cat. I sneezed.

Marty gathered up shoes and clothes lying on the floor, opened a door down the hallway, and tossed them in. "Deja, come out here," she said into the room.

This girl followed Marty out to the living room. A total Goth. Black fingernails, eyes caked with white shadow, black lipstick, cropped blonde hair streaked with black. She looked totally bored, and had a phone crammed into her neck.

"What?" she said.

Marty said to me, "This is Deja. You'll be sharing her room."

"No way!" Deja jolted to life and fumbled the phone. "She can sleep with Winnie! She never sleeps in her room anyway. I just got mine the way I want it."

Marty gave her that universal mother look.

"Deja, we discussed this. Winnie will be sleeping in her own room from now on, and it's too small for two beds. If you want to trade rooms with her, you can. Otherwise, you'll be sharing with Andie."

Deja gave me a look that could kill, like the whole thing was my fault, then went to her—our—room and slammed the door. I seriously considered sleeping on the couch with the creepy one-eyed cat.

Where did she get the name Deja anyway? Déjà vu? Did Marty just open the dictionary, close her eyes, and point to a word?

A man leaned against the kitchen doorjamb, watching the whole thing. At first I thought he was Marty's husband—my dad—and I forgot to breathe. But he was way too old. His hair was gray, and the skin on his face had white stubble like the soft pricklies of a windowsill cactus. He wore an Oakland A's T-shirt tucked into faded blue jeans with a big silver belt buckle, and a toothpick in his mouth moved side to side as he looked me over.

"She favors Russell," he said, like I wasn't even hearing it.

Marty sighed and looked at me, kind of dreamy. "Yeah, she does. More than Deja."

He sucked his toothpick, and then he plucked it out of his mouth. "I'm your grandpa, Carl," he said.

I tried hard to keep my chin from quivering. "My grandpa's in Pine Run." It came out snotty, and as soon as I said it I felt like a brat. But what could I do? It was the truth.

He put the toothpick back in his mouth and nodded. Marty touched him on the arm, and they exchanged a look as we walked on through. She asked him to get my boxes. I knew they'd be talking about me later, behind my back.

The kitchen counter was loaded with baked stuff. It was everywhere. Cookies and brownies and muffins. I got this sick feeling that maybe they'd planned some kind of celebration because of me. There was no way I was going to celebrate anything.

The rest of the house was small with puddles of junk on the tables and counters. Stacks of mail were shoved into corners, so I figured out that the house never got any cleaner than this. It was all a show for me. An ancient computer sat on a desk with *maybe* enough memory to hold my homework. Family pictures hung on the wall, and the eyes followed me when I walked by. I was pretty sure the cat had taken an unauthorized potty break somewhere on the carpet, but I didn't know much about cats. My sinuses swelled like a pop-up sponge.

"Do you have a cold?" she asked.

I shook my head. "I'm allergic to cats."

"Oh." Her shoulders sagged slightly. "You're allergic. Well, then." She looked around, unsure of what to do, but then she scooped up the one-eyed cat. "Sorry, Cyclops," she said. "You've been evicted." She rubbed a noogie on his head before pouring him out the screen door like a puddle of hot tar. He gave a squeak when he landed on all fours on the concrete.

Carl carried my suitcase and boxes to the bedroom. Deja rolled her eyes at him and stomped out. I wanted to be alone anyway. Even with my stuffy nose, I could tell she'd been burning something disgusting, so I pulled up the mini blinds and slid open the window. I stacked some of my boxes in the corner and shoved the rest under the bed, but I left my clothes in the suitcase. Why unpack? Soon I'd be going home.

I pulled two boxes onto my bed and dug out my Mom's red Bible, running my hand over the cover and tracing her name in gold on the lower corner with my finger. *Noelle James Lockhart*. I slid the Bible under the bed, making sure I didn't lose any of the stuff inside. I wasn't going to read it. I just wanted it handy so I could read Dad's little note on the inside cover and touch the verses Mom highlighted.

Winnie came to the door holding a rolled-up paper, bouncing on the balls of her feet. She looked harmless enough, but warning flags went up all the same. I'd heard stories about little sisters.

"I made this for you," she said. She unrolled the paper—a big sign that said WELCOM ANDRIA with little cartoon characters and balloons drawn around the edges.

"Thanks. It's really . . . good. My name's spelled wrong." Not to mention *welcom*, I thought. I didn't move any of my stuff for her to sit down.

"Oh, sorry," she said. She pushed aside my stuff and sat down anyway. Her butt fit right between the boxes I was going through. "Mom said you'd like it. She said you might feel funny being here at first." She tucked a stray strand of blonde hair behind her ear.

It was a bad idea to show any sign of weakness. "Yeah. Well, I never lived down the . . . I mean, in the valley before." I tucked a stray strand behind my ear, then untucked it.

With me diving elbow-deep into the boxes, you'd think she'd take the hint and move along. But, nooo. She just watched as I got out pictures and set them on the nightstand.

Winnie picked up a picture of us in front of the pyramids. "Is that your other mom and dad?" she asked.

My nostrils actually flared as I pulled the frame out of her grasp. "That *is* my mom and dad."

She flicked her blueberry eyes up at me and back to the picture. Her mouth formed a little O.

"Where is that?" she asked.

"It's the pyramids. In Egypt."

Her white eyebrows shot up. "No way! Wow." She picked up another picture. "Where's that?"

It was a picture of us standing in front of Cinderella's castle, and we were all wearing Mickey ears, for crying out loud.

"It's Disney World," I said very slowly, like she was impaired. As I took one photo away from her, she picked up the next. "And that one's San Francisco," I explained, not waiting for her to ask.

She glanced up at me like I was trying to fake her out, and looked back at the picture. "You went to jail?"

"It's not jail, it's Alcatraz. I mean, it used to be a jail. They don't use it anymore. You take a boat to the island, and you go into a cell and take your picture."

She handed it back. "Geez, you been everywhere. We never go out of Newberry, 'cept sometimes we go to the snow. And to Ginger's hospital, all those times."

Ginger. That was her other sister—the one who died. The one the hospital accidentally switched with me when we were born. That hospital ruined my life.

"You want to see Ginger?" she asked. "Deja's got a picture." She crossed forbidden territory and swiped a picture frame from Deja's desk. "This is old, before Ginger got really sick."

It was the picture in the tabloids at the grocery checkout.

I shrugged. "Yeah, I saw that already."

"I saw your picture too."

For four weeks my face was plastered next to Ginger's above headlines like BABY GOOF AT INTERFAITH HOSPITAL and A PARENT'S WORST NIGHTMARE until the story got old and they moved on to STATUE OF LIBERTY SENDING ALIEN MESSAGES.

"Grandma told me I looked like a blonde Xena in that picture."

Blonde Xena and the Powerpuff Girl. Ginger's cute little face had eyes like Junior Mints. Once I found Grandma holding Ginger's picture next to my mom's baby picture and *tsking* to herself.

Just to torture myself, I imagined the Powerpuff Girl in the Disney World picture with Mom and Dad instead of me. At least they never knew they had the wrong kid.

Cyclops pounced onto my bed and made me sneeze. Somebody must have let him back in. I pushed a box at him, and he jumped down. Right then, Newberry felt a lot like Alcatraz.

Winnie left and came back with gooey cinnamon rolls, one for her and one for me. I couldn't eat it, even though it looked like the perfect combination of cinnamon and icing and pecans. So she ate mine too.

"Wanna watch TV?" she asked, licking icing off her fingers.

I shook my head. "No, I'm tired. I'm going to bed."

"But it's not even dark—"

"Win," Marty called from the living room. "Come out here, baby."

The cat followed her out. I heard Marty tell Winnie not to bother me while she went down to help Grandpa open the drive-in, and to give me time. I rolled my eyes. Like there was enough time in the world to get used to living here.

I pulled out my Tinkerbell T-shirt and boxers that I always slept in. Eight thirty. Grandma and Grandpa would be asleep in front of the TV by then, even though it was still daylight.

I'd never had to share a bedroom before. Even at Grandma's the sewing room was all mine. Everything was so different here. The sheets had that foreign country smell. I hugged Grandma's beat-up afghan and breathed in the scent of her fabric softener. Pretending I was back at Pine Run, I pulled the afghan over my head and wiped my eyes with a corner of it.

On a chain around my neck were two wedding rings. They were scratched up, but once they were shiny gold. One was thin and one was fat. They fit around both my thumbs back when I was little and they were perfect. Like Dorothy clicking her ruby slippers, I squeezed my eyes shut and willed myself back home with Mom and Dad.

Sometimes my parents' faces were hard to see. If I tried long enough, I could picture Mom grading papers on the couch with a happy face stamp or Suzy's Zoo stickers. She always let me have one when I was little and jealous of all those kindergartners who hugged her every day. And Dad would be grading tests or writing lesson plans. I felt like a big shot, having two parents who were teachers in the school district, and sometimes I pushed the limits. I always thought I'd be in his class.

A string of *if onlys* popped up like roadblocks. If only Mom and Dad hadn't gone to Mexico. If only they had taken me with them, I wouldn't feel guilty for living. Sometimes, just to torment myself, I'd wonder if only I could save one of them, would it be Mom or Dad? Grandma obsessed about the fire alarm for a long time after they died. She tested it every day. I think she ran the battery out doing that. If only Grandma and Grandpa had a house, they could keep me.

If only Ginger hadn't contracted Niemann-Pick, no one would have ever known. I remembered the name because it reminded me of "seaman sick." If only they hadn't found out that Ginger's parents weren't carriers, then they would never have known they had the wrong kid.

It's hard to sleep in a strange place. I threw back Grandma's afghan for fresh air and blew my nose. Grandma would remind me to say my prayers, but God and I weren't speaking.

When I think about it, I guess Grandma was trying to help me get ready to go to Marty's, because one day she told me that God gives us power to do hard things. I think a fuse blew somewhere between Him and me, like when the microwave and the dishwasher and the toaster are flipped on at the same time. But all at once the lights went out and everything stopped running. We got disconnected.

He could have fixed it, if He really wanted to.

Bright lights scraped over the gloomy bedroom, giving it a surreal glow. I sat up in bed and looked out the window. Car headlights. A line of them, like migrating aliens catching a double feature. The light shattered into shards and splashed across the walls.

It was too bright to sleep. Even after the headlights died, the movie screen flickered on and Godzilla screamed faintly from the car radios—a giant night-light with sound effects. I lay back and stared at the ceiling, knowing just how he felt.

CHAPTER 3

Marty

I dreamed again—the exhilaration of weightlessness, the rush of speed, the summer wind in my hair. The warmth of Ginger's arm against mine. Calliope music played far below us, buoyed by the scent of cotton candy. Our heads rattled against the back of the seat as the car jerked and climbed, a giant bicycle chain spinning beneath us. We reached the top, and I turned my head to look at her. She laughed like she hadn't been able to in years, reaching freely for the sky. I raised my arms too, and in the breathless seconds before we dropped I saw a beautiful city flash like lightning in the distance.

I woke and hovered on the rim of sleep, unwilling to let go. Then I saw the angel bear on my grandmother's old dresser, the bear the hospice nurse had brought, and remembered that Ginger was with the angels now. I held on as long as I could to the warmth of her arm against mine.

The curtains above my head billowed and whispered in the breeze. Outside, the wind chimes passed their tones back and forth. I heard Dad working in the garage, listening to a tape of Marty Robbins. The house itself seemed to be holding its breath.

That first morning with Andie, I was fully aware that things were different. I had taken the day off from work, because it wasn't right to leave her at Deja's mercy on the first day. School would be back in session on Monday, and Dad's stint as babysitter would be over for another summer. It was too much to ask him to referee.

"Little armadillo, that's what she is." That had been Dad's observation on Andie's first night with us. "Curls up in a ball," he said. "A hide like armor."

I was helping him open the drive-in, and I'd paused from stirring the hot cheese into figure eights. "What did you expect, Dad? We took her away from her grandparents. Now she's living with strangers." I rubbed the back of my neck and rolled my head shoulder to shoulder. "Did we do the right thing?"

"Time will tell. Time will tell. She may loosen up." He made a stirring motion with his hand. "Don't let it scorch. I'll get another bag of chips from the back."

After we closed the snack shack in the middle of the second feature, I went back to the house and peeked into Winnie's room. Her breath came in rhythmic puffs, and the moonlight painted a swatch of light across her bed. Then I checked on Andie. With her head under that old afghan she'd brought, I could have sworn it was Ginger's form lying there. Changing the wallpaper and blinds hadn't really made much difference. The room still belonged to Ginger.

A fine residue of guilt dusted my conscience each morning, sifting into cracks in my defenses. I dragged myself from bed and stood in the shower until hot pins jabbed my scalp red. It was such an indulgence. Toward the end of Ginger's illness, when no one else could care for her the way I could, I had no time for myself at all, not even for normal things like bathing. More than once I'd jumped out of the tub still covered with soap when I heard one of the family call in panic that Ginger was in cataplexy or seizure. Later that day Deja would ask, "Gross, Mom, what's in your hair?" and I'd reached up to feel the crunch of dried shampoo. I couldn't even shave both legs the same day.

After we lost Ginger, I had all the time in the world to take long, luxurious showers, but it just didn't seem important any more. And I had time to clean the house so the girls could have people over, but by then Deja didn't want us to meet any of her friends.

Things were slowly—very slowly—beginning to matter again.

On that first morning, I wanted to be up before Andie. I got out of the shower and towel-dried my hair, pulling on shorts and a T-shirt. I slipped my feet into flip-flops and shuffled into the kitchen, twisting my hair into a scrunchie on top of my head. The thermometer outside the kitchen window read eighty-five degrees, and it was only seven o'clock. If I was going to bake, it would have to be in the morning.

I preheated the oven to 350 degrees, peeled overripe bananas, and threw them into the Mixmaster. Flour, brown sugar, white sugar, cinnamon, baking soda—all pulled from a giant file in my brain, just as dog-eared as any recipe card. One egg and oil. I chopped pecans when I found no walnuts in the freezer, and wrote *walnuts* on the magnetic shopping list on the fridge.

Only after sliding the loaf pans into the oven and setting the timer for fifty minutes did I pour myself a cup of serious coffee and turn on the little kitchen TV. The weather forecast said hot, dry, light winds and a high danger of fire with no end in sight. A high of 104 for the third day in a row. I wondered if Andie was used to the heat. From the look of the weather map, her little hometown was perched well above the heat of the Central Valley.

I wondered what she thought of us and our house. And of the drive-in.

Cyclops cried at the kitchen door, and I let him in to eat. He preened and practically grabbed the bag out of my hand when I filled his dish with crunchies. "Get used to the outside world," I told him, rubbing his jet-black head. "Things are going to be different around here."

Who would have guessed that Andie would be allergic to cats? I bet the kid never had a pet in her life. The only thing we could do was to keep him outside. Cyclops had been Ginger's and had earned his place in the family. He wasn't going anywhere.

When Andie came into the house the night before, backpack clutched to her chest, I got the feeling she was checking out the servants' quarters. It wasn't so much in anything she said, but in her expression and the way she gave the furniture and walls a wide berth. She never even put her clothes in the dresser.

She seemed mature for her age. Almost precocious. From what I gathered, she was the only child of schoolteachers with enough money saved to travel the world during summer breaks. Must be nice, I thought, until I remembered that it was on a vacation to Mexico that they had died.

If her parents had still been alive when we discovered that Ginger and Andie were switched at birth, I would have left her alone. Of course I would have been curious, but my first instinct would have been to protect Ginger. I wouldn't have given Ginger up, not in a million years. If she'd lived to be a hundred, I would never have admitted the little inconsistencies—the upturn of her nose, the roundness of her earlobes, the way she browned to caramel in the summer while the other girls burned and faded pale again.

I got up and dumped my coffee dregs in the sink, rinsing the cup and running the garbage disposal until it grated dry, remembering the day I called to tell Russell the news that Ginger wasn't our biological child. He was loading up his precious new boat for a fishing trip with some good old boys, and Starr told me he couldn't be bothered. She always ran interference between us. She probably thought I would ask for more money or (heaven forbid) for him to take the girls.

The two of them had been magically married since the day our divorce was final. Dad figured she'd been waiting in the wings all along. During that time Russell managed to move back home to Nevada, where he could go back to being a rodeo wannabe and acquire a speedboat, new truck, fifth wheel, and horse trailer. If Starr didn't keep a rein on his spending, they'd soon be out of money and I'd be out of child support.

When she wouldn't let me speak to him directly, I told her to make sure he picked up a Reno newspaper. He called me back that morning after he saw the story about the baby-switch. I suppose it was spiteful of me, but he had to cancel his fishing trip when I gave his address to reporters and they camped out in his yard. After the second day as prisoners in their home, as we were, Starr created some sort of diversion and he sneaked out to meet his fishing buddies, leaving the boat behind in the driveway. When the reporters discovered he'd escaped, they asked me where Russell liked to fish. I narrowed it down to three favorite fishing holes and offered to draw maps.

It was small consolation for the fact that, while I was taking care of our dying child, he'd had the nerve to say he couldn't handle it anymore and left. He even had the nerve to suggest that Ginger wasn't really *his*.

"There's never been any sick kids in my family. Look at her, for cryin' out loud, Marty. She don't even look like the others. Makes me wonder."

I was too incensed and hurt at the time to admit that I'd also wondered why she looked so different from Deja and Winnie. I put it down to recessive genes. My own mother was blonde at birth and turned dark-headed within months, just like Ginger. A niggling little thought had worked its way in at the time of her birth, in the form of an identification bracelet that had first been loose and then so binding that it left a mark on her newborn wrist. It made sense that the nurses had tightened it, and I'd quickly batted any suspicions into the outer reaches.

But the genetic disease—there had to be an explanation for that.

Ginger had been six when I first noticed her bobbing her head in front of the TV instead of moving her eyes to follow the action. As time went on, her speech began to slur, and she grew clumsier than normal. She had trouble keeping up in school. Eventually, the seizures began. Since so little was known about the disease, it went misdiagnosed for several years. As her symptoms progressed and my marriage floundered, I pulled inward, and it wasn't until she died that I had time to even question our part in it. Russell and I went in separately for tests, and we found that neither one of us was a carrier. The doctor took a hard look and noticed that her blood type on her birth certificate was wrong. Then it took forever to get the birth records opened. DNA tests revealed what I couldn't even imagine—that I'd raised the wrong child. *That I had buried the wrong child.*

I wouldn't be human if I didn't admit—only to myself—the horrible thought that went through my mind. That I had cared for someone else's sick child unto death. That I'd been cheated out of a healthy family, and my children cheated from a normal childhood, and I'd borne it alone without a husband, because he bailed when it got too hard. Then the guilt would set in, because I loved Ginger so much. I loved Ginger as part of myself. Part of me rested with her in that shabby little district cemetery on the edge of town.

A movement through the kitchen window caught my attention, and I realized I still had the empty coffee mug in my hand. Tiny yellow finches fought for position on a mesh sack of birdseed suspended from the roof outside, digging in upside down, eating their way around like a barber's pole, tenacious and undaunted by bigger birds. It was then that I heard ripping noises from the living room. Cyclops was finished with breakfast and was now clawing the couch. I set the coffee mug on the counter, sneaked up behind the cat, and scooped him into my arms.

"Honestly, in all that time outside you couldn't find somewhere else to sharpen your claws?" He growled low in his throat as I tossed him outside. "Find a nice shady tree," I said through the screen door.

The kitchen timer went off. I opened the oven to check the bread, releasing the warm scent of pecans and cinnamon, and sank a knife cleanly into the middle of a robust crack. I turned the loaf out onto a clean dish towel.

Winnie padded barefoot down the hall and into the kitchen, curling up in a chair at the table. I sliced two thick pieces of steaming banana nut bread and placed them in front of her with a glass of milk. She pushed back her hair and grinned.

"Sleep sweet, pumpkin?" I asked.

She nodded and picked at a pecan, flicking it off to the side. "If I sleep with you, then Andie can have my room. Deja won't be so mean to her." She blew steam away, sank her teeth into the slice, and washed it down with milk. White fuzz glistened above her lip.

I tucked a blonde lock behind her ear. "It's time you had your own room again. You're growing up, you know." *And I can't keep you close forever.*

"Is Andie awake?"

"I think she's still sleeping. We'll let her rest as long as she needs to. It's not every day that she gets a new family." I rested my chin in my hand and studied her. "So," I said, lowering my voice, "did she like your welcome sign?"

She shrugged. "Guess so." She nibbled the crusty edge in earnest and wiped her fingers on her pajama front. "She's been to Disney World. And jail."

I studied her face. "Jail?"

"She had pictures. In San Francisco. You have to take a boat there."

"Oh, you mean Alcatraz."

She nodded and finished off her milk.

"You've been there too, you know. You were only a baby, but we spent the day in San Francisco before Ginger got sick."

"Do we gots a picture? I want to show Andie."

"Maybe. Somewhere." It was with the others I'd pulled from our family album—all the ones with Russell in them, except for our wedding picture, which I'd thought was important in case they ever wondered if we'd actually been married. I'd resisted tossing them, for the girls' sake.

"Have I been to Egypt?"

I stifled a smile. "No. Why, has Andie been there too?"

"Uh-huh. Can I have some more?"

I went to the counter and cut another slice of bread. "Better go easy. Somebody else might want some." I offered it to her, then pulled back and waited. She took the hint.

"Please, Mommy," she said, grinning. It was a game we

played, called "remember your manners."

"Are you ready to start back to school next week?"

"Yeah." Her eyes flew open. "I hope I get Mrs. Orlando. I need a new backpack and a lunch box. Can we go to Target?"

"I think so. Your old ones lasted two years."

"Andie can go with us. Maybe we can pick out the same one."

I winced. "It would be okay if she picked out a different one, wouldn't it?"

She nodded. " 'Kay."

"So, did she say anything last night?" I asked. "You know, about being here?"

Winnie shook her head. "She's grumpy." She sprayed food, which I ignored for the moment, sensing her feelings had been hurt. "She's not like Ginger."

I motioned for her to sit on my lap. She climbed up without a word and rested her head against my shoulder in the curl of my neck. Her soft hair smelled of pillow and strawberry shampoo.

"She's not Ginger, honey, and it's not fair to expect her to be. She's Andie, and she's special in her own way. One of these days she'll seem like a sister to you."

Her head moved up and down beneath my chin, and her arm slipped around my waist.

"Remember that she lost both of her parents a couple years ago. And in a way, she's lost her grandparents, because the court said she has to live with us. We have to give her lots and lots of time. You understand?"

In my mind's eye, I saw her grandparents as we'd left them on the porch of their mobile home, leaning on each other like spent garden vines. This first morning without Andie must be like another death to them.

Winnie nodded and, after a moment, twisted around to pat my

cheek. She looked dreamily into my eyes. "You're pretty, Mommy. I love you."

"I love you more."

She tapped her finger on my chest. "I love *you* more."

I poked her back. "No, I love *you* more." Then I tickled her until I was afraid she'd wet her pants, and I let her slip off my lap. She ran cross-legged down the hall.

Her laughter came straight from heaven—a glimmer of hope that life could be restored.

If there was one good thing that came from Russell's abandonment, it was that we were pushed in God's direction at a time when we needed Him most. Something like being shoved onto one of those people movers at the airport, where you can stand still and make slow progress, or walk and make good time. I just stood, letting it pull me along, overloaded with baggage, relieved to be moving at all.

A nurse from the hospital had invited us to visit her little storefront church. The only reason I'd agreed to go was that she had promised to meet me at the door.

Her invitation came just in time. I think we would have unraveled completely if God hadn't rushed in to tie up our frayed ends. Except for poor Deja. Her raw ends were still exposed and tangled.

Lately my relationship with Him had stalled. I'd been reading a devotional booklet about overcoming loss, but I stopped when I came to a part about God bringing good from bad. It shocked me that anyone could even suggest that any good could come from losing Ginger. That was last winter, and we hadn't been back to church since.

I folded two slices of nut bread in a napkin and carried them out to the garage, to find Dad trying to resuscitate the lawn mower.

"Here, Pop," I said, handing him the bread. "Want some eggs to go with it?"

He smiled and wiped his hands on a rag. "No, this'll do." He nodded to a corner of the garage. "I'm cleaning up today. Got anything for the women's shelter?"

I knew what was in the corner—a folded wheelchair covered by a sheet like a little ghost.

"No, Dad. Not yet."

He kept his focus on the mower. "No hurry."

"You want a warm-up?" I motioned for his coffee mug.

"No, I'll float away."

When I got back to the kitchen, Winnie was on her fourth slice. "Mommy, Andie's up."

For a moment I wished I could suspend time and preserve the future I envisioned where we all blended like a beautiful jigsaw puzzle, blending into one another for a perfect fit without any missing pieces. But it was show time. I said, "Let's see if she's hungry."

I glanced at my reflection in the hall mirror as I passed and tightened my scrunchie.

We found Andie curled up on the couch with that ragged afghan, watching Saturday morning cartoons.

"Good morning," I said. "Would you like a slice of homemade nut bread?"

Homemade. What in the world made me say that?

"No, thanks." She kept her eyes on Tom and Jerry. Her short blonde hair was an explosion of soft straw around her head.

"We also have Cap'n Crunch, Pop-Tarts, instant oatmeal?"

"I'm not hungry."

Winnie settled in at the other end of the couch with the remote. "What do you want to watch?" she asked.

"I don't care." Andie pulled her oversize T-shirt down over

her knees and tucked it beneath her toes, covering every inch of her except her head. She sneezed and sniffled.

My first order of business would be to clean the carpets and furniture to try to get rid of some of the animal dander.

"Mom said we can go to the store today and get new backpacks for school," Winnie ventured.

"I'm okay," Andie said. Then she looked over at Winnie. "When does school start?"

"Two days. On Monday."

Andie hugged her knees to her chest and rested her chin on the top.

"If you want to take a shower," I said, "get a towel out of the hall closet where I showed you last night. If you can't find something, just look around or ask Winnie. And help yourself to anything in the fridge."

When she didn't respond, I left her to Winnie and went back to clean up the kitchen. I spent more energy than usual cleaning that Saturday. Really, how much stress should a thirteen-year-old induce in a grown woman?

Andie read on her bed all day or drew in her sketchbook, which she slammed shut when I stuck my head in to ask if she had any dirty laundry. She had made the bed and, except for a few photos on her nightstand, left no evidence that she'd even slept there. Her side had the temporary feel of a Motel 6.

Winnie tried to make her own bed without any coercion from me and cleaned off her dresser. She asked me if there were any frames she could have.

Deja brought out her laundry looking sullen, which I recognized as an attempt to discourage all communication. It didn't work.

"How's it going, honey?" I asked.

"Great." She dropped the basket heavily onto the floor and sorted her dirty clothes into piles of black, red, and skulls.

"Are you going anyplace with Summer today?"

She looked up and arched an eyebrow at me. "You think I'm leaving *her* alone with my stuff?"

It took a moment for me to realize she was talking about Andie. "Oh, come on, Deja. She's not going to bother your things."

She shook her head with a knowing smirk. "She could scratch my CDs or break my stereo. Or steal my money. No way."

I motioned to keep her voice down. "Deja, you're not being fair."

"I'm being smart."

"In more ways than one, young lady."

She rested the laundry basket on her hip and swaggered down the hall.

Winnie talked Andie into going with us to Target that afternoon. The Toyota was like an oven on wheels since the air conditioning had gone out, and we couldn't afford to get it fixed. Deja didn't go, and it was probably for the best.

Andie repeated that she didn't want a new backpack, and I let it go. We'd get one later if she changed her mind. I did insist that she pick out an insulated sack for her lunch, pointing out that the only time we buy school lunches is on pizza day. Winnie chose a backpack with wheels and a retractable handle—a large piece of carry-on luggage that would never fit under her desk.

Our first meal together tasted like cardboard to me, and we all breathed easier when Deja excused herself from the table. I'd settled on spaghetti, which was one of the few foods that got Andie's attention when I rattled off the choices. Winnie jabbered on, filling the silence with talk of school and friends she couldn't wait to see. I wondered if Andie missed her friends, and how she'd face the unknown on Monday, made up of kids who'd known each other since kindergarten and probably weren't interested in making room for strangers.

After dinner, while I wrapped brownies and Rice Krispie treats to sell at the drive-in, I decided to go to the cemetery before it closed at dusk. I slipped out by myself, picked up a bouquet of carnations from work, and drove out to Ginger's grave. I got out my trowel and gardening gloves from the trunk of the Toyota and pulled weeds around her grave, leaving the small dandelions because that's what Ginger would have wanted. I tossed the dead flowers from the vase and replaced them with the carnations. It was kind of a peace offering for the smallest—the tiniest—bit of progress I'd made away from the sorrow. And because we now had Andie, and life was moving on.

CHAPTER 4

Andie

Grant Charter School looked like a prison camp, with dirt for grass, rows of shabby modular classrooms, and a chain link fence surrounding everything. The only thing missing was barbed wire. Gang graffiti bled through fresh gray paint on the buildings. The color said you were here to learn and for no other reason. I couldn't believe it when they told me it was a K–8. Instead of going to a normal middle school, I was demoted to sharing space with kindergarteners and every grade in between.

Marty had already picked up my schedule, and we'd checked out the building the day before. When we pulled up to the front on the first day of school, I jumped out and backed away from the car, saying I was okay to go. I heard Winnie say she would help me. Like I would let that happen.

I shook off Winnie at the entrance, feeling a little like a rat about it, and jumped headfirst into the stream of kids feeding into the building.

Old-milk-carton-and-bologna-sandwich smell must be standard

issue to custodians. Do they dispense it in bottles so kids all over America feel at home when they're forced to leave their friends behind and start over at new schools? The doorway into the boys' bathroom smelled worse.

The little kids weren't intimidated by eighth-graders, either. Not even a tall eighth-grader. They pushed and shoved, using elbows and backpacks.

I found my homeroom and slid into a desk just before the bell rang. My homeroom teacher, Mrs. Bettencourt, was trying to look cheerfully stern, but how serious could she look with apples dangling from her ears and a *#1 Teacher* pin on her shirt? I wondered how she ended up teaching eighth grade, when her wardrobe so obviously said kindergarten.

The girl across from me stared until I looked over, and then she looked away again. I could see it happening out of the corner of my eye, over and over. I casually checked for opened zippers or buttons or boogers, and figured she must have heard about me. I wondered how many of the kids in the class knew that I was switched.

The PA system screeched to life. Feedback rang off the walls, and we all jumped and covered our ears. Obviously everyone was a little edgy that morning. We shuffled to our feet for the pledge of allegiance. It was half over before the back row made it to a complete standing position, and then they dropped back into their seats before "justice for all."

Two students started tag-team announcements over the PA, taking their jobs way too seriously. This was school, not an audition for news radio. I tuned them out and looked around. I wouldn't be here that long, so nothing they could say was important.

Tall windows opened to the soccer field and the ratty backyards of the houses past the perimeter fence. Trash pegged into the chain link holes was an especially nice touch. Metal slides and monkey bars from the Iron Age heated up in the morning sun. Fresh blacktop stretched for miles. The white-striped hopscotch and four-square lines soaked up enough rays to glow in the dark.

Inside the room, school spirit flags with the Grant Griffin and posters of authors and classics hung on the wall. A whole bookshelf at the front was devoted to literature. Not bad, but not as interesting as my dad's classroom.

I used to help my mom and dad get their classrooms ready every year. Dad didn't need as much help as Mom, because he taught eighth-grade English and PE. Mom taught kindergarten, so she needed me to trace letters, scrub small chairs, and label everything from crayon boxes to cubbies. Mom said my handwriting was artistic because I could copy the D'Nealian letter chart perfectly. I drew cartoon characters on her parents' newsletters and made up award certificates for her kids. She said she didn't know where I got my talent.

My dad taught the only eighth-grade English class at Tyson Burke Middle School. This year he would have been my teacher.

The air droned with happy kids chattering about summer camp or family vacations to Santa Cruz as they pulled out fresh yellow No. 2 pencils, bright sheets of blue-lined filler paper, and chunky pink erasers free of pencil jabs. The first day of school—the *only* day of the year when kids were actually glad to be there. Everything was fresh and new. I felt frayed, like a page out of last year's notebook with the holes ripped and the wire spiraling out. The scene telescoped away from me, muting all sound.

"Andrea Winslow."

The teacher repeated, louder, "Andrea Winslow."

No one answered. She stood in front of my desk looking down at me. My brain finally made the connection, and my stomach hitched.

"AnDRAYa," I said. "And my last name is Lockhart, not Winslow."

She started to argue, hesitated, then scribbled in her roll book and kept moving.

Mrs. Bettencourt wore the same kind of "teacher uniform" as my mom—a denim jumper with a blouse printed with pencils, crayons, and red schoolhouses. I focused on her pin. The apple had a happy little worm wearing a graduation cap. My mom always got a ton of gifts like that from her students.

This sob came out of nowhere. Followed by another. And another. I couldn't stop, and I couldn't catch my breath. I buried my head in my arms, burrowing toward the center of the earth away from everybody.

A grown-up hand patted my shoulder, but I didn't look up. Partly because my nose was running, and partly because it was a dark place, a black hole of escape that I didn't want to give up. When Mrs. Bettencourt decided I wasn't sick, she gave me some tissues and asked the girl across from me to take me to the counselor's office. I'm not sure how I got there. The counselor gave me a tissue and tried to get me to talk, but I knew all the tricks they use to try to get you to open up.

I missed first-period science sitting in the office. The bell rang, and I heard kids out in the hall. By the time I was in control enough to go back to class it was second-period algebra. It was excruciating, walking back in the middle of class alone with everyone staring at me like I was a freak. Mr. Hunt glanced at the pass that I handed to him, and then he raised his voice and tapped the math problem on the whiteboard to keep the kids' attention until I got seated. A pair of jerks snickered in the back of the class, and I tried hard to tune them out. I stared at the page in my math book until my eyes got blurry and the numbers wiggled all by themselves.

Everybody left me alone at lunch. I picked out a granola bar and a drink box from the lunch Marty had packed and tossed the rest. Winnie dragged her friends over to me on the playground. I didn't think we were supposed to be fraternizing. Dorky little fourth-graders.

Her friends lined up in front of me like I was a zoo exhibit. I guess they'd never seen anybody who was switched at birth.

"This is my sister," Winnie announced.

I flinched at the word. I didn't want to hurt her feelings. I was trying really hard.

"I'm Andie." (Not her sister, I added in my head.)

One of them whispered loudly, like I was hearing impaired, "She doesn't look like Ginger."

"Of course not, stupid," said another. "Ginger wasn't her real sister."

Winnie's face screwed up, and she clenched her fists. "Shut up, Cassie," she growled. "Ginger was my sister. Mom said we would always be sisters. Just shut up!"

The recess bell signaled the end of round one. I couldn't wait for this day to be over.

Mrs. Bettencourt came over to my desk during English to see how I was doing. She introduced me to Natalie, the girl who took me to the counselor's office. Natalie still watched me, but when I looked up now, she would smile and look shy.

When the bell rang at 2:40, Winnie met me outside and I followed her to our pickup spot. The Toyota was sandwiched in a long line of cars like a green pickle in a deli party sub. Deja sat in the front seat with Carl. I groaned under my breath and got in the backseat, kicking aside a pair of dirty gloves and a garden tool on the floor. Deja closed her eyes and screwed her earbuds in tighter, like she was afraid she'd hear me breathing.

Winnie yakked all the way home and all through supper about her new class and her new teacher. When she paused for breath, Marty asked how my day went.

Deja's white face came alive. "Pretty bad, I'd say. Sent to the office on the first day."

I choked on my macaroni. How did she know that?

She smiled wickedly. "Scott Worley is in your homeroom. His sister happens to be my best friend."

Great. Constant surveillance.

"What happened, Andie?" Marty asked. "The office didn't call about any problems today."

Deja balled up her fists and pretended to rub her mascaraed eyes. "She cried. Boo-hoo-hoo."

Carl snapped, "Deja, leave the table."

Deja rolled her eyes and pushed her plate away. "I'm done anyway," she said, giving him a rude look behind his back as she left.

Nobody brought up the subject of my day again. I wasn't hungry, but I picked at my food because I didn't have anyplace to go when I was done. There was no way I was going back to my room with Deja in there.

When Marty got up to clear the table, I rinsed my plate in the sink and went out to sit on the porch. The heat over the drive-in blacktop shimmered in deserted moonscape silence, but the cement steps were cool on my bare legs. Carl's country music warbled from the truck he had up on blocks. His legs stuck out from under the fender like it had swallowed him. The wind chimes jangled above my head in the hot breeze. A train whistle called, far away, headed for somewhere else and begging me to go along.

I squashed an innocent roly-poly with the toe of my shoe. Why had I come unglued at school? Maybe I was blindsided by the memories. My counselor, Mr. John, once told me about how everything has stress points, and how some things have more stress points than others. And when they add up—*kaboom!* Sometimes you're just a time bomb waiting to blow. I guess that's what happened. One stress point too many lit my fuse. I could only hope that it was out of my system, and that the points wouldn't accumulate while I served my time.

Marty looked at me through the screen door. "Do you have a list of school supplies?"

I nodded, and she said, "Go get it, and we'll run to Walgreens."

I fished out my list. She came back alone with her purse, wearing a fresh coat of lipstick. Winnie watched us leave from the screen door. Marty called to her, "I'll bring you some Hello Kitty folders, baby."

I wondered why she'd left Winnie at home. Winnie was a great buffer; she chattered like a pair of windup teeth.

Walgreens had everything I needed, except for some expensive calculator. Marty let me get some Lisa Frank folders and pencils. She went to look for allergy medicine and left me alone to wander down the candy aisle. Just as I was weighing the pros and cons of Baby Ruth versus a bag of Skittles, a bratty kid beside me started whining and worked himself into a major fit, rolling around on the floor at his mom's feet. I tossed the Skittles back on the shelf and watched, wincing at the decibels he was reaching.

Another movement distracted me. Past them, way off at the front of the store, the glass exit doors opened and closed. The setting sun winked at me. I rubbed my eyes. Opening and closing. The doors slid open and people walked out, bags slung over their arms, kids following. Opening and closing. Headed home.

Home. It would be so easy to walk through those doors and

keep on walking. Across the parking lot and through town to the highway. Maybe all the way to the moon. My heart banged away as I realized this was my first moment of freedom since Marty had taken me from Grandma. Until then, I'd been with Marty or Winnie or Deja, or in school with a teacher.

My feet pulled me around the bratty boy and his mom to the end of the candy aisle. The air seemed thinner there. The doors silently opened, teasing me. People came and went. Teasing me. Silently the doors closed.

Ten, maybe fifteen big steps, and I'd be gone.

Free.

Was this my chance? Was it worth it? It was crazy. I panicked a little, just thinking about it. If I walked out the door, what would I do once I got outside? I stopped past the cash register, staring at the opening door, feeling some magnetic field tugging me toward it. Out on the sidewalk, nobody would know me. I could just cross the parking lot and keep walking.

I thought that this must be how kids run away. On impulse. All a kid needed was a chance and a reason to take it.

I clenched my fists, trying to screw up my courage, rocking on my feet and feeling the warm Baby Ruth conforming to the shape of my fingers.

"This should work," Marty said, suddenly beside me, scaring me to death.

I stared into the shopping basket over her arm filled with school supplies, trying to focus. She was reading the directions on the back of some allergy medicine.

"But you can't use this every day, or you'll fall asleep in school. We'll get you an appointment with Dr. Shafer if this doesn't help." She looked down at my hand. "Did you pick out a candy bar? Better get one for Winnie."

I opened my fist and stared at the mangled Baby Ruth.

"What in the world happened?" she asked.

She studied my face for a split second and looked from me to the direction my feet were pointed, taking in the straight path to the door. Her expression changed. I swallowed and lowered my eyes. I must have looked really guilty.

Marty took the candy from me and turned it over in her palm. She looked at me kind of funny, but she couldn't read my mind. "You'd better go pick out a different one."

I didn't talk on the way back to the house because I couldn't tell if she was mad. But halfway home she broke the silence.

"Do you want to talk about what happened in school today?" she asked.

That's why she'd left Winnie behind. I shook my head.

She was quiet for a minute. "Deja's not always this bad. She really misses her sister. It'll take her awhile. It's hard when you lose someone." She shrugged a shoulder, looking embarrassed. "Well, you know that."

Suddenly I felt old—no kid should feel so old. "It hurts a long time," I said, "when somebody dies."

Marty looked over at me at the stoplight, her face hungry, like she wanted something I had. It still hurt whenever I remembered my parents, but not as bad as it used to. Sometimes I felt guilty, forgetting even a piece of the pain. Grandma said Mom and Dad would want me to get better.

I didn't know how long ago Ginger had died. Maybe time passes even slower when your kids go first.

"It gets easier," I said, which sounded lame, since just that morning I had gone ballistic. "After a while."

Marty wiped the corner of her eyes with her knuckles. Her long peach nails curled down, pointing to a silver charm bracelet on her wrist. On the bracelet was a charm, shaped like a little girl's head, and on it was engraved *Ginger*.

Right after I turned off my light to go to sleep that night, Marty came to my door and stepped into the darkness.

"Andie, I need to talk to you about something."

I scooted my feet up to make room for her to sit down on the edge of my bed, wishing I had faked being asleep.

She cleared her throat. "Starting this weekend, we'll need your help at the drive-in."

I let that sink in. "Like, how?"

"Nothing too hard. Probably selling snacks. The point is, this is a family business. We all chip in and help. You'll be earning a paycheck too."

I silently absorbed this information. Money could buy freedom.

"My point is, if you need anything between now and when you get paid, you know, for whatever you spend money on, we'll work it out. For candy or whatever. Just ask me."

In a flash of humiliation, I knew. She'd misunderstood the whole thing with the candy at the store. I remembered the look on her face, and it registered. She didn't think I was trying to run away; she thought I was trying to steal the Baby Ruth. Heat began as a pinpoint in my chest and radiated in a two-alarm blaze.

"But . . ." I began.

How could I tell her that? I'd have to come up with some other explanation. If she even suspected that I might try to make a break for it, she'd watch my every move. I'd really be a prisoner. Maybe it was just better to let her think what she wanted.

I squeaked out, "Okay."

She told me good night before she left and closed my door.

The impulse to run had frightened me, but it had also given me a sense of power. Soon I'd have a paycheck too. Money and power can come in handy.

CHAPTER 5

Marty

I received two calls on my voice mail while I was at work on Tuesday. Andie's counselor wanted to discuss a strategy to help her make a smoother adjustment. That translated into "We want to avoid any further outbursts in the classroom." Deja's principal called because in only two days Deja had managed to break every dress code and report late to every class. Mr. McNulty wanted to set up a plan to help Deja have a more productive year, which translated into "We're not going to put up with another year like the last one."

On Wednesday morning I dropped Andie and Winnie in front of the school, circled the block, and slipped into a visitor's parking space. I hoped neither one would have a reason to report to the office and see me with the counselor.

Mr. Lopez listened to the next chapter in our family saga. He was fully aware of what had gone on the past few years, after doing battle with reporters who wanted pictures of Winnie. His pen rested on a pad of paper the entire time without making a mark, and when I finished he just looked stunned.

"Sounds like Jerry Springer material, doesn't it?" I said sheepishly.

"No, no. Of course not." He rocked back in his chair and exhaled. "Do you have any suggestions that would make her transition easier?"

"I thought that was your job."

"Well." He sat up straighter and cleared his throat. "We like to partner with the family in situations like this."

I bristled. "You've had situations like this before?"

"No, we haven't, Mrs. Winslow." He grimaced. "And frankly, this isn't textbook."

"Look, I'm sorry. But you have no idea what my family has gone through in the past few years, and continues to deal with every day. Any help you can offer would be appreciated."

He looked at his hands and pursed his lips. "I guess the immediate plan of action would be to advise Andie's teachers of her situation in its entirety. If that's agreeable to you, of course."

"Whatever helps."

I left him, promising to keep in touch. My next stop was to the principal's office at Deja's high school. I hate to admit it, but all I heard from him was "blah-blah-blah." I'd been in his office so many times in the past year that I suspected he blamed me personally for Deja's behavior.

"Should I call Deja in for a conference?" he asked.

I looked him in the eye and said, "If you think it's best."

He reached for the intercom and hesitated. Then he put his hands back in his lap. "I don't really think it's necessary."

Over the next twenty minutes I promised to deal with her at home and support the school's authority, as always.

I clocked in at work an hour late. The store manager looked at his watch as I hurried to report to my register, tying my apron.

"Sorry, Robert," I called. "I'll make up the time."

Jo pooh-poohed him behind his back. "So, how's it goin'?" she asked over her shoulder.

If the main office had any idea how conversation-inducing it was to have checkers stationed back-to-back, they'd remodel the store in a heartbeat.

I forced a smile to my customer, saying, "Good morning." Over my shoulder I asked Jo, "What did I ever do to deserve all this?"

"Honey, some of us have bigger shoulders than others, but yours should have a weight limit."

Jo and I had grown up together at Elko High, and each moved to the Sacramento area separately. As fate would have it, I wandered into her checkout line a few months after Ginger passed away, and she talked me into applying for a checker's position. I'd wavered. Even though I badly needed the job to pay medical bills, I didn't yet feel even close to rejoining the human race. Maybe it was just so good to see an old friend, or I'd been out of touch for so long, that I applied. Actually, the real clincher was the 20 percent discount I got on everything in the store. I figured it could at least help to finance my baking habit.

Jo and I took our ten-minute break together in one-hundred-degree heat outside at the employees' picnic area, the only place where smoking was allowed. I put up with the bad air quality in exchange for sympathy.

Russell was the topic of conversation, since his child support check was late again.

"Tsk, tsk." She shook her hennaed head, taking a long draw and exhaling. "I warned you about Russell our freshman year, you remember? He's what my Jimmy calls a poser."

"Gigolo is closer to the truth."

She snorted. "Thought he was Clint Eastwood. Anyway . . ." She took another drag on her cigarette and blew it over her shoulder. "I'd like five minutes alone with him and my riding mower with a sharpened blade. I'd cut him down to size."

The air hung like an old blanket on the backside of the building near the dumpsters, and I got a dose of secondhand smoke. She dropped her cigarette and smashed it with the toe of her shoe. "I don't know what you ever saw in him."

"Jo, you were just as gaga over him as I was."

She chuckled. "You won the booby prize, I guess."

We went back through the employee entrance to our lockers. The gray metal stacks and combination locks sent us back to high school again.

"My mama always said, 'Pretty is as pretty does.' " She pulled out a huge makeup bag and dug around for lipstick. "I had more sense than to fall for a barrel racer. Bull riders were more my style."

I took out my cosmetic bag. "So you married an insurance salesman."

"Honey, there are advantages. I've got coverage for every major catastrophe, except in the event that I don't get to heaven. There's no kinda insurance for that."

"That's not what I hear." I smeared on some frosty gloss and pressed my lips together.

She studied me with her lip liner poised. "What do you mean? You going to church or somethin'?"

I tightened the scrunchie on my ponytail. "Maybe. Sometimes."

She turned back to her locker mirror and lip liner, and spoke without moving her lips. "You be careful. You don't want to go getting mixed up with a cult or something."

"Yes, Mom." I tossed my purse into my locker and slammed it.

At the end of my shift, I picked up a rotisserie chicken and some instant mashed potatoes for dinner, and tossed in a bag of chocolate chips to make chocolate-chunk brownies. Firing up the oven would heat the house to the level of a kiln. But the evening still loomed ahead when I'd have to deal with Deja, and I needed a shot of courage.

Later that evening, we ate dinner and sweated while the brownies baked. Winnie talked nonstop about school. Andie never made eye contact with anyone. She wasn't rude or disrespectful, just gave the facts and never offered more than anyone asked. She ate one small helping and excused herself as soon as possible, rinsing her plate in the sink. I could see her from the kitchen window reading a book under a tree.

I guess her books were an acceptable means of escape. I could think of worse ways.

The phone rang as I cleaned up the dishes. I ran back to pick it up in my bedroom because the cordless had disappeared. I should have let the answering machine get it. The client court specialist was calling to find out when I would be home so she could stop by for her initial visit with Andie. I told her to come sometime between dinner and dusk, when I'd need to help at the drive-in. When I hung up, I noticed how messy the house was. I called for the girls to get their shoes and backpacks so I could vacuum, feeling one more weight draped across my shoulders. I could only hope that Deja would be at Summer's when the worker showed up.

After I cleaned up the dinner dishes and the living room, I called Deja back out to the kitchen table. Dense brownies shouldered one another on a plate dusted with sifted confectioner's sugar. I knew she was at the volatile time of the month when chocolate could only help.

"Great," she said when she saw me at the table. "What did I do now?"

"Sit down, Deja," I said. "Have a brownie."

She sat down and tipped the chair back away from me as far as possible, cradling a brownie in her palm. "Did The Nut call you?"

The nickname had occurred to me too, but that wasn't the point. "It's Mr. McNulty. Don't be disrespectful."

She rolled her eyes.

"Deja, you know what's expected at school—"

"That dress code is so lame!" she exploded. "Who cares if I wear black or pierce my nose?"

"You know black is a gang color. It's for your own safety." I did a visual scan. "What do you mean, pierce your nose?"

She balanced the chair on its two back legs and looked off to the side.

"Deja?"

"I don't have any piercings. Not yet. It was a fake one, and you should have seen McNulty. He looked like he was going to totally flatline."

"What do you hope to accomplish by making him angry? It'll only get you suspended. Or worse."

She flashed her eyes at me. "What could be worse than two more years at Gale Langford High School?"

"Continuation school, with all the druggies and the pregnant girls comparing morning sickness." I paused for emphasis. "Or homeschool. Just you and me. Every day. Sitting at this table doing algebra and history. Together."

The chair legs settled heavily onto the floor. "But kids do worse stuff than that at school, and they don't get kicked out.

Justin Swartz brought a can of spray paint to school, and it fell out of his backpack and rolled to Mrs. Snider's feet in biology. And Lupe Alvarado started a fight in the girls' locker room and they had to lock down the gym for fourth period."

I ignored this tactic.

"Deja, you barely made it through last year. They know you've had some tough things to overcome, and they bent over backward to allow you time to get a handle on them. But like it or not, they expect you to at least try to cooperate. They're not going to tolerate another year like the last one."

She sat hunched and folded in on herself, sullenly picking her black nail polish.

I cleared my throat. "If you want to try counseling again, I could—"

"No. Way."

I folded my arms. "Well, Deja, since I haven't seen much improvement in your attitude, I'm postponing your driver's training again until you show some maturity and prove that you can handle the responsibility."

She bolted upright. "But Summer's already signed up, and she said they only have three spots left. If I don't get in now, I can't get in until spring."

"You'll have plenty of time to develop some maturity and save up money for the class."

"But all my friends will have their licenses by then. I'll be the only one!"

"It's up to you, Deja. When your grades improve and I see a change in your attitude, I'll reconsider."

I softened, remembering the disappointment at being the only one of my friends who had to wait to get my license until the insurance rates dropped when I turned eighteen.

"Honey, we don't even have a car for you to drive."

She looked up at me with her face set in stone.

"We would if Dad was here."

I blinked. "What?"

"If Dad was here, he'd buy me a car." She smirked. "He got Starr a Mustang convertible. A red one."

I collected myself before I let slip that the Mustang was part of his midlife crisis, and we weren't.

"Don't count on it, Deja. It's not that he wouldn't *like* to buy you a car," I lied, "he's just not very good at keeping track of his money. He thinks he has more than he really does."

"Well, I'm gonna ask him. He'll let me get my license."

She pushed out of the chair and marched back to her room. The door slammed, and pictures rattled in the hall. The brownie turned leaden in my stomach. I imagined her calling Russell and trying to get past Starr on the phone, and the rejection that would only add to her pain.

More and more she reminded me of my brother, Charles, in the months before he left the family. He'd checked out emotionally long before he took those first strides down the dusty road away from our little ranch in Elko.

I went out to where Dad was tinkering with the truck and asked if he would see that the girls got ready for bed. It was early, but I had a headache. He said he could open the drive-in alone and not to mind Deja. I guess he'd heard most of it, even out in the yard. I warned him about the lady from social services who could be dropping by any day unannounced.

I changed into a light camisole, crawled into bed without removing my mascara, and curled into a fetal position. I pulled the sheet up to my neck and lay there listening to the noises in the house, fighting the urge to get up and bake snickerdoodles.

Sometimes my life hung poorly, like a suit of borrowed clothes. It sagged and bagged and cinched up on me in the worst places. In the important places. If my life was really my own, wouldn't things work out better? Wouldn't it fit? Sometimes I felt like I was the one who got switched.

My mother's Bible sat on the nightstand, and I pulled it to me. It fell naturally open to Psalms. The words were carefully underlined with a straight edge in blue ballpoint. They promised restoration, and in the margin Mom had written *Charles*.

My family restored—that's what I wanted. Maybe then my life would fall into place.

As Mom's heart had ached for Charles, mine ached for Deja, for the day when she'd realize that her father didn't leave me; he left us.

CHAPTER 6

Andie

Friday was my first official night working at the drive-in. Imagine a huge bathroom at the public pool without the stalls and showers, and a funny smell you can't identify. Maybe dirty-sock smell. That's what I thought when I stepped inside the snack shack for the first time with the others.

"We all work on Friday and Saturday nights," Marty said, switching on the pizza ovens. "Sometimes it's crowded on Sunday nights too. Depends on the movie."

"Sometimes Deja ditches," Winnie said in a low voice while helping me refill the candy display with Skittles and peanut M & Ms. "Like when she has a big date." She looked up at Deja, who I noticed had one earbud dangling, not plugged into her ear. Deja mouthed *Shut up* to Winnie.

"Winnie, you know Deja can't date until she's sixteen," Marty said, shutting the door of the industrial-sized freezer with her foot and dropping an armload of pizzas onto the counter.

Winnie rolled her eyes. "Sure, Mom."

Marty poured some Pepsi into a cup at the soda machine. She took a swig and scrunched up her face. "Dad, you want to check the fountain?"

Carl came from a doorway and made some adjustments with the canister under the soda machine. Then he said, "Try it again," and filled a paper cup for her.

Marty guzzled it down. "Perfect."

Carl motioned for me to follow. "Come on back. I'll show you the projection room."

The projection room was small, hot, and windowless, except for a small opening in front of the projector. It smelled old too. Not the old-book smell of a library, soaking up the scent of cinnabar and great adventures, but a lifetime of James Bond, Disney, and Schwarzenegger sentenced forever to cheap seats and stale popcorn. Stale popcorn with extra liquid butter that squirts from a pump.

Like an old-movie graveyard.

"It works like this," Carl said. "You see these black disks?"

The giant disks hung suspended over one another with a black snake of coiled film spiraling from the top disk feeding into the projector.

"When the film for the first feature comes out here, it feeds back onto the empty platter in the middle. Then we'll play the second feature, which is on the bottom, and it will feed back onto the empty platter on top."

Something caught his attention on the projector, and he lifted his glasses and looked closely through the bottom. His hair had more blond in it than I'd first thought. Maybe he wasn't ancient, after all. He fixed his glasses back and looked at me over the top of them. For a second I thought I'd said it out loud. His eyes were that same funny gray color as Marty's. He squinched them up and asked, really serious, "You seen *Godzilla*?"

"I saw *Godzilla vs. the Smog Monster* and *Godzilla vs. Mothra*. *Mothra* was better, except those twin fairies were so annoying."

Carl gave me a blank look, and I realized we weren't speaking the same language.

"I didn't see the new one."

My parents were classic movie buffs. We owned a whole library. The first videos they ever bought were *Casablanca* and *Philadelphia Story*.

"I remember now. I think I took Marty to see *Mothra* when she was a little thing." He tapped the coil of film. "Scary movie, this new one." He snapped his fingers. "Oh, that reminds me." He went to the doorway. "Marty, remind me to call the distributor for that Disney film tomorrow."

Winnie met him at the door with a roll of pennies in her fist. "Which one, Grandpa?"

"*Parent Trap*. The newer one." He asked me, "You got an opinion on that one?"

An opinion? I begged my parents to buy a vineyard complete with horses after we saw it.

"It was good, especially for a remake," I said. "I'd say four stars."

"That good?" He rubbed his chin. "Better than Hayley Mills?"

"Way better. But my mom—"

I left the words hanging in midair. My mom loved the original.

Carl pretended to be interested in checking the feed on the projector.

"That's where I got my middle name—Hayley," I said.

He winked. "Pretty name."

Marty called me back into the snack bar. She was stirring

gallons of unnaturally yellow cheese in a pan on a warmer. She handed the ladle over to Deja. "Don't let it scorch," she told her.

"Andie, we're going down to open the gates. You want to work the admission booth or stay here in the snack bar?"

I looked around. "I'll stay here. But what do I do?"

"You man the cash register. The prices are posted on the counter by the cash register. Grandpa will take care of the pizzas, and Deja will do nachos. Everything else is self-serve. You just stay at the counter and take their money. Dad, can you show her how to work the register?"

"Sure can," he called.

Deja turned, dripping cheese from the ladle onto the cement floor. "But I do the cash register. Why does she get to do it? She'll probably screw it up."

Marty paused with her hand on the doorjamb, looking stern. "Deja."

Deja backed down a little, slashing me sideways with her eyes.

"Stay where you are," Marty told her. "She'll be fine. You watch the flame. The cheese is hot."

Marty glanced back at me, watching me arrange the candy, tapping her nails on the wood. "Andie, after the rush, you can have some nachos or popcorn. Or candy, if you want."

I felt my cheeks burn. She probably remembered the Walgreens incident and had second thoughts about letting me handle the money after all. "No, thanks," I said. "I'm not hungry."

The old-fashioned register had rows of buttons like stepping stones and a *ding* when the drawer opened. Carl practiced with me a few times, pretending to buy pizza, sodas, and a couple of homemade brownies that Marty had brought from the house. When he was satisfied that I knew what I was doing, he took the brownies with him.

The first car pulled in and parked at the front speakers. I dug in behind the candy counter, flexing my knees so they wouldn't lock. Carl cut up the hot pizzas and put two more into the oven. Deja ladled hot cheese onto boats of chips and lined them up, all drippy. I started to sweat, just waiting for the first customers to come in. Math was my worst subject.

A funny feeling cinched around my chest and slowly squeezed the breath out of me while I stood there waiting. It wasn't only the math. What if people saw me? People from school. I'd look like even more of a loser when they found me in this loser place. The cinder-block wall across from me looked like a giant dirty thumbnail had scraped away paint, digging through layers of color. The metal trash can near the pizza ovens had dribbles of cheese and other stuff that hadn't quite made it in. It looked like somebody had used the NO REFILLS sign for a target.

Carl tuned the radio to a country music station. I hate country music. The songs are always about married people cheating on each other or somebody dying.

I squeezed my eyes shut and pressed my lips together, fighting the urge to shout that I didn't belong there. My family had nice clothes and wore college rings and drove new cars, not dinged-up Toyotas with taped-on taillights. They didn't own run-down drive-ins. They had real jobs. We went fun places together and after dinner we played Uno and Clue, and I always got to be Mrs. Peacock. Our family had a dad.

Not only did my knees lock up; so did my throat. Tears stung the backs of my eyes. Oh, no, I thought. Focus. Not here. Not with Deja watching.

I blinked and glanced over at her. She was busy with the nachos. I could see people through the window getting out of their cars headed toward the snack shack. Little kids running for the door with money in their fists. Focus.

I flexed my legs and tried to take a couple of deep breaths. I gripped the counter two-handed and studied the price list taped down in front of me. CANDY BARS, 75 CENTS. EXTRA LARGE POPCORN WITH BUTTER, $4.00. PIZZA, $3.50 A SLICE. Gradually I felt myself get more in control. I could see the road ahead. *Just breathe.*

By the time the first kid slapped his money down I was steady enough on my feet to add together popcorn and a soda.

I sold a steady stream of nachos, sodas, pizzas, candy, and beef sticks for twenty minutes before the first feature. It went so fast I didn't have time to think. Everybody had tens and twenties, so I had to be careful making change.

Some kids looked over at me, whispering. At least, it seemed like it. I turned my back on them. *Don't look at me,* I wanted to yell. *I'm not really here.*

When the movie started, people went back to their cars and things slowed down. Most people sat in lawn chairs or on blankets spread on the blacktop instead of sitting in their hot cars. One lady set up a portable crib for her baby. I could hear him fussing all the way from the register.

It felt like someone had released the pressure valve, draining away my nerves. This wasn't so bad. I even smiled at a little kid using his red licorice for a straw in his Mountain Dew. Godzilla roared from the screen outside, flashing dry lightning at the window. A few people hovered around the snack shack, bees lingering over what's left of a picnic.

Winnie and Marty came back from the gate about thirty minutes into the movie. There was another rush of people in the snack shack during intermission before the second feature, right after Carl announced that we were closing the snack bar.

When the last customer left, we closed down the snack shack

for the night. We scrubbed the counters and the pizza and nacho pans, and emptied the trash cans. The trash cans were gross, and I heard Carl say he'd hose them down in the morning. People are animals.

"Do you want to watch the rest of *The Wedding Singer*?" Marty asked me while she counted out the bills in the register.

I shook my head, although I had never seen a PG-13 movie. Since I'd moved in with Grandma, I was lucky to go to the movies at all.

"Okay." She paused in her counting, but said without looking at me, "Why don't you take Winnie back to the house, and you two can go to bed. You must be pretty tired. Here, wait." She counted out five dollars into my hand. "This happens to be payday." She smiled as I stared at the cash.

I followed Winnie back to the house in the dark while Adam Sandler and Drew Barrymore exhaled from the speakers. It was 11:45, way past my bedtime. My feet hurt, and I wasn't used to staying up late, and I wondered if Marty would take back her five dollars when she figured out how much money I'd lost making change.

Back in my room, I found Cyclops sprawled on my bed like Superman in flight. I got so mad I dragged the bedspread off the bed, crash-landing him on the floor. I carried it to the porch to shake off the cat hair, and when I shook it out, the bedspread connected with the wind chimes over my head and they all clanged together. I almost had a heart attack. Maybe I was a little creeped out by being there alone with only Winnie.

The house echoed with Winnie's brushing and flushing, until she showed up in the doorway of the bedroom holding a ratty blue blanket and a stuffed Pooh. She curled up at the foot of Deja's bed like a little dog.

"You're brave," I said. "Deja will kill you."

"It's okay. Mom will get me when she comes back."

"Whatever." I put away my copy of *The Door in the Wall* and reached for the blinds at the window.

"Leave them open," she whined.

I pounded my pillow into a cloud and settled in, covering my face with the sheet to shut out the lights from the drive-in. I was almost asleep when somebody pulled Winnie's string.

"The drive-in's cool, huh?"

"What?" I backhanded dribble from my mouth. "Oh, sure. Great." I turned my back to her and snuggled into Grandma's blanket.

"I think it's fun, 'cept we can never go anywhere in the summer. And then we can't go anywhere after Thanksgiving because of the trees."

"The trees?"

"After the drive-in closes we sell Christmas trees. And wreaths and garlands and mistletoe. Grandpa sets up this big tent where he sprays them with fake snow, and he plays Christmas music all the time."

"When does the drive-in close?" I asked, hoping she'd say next week.

"The day after Halloween."

"People go to the drive-in on Halloween?" I asked.

"Uh-huh." I heard her shift and yawn really big. "Last Halloween somebody climbed up and threw a dummy over the screen. People ran into the snack shack yelling, '9-1-1! 9-1-1!' It was great."

Winnie's words slurred together, and the next thing I heard was puffy breathing from Deja's bed. Then I dreamed that I opened the door of my old house on Evergreen, and Godzilla—

the black-and-white Godzilla—said, "Trick-or-treat!" wearing a wedding dress and holding out his treat bag, but I was all out of beef sticks.

Marty never asked me for the money back, so the next time we went to Walgreens I used it to buy some pretty stationery to write to Grandma and Grandpa. The notepad had birdhouses on it, and the envelopes were blue with a birdhouse on the back. I knew Grandma would like it.

When I got back to my room, I propped my pillow against the wall behind my bed and sat with an extra pillow on my lap like a desk and a book on top to make a flat place to write. I peeled off a piece of birdhouse paper and took the cap off my pen. The paper was decorated around the edges with trailing vines and tiny bluebirds. It smelled like the strip of glue that held the notepad together on top, all fresh and new.

I wrote *Dear Grandma and Grandpa,* then sat back and tapped my pen against my chin, waiting for inspiration. I continued, *How are you? I'm fine.*

Well, that wasn't really true. I rubbed the side of my head with my pen. I scratched out *fine* and wrote *okay.* This could be tricky. I didn't want them to worry, but I didn't want them to think I was having a great time, either.

What now? I looked around the room. My backpack leaned against the wall under the window. I told them how I was back at school with little kids, but then I added that my class was in a different part of the school. I read the sentence over silently, and continued. *My first day was . . .* Hmm, it had been a no-good, very bad day, but I couldn't let them know that. I finished the sentence with *okay*. So I lied, just to protect them.

I added *Marty bought me*, then I scratched it out. I didn't think they wanted to hear about her. Instead, I wrote *I got Lisa Frank stuff*, then I frowned. They didn't know who Lisa Frank was. I sat back and tapped the pen on my bottom lip. *School picture day is next week. I will send you one. I work at the drive-in.*

Uh-oh, big mistake. I scratched it out. I forgot they didn't approve of movies, and they still thought I was ten years old. Even though they watched movies on TV, they said it wasn't the same. The only time I remembered hearing Mom argue with Grandma was over a PG movie that only had one bad word in it. Grandma didn't think Mom should let me go to see it. I went, but we kept it a secret from her, and here I was, keeping secrets from her again. Bigger ones, this time. Sometimes you have to protect people.

Just then the bedroom door flew open and slammed against my dresser, and I scribbled a big zigzag across my paper. Deja came in laughing and rolling her eyes. I turned my shoulder a little so she couldn't see that she'd made me ruin it, even though I didn't really expect her to get that close. She turned on her CD player and jacked up the volume until the walls vibrated. Then she started singing along. It was really bad.

I tried to concentrate, but it didn't work. I fished around for the cap to my pen and took my notepad outside to the porch, which is probably what she was hoping for.

I stretched out on my stomach on the porch so I'd have a flat surface to write on. The coolness of the cement soaked through my shorts and T-shirt. No wonder Cyclops camped out like that on hot days. A faint breeze lifted the wind chimes and brushed them together. Blue jays dove for yard snacks. An ant crawled onto my paper, following along the border of vines—clearly confused—and I flicked it away.

What could I tell Grandma? I put my pen to the paper trying

to force the words to come, but felt only grit between the paper and cement. I couldn't think of anything. I was Frankenstein's monster, caught between different worlds, unable to put two words together.

I wrote *Does anybody want to buy the house yet?* and *Is Grandpa watching his sugar?* Grandpa had diabetes and wasn't supposed to have sweet stuff, but sometimes Grandma felt sorry for him and let him have it anyway. He got really grumpy if she tried to stop him, but he'd already had some toes removed because he wasn't taking care of himself. He had to wear special shoes to help him keep his balance.

My elbows got sore on the hard cement, so I sat up and brushed off the dirt. I smoothed out the letter and took a closer look at it. Practically every other word was scratched out. Some scratch-outs were so bad that my pen had gone through the paper. It was a mess. Not even the cute little bluebirds could make it right.

Disgusted, I copied the letter over, but it ended up being only a half page long. It didn't say what I wanted to say. Everything sounded too normal. But my life wasn't normal. It wasn't going the way I wanted at all. And I felt like I was slowly being smothered by my cat allergies.

The shadows of the tall bushes grew longer, erasing my written words with darkness. I wandered out into the parking lot, tore the letter into specks as small as lint, and left it behind in a trash can. Before I climbed into bed that night, I took out a new sheet of notepaper and wrote without giving myself time to think, *Dear Grandma and Grandpa, I love you. Please let me come home. Andie.*

CHAPTER 7

Marty

Dad and I let the girls sleep in on Saturday morning and went down to Sam's Club during Gold Key hours to pick up supplies for the drive-in. We had a pretty good system worked out. I carried the checklist, and Dad pushed the cart loaded with paper towels, toilet paper, chips, cans of cheese, frozen pizzas, popcorn, candy, and sodas. At the last minute I tossed in huge bags of walnuts and chocolate chips for the school fund-raiser bake sale. It was the one time each year I splurged in bulk. At the checkout, I handed over the card and pulled out the business checkbook.

"You know, Dad, this will probably be our last trip for the drive-in this season. The next trip will be for the tree lot."

"Yup. Time sure flies, doesn't it?" He hefted the frozen pizzas onto the belt and grunted.

The checker said, "Sir, you can leave the heavier items in the cart."

"Don't mind if I do," Dad answered, straightening out his back.

I watched him out of the corner of my eye. He was still physically strong for sixty-nine years, but emotionally, I wasn't sure. Mom had died of breast cancer just before Winnie was born, before we knew Ginger was sick, and Dad hadn't truly recovered when we got hit with my divorce and then learned about the baby-switch. Just when he should have retired to paint, he got saddled with me and the girls.

The drive-in had been a godsend. There we were with a mountain of medical bills and me with no marketable skills, and suddenly there it was, just sitting on the edge of town as though a veil was pulled aside. Ancient and neglected—just an eyesore, really. But Dad found an old speaker system on eBay and repaired the screen to get us under way in months. Just in time for the first summer. It became a source of income year-round, with the tree lot at Christmas and farmers market in the spring.

I pocketed the Sam's card and receipt, and we steered the cart over to the seating area. I picked up two free coffees—our ritual after shopping. During the early morning business hours the store was quiet and empty, and we could talk without little ears hearing everything. Father-daughter talks that my daughters would probably never have.

I loaded Dad's coffee with cream and sugar and sat down across from him on the hard plastic bench of the picnic-style table. I had something on my mind that he needed to know.

"Next I'll get *The War Wagon*," he said, as I gathered my thoughts. I realized he was talking about his monthly Western.

"Two John Waynes in a row?" I asked. "You don't want to mix in a little Eastwood?"

"Only got time for one more before we close for the season. I lean toward the Duke." He blew on his coffee. "The screen will need to be painted before we reopen in the spring."

I cleared my throat. "Dad, I hate to say it, but I think there was money missing Friday night when we closed."

"You don't say." He thought for a long moment, sipping his coffee. "How much?"

"About ten dollars."

"This the first time?"

"As far as I can tell. But I haven't had time to add up our resale figures in a while. Andie was manning the register."

"Andie?" He chuckled grimly. "I thought you meant Deja."

"Deja?" I squirmed. "It could be her." Then I told him my suspicions with the candy at Walgreens.

He rubbed his chin. "Andie had the candy right out in the open? She wasn't hiding it in her pocket, or under her clothes?"

"No. She wasn't hiding anything. That I know of." I pinched my forehead, trying to remember. "It was more of a feeling that something was wrong. I couldn't put my finger on it. But you're right—a kid would hide something if she was trying to shoplift."

I caught him up on Deja's saga of school and driver's ed. It was mainly to keep him informed, because he could offer little except support. Life was much less complicated when he and Mom were raising Charles and me on our ranch in Elko back in the early seventies. Everything was "Mom and apple pie" in our little corner of the world. We were too young to be drafted and too busy with day-to-day life on a ranch to get into trouble. Mom ruled the roost with the threat of action taken by Dad as a backup. That pretty much kept us in line, although I do remember mucking out the stalls as punishment on more than one occasion, and Charles often having the keys to the truck taken away.

I got up and tossed my empty cup into the trash. "By the way, Dad, the Toyota's sounding funny. And the engine light came on this week."

He unfolded himself from the table and threw away his cup. "I'll keep my eyes open for a good used car. Make sure you keep water in the radiator. We need to nurse it along at least till spring. I don't know how many more hot summers it can take."

We loaded the groceries into the truck, drove home, and unloaded everything at the snack shack. Winnie and Andie were eating Lucky Charms at the kitchen table when I came back to the house.

"Where did you go, Mommy?" Winnie asked.

"Grandpa and I went to Sam's."

"Can me and Andie go swimming today? I told her about the pool at Tweedy Park."

I opened the dishwasher and started unloading the top shelf, feeling an old panic surface. I'd go a mile around to avoid that pool.

"I don't know, Win. There's a lot of work to do, and I have a nail appointment at five."

"We can help you, Mommy." To Andie she said, "We haven't been there for a long time."

"I've got housework to do, and laundry. Grocery shopping. You know Saturday is work day."

Winnie begged and promised everything but her firstborn male child in order to talk me into taking them. But Andie sat silently watching me, communicating in an offhanded way.

I absently pulled a dinner plate from the bottom rack. "Andie, what do you think?"

She looked me in the eye for the first time in days and said, "I like to swim."

It startled me how much she looked like an older version of Winnie. How could I turn down the first request she'd ever made?

"Do you know how?" I realized what a stupid question that

was. Any kid who's been to another continent has probably had swim lessons.

"I passed Tadpoles, Sea Lions, and Mermaids."

I was trapped. "Well, I guess we could go if you two will help me out."

They pitched in with a vengeance, and by one o'clock we were cruising for a parking space by the pool. We tailed a mother and child from the exit to their car and waited until they loaded the car with swimmies and coolers and blankets and pulled out of the space so we could pull in.

We unloaded the car, and I tried to act like nothing was wrong, but on the inside I was battling to breathe normally.

Winnie ran ahead, motioning to Andie and calling to me, "Come on, Mom. Hurry up."

When I paid for two adults and one child, I said to the pool attendant for no apparent reason, "We're only staying for a short time."

"Same price as all day," she answered, and stamped our hands with a starfish.

We found a dry space in the grass for our towels, and I set up my folding chair so I had a view of the deep end. Before they ran off, I insisted they lather up with SPF 45 suntan lotion. Their skin was so fair. They ran to the gate, then glanced up at the lifeguard tower and slowed to a race-walk.

Two towers perched over the pool with umbrellas covering the guards. They couldn't be the same ones. No, both looked like they were right out of high school, possibly younger—and the incident happened the summer before Ginger turned nine.

We'd practically lived at the pool that summer. Ginger's mobility had deteriorated, but we found that she could move easily in the pool. The doctor said it was safe with close supervision and great exercise for her. Unless she spoke, she seemed almost normal in the water.

We were all having fun in the shallow end when suddenly Winnie had to go to the bathroom. "Number two!" she frantically cried for the whole pool to hear. Mothers pulled their toddlers away from our area in panic, and I tried to get the girls out of the water as quickly as possible. Winnie kept whining and got the attention of the lifeguard, who had her whistle to her lips. I hoisted Winnie out just in time for her to scramble in the direction of the bathroom. Her little wet footprints chased her into the cement-block building full of strangers.

I hoisted Ginger up onto the edge of the two-foot end and ordered her to stay where she was. I raced after Winnie and found her shuffling toward a stall with her bottoms rolled down, binding her knees together like a rubber band. I got her settled on a toilet seat and raced back to the shallow end to find that Ginger had slid back into the water and landed on a two-year-old. The lifeguard was yelling at her to get out of the pool, fully expecting her to respond like any other child her age, and getting angry that she wouldn't. It was awful.

I yelled back at the lifeguard that Ginger had disabilities and then bore the shameful looks of mothers with the question hanging in the air: *Where were you?* We gathered our stuff, and I carried two crying girls out of the pool. We never went back.

And here I was. I never would have believed I'd come back in a million lifetimes.

I tucked my hair up inside my hat to keep the sun from bleaching out my color, and popped the top on a soda. I dug out my magazine and relaxed for the first time since I'd walked in the gate. It wouldn't be so bad to sit here in the sun for a couple of hours if the girls had fun together.

I glanced up from an article on "The New Dating Game," which I found riveting, and located the girls at the deep end. Andie climbed the high dive and jumped in without a pause. Then I watched Winnie climb up on the high dive and hesitate. She inched toward the end and stopped. She stood there too long. Kids behind her started yelling at her. A boy bounced the board, and she went down on her knees.

I dropped my magazine and jumped to my feet. The lifeguard blew his whistle and climbed down from his tower. The line of kids behind her parted. The boy who made her fall climbed back down, and Winnie shuffled uneasily back toward the ladder. The lifeguard put the boy in time-out, then bent down to speak to Winnie, who checked out her knees and nodded. Andie came over to them, and he said something to her. She nodded and pointed over to me. I raised my hand in a little wave, and the lifeguard climbed back up to his post.

Winnie ran over and showed me her knees while Andie queued up for the low dive. I gave Win a drink of my soda, which made it all better, and she turned to go back to the water.

"Winnie," I said, "what did the lifeguard say to Andie?"

A puzzled look briefly swept her face, then she brightened. "He wanted to know if our mother was here."

She ran back to the lower diving board and got in line behind Andie, who stood shivering in the sunshine with her arms wrapped around herself.

I had trouble concentrating on the article after that. Andie hadn't given the lifeguard a long explanation about her mother. She'd just pointed to me.

At 5:10 I raced into the Nail Palace, apologizing for running late, slid into the chair at Shirley's station, and handed over my check, which I always wrote at the beginning of the appointment to protect my newly polished nails from smudges at the end.

"Five more minutes and I would've rescheduled," Shirley said. "I'm booked till seven." She opened her drawer, deposited my check inside, and shut it. She pumped remover onto large cotton balls and sopped it onto my nails, tsking. "You lost three this time. I keep telling you they're jewels, not tools."

Shirley was kind of a know-it-all who liked to hear herself talk, usually about her previous customers. I knew enough not to give her any information.

She also tried to cultivate business for other areas of the shop for hair, facials, and pedicures. She pounced as I returned from washing my hands and was choosing a nail color for the next two weeks.

"You need a color."

I picked out a bright Romantic Red and handed it to her.

"Not that kind of color." She reached over and tweaked the ends of my hair. "You've got three layers going on here."

I'd been coloring my own hair for months. Carving out enough time to apply a thirty-minute color in my own bathroom was a challenge, but an hour and a half at a salon every four weeks was completely out of the question—not to mention the seventy dollars it would cost.

I decided to be frank with her, even though I'd probably be the topic of her six o'clock appointment. "I can't afford to do both. And I can't do nails."

She chuckled. "Honey, you can't do hair either." She rolled the bottle of color between her palms. The little bead inside tinkled gently.

I burned at the criticism, resisting the urge to clench my fists as she painted my nails. She had no idea what life had been like for me. I wished I hadn't been so generous with my tip, but now it was too late.

She must have sensed she'd offended me.

"Look," she said, leaning in, "the next time you color, keep it on the roots. Don't comb it through until the last five minutes, just to freshen the color. And get the ends trimmed."

She added a quick-drying topcoat and turned her desk fan down toward my hands. I glanced at my watch, and after three minutes cut the drying time short and got up from the chair, carefully keeping from brushing my wet nails on any surface.

"Here, let me." She reached into the pocket of my purse and set my car keys in my palm. Then she went to the counter and flipped open an appointment calendar. "Two weeks from today?"

I let the words hang in the air. Would it really do any good to change manicurists?

"I need to make it earlier next time," she said. "My niece is having a baby shower, and I want to be out of here by four."

"That's fine," I said finally.

She wrote out an appointment card and tucked it into my purse.

I smudged a nail when I got out at Shop 'n Save to pick up some hamburger for dinner and allergy medicine for Andie. When I cruised aisle ten for meds, I passed over the name brands for the generic ones. Even those were pricey, considering how often I purchased them for her. Either they weren't doing the job, or she was building up a resistance to the medicine. When I picked up a lower-priced box, the smudge on my fingernail caught my eye. How could I spend forty dollars to have my nails done every month, and begrudge the best to the girl who pointed me out as Mom?

I was exhausted on Tuesday from working overtime the day before, which was Labor Day. We'd come up shorthanded when all the new hires called in sick. They were the only ones who had nothing to lose by putting a sick day against the holiday. Robert promised some newbie heads would roll.

The house was a wreck when I got home at six, because the kids were out of school for the holiday and Dad generally stayed out of the line of fire. In an emergency, they knew they could find him in the garage or tinkering beneath the truck.

There's an unwritten rule floating in space that when your house is at its absolute worst, you'll have company. So of course, the doorbell rang. It was the client specialist from Family Court Services.

She introduced herself as Doris Wren. I invited her in, and she made simple conversation while taking in the cluttered counters, clawed screen door, and overflowing trash can. Her name fit her well. Just like the little birds that clung to my mesh birdfeeder outside the window, she seemed sharp, focused, and tenacious. And she was a foot shorter than I, which didn't help the visual I had of her pecking at my self-esteem with her pen and clipboard.

She opened the fridge, I guess to see if mold cultures were growing in the dark, flipped on the kitchen light to make sure we had electricity, and picked up the phone to check for a dial tone. What did she think I answered when she called me? Maybe she wanted to see if we paid our bills.

"Is Andie here?" she asked. "I'd like to see her room, please."

"Of course. I'm not sure if she's in her room, though. I just got home."

I led her down the hallway, and we stopped at the bathroom so she could flush the toilet. Maybe it was best that damp towels covered the floors.

Her brows knit together as she scratched at her notes.

I grimaced, embarrassed at the oozing tube of Crest and soap residue in the sink. "Just got home." I closed the door behind us as we left the bathroom.

Music pounded the walls, and I stepped ahead of Ms. Wren to knock on the bedroom door. Opening it, I spotted Deja sitting on her bed, and with a discreet, wordless slash to my throat, motioned for her to cut the noise. She looked up crossly, but when she saw my guest, she grabbed the remote and muted the music. I introduced her to Ms. Wren and breathed a sigh of relief that at least Andie's side of the room was straight.

Ms. Wren took in Andie's neatly piled boxes, clean dresser, and clear floor space, and glanced over Deja's side, taking in the Linkin Park poster, strewn underwear, and incense burning in a bowl on her nightstand. Ms. Wren's mouth drew shut, and she turned away from Deja's side.

"I assume this is Andie's bed?"

"Yes, it is. Deja, do you know where she is, by any chance?"

"No."

With all the incense in the air, there was only one place she could be. "I'll bet she's outside reading," I said, motioning back toward the hallway. The social worker followed me out the door.

We found Andie in the backyard under a tree reading a book. The worker asked to speak to her for a moment privately, and I went back inside. Five minutes later, Ms. Wren came back to the house.

She questioned me about any visitors we had, particularly any who stayed overnight.

"Overnight." I knew what she meant. I could tell by her demeanor, and the fact that she left these questions to the very end, that this was a part of the job she disliked. But this was the last intrusion I would bear. Did she think that as a divorced woman my house had a revolving door? In a controlled voice, I explained that the only people who spent the night in our home were friends of my daughters—girlfriends—and they were properly chaperoned. She seemed relieved and let down her guard a little, stressing that it was her job to make sure that Andie was safe and making some adjustment. She assured me that these questions were necessary. I told her I understood.

She said she would drop by for another visit soon. I watched her pull away in her car and realized I had picked the smudge on my acrylic nail into a white gash.

What had passed between her and Andie? Did Andie fill her ear about the family, about the arguments with Deja, about what a disappointing mother I was? Did she share how she was doped up with allergy medication because of the family cat that wouldn't stay out? Or how we "forced" her to work at the drive-in?

It was then that I realized how shaky our victory was, and how we could lose Andie—just like that.

CHAPTER 8

Andie

There was a letter waiting for me on the counter one day when I came home from school. My heart did a little flip when I saw Grandma's loopy writing. I picked up the letter like it was no big deal and went out to read it under a tree, far from the house.

I gently pried open the envelope so it wouldn't tear. The letter was short and hard to read. I decided to buy Grandma some stationery with lines printed on it. She said they were doing fine and not to worry. There had been a few calls about the house, but no one serious. She said they loved me. *We love you, sugar.* I carried it around in my pocket for days. *We love you, sugar.*

She didn't mention the letter I'd written to her, and I wondered if it got lost in the mail. You hear about mailmen who toss their mailbags into their backyards and stay home watching soaps all day. Maybe my letter was in someone's backyard.

Nobody at school seemed to recognize me from the Blue Moon, which was a major relief. Maybe they only went to real theaters, instead of loser drive-ins. At least no one teased me about it.

But October was coming. Once they realized I was a Halloween baby, I'd get plenty of it.

Natalie had asked me one day when my birthday was, but I'd sidestepped it. She was just trying to be nice, anyway, so it wasn't hard to change the subject.

After school a couple of weeks before Halloween, we picked up Marty at the Shop 'n Save where she worked. It was one of those warehouse grocery stores where you pack your own food. Grandma and Grandpa would like this place, except they would cause a major bottleneck for being so slow.

"Momma!"

Winnie ran to Marty, who stood at a checkout stand wearing an orange apron and a name badge with red letters and a Mickey Mouse pin stuck into the corner. I watched her push the buttons with the pads of her fingertips and wondered how she did it without breaking her long nails.

"Hey, guys," she said to us. "This is my last customer."

"Mom, I need mascara," Deja said, veering toward cosmetics.

Marty called after her, "Grab a jar of spaghetti sauce."

As she turned off her lighted number over the check stand and put a CLOSED sign on the belt, another checker came by.

"Hi, cutie," the woman said, winking at Carl. Her voice sounded like she had swallowed gravel. Her hair was a shade of red that clashed with her lipstick and her apron. She hugged Winnie's shoulder. "Hi, hon. Is this your new sister I've been hearing about? Introduce me, why don't ya."

I could feel my teeth grinding together. Not my sister, I said in my head. Marty smiled nervously and flicked worried eyes over to Carl.

"This is Andie," Winnie said, looking bashful. She hiked her thumb at the lady. "That's Jo."

The woman said to me, "So how's it goin'? You getting used to everything?"

She reached out and twirled a lock of my hair around her finger. It was getting long. Marty had told me it would look good if I let it grow out, but I wondered if she just didn't have money for haircuts. I pulled back from Jo's hand.

"Look at that hair," Jo said. "You fit right in, don't you? And those eyes. You're the spitting image of your daddy." She laughed evilly. "Ooh, honey. He was a looker."

The color drained from Marty's face. "Jo-ooh," she singsonged.

I mentally composed a reply as she went on.

"We been friends since high school," she said, with a choking laugh like her lungs were congested. "Good old Elko High. Your mom and me get ornerier every year, don't we?"

Carl blew out a breath and dug both fists into his front pockets, his eyes riveted to the gray linoleum. Marty looked like she was going to throw up or pass out.

"Winnie, take Andie to pick out some cereal," Marty said, careful not to look at me. "Aisle six."

"Gosh, Mom. I know where the cereal is. Come on," Winnie said to me. "It's not like they ever move things around here."

I could just imagine what they said behind my back.

We detoured through the Halloween section—a tunnel of fake spiderwebs and black garlands, where rats skittered and victims screamed. I could smell the candy corn. It had been hours since lunch, and I was starving.

"This is where we get our costumes," Winnie said, "because Mom gets a discount. Look at this!" She fanned out a Snow White costume. "I love Snow White. Maybe we should be Snow White."

We, as in Winnie and me? I had this sudden flash of myself dressed as Snow White with that patent leather hair and Deja holding out a poisoned apple.

"She was a victim," I said.

Winnie's brows scrunched together in a silent frown.

"She never did anything to help herself. She's like Cinderella. She just waited around for someone to rescue her."

Winnie turned away from me. I guess I'd shot down two of her favorites. She fingered a yellow dress with a brown wig and a fancy mirror.

"Belle was okay," I said. "She had guts, standing up to the Beast. And she didn't let Gaston push her around, either."

"Yeah," she agreed, thinking. "I like Belle. Maybe."

I spotted a stretchy costume with a communicator pin near the shoulder.

"I was a Star Trek commander last year," I said. "I wonder if Grandma still has my costume." I squeezed the pin, wishing I could beam out of there. Maybe Marty thought I was too old to go trick-or-treating. "I'm hungry. Let's find the cereal."

After supper I wrote back to Grandma, asking her when I could visit and if she could find the costume for me. This time I had more to say. I told her about that lady, Ms. Wren, who came to visit from the court and asked me all kinds of questions.

By now, Grandma's letter to me was mealy and creased in the folds—pretty mangled for only being a week old. Her handwriting wobbled like it had a life of its own, but I knew her words by heart. As I sealed my letter, Marty came into the bedroom with an armload of folded clothes.

"Here, you can put these away later," she said, dividing up the pile of clothes between my dresser and Deja's. "Did you finish your homework?"

"Yes," I said.

"Is there anything in your backpack for me? Any newsletters to read?"

"Here." I dug out a permission slip. "There's a field trip. Some museum."

Marty looked it over. "The Exploratorium. That's a fun place." She turned her back to me and separated my clothes into piles on the dresser. "Do they need parents to go along?"

I thought of the other paper in my backpack begging parents to sign up.

"No."

She wasn't really my parent, so technically it wasn't a lie, was it?

"Oh," she said. "Tell your teacher to let me know if someone drops out. I could probably take a day off. I went there with Deja's class."

Going with Marty as mother and daughter. Now that would be the real lie.

Marty left, and instead of putting my folded clothes into the dresser, I repacked them into my suitcase. The temperature dropped ten degrees when Deja came back from the bathroom after her shower. She turned her CD player up loud, I guess so she wouldn't have to hear me breathe. It wasn't because I ever said anything to her. The cat sauntered in behind her and jumped up on my bed. Sitting there with the walls pounding and my nose stuffing up, I decided that a Star Trek Federation officer would never allow herself to be victimized. I went out to find Marty, knowing I would pay for it later.

When I passed through the kitchen, a mountain range of iced brownies cooled on racks with chunks of chocolate the size of grizzly bears, but I couldn't smell them.

I found her in the laundry room.

"The cat's on my bed again," I said as she loaded the washing machine.

Marty's eyes narrowed, and she said under her breath, "I wonder how he got in," like she already knew the answer. I followed her back down the hall. She stood at the bedroom door for a moment surveying the situation with her hands on her hips. Then she scooped Cyclops off the bedspread and into her arms. "Deja, the cat does not belong in here. You know that."

Deja paused from putting away her clothes. Her face twisted up into a rude sneer. She glared at me. Like the crack of an ice floe, she said, "The cat belongs. *She* doesn't."

Marty froze. She looked like she wanted to slap Deja. Maybe if Cyclops hadn't been writhing around in her arms, she would have. Her next words were daggers, unsheathed.

"You're grounded. All weekend. Turn off the music and go to bed."

Marty left with the cat, and the temperature dropped another fifty degrees. Deja slammed her drawers shut and combed out her wet hair like she had no feeling in her scalp.

I'd never had a true enemy before. And for sure I'd never slept in the same room with one. If Deja was going to be grounded at the house all weekend, maybe this was a good time to go back to Grandma's for a visit.

I looked at the letter I'd written, folded it up, and stuck it in my pocket. I went back out to the laundry room to find Marty. She was talking to herself and doing a sloppy job of folding clothes.

"Marty, do you think . . . I mean, um . . ."

She stopped and looked up at me. I licked my lips. What if she said no? She probably wasn't in a good mood for me to ask, but I blurted it out.

"Can I go to Grandma's this weekend?"

Her shoulders sagged. "This weekend? Well, I don't know. It hasn't been that long." She sat down on a laundry hamper.

Her Mickey pin winked at me from her collar. He was sitting on the beach under a palm tree.

"I have a Mickey pin," I said. I got closer and reached up to touch it. I liked the way it felt smooth under my thumb. "Mine's riding a surfboard." I turned her pin over. "You have one of the old pin backs. These fall off too easy. The good ones are rubber and are shaped like Mickey ears. I have extras, if you want one."

She didn't say anything. I pressed the back on tightly and smoothed it. "I have a ton of trading pins. Some are from Disney World, but most of them are from Disneyland. Where did you get yours?"

"Uh . . . Disneyland. There was a foundation, you know, that grants wishes for . . . for sick kids. They paid for us all to go."

I looked up at Marty. We were really close, and she had a funny look on her face. I let go of her pin and stepped back.

"Can I go to Grandma's? I haven't seen them for a long time, and they really miss me. And they need some help." I tried to think of stuff I used to do for them. "It's getting cold up there already, and Grandpa might try to clean out the gutters, or something dangerous like that."

She gave me a strained little smile, like she wasn't buying it. She rubbed her forehead. "Well, I don't know. I have to work all weekend."

I stood there, willing her to say yes. "We could go right after school. It's not that far. You could get back before the drive-in opens."

She looked past me down the hallway toward our room. Deja's music blared, and she was still slamming drawers. Marty sighed and narrowed her eyes. "It might be a good time to go, since Deja's grounded anyway. Why don't you call your grandma tomorrow after school and tell her you're coming?"

"Thanks, Marty," I said. "I'll pack right when I get home." I was so happy, if she'd been someone I hugged, I would have hugged her. I danced down the hall and didn't even care if Deja saw me.

Yes! Only two more days and I'd be back home at Grandma's.

CHAPTER 9

Marty

Win and I drove Andie up to Pine Run straight from school on Friday and dropped her at her grandparents' mobile home. The FOR SALE sign in the yard looked faded and weather-beaten. It was chilly, in more ways than one, and Winnie was unusually quiet as we left the mobile home park. I pulled into a drive-through on the edge of town for hamburgers before hitting the interstate, which cheered her up. The burgers turned out to be big and sloppy, so we pulled over to eat them in the parking lot.

The scenery was beautiful. No wonder Andie was anxious to get back. I rolled down the window to breathe in the fresh air. On a distant hillside, an Amtrak train wove through the forest, a gleaming satin ribbon gliding through an eyelet of sugar pine and cedar.

Stuffing her mouth with french fries, Winnie observed, "She's different."

"What do you mean?"

She shrugged and washed down food with a drink. "She never laughed before."

I thought for a second. "You're right." I thought about how Andie had become alert as we'd entered the park, how she'd bolted before the truck was completely parked, and how her solemn face had lit up in her grandmother's arms.

"Mommy, does she love them more than us?"

I squirmed a little, not wanting to hurt her feelings, and feeling hollow myself. "It's natural that she would love them more, Win. She doesn't know us very well, and they're her grandparents. They've been taking care of her since her parents died."

She reached greasy fingers over to caress my cheek. "Does that make you sad, Mommy?"

I grabbed her hands and planted a kiss on her salty fingertips. "No, sweetheart. It's good that her grandparents love her so much. You can never have too much love. You just watch—one day she'll be laughing with us."

Winnie licked some catsup from the side of her mouth. "Jimmy Cochran at my school, he lives with his grandma because his mom and dad are in jail. He doesn't like it, 'cause she makes him go to bed at eight and she won't let him play any video games."

Like I said, food does wonders for Winnie's frame of mind. She jabbered like her old self all the way back to Newberry.

We pulled in at dusk, just before the drive-in opened, and cruised around a line of cars waiting to get in. Winnie hopped out to open the gate so I could drive through. I found Dad working all by himself, because Deja had told him she was sick with cramps. It was her little way of getting payback for the fact that she was grounded.

After we got the snack shack in order, Winnie stayed behind with Dad to be an extra pair of hands, and I went down to the admission booth to open the gate. I spotted a car with the back end practically dragging on the ground, and I told the driver to pop the trunk. When he argued, I told him to come back on Tuesday nights, because it was family night and he could bring his trunk full of friends for $4.00. He made a U-turn and left.

I spent the rest of the evening thinking about what I'd said. What was a family? Here we were, a grandfather helping to support his single thirty-something daughter and her kids. Did a "normal" family exist anymore?

At unguarded moments we still connected, except for Andie, who needed time. We'd laugh together, and I'd see glimpses of our old selves, before our lives got hard. But more often than not, we were fragmented. Deja was gone mentally and physically with her friends, which was scary. Dad withdrew in frustration more and more whenever Deja showed her colors. Off and on since we'd lost Mom, he'd left us for several weeks to paint after the Christmas holidays, except when Ginger's health was at its worst. While he was away I'd have to work overtime to make ends meet, and the girls would be home alone most nights.

And of course, there was Russell. If I really wanted to blame someone for the way our family turned out, it would be him.

At least he'd never wanted to share custody. He never even wanted the girls for weekends or holidays, so I always had them with me at the most important times. Starr blocked any attempts by Deja or Winnie to contact him. It was her handwriting on the birthday checks they received, not his. She didn't know it, but her actions probably had spared them even more pain and disappointment. If I knew Russell, he'd promise them the moon, but he wouldn't deliver.

Starr was effectively erasing him from their lives. One day, maybe I'd thank her.

Later that night, after we closed down the snack shack, Dad made himself a buttery tub of popcorn and set up a lawn chair within earshot of somebody's car radio to watch the second half of *The War Wagon*. I headed back to the house. Deja's music blared, even though it was after eleven. I knocked once and peeked into her room.

She looked younger in her blue monkey pajama pants and T-shirt, without her black-and-red armor. Her head was crooked against the phone. "What?" she challenged.

"I see you're feeling better."

Her eyes got big, and I could see she remembered the lie she'd told Dad to get out of helping at the drive-in. "Yeah. I took some medicine."

"We're going to bed. Would you mind turning down the music a little?"

She wordlessly grabbed the remote to her CD player and clicked it down a few notches. It was still loud, but at least she didn't argue.

Instead of doing battle, I simply said, "'Night, honey. Love you."

She was probably expecting me to pounce on her for ditching the drive-in, so I think I surprised her. The corner of her mouth turned up just the slightest bit. "'Night."

I got ready for bed and was just turning off the light when Winnie knocked on my door.

"Mommy, can we have a sleepover?"

Her tummy showed beneath her baby-doll pj's, and she clutched her blanket like a four-year-old.

"Hm, I don't know. You kick. And you talk in your sleep."

"Oh, Mommy," she scolded.

"All right. If you promise not to kick."

She made a running jump onto my bed and burrowed in beside me. I reached past her to turn off the light and wrapped my arms around her. She smelled like all the summers of my childhood. It was comforting to have someone who would receive my love without question.

I lay contentedly listening to Winnie's steady breathing, thinking about Andie looking at my pin, so close that I could have grabbed her and hugged her. Any sudden movement would have frightened her hummingbird hands away.

How did I feel with her gone?

Worried that the baby steps she'd taken toward us would be erased by giant steps backward after spending time in Pine Run. Afraid that her grandparents would poison her against us. And guilty, when I realized that I also felt relief and that we all really needed a break from the stress.

Winnie shifted and sighed. I rested my cheek on her silky head and thanked God for this family, as flawed and imperfect as it was, thinking how He had let me curl up beside Him when I'd needed Him most.

CHAPTER 10

Andie

My stomach danced like Christmas morning the closer we got to Grandma's. Winnie had let me borrow one of her scrunchies. I tightened it and picked the cat hair off my clothes.

Marty parked the pickup in front of Grandma's. Yes! The realtor's sign hung in the yard. I slid out and ran to the door without waiting for Marty or Winnie.

Grandma opened the screen door. "Andie, sugar!"

I almost knocked her over when I hugged her. She fit lower in my hug than I remembered.

"Let me look at you," Grandma said, squeezing my chin in her cold fingers. "I declare, you've grown five inches."

"Hello," Marty said behind me, with Winnie hiding behind her.

Grandma said hello back, but she wasn't very enthusiastic.

I held the door back so Marty could bring in my suitcase. She took it into the living room, and we followed. She said hi to Grandpa, but he only nodded.

She set the suitcase in the corner. "Andie, remember that Carl will be back Sunday about four to pick you up. I guess we'll see you then. Have fun." She turned, and Winnie gave me a baby wave before they left.

Grandma watched her go. "Does she have to wear her slacks so tight?" she said, shaking her head. "And those fingernails. So gaudy."

The screen door slammed. I winced, hoping they hadn't heard.

The next morning at breakfast she asked, "Don't they ever cut your hair?"

"I'm letting it grow out," I said, tucking a stray piece behind my ear. "I never had long hair before."

She flipped a lock of my hair. "But it's so stringy."

I pulled away from her hand. "Grandma, I got a haircut in the summer."

"Your mama always looked better in short hair," she said, stirring her coffee white with cream. "When she was a little thing, I would put her hair in pin curls on Saturday, and it would stay so nice all week. She had a natural wave."

My hair was bone straight. It wouldn't even stay in Winnie's scrunchie.

Grandma washed all my clothes again, even though they were clean.

"They smell funny," she complained. "Maybe it's her machine. Sometimes a washing machine can have a sour smell. Especially an old one. And what's all this black hair on your pajamas? Do you sleep with a dog?"

"It's cat hair—"

"Cat hair! Land sakes, don't they know you're allergic to cats?"

"They keep him outside. He . . . he sneaks in sometimes. I guess he used to sleep on my bed. I take allergy medicine when I need it. It's okay," I lied.

She asked me questions about Marty, without actually saying her name. I tried to answer without giving any details. She asked me how "the others" were treating me, like they were from some strange planet. But I didn't tell her about Deja. Why make her worry?

I made the mistake of telling her that I worked at the drive-in on the weekends. I don't know where my brain was. She started complaining that I shouldn't be around those kinds of movies, and I explained that they only showed family movies and Westerns. And when she said they had no business putting me to work because I was too young, I started getting mad. She was always treating me like I was still a little kid.

Grandpa felt better in the afternoon, so when their social security checks came in the mail, we went to Safeway. Grandma drove so slow. Now that I didn't have to hide in the backseat, I wanted to. When she pulled into the parking lot, she barely missed a line of shopping carts a courtesy clerk was steering in the front door. Then she parked way over the line, and Grandpa swung open the Lincoln's door and smacked the car door next to us. I tried to hurry them into the store before the car's owner came back and noticed what happened.

We looked like a field trip from the opportunities class; Grandma leaning on her cart, Grandpa shuffling along in his special shoes like he was tethered to her, and me following with coupons, my eyes sweeping side to side, hoping not to be recognized.

It took hours. I mean, how hard is it to pick out milk? A quart jug of Crystal Dairy's whole milk—the same kind she'd bought every week since I could remember. All she had to do was to check the expiration date. She squeezed every loaf of bread on the discount rack and then decided she didn't need any. We ended up in the bakery section, where she let Grandpa put some sticky buns in the cart, even though he can't have sugar. By the time we got back it was getting dark, and Grandma turned the thermostat up to eighty.

I Love Lucy was the only thing worth watching on the three TV stations they got. Grandpa snorted and startled awake when I laughed, and then nodded off again when he realized it was me. After that, I didn't laugh so much.

I wondered what my friend Kayla was doing. I still had the friendship bracelet she gave me for my birthday in sixth grade. But then she started practicing cheers with Jennifer down the street from her and spending her allowance on lip gloss and body glitter. Grandma wouldn't let me play her Java Punks CD at the house the last time she came over. I hadn't seen her since school was out in June, and wasn't sure she even wanted to talk to me.

We didn't go to church the next morning because Grandpa's sugar was out of whack and he stayed in bed. The realtor called when we were eating macaroni and cheese and wanted to show the house in the afternoon. Grandma told her it wasn't a good day, but to try back later in the week. It took a day or so for Grandpa to get through these spells, she said.

Grandma and I spent the day looking at her photo albums. It used to make me sad to see pictures of my parents when they were young, but now it felt good to hear the same stories over again. I was a kite on a string, with the memories reeling me back to them.

Like a photo in my mind, I remembered the last time I saw my parents. We were at the airport before they left for Mexico, and they were wearing their new aloha shirts. Dad had his sunglasses propped up like his eyes were on the top of his head, and Mom had a new vacation purse made out of straw. It scratched my arm when she hugged me. We couldn't go all the way inside the airport and wait with them for their plane. We had to kiss them good-bye at the security checkpoint where only people with tickets could pass. Mom smelled like suntan lotion because they planned to go straight to the beach after they checked into the hotel.

Right after we heard about the hotel fire, and it was sinking in that they weren't coming back, we got a postcard in the mail. It was a picture of their hotel on the beach. Mom said they were having fun and they wished we were there too. She had bought me a souvenir, but it was a surprise. For a second I thought it had to be a big mistake. How could Mom and Dad send me a postcard if they were dead? It was all a big mix-up, and their plane would come back, and boy, would somebody be in trouble then. But Grandma showed me the postmark. It was mailed the day before the fire. I never did find out what Mom bought me.

I wondered how many other families got postcards. Postcards can be a bad thing. That postcard was tucked into Mom's Bible, and every time I read it, *Wish you were here* meant they were waiting in heaven for me.

We came to some pictures of my Uncle Greg and Aunt Robin in Canada with my three boy cousins. Grandma traced her finger around Tyler's picture. He was the reason I didn't have any brothers or sisters. He was a couple years older than me, and by the time I was five he was sick. My parents figured they just got lucky with me, because I was healthy, and they were afraid to take a chance on having another kid.

Once I looked up Niemann-Pick on the Internet. Scary stuff. It can take out a whole family before they even know what hit them.

"Little Tyler. He had that disease, you know. Poor Greg." Grandma studied it like she was trying to memorize his face.

My other two cousins were younger than me. "Are Brent and Kyle still okay?"

Her forehead creased. "So far as I know." She closed the book and put it back on the shelf. "Greg said they might come out for Christmas. I declare, I don't know where we'll put everybody."

"Don't worry about it, Grandma," I said. "It'll work out."

Uncle Greg said that every year, but they never came.

"Your mama was so good about visiting. She sent cards and letters all the time. But you know what they say: 'A daughter's a daughter all of her life, but a son's a son till he takes a wife.' "

Whatever. I guess she had to make excuses for Uncle Greg. For the rest of the afternoon, Grandma called me Noelle. That was my mom's name. It was still hard for her, I guess, just like Marty missing Ginger. A daughter's a daughter all of her life.

Before Carl came to get me, I dug out my Star Trek costume from the closet, just in case, and stuffed it into my suitcase. Then I opened some boxes of my stuff in the sewing room closet and pulled out a few books that I'd already read. I couldn't stand to be without a book, even if I already had it memorized.

At five minutes till four I heard the Dodge Ram pull up. I went into Grandpa's bedroom to say good-bye and then walked with Grandma out onto the porch with my suitcase.

"Are you sure Grandpa's gonna be okay?" I asked her while Carl threw my suitcase into the back.

"He'll be right as rain in a few days." She held on to my arm on the wobbly front steps. "Don't worry, honey. We'll be all right."

Then she raised her voice loud enough for Carl to hear, "And we'll let you know when we hear something from our attorney."

"I'll come back soon, Grandma," I said, wrapping my arms around her.

"Sure, honey. You just let me know when you're coming. We'll be here." She squeezed me hard, smelling like White Rain hairspray.

To Carl she said, "Sir, you take care of my granddaughter."

"Yes, ma'am, we will. Anytime she wants to come back for a visit is fine."

I waved at Grandma until we rounded the corner. I saw her dig into her pocket and pull out a tissue. Tears welled up in my eyes. It wasn't fair. They needed me, and I missed them. Then I remembered about the rain gutters and wondered if Grandpa would try to clean them out for real.

Carl got me a Blizzard at the Dairy Queen on the way back. I guess he thought food would make me feel better. He was an okay guy. It seemed funny that he was a grandpa, because he didn't act like one.

Cars had their headlights on by the time we pulled up at the drive-in. It was only six o'clock and already getting dark. The drive-in was opening earlier every night, with the darkness chasing it.

The marquee at the entrance had changed. It said PARENT TRAP and EVER AFTER. More oldies. We parked and went straight to the snack shack to help Marty open up. I felt a little nervous about seeing her, because of the snotty things Grandma had said about her, but she smiled when she saw me. She asked about my weekend and how my grandparents were doing, just like nothing had changed. Maybe she hadn't heard, after all.

Sunday nights were slow, so I got to watch *Parent Trap* instead of working. I didn't want to talk to anybody. I felt homesick for

Grandma and Grandpa. They had seemed really delicate, like old books that crack and flake when you turn the pages. I worried that Grandma wouldn't make Grandpa eat the right stuff and then she'd blame herself if he got sicker. Inside, I knew you can't make people do what you want, but you can still blame yourself, just the same.

Marty took Winnie and me back to the house after the first feature since it was a school night. On the way across the parking lot I remembered that I was the reason Deja got grounded. My feet slowed like they were slogging through wet cement.

Marty glanced back at me. "Deja's not home. She's spending the night with Summer. She was gone as soon as her time was up."

Could she read my mind?

"Was it bad?" I asked.

Marty snorted a laugh. "She was awful. But don't you blame yourself. This is something Deja has to sort out on her own." She gave my shoulder a squeeze before going in.

Marty helped Winnie get ready for bed. I unpacked my suitcase and put my clothes in the dresser. Then I thought about it and put them back in the suitcase. It was a sign of surrender to unpack.

Marty came to my door just as I was getting into *Johnny Tremain*.

"Do you need anything?" she asked.

I shook my head.

"Got any dirty laundry? Any cats to throw out?"

"No." I switched off my reading light and sat there in the dark, but she didn't go away.

"Marty?"

"Yes?"

"They don't have anybody else but me."

She stood backlit by the hall light with her arms crossed, leaning against the doorjamb. The shape of her head looked like an old-fashioned silhouette, with her corners softened. "I thought they had a son," she said.

"Uncle Greg. He hasn't come to see them in two years."

Marty nodded. "I know how much you love them, Andie," she said. "But you're only thirteen years old. You have to take care of you."

"I'll be fourteen next month. I can take care of me and them too."

Marty dipped her head. "Why don't you write to your aunt and uncle? Maybe they don't know how your grandparents are. Sometimes when you're far away from people, you remember them the way they used to be." She paused. "Or the way you want them to be."

"They live in Canada. I could get the address from Grandma next time. I told them I'd be back soon."

"Sure. You'd better go to sleep now. School tomorrow." She switched off the hall light. I couldn't see her face, but her voice was gentle. "Sleep tight, Andie."

After she left, I switched my light back on and fished around under my bed for Mom's Bible. Its ragged cover was the color of old beets. Flicking off dust bunnies and cat hair, I flipped open to the inscription: *To my loving wife, Noelle. Psalm 84:11. Forever yours, Gary.* Dad's handwriting was spiky and cramped. He said college ruined his penmanship, taking notes so fast.

Psalm 84:11. Maybe one day I'd actually look it up.

CHAPTER 11

Marty

The school's Harvest Fair was held on the first Saturday in October, and I naturally signed up to work the baked goods booth. Early in the morning, I double-parked in front of the school cafeteria, unloaded my trunk with the girls' help, and went back to move the Toyota while they headed for the playground before the fair got under way. Apple pies, pecan pies, walnut brownies, caramel delights, molasses joes, chocolate chips, cashew brittle, and cinnamon rolls represented my year's contribution to the school, since giving cash, as other parents did, was out of the question for us.

Dot, the PTA mom in charge of the booth, praised the massive amount of goodies I'd brought. I'd met her the year before, and for once someone remembered me because of my cinnamon rolls, not because of the baby-switch fiasco. Together we priced items and arranged the table, putting tiny samples on a plate to entice hungry parents and children to spend their scrip.

People arrived along with the sun. Out of necessity, the baked goods booth was always in the shade of the cafeteria. No one ever bought melted chocolate anything.

Dot was nice, but she filled the morning with nervous chatter. When her daughter, Natalie, came running up to the booth with Winnie and Andie in tow, I recognized Natalie as Ginger's friend from first grade. I realized then that Dot was afraid of saying the wrong thing, and couldn't stop herself from babbling. I could understand, but I hated it that people felt they had to tiptoe around me.

The girls begged quarters to buy scrip because the vice principal was in the hot seat in the dunk tank. I felt pleased that Andie seemed to be having a good time, since she hadn't wanted to come.

The smaller items sold quickly, and as usual, the pies were among the last items to go, even though they looked great and were no ordinary pies. Dutch crumb cinnamon apple and hazelnut crust pecan—my own twist on the originals.

Russell had always been uncomfortable with anything fancy. "Give me plain old American apple pie with nothing special about it, just like my momma used to make it." That didn't say much for his momma. After he left, I vowed never to make "plain old apple pie" again.

About midmorning, a man came up to the booth looking like an updated version of Bobby Darin. Dark hair, polo shirt, clean-cut, sunglasses. His unexpected good looks befuddled me, and I could hardly keep from staring. That hadn't happened to me in a long, long time. He stuck his sunglasses on top of his head, and Dot introduced him as Julian Barrett, the county health inspector. My defensive antennae went up immediately and mingled with the danger signs of attraction.

Wariness kicked in from my days of working at Leidig's Bakery when we were newlyweds—the owners used to go into a panic at the mere mention of the health inspector. Ursula and Guy were from the "old country," where authorities could shut down your livelihood without cause, with only a word. If we heard that another bakery in town had had an unannounced visit, it triggered a flurry of scouring and cleaning that seriously affected our output for the week.

Julian gave me a warm, easy smile and reached out to shake my hand, which I realized too late felt sticky and would send up flags that I was handling food without gloves. I wondered if a school bake sale fell under his jurisdiction. Then Dot gave him a sample of my molasses joes. He took a bite, and his eyebrows shot up. He nodded his head in earnest.

"That's very good."

"Marty made them. She's quite the baker." Dot handed him a sample of caramel delight. "Here, try this."

Honestly, his eyes rolled back in his head. I bit my lip to keep from grinning.

He asked, "Do you work in a bakery?"

A bakery? My suspicious mind spawned irrational thoughts. Was it a trap? Did he know I sold homemade treats at the drive-in without a license or a proper kitchen? So far, our little business hadn't attracted any attention from the health department, and we wanted to keep it that way.

I laughed it off, trying to sound nonchalant. "A bakery? Of course not." But his next words crystallized everything for me.

"Well, maybe you should consider opening one."

The universe hiccupped, and I blinked at him.

"Me?" Was he serious, or was this just a line to throw me off guard? Was I paranoid? I slowly shook my head. "Not in a million years would I open a bakery. I enjoy baking too much."

Leidig's Bakery had been a source of pride to the owners, but it had totally consumed their lives. The day-to-day operation of owning a bakery would take all the joy out of it for me.

"That's a shame," he said, digging in his pocket and handing Dot scrip for a mixed plate of molasses joes and caramel delights. "I should know. I visit a lot of bakeries in Whitcomb County. Maybe you should think about it."

He asked us to set the plate aside for him so that he could pick it up on his way out. When he said good-bye he caught my eye, and I immediately busied myself. Russell used to brag on my baking too, until he felt threatened by my success.

I'd started baking in elementary school, so when I landed my dream job at the bakery in the old part of town right after we were married, I was the happiest I'd been since I was sixteen and Russell first looked my way. We lived over the bakery in a little apartment, and it smelled like rising bread and sweet rolls around the clock. The scent of heaven. My feet never touched the ground.

Ursula and Guy let me experiment with my own creations as long as I produced a saleable product. After the first six months, they were featuring one of my items every week. Eventually my little accomplishments bothered Russell. And I think Ursula recognized jealousy when she saw it.

"Do not let anyone keep you from your gift, Marta," she said, pointing a floured finger at my apron front. Ursula refused to call me Marty, which she considered a boy's name. "You were born to bake. Do not let anyone steal your joy."

But by the end of the first year, Russell had started complaining about my schedule. The early shift was a rotten one for newlyweds. I was gone before sunup and asleep by eight thirty every night. One day he announced that we were going to California for a job he'd seen on the Internet. And the next day, we were gone.

Dot continued to fill me in on Julian. "He seems like such a lovely man. He goes to our church, you know. I think I've seen you there too."

My head snapped up. "Newberry Community?"

"Well, not lately. But before . . . I mean . . . you used to come."

I scooped cookie crumbs from the table into my palm with a cupped hand and dumped them off to the side, wiggling my fingers to free every crumb. I didn't remember seeing her at church, but I'd pretty much kept to myself. "It's been a while."

"Julian comes just about every Sunday. Well, he misses once in a while; who doesn't? But I think his job must be demanding. Maybe he has to travel. He seems to be a very dependable type."

The way she was promoting him, I think she wished she could say he was visiting his elderly mother.

The drive-in and the farmers market hadn't had an inspection in years. "I haven't seen him before," I said. "How long has he been here?"

"He started coming to church about six months ago, I think."

I rearranged the remaining baked goods, thinking that I'd have to warn Dad about the new health inspector. We kept a clean place, but it wouldn't hurt to brush up on the basics.

Throughout the day I found myself occasionally scanning the other booths for his dark head, like a silly teenybopper with a crush.

Sometime during the last hour of the fair he was back for his plate of goodies, still looking debonair, but wilted from the heat. He lifted up his sunglasses and stuck them back on top of his head. "If you have any more molasses joes, I'll take those too. What do I owe you?"

"We have a few," Dot said, flying into action. "I'll bag them up for you."

She turned her back, digging for a plastic baggie, and Julian pointed to the cinnamon rolls, mouthing the word *Yours?*

I nodded, noticing he had a dark shadow on his upper lip and it wasn't past noon.

He cleared his throat. "I'll take this plate of cinnamon rolls too," he said.

Dot ripped off a section of foil and tucked it around the rolls. "That'll be ten dollars."

He pulled out a twenty and told her to keep the change.

"Is there any chance we'll be seeing you in church again soon, Mr. Barrett?"

He paused and tilted his head.

"You *do* go to Newberry Community, don't you?" she asked, handing him the plate.

For some reason, his eyes briefly slid over to me. "Whenever I can make it."

A growing panic started at my legs, which wanted to buckle, or wanted to kick her in the shin for what I was afraid she was about to say.

"Marty has been to Newberry Community too. Although it's been a while. I was trying to convince her to come back sometime soon."

I pressed my lips together. She had no business being pushy with me. The panic had reached my chest. What if she mentioned Ginger?

He must have read my discomfort, because he said the perfect thing. "Perhaps if you held a bake sale."

Her mouth made a little O and she nodded knowingly, as if she recognized his cunning. She had no idea he'd neatly moved the question of my church attendance from personal to neutral ground. I met his eye, and he disarmed me with a smile.

"Thank you, ladies," he said, popping on his sunglasses and

gathering up his purchases. He briefly dipped his sunglasses down and looked at me. "Remember what I told you."

We stood watching him go. The sun had moved, and the corner of our table now caught direct rays.

"He's right, Marty," Dot said. "You really should think about opening your own bakery. I bet you'd be good at it."

I shook my head. "No, I used to work in a bakery, and I know what it takes to operate one. Up at four every day, six days a week, standing on your feet, dealing with customers, vendors, and landlords. Health inspectors. Doing bookwork until late at night, up again at four the next morning." I shook my head. "It's hard on a family."

We moved the table back into the shade for the rest of the day. When my shift was over, I helped Dot get the booth cleaned up and went looking for Andie's homeroom teacher. I found Mrs. Bettencourt at the drug-free booth inflating balloons. She said Andie hadn't had any more outbursts that she was aware of, but that she didn't participate in class discussions and it was affecting her English grade. I was relieved to find that she seemed to be adjusting, and wasn't really concerned about the grade. One step at a time.

I sincerely hoped I wouldn't run into the health inspector before I got the girls corralled, packed up, and out of the parking lot. He seemed smooth and dependable, but so was my Frigidaire. I wasn't in the market for a relationship of any kind.

The encounter did complicate things. Over the last few months, I'd actually toyed with the idea of going back to Newberry Community. Now I worried about running into Julian, and how I would feel about it.

After dropping the girls at home, I stopped by Ginger's grave and barely made it on time for my nail appointment. Shirley complained about the dirt under my nails and mentioned that, by the way, my knees were also a mess. I wasn't about to explain to her about tending Ginger's grave, so I let her go wild with spider decals to distract her. I scheduled another appointment, trying to stretch it out to three weeks this time. She pressed me to schedule my following appointment while I was at it because her times filled quickly around the holidays. I agreed, knowing it would probably be my last appointment for several months. I felt guilty enough having my nails done when we had to scrimp so.

The time between the tree lot and drive-in always stretched into a long winter until the farmers market opened in spring. That called for serious belt tightening. I was considering trying to sell my baked goods at the market this spring, only to the vendors early in the morning before the market opened, just to see how things went. But what if the new health inspector showed up?

My yearly mammogram was scheduled for that week with a big circle around the date in my pocket calendar. I wasn't even forty yet, but Mom had died of breast cancer at sixty-four, and the doctor wanted to get a baseline to watch me closely.

I sat in the little closet wearing my drafty gown, clutching it shut in the front, and felt a shroud of depression across my shoulders. I endured the whole routine and was ready to get dressed, but the technician said to wait. There were more pictures she needed to get. That could only mean that she'd seen a shadow or something out of the ordinary.

I gathered my gown tighter and shivered in that pale green cubicle with the piped-in elevator music and smudges on the handle of the accordion door. Could my mammogram really show an abnormality? How would my little family cope if I got breast cancer? Who would take care of me?

I'd sat with Mom in the oncologist's office every week for six months, watching the tube of red chemicals feed into the catheter implanted in her chest as she reclined with a blanket across her lap. The catheter was necessary because her veins collapsed and her blood seemed to dry up whenever a needle was present. She said she felt like a science experiment, and that was on days when she felt well enough to joke around.

That was before Winnie was born and before Ginger got sick. Mom never even got to see Winnie.

The magazine in my lap was at least five months old, featuring egg bread for Easter on the cover, and I thought about what Julian Barrett had said. Deep down, in my most secret longings, I did sometimes dream of having my own bakery. But it was like a glint of refracted light from a diamond that splashes on the wall and disappears. It's beautiful and alluring, but intangible as fairy dust. You turn to look and it's gone.

Finally the technician came back and told me to dress. When I asked her if there was a problem, she said she wasn't supposed to say, but it looked okay to her. If there was a problem, she said my doctor would be notified.

I called my doctor's office every day that week until they told me they'd gotten the results, and they were clear. By that time, I really didn't care if they thought I was a pest. I couldn't stand not knowing.

I expected to feel relief when I got the good news, but my spirits didn't really lift. Ringing up cans of soup ten for a dollar at my checkout stand, I finally put my finger on what I was feeling. Carlos moved among the endcaps, refilling the magazine racks with the latest November magazine issues. Glossy turkeys and gingerbread houses took their places alongside jack-o-lanterns and autumn scenes.

The holidays were coming. I had the weirdest feeling that I stood on the edge of a vast desert, dry and barren, and on the other side was Life After. How would I make it safely across? Would I have a meltdown during the next few months?

My check stand was as far as I could possibly get from the magazine section, and my endcap never had anything but candy. Robert had made that concession for me when I was hired. There were times when I could hardly function with all the reminders of the holidays to come. But that was then, and I couldn't avoid the magazine rack forever.

The first bit of quicksand I'd have to navigate was Andie's birthday, which was also Ginger's birthday. And Halloween. Ginger had dealt with stupid jokes about being born on Halloween, and I'm sure Andie had too. I owed it to Andie to do my best to make her day special.

Plans for her birthday took shape in my head while I checked out customers. I'd been doing the job long enough to multitask, writing internal grocery lists, planning weekly menus, and creating new recipes. We would take Andie out for her birthday dinner, and I'd make a really special cake. Something with beads and rosettes. She seemed like the rosette type. And I would arrange with her homeroom teacher to surprise her with cupcakes. That wouldn't be so hard, would it? Of course we'd give her a little gift. I had no idea what. Maybe Winnie would have some suggestions.

For her last birthday, Ginger had wanted a CD by a boy band, just like some of her friends from school had gotten for their birthdays. We all pretended to like the music, since she played it over and over again. I'm not all that sure she liked it herself. She wanted so desperately to forget that she was different.

Ginger was mainstreamed in regular classes up until the last few months of third grade, mainly for the social interaction, because she couldn't keep up with the work. All the research said that when a child gets Niemann-Pick Type C as an older child rather than as a toddler, they have a reference point of normality. They remember when they were just like everyone else. Their self-esteem suffers because they know how they now appear to their peers. Geeks. 'Tards. All those horrible words kids use to wound each other when they don't know how to react. Slurred speech, impaired motor coordination, seizures—all embarrassing to a kid who remembers how she used to be.

That night when I picked up some cupcake papers on my way out of work, I also grabbed some canned pumpkin and cream cheese for a pumpkin cake roll, and some dried cranberries for scones. I threw in a Mylar birthday balloon for Ginger's grave.

The next day I called Andie's teacher, and we agreed on the following Thursday for the cupcakes. Then on the night before, I waited for the girls to go to bed and started baking.

That particular day had been hectic. My register was down, so I had to move and ended up by the magazines at check stand 10. The holiday magazines. I assured Robert I was okay with it. No problem. But I guess being around all that holiday cheer must have affected me more than I knew.

I mixed up the batter from scratch and poured it neatly into the pastel papers nesting in the cupcake pan. Then something happened that hasn't happened to me since elementary school. When the timer went off, I peeked in to find that the cupcakes had sunk in the middle like oceans on the moon.

I stared at the twenty-four little failures until the heat soaked through the potholder and scorched my hand. I felt personally affronted. What had I done wrong? Was the baking powder old? Did I leave something out? I sagged into a chair and put my head in my hands.

Had I lost my touch? Did I sabotage myself?

What would I do without cupcakes?

Think. I couldn't reschedule with the teacher. It was too close to all the Halloween activities at school. Maybe I could just forget about it. Since Andie didn't know I was bringing cupcakes, she wouldn't miss them. But what if Mrs. Bettencourt had accidentally let it slip? Andie would be disappointed and think she'd been set up.

I felt cornered and did something I'd *never* done before. I drove to our competitor, Food Town, and bought prebaked cupcakes. Then I scraped off all the icing, whipped up my own buttercream frosting, and topped the cupcakes with sprinkles. The perfect crime.

I quietly cried as I iced them, because in my mind, giving less than my best to Andie was the same as cheating Ginger.

CHAPTER 12

Andie

When I was a little kid I used to think everybody dressed up in costumes on their birthdays, just like me. In kindergarten, I realized that my birthday and Halloween were two separate things. It was kind of disappointing. I started celebrating my birthday two weeks early so I didn't have to decorate with orange and black.

I didn't expect an actual party this year. But Grandma did send me a check for twenty dollars in a birthday card. Not enough for a cell phone or an iPod, which was what I wanted. I didn't expect to get anything from Papa Jack and Grammy Lockhart, because I was pretty sure they didn't know where I was now. I got the feeling that they wanted to forget I ever happened.

"When's your birthday?" Winnie asked, spraying crumbs.

We were doing homework at the kitchen table, and she'd crammed a whole milk-soaked oatmeal raisin cookie into her mouth.

"October thirty-first."

Her glass of milk paused halfway to her mouth. Chewing,

Winnie glanced over at Marty by the sink. "That's like . . ."

Like Ginger. Hello, we were born on the same day at the same hospital.

"Do you want to have a party?" Marty asked, sounding a little too perky. "You can invite some friends from school if you want."

Friends? From school? My only friends were left behind in Pine Run.

"No, thanks. I don't want a party."

Winnie bent her will on choosing between the three kinds of homemade cookies on the plate.

"You get to pick where we eat your birthday dinner, right, Mom? Any place you want."

"Any place within reason," Marty said, whisking away the cookie plate before Winnie could reload. "And we'll come home for cake and ice cream afterward."

I shrugged. "Sure. Whatever. It's no big deal."

"You said it," Deja agreed from the couch.

A few days before my birthday Mrs. Bettencourt said, in the middle of English, "Andie, your mother is here."

I looked up from *The Yearling* to see Marty balancing two trays of cupcakes, trying to make room to set them down on the desk. She was talking too loud and smiling too big. I'm sure she made a mental note to warn Mrs. Bettencourt about calling her my mother.

I guess it wasn't her fault. But the word shot through my chest like a silver bullet.

"Come up to the front and pass them out, Andie," Mrs. Bettencourt said. "This is a good time for a break."

I closed my book and stuck it in my desk. I really wished Marty hadn't made a big deal about my birthday—I was fourteen, not four—but I guess I shouldn't have been surprised that she'd bring treats. It was like the ghost of a dead pastry chef had possessed her body. We were wading in cookies, scones, and cinnamon rolls at the house. Funny, I don't remember her eating any of it.

She smiled in a kind of relieved way when I took the cupcakes.

"So it's your birthday today, Andie?" Mrs. Bettencourt asked.

Before I could stop her, Marty answered, "It's not actually until the thirty-first."

Snickers broke out from the fourth row where Scott Worley sat with two other rejects. I was surprised how quickly they connected the date with Halloween. At least one of them had a spinal cord that connected to his brain.

"Queen of the undead" floated to the front. "Alien pods mix-up."

Natalie turned to them and mouthed words I could only think in my head. I thought I saw flames shoot from her mouth.

They hooted and laughed until Mrs. Bettencourt announced, "You three boys have lunchtime detention."

That sobered them up. Marty tried to distract me, touching my shoulder lightly.

"Andie, I've got to get to work. I hope you like them. The cupcakes." She pointed to Scott's group. "Forget them."

I nodded and tried to smile. I kept thinking about the stupid Satan's spawn and Mummy dearest jokes that would be coming now that everyone knew my birthday. The baby-switch would add a new dimension this year.

"They're immature jerks," Natalie said at lunch. "Don't even listen to them, Andie. Scott will probably be in juvey before he's sixteen."

"I'm used to the Halloween jokes. They don't bother me anymore," I lied.

"Are you guys going trick-or-treating?" she asked. "The

church has a carnival that's pretty fun. I mean, if you want to come. I go with my little brothers." She sucked down her diet soda. "Your moth—I mean, Marty knows. It's the church where they went after Ginger died."

"I don't know. Maybe," I said.

She worked at peeling the label off an apple for longer than she needed to. I wondered if she used to be Ginger's friend.

The next day in English, Mrs. Bettencourt passed out oversize papers of a tree with spaces to fill in. "Tonight you will begin filling out your family trees. You may use any records that show birth, death, and marriage dates. This assignment is due on Friday, so this gives you three days. Plenty of time. And please use colored pencils to decorate them."

That night at the house, Deja was really losing it, so I didn't even try to do my homework in our room. I dumped out my backpack at the kitchen table, and Marty saw the family tree assignment. She immediately dug out albums and boxes full of pictures and started showing me photos of old people and young people, in black-and-white and color. Most of the old ones were on some kind of farm or ranch, or at a rodeo or on a horse. So I was related to Yosemite Sam?

Marty sometimes got Winnie's and Deja's baby pictures mixed up, they looked so much alike. Deja and Winnie looked like blonde blobs with dots for eyes. Ginger looked like a neighbor kid who wandered into the pictures.

Winnie noticed what we were doing and left the TV to Carl.

"Here's Grandma and Grandpa," she said, showing me a really old black-and-white picture of two people standing beside a picket fence. There was a horse between them with a little girl in the saddle.

"What was your horse's name, Momma?" Winnie asked.

"Tipper."

"Where's your bride picture?" Winnie asked, flipping through the album. "Here, look."

A younger Marty with big hair, in a wedding gown, clung to the arm of a tall man in a western-style tux and cowboy hat.

"That's our dad," Winnie said. "Isn't he cute? He lives in Nevada. We never get to see him."

"There's a very good reason for that," Marty said, pulling the album out of Winnie's hands and closing it.

She pointed to the first box at the top of my paper with a black fingernail with a spiderweb decal. "Here, we'll start with your great-grandparents, Arla Jean Miller and Oscar Browne McAlister. Then under that put Carlton Dean McAlister—that's Dad—and my mom, Betty June Troy. She died in '97, before Winnie was born."

She paused for me to catch up.

"Then put my brother, Charles Monroe McAlister. He never married and has no children—that we know of, anyway. Then under that put me, Matilda Inez McAlister, and John Russell Winslow. He's . . . he's your father." She tapped her nail on the box. "Then under that write Deja Michelle, and then your name."

I wrote Andrea Hayley, just to get it over with.

"Then put Winona Jade. That's Winnie. And that's it for our side."

Winnie looked cross. "Momma, you forgot Ginger."

Marty sighed. "I didn't forget her, Winnie, I—"

"But Momma, you said—"

"I know, honey. I know." She reached across and covered Winnie's hand with hers. "We'll always love Ginger, honey. But this is Andie's homework."

Winnie pulled away, and her face screwed up.

"There's room under my name," I said. "Right here. What's her middle name?"

Marty cocked her head at me and gave me a funny little smile. "Celeste. Ginger Celeste."

Her name ran into mine on the page like we were one person.

Satisfied, Winnie opened the album with Marty's wedding picture again.

"Here's Christmas!" She pointed at before-and-after Christmas tree shots. "Here's the tree before we started. Here we're putting on the ornaments. I got to put the unbreakable ones around the bottom 'cause I was little. Here's Cyclops playing with a garland. And this is after we're done."

Three little girls in their jammies smiled in front of a leaning tree. I recognized that it was in this same house. Next to that was a picture of Marty, husband, and baby sitting in front of a small Christmas tree. They looked so young, like they were only playing house.

"Deja's first Christmas," Marty said.

"Look, here's Mom and Dad at the prom."

In that one, Marty's big hair and yards of frou frou lace looked out of place with the cowboy beside her. His right arm was draped carelessly over her shoulder, and his left thumb was hooked in the belt loop of his straight-legged jeans.

"And this one's their honeymoon. They stayed at a casino."

"Is this Las Vegas?" I asked. I'd never been there, but I was not impressed.

Marty snorted and shook her head. "Not even close." Then, under her breath, "That should have been a clue."

Winnie complained when Marty took back the album.

"That's enough. No, Winnie, I'm putting these away now. Go get the movie we rented."

"Can I call Grandma?" I asked. "Her letter said Grandpa was sick, and I wanna check on him. See if he's okay."

"Sure. Use the phone in my room."

I went down the hall into uncharted territory and pushed open Marty's door. Her room smelled like vanilla and reminded me of an old-fashioned ice cream parlor. I went in and sat down on the edge of her white iron bed, triggering an avalanche of lacy pillows. I reached for the phone.

Beside the phone on the nightstand was a photo of a birthday at Chuck E. Cheese with Ginger and Marty wearing party crowns. I picked it up to look closer, careful not to disturb anything. Ginger looked different from the tabloid photo. She leaned toward Marty like she was slowly falling over. I expected her to tumble out of the picture onto the bed beside me. She looked bigger, but not older, like a big goofy puppy. Then I looked closer and felt my insides fall down to my toes. Maybe I'd feel goofy, too, if I had to go to Chuck E. Cheese in a wheelchair.

It was then that I noticed the trash can by the bed overflowing with wadded tissues. I was pretty sure Marty didn't have a cold.

Mom and Dad never talked about my cousin Tyler, except in whispers when they thought I couldn't hear. I heard my mom say once that he was having a hard time because his friends were calling him a retard. I wondered if Ginger knew what was happening to her too.

I remembered overhearing my parents arguing about me. Dad telling Mom she needed to let me be a kid, that she was smothering me. It scared me at first, picturing pillows in the night, because I didn't understand. I'd fallen at school, and Mom had taken me to see Dr. Barber again. I only had a skinned-up knee and some bruises from falling off the monkey bars, and the doctor seemed a little bit tired. He patted Mom's arm and told her it was normal for kids to fall. I don't think she believed him. She worried like that.

I wanted to believe him that I was normal, but I wasn't sure because Mom worried so much, and because of Tyler. Sometimes

I'd felt like a shadow followed me that I couldn't quite get into focus, and couldn't talk about to my parents. My little ghost.

A burning taste soured my throat. The little ghost finally had a face—the face of the kid in the wheelchair.

All that time growing up I was waiting for something bad to happen, feeling like I was doomed. But it was all for nothing. It happened to Ginger, not to me, and she didn't even see it coming.

A mean thought came into my head. A terrible, mean thought. Right then I was a little bit glad for Mom and Dad that the whole baby swap happened. That way they didn't have to suffer like Marty did. She took their pain for them, and they never knew it. But in a way I guess they felt a different kind of pain, just waiting for me to get sick all the time.

Ginger looked happy in the photo. Silly happy, with that giant mouse in the background. Marty had her arm around her. My mom would've worried about her the same way she worried about me. I couldn't take my eyes off the picture, imagining my mom with her arm around Ginger.

I picked up the phone and punched in Grandma's number.

Grandma asked me what was wrong. I could never fool her. I said I was getting a cold and made up something about being tired. Then I asked about Grandpa to change the subject. She said he was doing a little better, and that the real estate agent had brought some people by that day to look at the mobile home. They hadn't heard anything yet, though. We made plans for me to come at Thanksgiving. I said I couldn't wait.

After talking to Grandma, I buried the family tree in the bottom of my backpack, and the next day I asked for another blank one from Mrs. Bettencourt. Secretly, I made a Lockhart family tree and turned that one in instead. I didn't have many dates or complete names, but it was my real family.

✦ ✦ ✦

We went out for pizza for my birthday on the weekend before Halloween, and they gave me the *Lord of the Rings* boxed set as a present. Marty asked me if I'd read them, and I said yeah, but I loaned them to my friend Holly, and she moved away and I never got them back. Carl drew a picture of me riding a horse with its front feet up in the air like Zorro on the inside of the first book. He's pretty good.

The birthday cake Marty made had two levels draped with icing beads and yellow rosettes. The only thing missing was the bride and groom.

I said, "Maybe you should open a bakery or something."

Marty looked at me funny, and for a second I felt stupid, like I'd said something wrong, but then she smiled and thanked me. Go figure.

Carl had ordered *The Ghost and Mr. Chicken* to show at the drive-in for Halloween night. It was a really old movie, and I think he just picked it out for himself, because nobody goes to the movies when you can go trick-or-treating—I don't care what Winnie says.

Halloween night was a shocker. Marty came out dressed like a cat in a skintight black leotard and black satin Daisy Dukes over it, a headband with cat ears, and penciled-in whiskers. She didn't grab a pillowcase for candy, but she did have a camera.

Winnie wore a Belle costume. I had squeezed myself into my Star Trek uniform. The stretchy material plastered the chain and wedding rings against my skin.

"Stand next to Andie so I can get your picture," Marty said, maneuvering to get us both in.

I wasn't sure how she could take pictures with her long nails covering the lens, but I didn't want to end up in the photo album. I moved out of camera focus and reached for it. "Wait. Let me take a picture of you and Winnie instead."

Marty looked like she wanted to argue, but she handed it over. I squinted through the lens at them. Marty scrunched down to be level with Winnie, and when she smiled, her whiskers wrinkled into wiggly lines.

We drove across town to a fancy neighborhood where the houses dripped creepiness and munchkins fearlessly crossed the street. The money these people spent on Halloween decorations would feed a family of four for a month. When the doors opened to our "Trick-or-treat," I could see into formal living rooms where no one ever sat, or family rooms with big-screen TVs. My house on Evergreen was like that.

After hitting every house, we stopped by the church for the carnival. The church wasn't a regular stained-glass building with a steeple. It was a storefront in a strip mall, right next to Jiffy Hardware. I wondered what we were stopping for until we got out and I saw the church sign.

Natalie was there, dressed as a rock star. We were the oldest ones, so we helped out with the games for candy and prizes, and then we helped to keep the little kids quiet while they listened to a story about two pumpkins. One pumpkin was all rotten and dark inside with a sad face cut into it, and one was smiley and had a bright candle burning inside with a heart-shaped opening cut into the back. That's how they put the light inside, through the heart. They said that Jesus came into your heart and brightened your life and kept you from rotting. The bad pumpkin reeked like the dumpster beside the Shop 'n Save, with tiny gnats buzzing around it.

I'd asked Jesus into my heart when I was six, but all I could smell was the garbage. Maybe there was more to the story, and I just didn't hear it. Maybe my heart-shape was plugged.

Before we left, I heard Marty promise the pastor we would be back soon.

When I got ready for bed that night, I found I had the perfect outline of the chain and wedding rings pressed into my skin.

Deja came home late that night. She stumbled in our room and must have hurt herself, because I heard her swear. I pretended to be asleep, but I could smell something funny. Not the usual funny smell of her perfume or incense. More like the way Uncle Greg smelled by the end of the Super Bowl.

CHAPTER 13

Marty

"Think that turkey's big enough for the five of us?" Dad asked as we pushed the cart over to the seating area at Sam's. We had switched from a flatbed to a cart since we didn't need resale items at the tree lot.

Nestled beside packs of Styrofoam cups, hot chocolate mix, candy canes, and assorted two-inch-wide rolls of wire ribbon for Christmas wreaths sat a twenty-one-pound turkey and other fixings for Thanksgiving dinner.

I filled two cups with free coffee, loaded Dad's with cream and sugar, and carried them to the table. "Dad, the turkey needs to be big. You want leftovers, don't you? Turkey potpie, turkey soup, turkey salad. Turkey surprise."

He blew on his coffee, making little whitecaps. "I'm not sure about that last one. We'll eat our weight in turkey sandwiches while we're getting the tree lot going, I suppose. Did you ever find out if any more money's missing?"

"I haven't been able to do the books yet. Andie wants to spend

Thanksgiving with her grandparents. Maybe I'll find time while she's gone."

"Too bad," Dad said, and slurped his scalding coffee. "We could use an extra pair of hands then. How's she doin'?"

I shrugged. "She's making slow progress. Her teachers say she doesn't participate in any discussions, but she hasn't had any more outbursts. She still keeps her clothes in her suitcase. She doesn't let Deja intimidate her, though." Any other child would have been driven out to the living room couch by now. I pinched a pattern around the lip of my paper cup. "The holidays are coming. I'm not sure what will happen then."

"They'll be hard on all of us," he said.

I looked up to meet his eyes. He looked away and rubbed his nose.

I'd noticed in the last few years that Dad was easily moved to tears, especially about Mom. I felt like a very bad daughter just then. I wasn't mourning in a vacuum.

"Mom's birthday's coming up, isn't it?"

"The thirtieth."

"I'll fix something special that day."

"Darlin', you fix somethin' special every day."

I reached out and patted his hand. "Andie told me that it hurts for a long time when someone dies, but that it slowly gets easier. She's pretty wise for a fourteen-year-old."

He nodded, unable to speak. Finally he said, "She comes from pretty amazing stock."

We talked about the tree lot, and he gave me a list of three kinds of trees to order online. We made our wreaths by hand from leftover cuttings. When we were ready to go, I tossed our cups into the trash while he untangled himself from the bench and took over the cart. I dug out the receipt as he pushed the cart.

"I have to take the girls clothes shopping today."

"You know how to give an old man the frights," he answered.

"Don't worry—it's Russell's money. His check was on time for a change."

As we waited in line at the exit, Dad said, "You need to think about using some of Andie's money. That's what it's there for."

I greeted the associate and handed over the receipt. "I don't want to touch her parents' money, Dad."

"Girl, you *are* her parent now."

The associate put a big check mark on my receipt and handed it back. My reality check.

"But using their money would seem like they were the ones still taking care of her, not us. I didn't even dip into it for her birthday."

Andie had seemed pleased with the small celebration for her birthday, and she'd even told me I should own a bakery. The thought still warmed me. "That money's for college."

"How do you know she'll want to go to college?"

"Dad." I looked at him pointedly. "She's the only sharpened pencil in the pack."

He nodded in agreement. "I see what you mean."

The line moved along slowly through the exit. "I'll have to take her to the doctor soon. That over-the-counter allergy stuff just isn't working."

I waited at the curb with the cart until he brought the truck around for loading. Maybe Dad was right. Money was so tight that for the first time I actually toyed with the idea of tapping Andie's monthly allowance.

No one but a fellow sufferer understands the cost when your child has an extended illness. There were so many expenses not covered by our insurance, including loss of pay when I missed work to take her to the university hospital, and food and lodging while we waited to see specialists. And the wheelchair. You don't even consider the cost when your child needs a wheelchair; you just get it and figure out later some way to pay it off. Sometimes there's help, and sometimes there's not.

Now the wheelchair sat folded up on itself in the garage, covered with a sheet like a little ghost mourning the loss of its companion. One day, when I was ready, I'd give it to a family who needed it—one of the families we'd met who'd lost one child after another to this dreaded disease.

Dad pulled up and loaded the truck, and we headed for the lumberyard for some posts and wire for the fencing and plastic sheeting for the tree lot shed. We also replaced the space heater, since the old one almost burned down the shed the year before.

In the afternoon, while Dad was hammering away, Winnie, Andie, and I rifled through a box of last year's winter clothes to see what was usable. There were two coats. One was too small for any of them, and the other was an old one of Deja's. Winnie grabbed it and tried it on, saying that she loved it, but the sleeves dragged past her knuckles. Even when buttoned, the coat wouldn't stay up on her shoulders without her constant shrugging.

Andie's face was stormy and dark. It was obvious that the coat would fit her better—and that there was no way she would wear a hand-me-down coat from Deja. I didn't even suggest that she try it on.

I knelt down by Winnie. "Let's roll up the sleeves. Maybe if I move the buttons over . . ." I overlapped the buttons by two inches. "It'll work. We'll see if we can find a coat on sale for Andie."

I asked Deja if she needed a coat, but she said she had one of Ridley's. The thought occurred to me that she might be without a coat if and when they broke up. But of course I kept that thought to myself. I told her that she and I would go shopping alone some other time for clothes.

Winnie and Andie went with me to shop for jeans and warm tops. Andie gravitated toward dark, somber colors and styles, while Winnie went for bright purples, pinks, and frills. The little old woman and the baby of the family, I thought privately. We managed to find a decent coat on sale for Andie. Even though Deja lived in Ridley's jacket and told me she didn't want a new one, I dreaded her reaction when she saw Andie's new coat.

When we got home, I asked the girls over grilled cheese sandwiches and tomato soup, "What do you girls think about going to church again?"

Winnie swallowed. "You mean our old church? Bertney goes there."

"Brittany, honey." I nodded. "Yes, Newberry Community." I said to Andie, "Natalie's family goes there."

She dipped her sandwich in tomato soup. "She told me."

"Have you been to church before?"

She nodded. "In Pine Run."

"We'll shoot for a Sunday after Thanksgiving, okay?"

They agreed. I knew I'd need all the heavenly help I could get during the coming holidays.

We got their winter clothes just in time. Monday morning we woke to pouring rain and wind. I pulled up in front of the elementary school to let the girls out, and just caught myself before I repeated what my mom used to say to me: Don't melt in the rain, sugar cube. I wasn't up to ridicule by the sullen teenager in the front seat.

We were at the tail end of the long line of cars in front of the high school, undulating like a slow inchworm, and Deja jumped out before I was even close to the entrance. She hooked up with some scary friends in black trench coats and never looked back. I breathed a prayer for her, with the rain pasting her hair to her head and her blonde roots showing through. Ridley joined them and draped an arm across her shoulders. Then he gave her a kiss and whispered in her ear. The car behind me honked, and I realized the line was moving—way too fast now for my comfort.

I went on to work and parked in the employee parking lot on the edge of civilization. I was soaked by the time I got inside the building. I muted my cell phone and stuck it in my pocket, and when it vibrated later in the morning, I tried to ignore it. I glanced at the caller ID. It was blocked. I hesitated. Probably the school, but which school? Oh, well, if it was a true emergency they'd call the manager's office and track me down. There was nothing I could do from work.

Jo and I managed to have our lunch breaks together. The break room was unusually crowded since no one wanted to go out in the rain and wind. I peeled open my miniature can of tuna and mixed in mayonnaise and relish. Jo heated up her soup in the microwave, grimacing at the traces of other lunches that had exploded or boiled over on the turntable.

"Health inspector would love to get a load of that microwave," she said quietly to me as she sat. "He'd put the fear of God in them."

I paused with the tuna-laden cracker almost to my mouth at the reminder of Julian Barrett. "I don't know. He seems like a nice guy."

She turned her head to me and her penciled eyebrows shot up. "You know him?"

I shifted in my chair. "No, I don't *know* him," I said, lowering my voice. "I just met him once at the girls' school."

She cocked her head. "And?"

"What do you want me to say?"

"So, is he cute?" she asked. She stirred her soup without taking her eyes off of me.

"I don't know. All I said was that I met him and he seems nice. Don't read anything into it."

She looked offended. "You don't have to get all worked up about it."

"I'm not getting worked up." I picked up the weekly ads someone had left on the table and tried to read.

"Well, all I know is this is the first nice thing you've said about a guy in a couple of years—"

"Jo, just drop it."

She glanced over her shoulder, and I remembered we weren't alone in the lunchroom.

"How're things at your house?" I asked, trying to change the subject.

"Well." She broke crackers into her soup and brushed off the crumbs from her palms. "Not so good. Dr. Barry says Walt's diabetic."

"Jo, I'm so sorry." I felt like a self-absorbed toad. "When did you find out?"

"Last week. He was losing weight and just didn't look good." She chuckled. "That's what you call an oxymoron, isn't it—losing weight and *not* looking good? Doctor put him on medication, and he's feeling better. But we're exercising and changing the way we eat." She nodded toward the soup. "We're both bound to get healthy."

I spread tuna salad on another cracker. "He's not on insulin, is he?"

"Not yet—not as long as he takes care of himself. We're getting a home gym."

We chatted about sales in the paper, and Jo told me her plans for her garden next spring.

"Is Andie fitting in?" she asked.

I thought for a moment and glanced around, not wanting my private life to be the topic of the next lunch break. "Jo, when your kids were young, did you ever read them the story of the snow child?"

She laughed. "Are you kidding? Bob and Walt Jr.? The only thing they wanted me to read was the back of the cereal box."

I gathered up my trash and packed it in my lunch sack. Maybe this wasn't a good time.

But she prodded. "No, no, hold your horses. So what about the snow child?"

"Okay. The snow child comes to this old couple because they're lonely, but she has to leave them when the snow melts. She promises to return the next winter, when it snows again."

She pursed her lips, considering me. "So she's melting, and you're afraid she'll freeze up again and go back?"

"She's not melting that much. Not like I expected."

"Well, she's only been with you for, what, three months? It's not really that long." She snapped the lid back on her plastic container.

"I know. Maybe I'm expecting too much. Or maybe she should never have left the old couple in the first place." I sighed. "I just want her to be happy."

"Honey, you want everybody to be happy," Jo said, rising to gather her purse and trash. "Sometimes 'happy' is up to the individual."

I threw away my trash and followed her out the door. Then I

remembered about the call I'd gotten, and pulled out my cell phone.

Jo peered over my shoulder. "Who you trying to avoid now?"

I sighed. "It's probably Deja's school. You go ahead; I need to see what they want."

It was the school attendance line. Deja must've cut class with her friends, right after I'd pulled away from the school that morning. Where in the world could they go in this horrible weather? I closed my eyes, imagining the worst.

When I got home, I asked Dad if he'd picked up Deja after school and how she seemed. He said that he'd picked her up as usual, and that she seemed edgy. Nervous. I told him about the phone call from school, and he followed me into her room.

Deja sat up in bed and clutched her pillow in front of her like a shield when we came in. I glanced over at Andie sitting on the other bed and asked if she would please let us talk to Deja in private. She grabbed her book and left.

I walked up close and looked Deja in the eye. Her pupils were normal, not dilated or red. She didn't smell like alcohol or have visible hickies.

"What?" she challenged, squirming a little.

"Where were you all day? The school called."

She hugged her pillow closer and didn't answer.

"Deja, we know you cut. Where did you go?"

"Nowhere."

Anger built inside me, and I had trouble controlling my voice. "I want the truth, Deja."

She looked up at me, with tears glistening her eyes. "We didn't go anywhere. We sat in the parking lot all day." She punched her pillow. "He didn't have enough gas to go anywhere."

I breathed again. At least some of my fears were relieved. "Did you really think no one would notice that you cut?"

She didn't look at me or at Dad, but said to her pillow, "I don't care. We talked, and we slept, and it was like being in a safe cocoon with the rain running down the car windows."

We both stared at her, unsure how to respond. Safe? Safe from what? And—sleeping!

Finally I said, "Is there anything else you want to tell us?"

She shook her head.

"Well, you know this postpones your driver's ed even longer."

She didn't answer, but flopped over on her stomach and covered her head with her pillow like she was trying to suffocate herself.

Could this boy mean so much to her that it was worth losing her driver's ed?

She didn't come out to supper later, which was no surprise. I didn't eat much myself. It worried me that she would turn to a boy to feel safe and secure. I knew from experience that was no way to live life. But something about her had seemed vulnerable. She didn't lash out and give us the attitude I'd expected. Had something happened? Was it normal boyfriend trouble, or something more?

CHAPTER 14

Andie

The Blue Moon sign read CLoSed 4 sEAson. We worked one last day, cleaning out the snack shack freezer and boxing up the candy and supplies. Marty emptied the cash register and paid us all one last time. We loaded our arms with leftover frozen pizzas that she said wouldn't last until next summer. Then we locked up and headed across the parking lot back to the house.

It felt great knowing I didn't have to work the drive-in anymore. I'd be gone before it opened again. I turned to look across the parking lot. The building looked lonely with its windows boarded up and a huge padlock on the door between them—like a big sad face.

I hid my money in my suitcase. It wasn't a very good hiding place, but at least it was out of sight. I didn't trust Deja. She wasn't there very much, but I still didn't want to take any chances. No one had said anything about an allowance.

Carl went to work on the Christmas tree lot, setting up a fence and surrounding it with twinkle lights. Then he framed up a small building and tacked heavy plastic on three sides. Winnie said that's where he sprayed the trees with fake snow.

My allergies didn't go away. One day I woke up with a sore throat, and Marty put her cool hand on my forehead and cheeks and decided I had a fever. She called in my absence to the school and took me to the clinic. I felt lousy, all achy and shivery sitting there in a cold plastic chair in a big gray room that smelled like BO and echoed with babies crying. Little kids stepped on my feet, and old people coughed so hard that I was afraid they would die right there in front of us.

Dr. Barber back in Pine Run had cushy chairs, gossip magazines, and a giant aquarium with a shark. One corner was always set up with toys and puzzles and blocks to keep kids busy so they wouldn't think about getting shots. He had soft music playing out of the ceiling and nice nurses who smiled and looked sorry that you were sick. He even had a funny little sign that said The Barber Will See You Now. According to Mom, it was a play on words.

Dr. Barber had known me since I was a baby. When you're sick, you feel better when somebody knows you and can pronounce your name right.

The doctor gave Marty two prescriptions for me. One was a smelly pill for my sinus infection, and the other was allergy medication I had to take every day. I overheard him say to get rid of the cat, or vacuum and wash my stuff every day.

I felt a flicker of hope. I thought, they'll never get rid of Cyclops, and if I'm too much trouble, maybe she'll send me back to Grandma. I must have been delirious with fever.

I missed three days of school. Marty asked me again if my class needed chaperones for our field trip to San Francisco, but I said no. I felt a little bad lying to her. Marty wasn't bad, but I couldn't handle a mother-daughter thing.

✦ ✦ ✦

The morning of the field trip, I threw two books into my backpack with my book light, just in case. I could escape any situation, burrowing into a story. The bus ride took two hours. It was dark when we left the school, way before school actually started. Everybody was pretty quiet until the sun came up, but the brighter it got inside the bus, the louder they got. Natalie kept talking to me and wouldn't take the hint, so I finally put my book away.

I noticed some of the parent volunteers looking back at me from their seats and whispering. I thought grown-ups would have better manners.

Just before we got to San Francisco, huge patches of glistening water opened up out of nowhere. I closed my eyes when we crossed the Bay Bridge because the bus was so high over the water. A blast of crisp ocean air hit my face. Somebody must have put the window down. Then everybody started putting down their windows until we had a wind tunnel inside the bus and the chaperones made us close them again.

Finally we parked and got out on the street. Mrs. Bettencourt marched us inside the Exploratorium and told us when and where to meet back for lunch. Everyone scattered like rats. Natalie and I goofed around in the photo exhibit, throwing our silhouettes against the giant screen in weird poses until one of the parents told us to stop hogging it. For lunch the bus took us to a huge park with a view of Alcatraz and the Golden Gate Bridge. We ate on the grass with the wind blowing our trash everywhere.

"Have you been over there, to Alcatraz?" Natalie asked me, peeling her banana.

"Yeah." I swallowed a mouthful of peanut butter and jelly sandwich. "I think I was six."

"We went last year at Easter break. My brother Ryan got sick on the boat ride and threw up in the bushes when we got there." She ate a bite of banana. "He was sick the whole time we were on the tour. Then he started crying when Mom said it was time to get back on the boat."

Natalie told me funny stories all day. She made it sound like having a big family was a blast.

When it was time to leave, Mrs. Bettencourt and some parents had to track down Scott Worley and his band of nerds. It took an hour to find them, so we were late getting back to school. They were banned from any future field trips.

The next night was open house. When I saw in homeroom that our family trees were on display, I tried to fake being sick at dinner that night. Marty wouldn't buy it. It turned out that I couldn't eat much because my stomach was doing flips, so it was true.

We spent a long time in Winnie's classroom, where the walls were filled with turkeys and Pilgrims. Finally we had to go to my homeroom. Natalie was waiting and dragged me over to meet her mom. She already knew Marty. I watched Marty read my Lockhart family tree on the wall. It was full of doodling and decorations, not like the one I did of her family, which was plain and sloppy. She seemed disappointed at first that hers was missing, but she covered it up really well. She reached up with her finger and touched the characters I'd drawn to show each one of us Lockharts, and bit her lower lip when she got to my cousin Tyler.

That week the weather got colder, and Marty dug out some boxes filled with winter clothes from the garage. I didn't have a warm coat, and when she pulled an old one out of the box, I knew it was Deja's. There was just no way I was gonna wear it, and I think Marty knew that because she skipped over me and offered it to Winnie. She took us clothes shopping and bought me a new coat at Target, and it was the first time I think I made Deja jealous. It was just an okay coat, but it was new. It wasn't like Deja needed one, anyway. She lived in her boyfriend's old jacket. I think she only took it off to sleep.

I got some bad news just before Thanksgiving break. Grandpa got the flu, and Grandma said it was better if I came some other time. I was so disappointed that I cried in the bathroom with my face buried in a towel so no one could hear me. It hurt my feelings, because I could have helped them out. But Grandma said he was contagious, and I'd just gotten over a sinus infection, plus, I didn't need to expose everyone else. So I spent Thanksgiving in Newberry.

Thanksgiving Day started early there at Marty's. The turkey was already sitting shiny brown on the platter when I got up at ten. A pumpkin cheesecake and iced brownies cooled on racks on the counter, and Marty was whipping cream in the mixer. I wondered if she'd slept at all the night before.

"Good morning! Have a cinnamon roll," she said, pausing in her chopping to wipe her hands on her apron and hand me a plate with a gooey iced bun. "But don't fill up on them. We're eating early."

I got the feeling it was best just to take the bun and fake it that I wasn't hungry.

Winnie sat balled up in the afghan on the couch watching the Macy's parade.

"You missed the Snoopy balloon," she said, licking her fingers. Icing clung to the front of her gown.

I sat beside her on the couch and crisscrossed my legs, tucking my nightgown over them one-handed. "Why do we have to eat so early?" I asked. I sank my teeth into the roll, and gooey warm dough and cinnamon melted in my mouth.

"Grandpa's setting up the tree lot. The trees came last night."

I had visions of Christmas trees marching down the driveway and settling in for a double feature.

Marty's super-hearing must have been activated, because she called, "He likes to get a jump on the competition. You'll be surprised how many people buy trees on Thanksgiving Day."

Marty went all out, putting a Thanksgiving tablecloth on the table, setting out china and crystal and cloth napkins. She even had Pilgrim salt-and-pepper shakers. Deja woke up right before we ate dinner. She looked like a slug that had slithered in from the garden and pulled out a chair at Marty's fancy table.

"Deja, go comb your hair and get dressed," Carl said. He had washed up and changed into a clean T-shirt, and smelled like sap.

Deja left the table for so long that Carl yelled for her, but she didn't look much better when she came back. I could tell the scent of turkey was driving Carl crazy, because he frowned, but didn't insist on a do-over.

Marty said, "Andie, before we eat on Thanksgiving, we go around the table and everyone says something they're thankful for."

My chest tightened.

"You don't have to do it, if you don't want to."

"I wanna start," Winnie said. She scrunched up her face like she was having a brain spasm. Then she said, "I'm thankful that I only got one C on my report card."

Marty went next. She took a deep breath and said in a quiet voice that crumpled at the end, "We made it through another year." She tried to smile and wiped her eyes. Carl gave her an affectionate wink.

"Deja?"

Deja cocked her head, looking very bored. I avoided eye contact. Would she make up something obnoxious about me, or chicken out in front of Carl?

"Oh, yeah." She curled her black fingernail around a lock of split ends. "I'm thankful . . . that . . . Madonna's coming out with a new album. And I hope it's better than her last one because it sucked."

Marty looked down at the table and exhaled. Carl stared at Deja for a second, sucking his teeth.

Marty turned to me and asked timidly, "Andie, do you want to say anything?"

My mind was like a blank journal where you're expecting to see words, but there's just frightening white space.

"Um . . . " My knees bounced under the table until the candles and the salt-and-pepper shakers wobbled. "I . . ."

Everyone waited. Deja yawned loudly.

"I'm thankful . . . that . . . I . . . get to go to Grandma's for Christmas."

Deja gave a nasty little smile that said she agreed with me.

Carl said a prayer that covered *all* the bases. Maybe it was his prayer for the year—I don't know.

It was the weirdest Thanksgiving dinner. Too quiet. I missed all the friends and relatives my parents used to invite to dinner. I missed squeezing people into the dining room, and being in charge of the kids' table. Marty had knocked herself out, but it was still like any other dinner. Just the four of us ignoring Deja.

Last came the pumpkin cheesecake. We sensed that it would not be smart to say we were too stuffed, so we ate it. I unbuttoned the top button of my jeans and considered ralphing in the toilet, but that would have been hard to hide.

After the last bite, Marty jumped up and started clearing the table. Carl picked his teeth with a toothpick for a while. I think he was too full to move, or the tryptophan was working its magic. Winnie played with the flame of the candle until I told her to stop spilling wax on Marty's tablecloth.

Finally Carl got up and put on his coat. Winnie and I grabbed ours, and he told Deja to come with us. We all waddled down to the lot behind him like a line of ducks.

The Christmas trees smelled so good. No matter how old I get, I'll still be a Christmas bloodhound when I get the scent.

Carl explained the setup at the little shed.

"These six-foot trees are all $19.99. They're Monterey and Scotch pine. All these rows"—he pointed to the left corner—"these are silver tips. They're $40 for small ones and $50 for the five-foots. Now, the customer will pull the tag off the tree he wants and bring it in here to the counter. Then they pay for it, you stamp it *paid*, and they'll bring the tag out to me to load the tree. If they want it flocked it's an extra $5 a foot, and they can pick it up in a couple hours.

"Deja, find the extension cord and start the hot chocolate. The big coffee pot's inside." He dug in his pockets. "Winnie, take my keys and go up to the snack shack for stir sticks. It's the green key. Make sure you lock it back up. Andie, find the candy canes in the back and put them out in a basket. And look for the box of spoons and the tape recorder. Play this when the power's hooked up."

He handed me a Christmas tape by somebody named Chet Atkins with a guitar on the front. It had to be country music. I weighed it in my hand, thinking maybe the boom box would chew it up.

The music wasn't all that bad after all. Chet was pretty good on the guitar. With him playing "Jingle Bell Rock" and the trees looking like a miniature forest, the excitement stirred inside me, like cream swirling in Grandma's coffee. It made your mouth water even if you knew it wouldn't taste like you expected.

I wandered the lot looking at the trees to make sure I could tell the cheap pines from the silver tips so I wouldn't screw up. It wasn't hard to know the difference. The silver tips were perfect and small and smelled like Christmas. The pines looked like a little kid had drawn their outlines and scribbled them in.

The first customers showed up at four o'clock, and I felt the same old panic squeezing my insides that I'd felt my first day of working in the snack shack. But soon there were so many people buying trees that I was too busy to think about being nervous.

Three people wanted their trees flocked. Carl blew flocking on them with a blaster that sounded like a 747 taking off. They smelled more like hazardous chemicals than Christmas trees. Maybe the flocking kept the needles from falling off so they'd look good all the way until Christmas Day. We always bought our tree two weeks before the big day. We'd drive to a Christmas tree farm up in the mountains and ride a wagon to find the perfect tree and cut it down ourselves. Then Dad would hold the thick end of the trunk and Mom would grab the middle, and I would reach into the prickly needles to hold the top where the angel would go, and we'd carry it back to the car. Sometimes there were even patches of snow on the ground. Real snow.

We saw Marty back the car out and leave, and I wondered where she was going. Maybe she needed something from the grocery store. But then I remembered that she said the store was only open in the morning because of the holiday. When she stopped by later to see how things were going, there was dirt on the knees of her jeans and her eyes were all puffy. I gave up trying to figure that one out.

When the hot chocolate ran out, Carl told us to tell Deja to make some more, but she was gone. He was mad when he found out she just took off, and said something under his breath that made Winnie laugh. Winnie and I had to make the chocolate ourselves, but it was pretty bad. One thing I can say for Deja—she knew how to mix hot water and powdered drink mix and make it turn out right.

When it got dark, the Blue Moon sign lit up at the entrance with XMAS TREES 4ROM $19.99. Carl rolled out a barrel and made a fire in it. People stood around the fire drinking hot chocolate, but the little kids got too close to it, and that bothered me. Their parents weren't even watching them. The kids started throwing pine needles and twigs into the fire and jumping back when showers of sparks popped and sizzled in the air. They'd laugh like it was the greatest thing. They had no idea.

Worrying about the fire kept me from paying attention to what I was doing. One customer snapped his fingers in my face, and another told me I'd given him too much change. After that, I stayed in the shed and tried to ignore the fire, but it was hard. When I stood at the counter, I could see the flames out of the corner of my eye.

Finally Carl put the lid on the barrel and snuffed it out. The last people paid for their trees and went home, and he locked the big fence around the tree lot. Then he turned off the Blue Moon sign and put a chain across the entrance. We turned off the music, locked up the shed, and went back to the house.

It smelled like turkey and pumpkin pie when we opened the door, and I remembered it was still Thanksgiving. Marty made us sandwiches with turkey and dressing and cranberry sauce, and set out a plate of three new kinds of cookies and the pie. It seems like she would have been tired of cooking. My mom always said she was too exhausted to eat by the time dinner was ready on Thanksgiving Day.

I glanced over at Marty when she wasn't looking. She smiled when anyone talked to her, but then her face drooped, like she couldn't keep it propped up. If she was that tired, she should've watched TV. We knew how to make sandwiches.

The next morning we all went down to the tree lot after breakfast, except for Deja, who slept in. What a slacker. No one complained, though. It was better without her.

Winnie was really enjoying herself, turning the little shed into a playhouse. That is, until a man and a little girl walked in like they owned the place. Winnie's head jerked up when she heard him giving orders, and her face fell when she saw the little princess prancing along behind him. The girl's ski jacket was glittery pink with white fur around the collar, and her hands were tucked into a fancy muff. Even her boots were trimmed with fur at the top.

"Oh, not Marissa," Winnie moaned under her breath.

"Who's she?" I asked.

"She's in my class. I hate her. She thinks she's so cool."

The man was tall, so that the girl had to almost run to keep up.

"Hi, Winnie," she said when they got to the counter.

"Hello, girls," said the man, pulling a crisp fifty, twenty, and a five from a money roll. "There you go." He slapped down the tree tag. "One five-foot silver tip. Flocked."

I stamped *Paid* on his tag and thanked him. He took off to find Carl, but Marissa stayed behind.

When her dad was gone, she looked around the hut really snottylike. "You have to work here?"

"Sure. It's fun," Winnie said. She shrugged Deja's old coat back up onto her shoulders because it kept sliding down. She had to roll the sleeves up so they wouldn't get in the way.

"Want a candy cane?" I asked her.

Marissa dug into the basket of candy canes and shoved a bunch into her pocket.

"Hey," I said. "You only get one. Put the others back."

Marissa wrinkled up her nose. Did she smell something? "You're . . . her . . . um . . . "

"She's Andie. She's my sister," Winnie said. "You get *one*."

Marissa rolled her eyes and kind of pitched the candy toward the basket. "Santa's Treeland has better candy canes anyway. They're big and they come in root beer and grape too. That's where we're going for our wreath. Dad says they stay green longer than yours. He got one here last year, and it died before Christmas."

She stuck her hands in her muff and almost waved it in our faces.

"Is that real?" I asked.

"It's rabbit," she said. "My mom ordered it online."

I said, "Some poor white rabbit gave its life so you could pretend to look cool."

Marissa didn't know what to say. She opened her mouth, closed it again, twisted her face into a tight knot, and took off. So what if I got into trouble? I didn't care.

Winnie stuck out her tongue as soon as Marissa's back was turned.

After they left, Carl called from the Scotch pines. "Andie, run up to the house for me and get my other work gloves."

"Okay." Any excuse to go back inside. "Where are they?"

"In my room. Could be on the dresser. Look around."

I trudged back past the silent speaker poles in the parking lot and into the house. It was quiet, so I figured Deja was still asleep.

Carl's room was at the other end of the house, just past Marty's.

I pushed the door open and peeked inside. In some ways, it didn't look like a guy's bedroom. Except for the socks on the floor and the dresser covered with small tools and loose change. But on the walls were beautiful paintings and drawings.

I stepped closer to a shimmery pastel desert, where flowers dotted the sand like sea anemones on the ocean floor. Beside it was a picture of a beautiful black-haired woman in buckskin cradling a baby. Charcoals of Indian children in a wagon, horses running in a meadow, a horse bucking a cowboy—they were perfect.

Carl had never struck me as an art lover. I read the intertwined *CMcA* in the corner. It took me a second to realize they were his initials. Carl McAlister. I looked up at the woman again. My breath seemed to move her feathery hair.

One picture had a blue ribbon that said *Elko County Fair* tacked to the frame. Then I knew it was his work, for sure. It was a pencil drawing of Marty and Tipper, standing by a fence.

I had a blue ribbon too. I'd won it in a contest at the recreation park when I was nine. It was a colored pencil drawing of a carousel horse, with streamers and flowers, like a fairytale unicorn. But it was no way as good as these.

Cyclops rubbed against my leg, screeching his weird other-world meow, and I remembered what I'd come for. I sneezed and pushed him away with my foot, and went to the dresser where Carl said the gloves would be. I opened the top drawer, thinking that maybe he'd dropped them inside.

"Get out!" Deja suddenly roared behind me. She blocked the doorway, a demented dragon in plaid boxers and fuzzy claw slippers. "What are you doing in here?"

My lungs were a vacuum.

"I— I—"

She smelled fear, and kicked it up a notch.

"Get out!" she shouted again, eyes bulging in her white face, morning-hair splayed out from her head like retractable armor. "Who said you could go into Grandpa's room?"

Was that smoke shooting from her nostrils?

Cyclops bolted under the bed.

"I'm—"

"You don't belong in here!" she screamed. "When I tell Grandpa—"

I slammed the drawer hard, rattling everything on the dresser. "I came for his gloves!" I shouted back. "He sent me for his gloves."

"His gloves." She folded her arms across her chest and arched one eyebrow to the ceiling. "So, where are they?"

"He said they were on the dresser, but they aren't, so—"

"So you went through his private stuff?"

I searched the room visually, hoping they were in plain sight. Then I saw them on the bed, half hidden by his bath towel.

"Here they are." I scooped them up and pushed past her. "I told you so."

"You are so busted if you're lying, you little—"

I left the house and stomped back to the tree lot.

"Here." I thrust them at Carl, and his eyebrows shot up. I guess I was having trouble getting my controls on.

"What's wrong?"

"Deja's awake."

He said something under his breath I wasn't supposed to hear. Then he added, "Don't let her bother you."

I had to walk it off. I kicked pebbles, imagining her face on them until I'd powered down. Getting back to work helped me shrug it off some, listening to Chet play "Silent Night" on the guitar. And hearing Carl grumble about how much he hated fake trees.

"What's the world coming to? The whole point of having a tree at Christmas is that it's symbolic. Why get a tree at all, if you're gonna get an ugly one that you take out of a box and put together like bottle brushes?"

Marty caught my eye when she heard him start to rant. She smiled and shook her head behind his back.

We worked the tree lot every day after school, until I started falling behind in my homework. It got kind of embarrassing to see kids we knew from school. Constantly on alert, I hid out when I saw someone I recognized.

One Saturday night Marty sent us back early to get ready for bed because we were going to church the next morning. Winnie was happy, but Deja had rolled her eyes and said, "Knock yourselves out. Just don't wake me up when you leave."

Carl geared up to do battle with her, but Marty gestured for him to let it go. I figured church couldn't be as bad as spending Sunday morning with Deja.

When I got out of the shower that night, I looked in my suitcase for my nightgown. No luck. So I checked the laundry. The dryer was full of socks and underwear, but none of my stuff was out in the piles of dirty clothes. Marty usually folded my clean clothes and set them on top of my dresser. Then I would put everything back in my suitcase.

Only one other place to look. I yanked open a dresser drawer, and there they were. Neatly folded tees, underwear, socks, and jeans. Maybe she was just being helpful, putting them away for me. Or maybe she was trying to force me to give up, to fit in. It didn't matter which. I scooped up armfuls of clothes and threw them into my suitcase.

Winnie said we didn't have to dress up for church, so I didn't. When we got there the next morning, people were standing by their folding chairs, clapping with the band that was playing at the other end of the room. The pastor was wearing jeans and a blue aloha shirt. It wasn't like any church service I had ever been to. At least they didn't make me stand up and be introduced to everyone.

After the service, people stood around drinking coffee and punch. Winnie was stocking up on cookies when a lady with a clipboard got us in her sights.

"Hello, girls. I'm Mrs. Keifer. We're putting on a Christmas play in a few weeks, and you two would make perfect angels. Would you like to be in it?"

I shook my head, but I could tell Winnie was already writing her acceptance speech.

The woman said, confidentially, "You know, blondes make the prettiest angels."

"Okay," Winnie said, looking bashful.

I rolled my eyes. So much for being politically correct.

"Where's your mother? We need to talk costumes."

Winnie dragged Mrs. Keifer over to Marty.

Natalie made her way over to me through the crowd of hugging, noisy people. "Mrs. Keifer talk you into doing the play?" she asked.

"No, but she got Winnie. Are you in it?"

She nodded and shrugged.

"You're an angel too?" I asked.

"With my hair?" She tugged on a dark curl. "I get to be Mary. I was Mary last year, and the year before, and the year before that. The little kids think that's my real name." She hugged her Bible to her chest. "We're going Christmas shopping at the mall. You wanna come? We eat lunch at the food court."

A slow, creeping panic cinched my stomach. Part of me wanted to go. I knew it would be fun. I hadn't been to the mall yet. But I felt weird—like if I went, I would cross some line, some invisible point of no return. I guess I wasn't very good at hiding my feelings.

"Forget it. It's okay," Natalie said. "We might be too busy to go anyway."

"No, it sounds like fun. But I think we're doing something."

"Sure. Don't worry about it." She looked around for her mom. "Well, I gotta go. See you tomorrow."

I felt like a creep. But in a way I felt relieved, like I had narrowly missed capture.

CHAPTER 15

Marty

"Guess what we got for Christmas, all the way from Florida," I announced as I popped open the car trunk. Inside was a box of beautiful oranges with a brilliant sun on the wrapper.

Dad climbed down the ladder, letting the string of Christmas lights dangle from the roofline, and swore under his breath. "Doesn't he know we have all the oranges we need in California? He'd know that if he ever bothered to visit."

My brother, Charles, was the prodigal son, and Dad never forgave his ramblings, especially the fact that we hadn't been able to reach him for Mom's funeral.

"It's the thought that counts, Dad. He's trying to keep in touch." I looked at the return address. "At least we know he's still in Plant City."

He made a sour face. "Still single's my guess."

"So am I. Now will you please quit being grumpy and carry the box into the kitchen?"

Dad hoisted the box from the trunk and deposited it on the

kitchen counter. Then he returned to the ladder, mumbling his displeasure about his only son.

I picked out an orange from the box and peeled it. The orange was ripe and juicy, and its skin peeled easily away. I wondered if Charles was happy and whether he'd ever been able to shake off the years of father-son dysfunction. Did he miss us, especially at this time of year?

Christmas was three weeks away. Winnie had been fitted for an angel costume and had to be driven to practice several times a week, but I never stayed to watch. My favorite oldies radio station was playing Christmas songs twenty-four hours a day, so I switched to smooth jazz where they weren't quite so recognizable. A giant tree lit up the old town square, decorations dangled from the streetlights, and the local cement company had decorated its building with enough Christmas lights to short out the whole Sacramento region. I considered taking a detour to avoid it all, but resigned myself to endure it for the girls' sakes. It was time for me to get used to the holiday.

We had come through Thanksgiving pretty much unscathed, but Christmas was a potential minefield. This was the second Christmas since we'd lost Ginger, and I was determined to keep it together for the family's sake. This year, there would be a tree.

Andie came out to the kitchen and asked my advice about what to get her grandparents for Christmas. I had a brilliant idea—one that would allow me to spend some quality time alone with her.

"Winnie's spending the night at Brittany's. Go get your money, and we'll do a little Christmas shopping."

I waited to see if she recoiled from the idea, but instead, she smiled. I tossed her an orange to eat in the car, and she ran to get her money.

After hours of shopping, she finally decided on a wall clock with large numbers. I couldn't shake the suspicion that had begun with the Baby Ruth in Walgreens, and found myself casually watching her while we shopped. She never gave me any reason to doubt her honesty. Nevertheless, I didn't completely relax until we left the store.

We stopped at a crowded burger joint for lunch, the retro kind that played Elvis and the Beach Boys. They had added "White Christmas" and "Jingle Bell Rock" to the jukebox's lineup. After the waitress took our orders and an awkward silence descended, I realized how few private conversations we'd really had.

I asked Andie what she thought of our little storefront congregation.

She shrugged. "It's different from my church in Pine Run. The singing and stuff."

"But I bet the message is the same. Did you follow the sermon?"

She dunked a french fry in catsup and twirled it into a pattern. "Yeah, but I don't believe some of it."

"You don't?" I sprinkled too much salt on my fries. "What is it that you don't believe?"

"How God always answers prayers. What about people that die? Somebody probably prayed for them. It doesn't always work."

Wow. I wiped my mouth with a napkin and paused to gather my thoughts.

"We all die eventually, Andie. It's part of life. Of course, that's no consolation when it's someone you love, or when it happens unexpectedly. It doesn't seem fair." I took a bite of french fry, then pointed it at the ceiling. "Believe me, it's something I intend to ask God about when I see Him."

She was quiet after that, and I wondered if I'd done any good or had just raised more questions. On our way home she asked me, "Are you mad at God?"

I thought for a moment and decided on honesty. "Yes. Sometimes."

"You still talk to Him, even when you're mad?"

"Yes, I do." I glanced over at her. She stared out the window into the December grayness. "What about you?"

She shrugged without breaking her gaze. "I think my heart-shape is plugged."

Winnie brought the mail to the dinner table one night, and one card stood out from the rest. It smelled heavenly, which could only mean one thing.

"Here's your Christmas card from Ruby, Dad." I tossed it across to his plate, none too gently.

He pulled out his glasses and positioned them on his nose. Then he examined the return address and used his dinner knife to slit open the envelope. Inside was an ornate card with a glamour photo tucked inside. His lips moved as he read it silently.

"She's shameless, Dad. Throwing herself at you like this every year."

Her card had the power to turn me into a jealous daughter. I didn't know which was worse, the thought of Dad leaving us for Ruby, or the thought of sharing a kitchen with her here.

He closed the card, then opened and studied it again. "Shameless."

Winnie grabbed the glamour photo and passed it around. "Grandpa's got a girlfriend. She was our Grandma's best friend, and she sends him a card every year."

He dipped his head down to look over the top of his glasses at Winnie. "Why do I need another girlfriend? Got one right here." He reached over and tickled Winnie until she screamed.

Andie sat very still, watching and looking faintly expectant. He must have seen her out of the corner of his eye, because he reached over to his right and tickled her until she doubled over with laughter.

Laughter. It was beautiful, unfettered. I felt tears sting my eyes. And for some odd reason, I had to give myself permission to enjoy it.

Then I noticed Deja. Watching stony-faced. Needy. This poor girl who desperately needed a father's love and would never know it.

She pushed off from the table and threw down her napkin. "I'm done."

The others stopped abruptly and looked up in surprise. I briefly locked eyes with Dad, whose initial irritation softened when he read my unspoken words. We watched her retreating back, and with the mood broken, we went back to eating in silence.

My fear was that, to Dad, Deja was becoming more like my brother with each new problem. Charles had never amounted to much in high school. He'd barely graduated. Dad didn't know how to deal with the disappointment he felt, so he shut down. Just stopped communicating with him. Disapproval was all Charles ever got from Dad after that, and he finally left.

I couldn't allow that to happen to Deja, even if I erred on the side of leniency. I knew, deep down, that Dad wouldn't want it either.

Deja had made some bad choices. Sometimes she made me so mad that I almost forgot how to love her. But silence and disapproval would never create a bridge between us.

I asked the girls to clear the table, and I went to her room. She was putting her clothes in her drawer, and I came up behind her. When she turned around, I grabbed her in a bear hug and wouldn't let go.

"Gosh, Mom, stop!" She squirmed, but not very hard.

"I haven't hugged you today." I playfully rocked her from side to side, just like she was five again.

"What do you want? Stop!"

"I'm not letting go. I love you."

Her squirming quieted. She stood there with her arms at her sides, not hugging back, but allowing me to love her.

She endured it for a while, then finally said, "Okay, Mom," but there was no bite to it.

"Not until you say it."

She sagged in my grasp. "Say what?"

"You know," I said, gently rocking her side to side. "I . . . love . . . you. Go on."

"Love you back," she said in tones only audible to a mother's acute hearing.

I kissed her a big sloppy one on the cheek and released her. She backhanded it from her cheek, but I wasn't offended.

"Sunday, after church, you and I will go Christmas shopping. You need some jeans."

She looked suspicious. "After church, as in you'll come back and pick me up?"

"Come on, Deja, church isn't that bad. You know what it's like."

"When's it over? I'll be ready when you guys get home."

I put my hands on my hips and considered fighting, but one battle a day was enough. Besides, I didn't want to lose the small piece of ground I'd just won. "Okay, this time you can stay home. But the next Sunday, you go."

She shrugged, not committing.

But on Sunday, Deja woke up with cramps. I suggested rescheduling our shopping trip, but she wanted to go anyway. I prayed through the whole church service that she would feel better and that we'd make some progress.

I couldn't help scanning the crowd for Julian, but he wasn't there.

When I brought the girls back home from church to help Dad with the tree lot, Deja was ready to go. When I'd told him how important this time was with Deja, he'd asked his friend Ty to help him at the lot. I kissed Dad's cheek, and he wordlessly patted my shoulder.

"You two have fun," he said.

Deja and I drove to the mall and scouted out a parking space. Santa was holding court in the center of the mall, and happy little Christmas elves in short pants kept order with unruly parents and tired kids.

Deja kept two steps ahead of me. I followed her around the mall, feeling like I was walking on eggshells. We went into her favorite store, which got more bizarre the farther in you went. Most parents hovered around the front where the Rainbow Brite T-shirts and fuzzy purses were stacked, and avoided the far corners with the skulls and studded paraphernalia.

Nothing fit there, thank heavens, so we went to the candy store for truffles and butterscotch lollipops. Chocolate fixes everything, especially at that time of the month. We did finally locate a single pair of jeans Deja was happy with. I sighed at the price and pulled out my checkbook. Well, if Russell wasn't going to spend time with her, he could buy her fifty-dollar jeans. On the way out of the mall, we wandered into the bookstore. I bought a mocha and settled in a comfortable chair at the attached cafe while Deja listened to music.

Unexpected memories awaited me. The first time I drove to the mall after Ginger died, it had been so long since I'd driven on the freeway that I pulled off at the very first exit, shaking like a teenager who'd failed a driving test. I managed to get back home, and Dad stopped what he was doing and drove us to the mall himself. I ended up hiding out in a chair at this very same bookstore waiting for him and the girls to come and find me. After being home for years with Ginger, I'd been overwhelmed by seeing so many people in the same place. And here I was trying to help Deja move past the pain in a different way.

When Deja found me, she had a CD she wanted me to spring for. I agreed to buy it, but insisted that she wait until Christmas morning to open it and to act surprised when she did.

All in all, I'd say the day was a success, although once back in the family fish tank, Deja fell back into her old swim pattern. I went down to the tree lot and relieved Ty, so he could go home to his family.

Falling into bed that night, I felt encouraged. I hadn't come unglued at all the Christmas frenzy at the mall. I'd seen a glimpse of what God could do when you were willing to be vulnerable and reach out to someone. I didn't expect Deja to have a miracle turnaround. But for now, she knew that I loved her. Even with all the poor choices she'd made, I still loved her, and she knew it.

Just before school was out for Christmas break, I asked Dad to bring a tree up to the house and dig out the tree stand from the garage. I wasn't sure how I'd feel seeing Ginger's ornaments again, but I had to try. Dad set the tree in the stand and struggled to get it to stop wobbling. That tree could have been me facing the holidays. Luckily, we both stayed on our feet, so to speak.

Ironically, the worst thing that I thought could possibly happen turned out to be okay after all: The girls broke one of Ginger's baby ornaments when they were decorating the tree, and I weathered it. I initially became unglued, of course, but once it was over, I experienced a curious sense of relief. Something irreplaceable had broken, and I was sad, but I still had memories that couldn't be broken. At least, that's what I told Winnie, who bore the blame for the accident.

At the start of Christmas break, we sent Andie off with Christmas gifts to spend the holidays with her grandparents. I wanted to hug her, but I just wasn't sure she was ready for it yet and didn't want to push her.

I baked so much over the holidays that I gave away goodies at the tree lot for free. I wondered, if I ever did open a bakery, what would my therapy be then, and would it take away my need to bake altogether?

The children's nativity was performed at church on the Sunday night before Christmas, and Dad went with me. Winnie was disappointed that Andie missed it, but she did a great job and flawlessly delivered her one line. She looked adorable in her blonde ringlets and garland halo. I could hardly watch, imagining my little Ginger singing before the throne with the angels. I hovered at the back in case I needed a quick exit.

After the last carol we joined everyone for cookies and punch, where I met other parents whose children were in the play. I recognized a familiar dark head and disarming smile coming my way, and smiled in spite of myself.

"I thought those were your caramel delights," Julian said. He held the hand of a little girl with dark hair wearing a shepherd's costume. "Have you taken my advice yet?"

I felt myself blushing. "Well, you know, with the holidays there hasn't been much time."

The little girl looked up at him, licking her fingers, and said, "Mommy said I have to take off my costume now."

"Okay, kiddo," he said. "Off you go." The child ran off toward a beautiful young woman who smiled at Julian and took the child's hand.

My smile faded.

Dot never mentioned if he was married or had a family that day at the Harvest Fair. Maybe she didn't know. But why else would he have been at the fair that day, unless he was supporting his child's school? I didn't really think he was there in an official capacity.

Suddenly I felt like a fool. A stupid, foolish woman who'd fallen for a guy because he'd praised her cooking. All the attention I'd received from him must either have been misunderstood, or something I didn't want to be part of.

People moved around us and in between us and greeted us. We stood awkwardly, and when the conversation became one-sided, Julian stopped speaking altogether. The child ran back a few minutes later to the cookie table.

"Uncle Julian, Mommy says we have to go. You promised we could look at Christmas lights."

Uncle Julian? My gaze dropped to the carpet at my feet so he couldn't read my embarrassment.

"Hold on," he said to her. "I didn't introduce you to Mrs. Winslow."

I looked up to see the child standing in front of him, his hands resting on her shoulders.

"I'd like to introduce my niece, Sarah. Sarah, this is Mrs. Winslow. She made those wonderful caramel delights."

I smiled sheepishly and asked if she knew Winnie. She said Winnie had helped her pin her dish towel on her head. Then Julian told her to scoot and tell her mother that he'd be along. He leaned in toward me slightly and said, "Merry Christmas, Mrs. Winslow."

✦ ✦ ✦

By choice I worked the last shift on Christmas Eve. Maybe I'm a bad mother, but I had to keep busy. I got home at six o'clock. We ate. I don't remember what. Watched a Christmas special on TV. Deja made hot chocolate. Carried Win to bed at eleven. Baked coffee cake at midnight. Took a sleep aid at 2:00 a.m.

Christmas morning, five o'clock, Winnie climbed in bed with me and begged me to get up. We opened gifts. So groggy, I could hardly focus. Dad made strong coffee to go with the coffee cake. Fell asleep on the couch amidst the wrapping paper and ribbons. Meant to call Andie, but forgot. The sun went down, and I exhaled.

CHAPTER 16

Andie

Even with the tree lot and her nine-to-five job, Marty managed to bake chocolate dandies, stained-glass cookies, scotch bars, butter horns, peanut butter cups, molasses joes, Sacher torte, and a buche de Noel. That's a cake that looks like a log.

The scent of candles and baking gingerbread boys gave me terminal munchies. Winnie carried cookies in her pockets, leaving a trail of crumbs behind her like Hansel and Gretel.

The whole living room had to be changed around to fit the Christmas tree in front of the picture window. Carl made sure the tree was standing straight, and told us to have fun before he took off. Winnie dragged boxes out of the hall closet and started pulling out Christmas decorations.

"Wait until I get the camera," Marty said, jogging down the hall.

Winnie pulled out a Nike shoe box and opened it.

"This must be Deja's stuff," she said, dangling a felt reindeer cutout with Deja's school picture pasted over its face. "I think this is from kindergarten."

What a crack-up! Deja was missing two front teeth, and her hairband pulled her hair so tight it made her ears stick out from her head.

The phone rang. Marty must have answered it back in her bedroom.

"Where's my shoe box?" Winnie dug in the storage container. "Maybe this one."

She pulled out a box and opened it. "This is Ginger's stuff."

Ginger's stuff. I almost expected it to glow in the dark.

How would it feel to know you wouldn't be celebrating any more Christmases?

Winnie set the box on the edge of the coffee table and started pulling out tissue paper. On the top was a felt reindeer with Ginger's face. She had dark curly hair, and I reached up and tucked a stray hair behind my ear. How stupid could they be? Couldn't they see she didn't fit in this family?

For the first time it was so obvious. How could my *own* parents not see the difference? Between the straight blonde hair and the fact that I was never sick, no matter how many times Mom took me to the doctor, did they ever suspect the truth? Did the thought cross their minds in some quiet moment? Maybe they watched me for signs that I was really theirs; for Dad's eyes, Mom's smile. Some family quirk.

I remembered one time when I was watching Bugs Bunny and caught Dad looking at me over the top of his newspaper. For a split second he looked really serious—almost sad—and I yelled, "Rabbit season!"

"Duck season!" he yelled back. But it was weird. Almost fake. And his smile never made it all the way to his eyes.

I finally got it. He wasn't looking at me; he was looking for her.

In Ginger's reindeer picture, I saw Dad's eyes. I felt an overwhelming urge to break every ornament in the box. To stomp on that shoe box until every trace of Ginger was crumbs.

"I had Mrs. Maginetti in kindergarten," Winnie said, startling me. "We made a wreath with pretzels. Wait till we get to my box."

Marty called from the back bedroom. "Winnie, wait for me. I'll be there in a minute. Don't get anything out."

"O-ka-ay," Winnie singsonged, but she kept pulling out decorations from Ginger's box.

"She said to wait," I said. But I really wanted to see what else was in it. I felt the delicious sting of medicine in a cut, the kind of pain you weirdly enjoy.

"This is a candy cane she made in Sunday school." She held up the twisted red-and-white pipe cleaner candy cane, and then rummaged deeper. "Oh, I remember! Grandpa got us these on a trip."

Tiny moccasin booties made of soft leather and beadwork dangled from a hook. On the back was stamped WILLIAMS, AZ.

"I think they're from Arizona," she said.

"No duh, it says so on the back," I said, feeling uncomfortable. "You better wait for your mom."

Cyclops landed on the coffee table, scattering wads of newspaper and slinking around boxes. He nosed into tissue paper, pushing Ginger's box to the very edge.

"Cyclops, get down!" I sneezed.

Winnie pulled out a Baby's First Christmas ornament with Ginger's name and birth date painted on it.

"We all have one of these. Mom painted them," she said. Dangling it from her finger on the thin wire, it caught the light like a huge diamond.

Cyclops locked onto his target and launched. He tackled, tucked, and rolled. Pop! The ornament burst like a bubble.

"Winnie!" I yelled.

Cyclops jumped up like he'd been shot, shook his paws free of glass, and darted under the couch.

Winnie sat there looking like she'd been hit with a stun gun.

Marty raced down the hall with the camera in her hand. "What happened?"

She took in the glass and the opened boxes in one glance. Then she grabbed Ginger's box from the edge of the coffee table.

"What happened? Did something break?"

I looked at Winnie, but she just zoned. Why did I have to be the bad guy?

I said, "Winnie was . . . showing me an ornament and . . . Cyclops jumped on it and it broke."

Her eyes got wild. "Which one? Which one was it?" Marty let the camera slip out of her grasp. Then she set the box back on the table and reached down to pick up a glass shard with part of Ginger's name on it. "Winnie?"

Winnie buried her face in her arms and began to sob.

Marty towered over me.

"Which one, Andie?" she asked, huffing like she was hyperventilating.

"The . . . the shiny one. The one with Ginger's name."

Her face twisted and her nose flared to let in more oxygen, because it didn't look like she was getting enough. Then she blew.

"I told you to wait for me! You had no right to get into Ginger's box!"

"It wasn't me! It was Winnie. I tried to stop her."

Maybe it showed, how guilty I felt, because for a second she looked like she didn't believe me. I'd wanted to see what was in the box in the worst way. And I'd wanted to break her stuff myself. I guess it was written all over my face.

"Winnie . . ." Marty closed her eyes, and her shoulders heaved. "Go. Just . . . go to your room."

Winnie stumbled up, scattering tissue paper and boxes, and ran sobbing down the hall. I'd never heard Marty yell at anyone but Deja. She knelt down and started picking up the glass. She sifted the pieces in her palm with a long red nail with holly decals. Then she sat back on her heels, and her whole body sagged. Her face screwed up, and big tears rolled down her cheeks. She wailed like a wounded animal.

It's scary, watching grown-ups cry. I mean, if they're not in control, who is?

I was trying to think what to do, and keep myself from crying, when Carl opened the front door. He wiped his feet on the rug, and I looked up helplessly into his startled face.

"What happened?" he asked. "What's wrong? Marty?"

I gestured at Marty. "Winnie broke an ornament."

He looked down into the pieces in Marty's hand, and he kind of deflated. He leaned down and rubbed her shoulders with his big hands. Then he kissed the top of her head. "Come on," he said, helping her up.

She sniffled down the hallway into her room, and just before she closed the door, I heard her call him Daddy. Then he went down the hall to Winnie's room and went in, blowing his nose with a big white handkerchief and closing the door behind him.

I sat in the middle of the mess with Johnny Mathis warbling in the background about being home for Christmas, feeling like the lone survivor at ground zero. I sniffled a little out there, sitting all by myself and thinking I didn't belong here, didn't deserve this. I wanted to call Grandma, but I couldn't ask right then and didn't want to take the chance of making things worse. I missed her, and I needed to talk to someone who loved me.

Eventually I got out the vacuum and picked up most of the glass, saving the piece with Ginger's name.

Carl finally came out of Winnie's room and sank onto the couch. He rubbed his face with his hand and exhaled. Then he patted the seat beside him, and I sat down.

"Marty's having some trouble with the holidays. This is only the second Christmas since we lost Ginger." His sad blue eyes absently studied the ornament box. "She'll get through it. We all will, I guess." He shook his head. "Last year we skipped Christmas altogether. It'll be a hard thing."

I nodded. "Yeah, I know."

He considered me for a moment. "I guess you do. It can't be easy, losing your folks so young like you did."

He caught me off guard. I didn't know how much of the truth he really wanted to know.

"I'm okay. It's not so bad this year." At least not yet.

Carl waited for me to go on, but when I didn't, he said, "Listen, if you ever feel like you want to talk to somebody . . ."

I nodded.

"We all might be twenty pounds heavier by Christmas, if Marty doesn't slow down on her baking. But I guess there are worse ways of coping." He looked around at the mess of boxes. "Just leave this stuff where it is for now," he said. "They'll feel better about things later."

I watched *Andy Griffith* out there by myself after he left. I tried not to laugh because it didn't seem right, but it was hard because Barney looked so goofy in a wedding dress. Marty came out with her eyes all red and swollen and went into Winnie's room. I guess they made up. Later, when the tree was all decorated, I didn't argue with Marty when she asked me to be in the picture. It wasn't that big a deal.

✦ ✦ ✦

We went Christmas shopping before I went to my grandparents', and Marty helped me pick out a gift for them. It took most of the money I'd saved from working at the drive-in. So when Natalie gave me a gift at school, and Winnie told me she had picked out something I'd really like, I had to scramble to come up with something cheap for them.

I wrapped a basket I'd made in school for Marty and Carl. It was kind of lopsided, but it was only my first basket and it didn't cost me anything. For Winnie I got some hair clips, and for Natalie a journal from the Dollar Barn. Deja didn't deserve a Christmas gift, except some coal for her stocking.

Winnie was making a graham cracker gingerbread house the day before I left for Grandma's, using candy canes, Tootsie Rolls, Life Savers, ribbon candy, and gumdrops. She asked if I wanted to make one, so I made mine sideways into a mobile home and put Tootsie Roll steps going up to the door. I'm not sure, but I think Winnie was trying to make hers into a castle. It was a gooey mess, but I told her I liked it anyway.

Carl drove me up to Pine Run early on Sunday morning at the beginning of winter break. The tree lot didn't open till noon, and there weren't many trees left, and he had time. Marty loaded me up with fudge and peanut brittle to share with Grandma and Grandpa, and a gift for me to open on Christmas morning.

By the time we got to Pine Run, Carl had to turn on the truck heater. Lumps of snow piled up in the shaded banks of the highway and dark crevices between the houses, and melted snowmen drooped in people's yards. I rolled down my window. The sky looked sooty and smelled like snow. I thought how great it would be if I got snowed in here for weeks and weeks, one storm rolling in after another.

Carl pulled into the mobile home park, inched the Dodge Ram over the speed bumps, and parked behind the Lincoln. Bilbo was half buried in snow by the For Sale sign. Grandma's TV was so loud I could hear it when I got out, even with the house shut up tight. I jumped out and ran in without waiting for Carl.

Grandma opened the door. "Andie, sweetheart, come in before you catch cold," she said, squeezing me hard. Then she saw Carl. "Shut the door behind you, please, Mr. McAlister."

I heard Grandpa call, and followed the plastic carpet runner into the TV room. The room smelled gross, like rotten eggs.

"Hey, Grandpa. You feeling better?" I hugged him, tripping on a folded-up walker beside his chair. Where did that come from?

"Oh, best as could be expected," he said so loudly he startled me. "Had a touch of the flu, and then my leg give out on me. Dr. Owen makes me use this old thing." He nodded toward his walker like a sulky kid.

Carl followed me into the TV room and set my bags down in the corner.

"Morning, Mr. James. Merry Christmas," he said loudly.

"Merry Christmas to you too, sir. Our Andie behaving for you?"

"Good as gold." Carl winked at me. "I've got to get going. I need to get back and sell some trees. You all have a nice Christmas."

I walked Carl to the door.

"I'll be back New Year's Day," he said. He paused, then leaned in and said quietly, looking me in the eye, "You have any problems or anything comes up, call us. You got the number?"

"Yeah. We'll be okay."

He hesitated. Then he said, "You know, it's probably best for you to stay here anyway. Maybe next Christmas will be a happier one at our house."

I thought to myself that I'd never know. I'd be moved out by then.

After Carl left, I grabbed my suitcase and headed to the sewing room.

"I've got a present for you, Grandma," I called. "Where does it go?"

The clock with large, easy-to-read numbers, wrapped in penguin paper, was buried in my suitcase between socks and underwear. The bow was smashed flat, but the penguins still looked jazzed.

"Just set it on the counter," she said. "We don't have a Christmas tree this year. It's too much trouble for us old folks."

"That's okay." I shrugged, feeling a little disappointed. "I don't need one."

Their only decorations were some Christmas cards Grandma had taped around the doorway. It didn't look like Christmas there at all.

"I haven't got around to putting up any decorations," Grandma said. "See what you can find in your closet."

I pulled off my sweater. It felt like a sauna, and Grandpa still had a blanket on his lap. The TV tray beside him overflowed with prescription bottles and empty cups. How could he keep them all straight?

"You keeping your grades up?" he shouted.

"Yeah, pretty good," I answered.

He put a hand to his ear and shook his head.

"Yeah, pretty good!" I shouted.

He nodded. Geez, when did his hearing short-circuit? I saw his hearing aid mixed in with the pill bottles. Why wasn't he wearing it?

I carefully brought out the boxes. Grandma's Christmas decorations were ancient. Frayed garlands and fragile bulbs with the color worn clear in spots. I put the old nativity scene on the counter, but Baby Jesus wouldn't stay in His manger. Maybe He was creeped out that His mom's face had worn off and one of the sheep only had three legs.

I found some of the Christmas decorations from our old house on Evergreen. There was a grapevine wreath, Santa's sleigh, and a giant reindeer that used to sit by our fireplace. It felt good to touch them again. I smoothed out the silk holly and poinsettias, and fluffed up the big plaid bows. When Grandma wasn't looking, I buried my face in the reindeer's bow and breathed deep. Smells can take you years away.

We were trying to untangle a knot of twinkle lights when someone knocked at the door.

"I'll get it, Grandma," I said. I figured it was a neighbor, and it was okay now because I was just a temporary visitor. When I opened the door, Carl stood there with a big box under his arm.

"I brought you something," he said, wiping his feet and coming inside to stand the box upright in the corner. "I saw your grandparents didn't have a Christmas tree, so I got you one."

The skinny box had a picture of a Christmas tree on the side. I looked blankly at him. Carl with a fake tree? What was wrong with this picture?

By that time, Grandma had shuffled in.

"I brought Andie a small Christmas tree, if it's all right with you. It's pre-lit, so it shouldn't be any trouble."

"Where did you get it?" I asked.

"I stopped by the K-Mart on my way out. You all have decorations for it?"

"Yeah, we have boxes of stuff." I couldn't believe he would do this for me, especially knowing how he felt about fake trees.

Grandma wasn't saying anything, but she looked at the box like it had lice.

"Grandma, it's okay, isn't it?"

Her mouth puckered shut, and then relaxed. "If Andie wants it, I guess we can find a place for it."

"Thanks, Grandma."

I ripped open the box and dug out a bristly green stick. I smiled up at Carl.

"It looks pretty good, for a fake tree," I said.

"Yeah, it'll do." He opened the door. "This time, I'm really going. Bye, punkin." He chucked me gently under the chin, like he would do to Winnie, and he left.

I cleared a space in a corner of the living room and set up the tree. It looked pretty real, once I got the ornaments and garland on it. I made a paper-plate angel for the top.

Grandma was grumpy after that. I couldn't figure out what was bothering her until I overheard her talking to Grandpa, which wasn't hard. She said Carl only brought the tree because he was trying to win me over. And he called me *punkin*—that bothered her too. She sounded a little jealous and a lot suspicious. She said something about him wanting my insurance money, but I didn't know anything about money. He was just being nice, wasn't he?

I remembered the goodies Marty had packed for us, but decided not to spring them on her right away.

"Grandma, I want to bake some cookies."

"Sure, hon. Look in the cupboards. It's been so long since I baked, I don't know what I've got anymore. Maybe we should pick up some slice-and-bake cookies when we run to the Safeway."

The sugar cookies we baked didn't compare to Marty's peanut brittle and fudge, but we had fun making them together. And

Grandma didn't bad-mouth Marty's goodies so much when I brought them out later.

It was good to be with Grandma and Grandpa, but it was quiet and a little sad. And boring. I did some cleaning for Grandma, things that hadn't been moved or dusted in years.

On Christmas morning, Grandma asked me to read aloud from the Bible about Jesus' birth before we opened our gifts. Grandma wiped her eyes. I could tell the story meant a lot to her. But why couldn't a God who made those miracles happen protect my parents? He protected Mary and Joseph; why couldn't He have warned my dad in a dream, or sent an angel to them?

I knew the answer. We just weren't that important.

We listened to Christmas carols on the radio and watched a marathon of *It's a Wonderful Life*. The weather was stormy, and Grandma kept checking the phone to make sure there was a dial tone. If the power had gone off, I think I would have cried. I just wanted the day to be over.

Winnie gave me a craft kit to make jewelry. Marty and Carl gave me a sketchbook and set of colored pencils, so I got them out and doodled, just to make the time go by. I wondered how Winnie and Natalie did in the church play. Maybe I'd call Natalie when I got back.

On New Year's Eve I took down the tree and the decorations and put them in my closet. Just before Carl got there on New Year's Day, I remembered to copy down Uncle Greg's address and phone number. That's when I realized that he'd never even called Grandpa and Grandma to wish them a Merry Christmas.

CHAPTER 17

Marty

I taped an index card with emergency contact numbers to the passenger's visor of the truck. "Where do you think you'll end up, Dad?" I asked.

"I'm shootin' for the South Rim again." He checked the snow chains and the toolbox in the truck bed. "If the weather's bad, I'll move farther south toward Tucson."

"Tucson. The saguaros calling you?"

"Every night in my dreams." He cinched up his tie-downs and tucked the ends under the tarp. "Way too early for blooms, but I'll take what I can get."

"Have you got your thermals?"

He nodded. I hated to mother him, but he was headed for some rugged weather, and it could be a month before we saw him again.

I packed extra blankets in the truck bed and tried to smile for his sake. All year he looked forward to this time when he could travel and do what he loved best—paint. And this time in the dead of winter, between the tree lot and the farmers market, was the only time he could get away. Enjoying life is what retirement should be about, not babysitting your grown daughter and her children.

The Grand Canyon was Dad's favorite place to paint, with the desert a close second. It sent chills up my spine to see the angles he reached painting the canyon floor. I didn't want to know what chances he took for the sake of his art.

As he packed, he hummed an old cowboy song, "Blue Bonnet Girl." He was happiest on the open range or in the saddle. Dad would've moved back to Nevada in a heartbeat after Mom died if it hadn't been for us, even though the family ranch had already been leveled for a golf course.

After Ginger died we discussed moving back home outside of Elko, since we no longer needed to be close to her specialists. There's something healthy about growing up in a small town with animals and wide-open spaces. But we decided that Winnie and Deja didn't need to be ripped from their friends and school when things were finally settling down for them. Besides, Russell and Starr had moved back to Elko, and I really didn't want to run into the happy couple. I felt it was best for the girls to have as little contact with him as possible.

Dad popped open the glove box in the truck cab, tossed in extra flashlight batteries, and slammed it shut. Then he scanned the contents of a box on the floor—mostly maps. He left space for his paints and canvases on the passenger's seat, mumbling to himself while he went over a mental checklist.

"Did you refill your prescriptions?" I asked. "What about antacid?"

"Got them in my kit."

He checked the air pressure in the front tires.

"Is your cell phone charged? Have you got the charger?"

"Yup. But I don't count on getting a signal where I'm goin'."

"When do you think you'll be back?" I asked.

"Oh, better count on a month, just to be safe."

I tried not to let my disappointment show, but he glanced up from the tire gauge and saw my face.

"It'll go fast. You and the girls'll be okay."

"I don't mean to sound like a worrywart, but which route are you taking? Will you go by Reno?"

"Not likely. All depends on the weather. I'll probably come up the same way as I go, through Barstow and Kingman."

I breathed a little easier. If the weather was bad, he wouldn't take a chance on coming back through Salt Lake to Elko. And see Ruby.

My paranoia about his sneaking off to see Ruby was unfounded. I paid the gasoline bills; if he went anywhere near northern Nevada, I'd know. Not that it would make any difference. He was a grown man, not a runaway teenager.

I sounded like a jealous wife.

Never in a million years would I stop Dad from being happy if he really cared for another woman as he had for Mom. But I didn't want to deal with it, just the same. If Dad left, it would be too much like Russell leaving us all over again.

I lay awake long into the night mentally going over every scenario and trying to remember what he might have forgotten to pack. What would I do if he didn't come back?

I remembered coming out of the doctor's office just after we'd found out that Ginger had been switched. Standing in the parking lot scratching the paint around the keyhole of the car door. The key had fit before we went in, but it didn't after we came out. It had swelled or twisted, and wouldn't go into the lock. I glanced around and said that maybe we had the wrong car. Dad gently took the keys out of my hand and unlocked the door for me. I would still be in that parking lot now if he hadn't been there. Nothing fit the same after that.

I switched on my light and pulled my Bible from the nightstand. Searching the Psalms, I finally found one of my mother's favorite verses—Psalm 46. She had underlined the first verse in blue ballpoint. *God is our refuge and strength, an ever-present help in trouble.*

As I read through the chapter I felt encouraged, especially when I got to verse 10: *Be still, and know that I am God.* It came to me, an unexplainable peace threading its way in among my fears and anxiety. God was my strength, not Dad. Dad was an important part of God's plan for us, but he wasn't the plan. God's plan was for us each to come to depend on Him, not on other people, as much as we love them. The time would come when Dad would leave us. But God never would.

I talked to Him for a long time, just like He was there in the room with me, with His nail-scarred hands and His kind eyes smiling. He was so very real to me that I fell asleep feeling He was keeping watch.

Early before sunrise, Dad packed his art supplies carefully into the front passenger's seat. I loaded him up with a thermos of strong coffee, plenty of sugar and creamer, a package of warm cinnamon rolls, three kinds of cookies, and sandwiches. The girls shivered with me in our pajamas on the porch while we said our good-byes. Exhaust curled into the frosty air as the truck sat warming up in the driveway.

I hugged Dad tightly, trying to hold myself together. "Where will you stop tonight?"

"Kingman. I'll call you girls from there."

Though I fought it, that old feeling of abandonment crept into my heart, and my face crumpled. He gave my shoulder another squeeze and brushed at his eyes. "Now, I always come back, don't I?"

I could only nod as I stepped aside for Winnie and Deja to hug him. Andie stood wrapped in her blanket looking worried, but she smiled shyly when he chucked her affectionately under the chin.

Long buried feelings surfaced as we watched him climb into the cab. Memories of Russell pulling away with a loaded car, walking out on our lives forever. Leaving us for someone new.

Lord, help me to forget.

Dad waved and backed the truck out of the driveway. Winnie wrapped her arms around my waist as he drove off into the parking lot toward the gate. She whimpered, and I pulled her tighter.

"He'll come back, Win. He always does."

"Not like Daddy," she said.

My heart nearly broke. "He's nothing like Daddy, angel. We'll miss Grandpa while he's gone, but he will come back."

I shooed them inside out of the cold, knowing that the feeling of loss would stay with us all day. I forced myself into Mommy mode, acting more confident and positive than I actually felt. Dad was in good health and had more wisdom and common sense than anyone I knew. He'd come back to us, if it was humanly possible and if God was willing.

That night, after he checked in with us from Kingman, I realized there was a fine line between praying for him constantly and worrying about him. Somewhere I had to find balance. Just like the pastor had said in his sermon on Sunday, I had to let God keep him, and that meant letting him go.

I picked up my new work schedule on the day after Dad left. Robert had given me all the extra hours he could to help with our finances, except for Sunday mornings, which I'd specifically asked to have off. I'd decided that church was going to be a priority this year, no matter what. We all needed it, especially with Dad gone. I'd even get Deja there eventually, and we'd be a family together. The thought kept me going.

On New Year's Day I'd done a complete cleansing of my kitchen cabinets, replacing old spices, baking supplies, and staples with new ones, lining the shelves with fresh paper, and rearranging my work station to be most efficient. My new schedule didn't allow much opportunity to bake, and every minute spent rummaging through messy cabinets would be lost time.

"Too bad about your dad being gone," Jo said on our ten-minute break. "If you got a big problem of some kind and you need a man, I'll send one over." She took a long draw on her cigarette and blew it to the side. "But you can't keep him."

"Nothing will come up that we can't handle or a plumber can't fix," I assured her.

"Just in case. I'm only offering."

I splurged for our first official girls' squad meeting and brought home a tub of fried chicken and a liter of root beer. Paper plates were the order of the evening. Until Dad came home, we'd make life as simple for ourselves as cheaply as possible.

My last nail popped off when I dug out a pencil and paper from the kitchen junk drawer for the meeting after dinner. I fished it out from the back of the drawer—pretty and red with a snowflake on the tip—and tossed it into the trash. It would be two months or longer before I could afford a new set. I knew I should rethink the whole acrylic nail indulgence anyway. It was part of the makeover Jo had convinced me to get, but the nails got in the way of everything I did. Sometimes they even made it hard to bake.

I couldn't afford them, and I suppose some people would think they were gaudy. In a fleeting, renegade moment, I wondered what Julian thought of them, and I shook my head. What difference did it make? I looked at my own nails and grimaced. They were paper-thin and torn with white blotches stained with stubborn red polish. Maybe the fake ones served a purpose, after all.

Winnie, Deja, and Andie joined me at the kitchen table for our annual strategy meeting. Winnie opened with a brief explanation for Andie.

"Okay, ladies," I said when she was done. "Most of you know the drill. This meeting is for the division of duties and to set a menu. Now's the time to speak up if you have any preferences."

"Andie and me wanna load the dishwasher," Winnie said, her legs bouncing the seat.

Andie's forehead creased, and she looked irritated. To this point, she'd been very patient with Winnie, but it looked as though Winnie may have finally crossed the line.

"Is that okay with you, Andie? There really aren't that many dishes since it's only the three of you."

"I guess so," she said.

I listed Winnie's and Andie's names on the small whiteboard under DISHES.

"What about you, Deja? Your turn to pick."

She tipped her chair back, her eyes slits. "I'll feed the cat."

"That's good for starters, and what else?"

"Bring in the mail."

"Very funny. Okay, I'll assign you to bathroom duty."

"Wait—"

"Too late. We'll rotate next time."

All four legs of her chair set down heavily onto the floor. "Well, if I have to clean the stupid bathrooms, they should have to vacuum all the rooms."

"Yeah, we'll vacuum," Winnie said. "And we'll dust too."

Andie's jaw dropped. "I can't dust. It makes me stuffy."

"You're right. Winnie, the job's all yours. Andie, you could unload the dryer and fold clothes."

She considered it. "Okay."

"Which means, Deja, you sort and load the washing machine."

"Why can't she load it too? I have a lot of homework," Deja argued.

"There's too much cat hair and animal dander on dirty clothes because *somebody* keeps letting the cat in."

Deja sneered at Andie, who beaded her eyes and met Deja's look with a steely gaze, not flinching. Good for Andie! I buttoned my lips together to keep from smiling.

"We'll keep this schedule for one week," I said. "Now, about food. What do you want me to pick up that's easy to fix?"

"Ramen," Deja said. "Beef and chicken, not that gross shrimp kind. And Oriental salad."

I started my shopping list. Winnie wanted peanut butter and jelly, and instant macaroni and cheese. Andie suggested grilled cheese and tomato soup.

"You know how to fix that?" I asked.

"My dad showed me. And scrambled egg sandwiches and sloppy joes too."

Winnie studied her with a frown. Finally she said, "My dad showed me how to pour beer without getting it all foamy."

Andie's eyebrows lifted. "Nice."

"That's enough, Winnie. Now, we won't be eating out until we get a check from your father. So tighten your belts."

"I can cut out coupons if you want," Andie offered. "To save money."

I smiled. "I wish I could take you up on that, Andie. But they won't let me use coupons on top of my employee discount."

Deja snorted, and the look on Andie's face made me wish I'd taken the coupons anyway and just pretended to use them. "It was a great idea, though," I said.

They added teriyaki bowls, potpies, and SpaghettiOs to the list.

"Deja, I want you to be in charge of the oven when it's used."

I made out a menu for the week and posted it along with the job list. "Okay, I think we're set. One warning." My eyes swept from Winnie and Andie to Deja. "Anyone who doesn't do her jobs this time around gets double the next. Understand?"

The younger girls agreed. I waited, and Deja finally said, "Fine."

The first week was slow going, like a great locomotive trying to gather steam, but they finally got used to the idea of my getting home at ten o'clock. There were no major mishaps, just minor glitches, for which I was grateful, and they rarely called me at work. I came home exhausted every night, ate peanut butter and jelly or a can of soup, and went to bed. By the weekend I was slowly adjusting to the longer schedule, though I almost nodded off during the sermon on Sunday morning. After church that day, I fell asleep on the couch trying to stay awake to watch a movie with Winnie and Andie. When I woke up it was dark, and they were in their rooms. I felt like a bad mother. On Monday night we had another meeting to switch some of the jobs around and adjust the grocery list. They all agreed there were no major problems to report—everyone seemed to be doing her job reasonably well.

It killed me to even occasionally buy packaged goodies for

their school lunches, but I had no choice. There just wasn't enough time in the day to bake on top of everything else. But when withdrawal got too bad I baked at midnight, although I always regretted it in the morning.

When Russell's check came we splurged on Chinese takeout from Lucky Dragon and rented a movie. Of course, the movie didn't interest Deja, but it was a chance to catch up over dinner.

I knew it was too good to last. Halfway through the month, Deja got lazy and quit doing her jobs. I wished more than ever that I could be home with them. Especially when the court worker came to visit, and the girls were there by themselves.

Dad checked in with us from Tucson and Nogales. He called again from Old Smokey's Restaurant in Williams, south of the Rim, just before he started home. He'd caught on canvas a perfect sunset and a Navajo child in the snow with shades of purple. He sounded happy. Contented.

I told him he had been right, that we were getting along fine so far and that hopefully the end of the month would turn out as uneventful as the beginning.

Dad wasn't what you'd call religious. But going to church and reading my Bible were slowly making a difference in me, and I couldn't keep it to myself.

"Dad, I pray for you every day," I told him on the phone before we said good-bye.

There was silence on the other end of the line, and I was afraid we'd been cut off. "Dad?"

"It's working, girl. Keep it up."

CHAPTER 18

Andie

We had a powwow right after Christmas to split up the jobs and figure out how to survive until Carl came back.

"First we give up sodas. And ice cream and candy," Winnie explained. Both the tree lot and the drive-in were closed, and we couldn't spend the money on junk food. "And we eat the frozen pizzas left over from the drive-in. But you still bake, right, Mom?"

"When I can. But not as often."

Winnie hadn't figured out that stress was like jet fuel to Marty.

A thought occurred to me. If money was so tight, maybe Grandma was right. According to her, I was supposed to be getting some kind of insurance money. Maybe Marty wanted it.

"Mom works overtime, so we have to clean up the house and do the dishes and wash clothes. Right, Mom?"

Marty looked kind of embarrassed. "You're not sentenced to hard labor, Winnie. I just need some extra help, that's all."

Winnie dissected an oatmeal cookie, flicking out the raisins.

"When Grandpa gets back, he's gonna have new pictures to sell at the farmers market."

"Where's that?" I asked.

"Here." She slurped down her milk. "On the weekends. People bring their crafts and vegetables and junk to sell in the parking lot."

Of course they do. Dumb question.

We decided on some easy dinners that we could fix if Marty wasn't home to eat with us. I think she was surprised that I wasn't totally kitchen impaired.

Carl left right after New Year's, and we didn't hear from him very much. I think Marty worried that he was stuck somewhere, because she'd shush us and freeze when news reports aired about stranded motorists or lost hikers on TV.

The whole idea of us being a cleaning service would have worked, except that toward the end, Deja was a slacker. And she let the cat in every night. Winnie and I would have to chase Cyclops around to lock him in the garage. He knew what we were doing. It was cold out there.

Most of the time we were already in bed when Marty got home, so we couldn't really complain to her until the weekend. Once, when it was Winnie's week to load the washing machine, Marty said that if Deja wasn't doing her part to just stop doing her laundry. That got her attention.

"Hey, where's my stuff?" Deja demanded one night, digging through the laundry basket. "Nothing in here's mine."

Winnie chewed her bottom lip and flicked her eyes over at me. I wondered if Deja scared her.

"Look on your floor," I said.

She ignored me and went to the laundry room. I heard the dryer door slam, and she came back out to the living room.

"Nothing of mine is *clean*?"

I could see Winnie beginning to squirm. I jumped in so she wouldn't cave. Nobody likes a bully.

"I don't know," I said without taking my eyes from the TV. "What about you, Winnie?"

I could see Winnie shaking her head out of the side of my eye. Deja positioned herself between us and the TV. I think she was trying to cook the air between us with her laser eyes.

"It's your job to load the wash," she said to Winnie. "I need my red sweater for tomorrow. Now, do it."

"No can do," I said. "Marty told us to quit washing your clothes."

Her eyes squinted up so small that I thought they might get sucked into her black hole of a brain. "You're lying. Why would Mom say that?"

"Hm. Maybe 'cause we're tired of covering for you." I looked over at Winnie, who was practically cowering. "Yeah, that's it. You're a slacker, and we're not covering for you anymore."

I think I threw her. I'd never really stood up to her before. Mostly I tried to ignore her or stay out of her way, but she'd pushed me to the edge.

Deja said something really disgusting, and I think not humanly possible. Winnie looked like she was going to need CPR.

"Okay, brain death," Deja spewed. "How—exactly—are you 'covering' for me?"

I looked over at Winnie. "Let's see, Winnie cleaned the hall bathroom for you last week, didn't you, Winnie?"

Her head made the faintest movement in agreement.

"And Marty said for you to fill the dishwasher, but I've been doing it every night."

"I have tons of homework. There's no way I could do all that and keep my grades up."

I couldn't help myself. "I didn't know Fs were that hard to keep up."

Deja's head snapped back like I'd slapped her. I could hardly believe it myself. It was the meanest thing I'd ever said to anybody. Boy, was I going to pay.

Deja locked me out of our room. I was a little bit worried that she might hurt something of mine, but I reached up and touched the rings on the chain around my neck. They were the only thing I really cared about that couldn't be replaced. I had some stuff in boxes that were taped shut, but she didn't know what was in them. Grandma had copies of all the photos of my parents. I thought of Mom's Bible. I didn't think even Deja would have the nerve to destroy a Bible.

When Marty came home and saw me almost asleep on the couch, she and Deja had a talk in Marty's room. I heard the washer running, so Deja must've washed her own sweater after all. But she wasn't any better about doing her jobs after that. If anything, we saw less and less of her. No loss.

Some nights Deja didn't come home until ten, just before Marty. I didn't say anything at first. Marty could hardly drag Deja out of bed for school the next day.

I tried my hand at vacuuming. I did it really fast, just to get it over with, but my allergies got worse from the cat hair. My prescription got kicked up a notch and made me feel like a walking zombie until I got adjusted.

But that wasn't the worst thing. One night right after Marty got home, I climbed under my covers to read *The Hobbit* after my shower, and I reached up out of habit to curl my finger around my chain. It wasn't there. The chain with my parents' wedding rings was gone.

I searched the bathroom and my night table and the bed. I was tearing apart my suitcase when Deja asked from her bed, where she lay sprawled reading a magazine, "What're you looking for?"

It shouldn't have taken me so long to figure out. Two things were odd. One, she never, ever spoke directly to me in a normal tone of voice, and two, she never, ever paid any attention to anything I did. Why should she now?

I whirled to face her. "You havc it."

She gave me a fakey *whatever* eye roll. "Have what?"

"My chain. My chain with the rings on it. Give it back." I advanced on her.

"Back off," she barked. "I don't have your lame chain."

She flipped through her magazine. I knocked it out of her hand.

She smiled evilly, in a satisfied way. Then she jumped up from the bed, giving me a wide berth with her hands out to block any blows.

"Mom!" she called, stomping down the hallway toward Marty's room. I took the advantage and attacked her drawers.

Bizarre. That's what I'd call the junk filling her drawers. A studded collar, broken pencils, empty soda cans, food wrappers, Ramen crumbs, popcorn kernels, tardy slips, loose tobacco, money, a toe ring. When she came to the bedroom door with Marty, I was pulling out a chain from a pile of holey socks. The chain wasn't mine, but the dog tags on it did suit her.

I slammed the drawer and turned to Marty.

"Deja took my chain with the rings on it, and she won't give it back."

Marty looked at me, and then at Deja, waiting for her response.

"I did not take her stupid chain," Deja protested. "I don't even know what it looks like."

"It's a plain silver chain with two gold rings on it. And one of the rings had a swirly pattern on it." I willed my bottom lip to stop trembling. I would not cry in front of her. "They belonged to my mom and dad."

"When was the last time you saw it?" Marty asked.

"I took it off to take a shower. And when I got into bed, it was gone."

"And you looked all around for it?" she asked.

"Everywhere. In here, in the bathroom, even my suitcase."

"Well, Deja?" Marty asked, sizing her up.

"What? Gosh, Mom, I don't believe this! You believe her over me?"

Marty turned to the dresser and started rummaging through the drawers herself, elbow-deep in clothes. She dumped the drawer on the bed.

"I don't have her stupid chain!" Deja said, scooping up a heavy sock and stuffing it in her pocket. Then she gathered up clothes and shoved them back into the drawer.

"Deja, I wish I could believe you," Marty said with her hands on her hips. "I'm really tired. Just make it easier on all of us, and tell us where it is."

Deja looked from Marty to me, and bared her teeth.

"You'll never find it in my stuff, because I don't have it." She stormed off.

We looked for a long time, but we didn't find it. I wondered if Deja would try to get rid of it, now that she knew her mom considered her a prime suspect. She wouldn't want to risk having it found in her possession.

Then I ratted on her. I told Marty how Deja was gone so much and how late she came home most nights. I thought it would make me feel better, but it didn't. When Marty rubbed her temples, I saw her fake nails were gone. Her own nails were stubby and broken. I guess we were all making sacrifices.

While Deja was in the shower, I pulled out Mom's Bible. I flipped through, and it naturally fell open to a wrinkled page, creased and dog-eared with lots of highlighter in different colors. Psalm 84. In the margin was my name with an arrow pointing to a verse in yellow. It startled me at first, like a message from beyond. It was verse eleven, the verse Dad wrote in the inscription in the front. It said, "No good thing does he withhold from those whose walk is blameless." I guessed Mom meant that I was the "good thing."

If Mom believed that verse, then maybe it was true. I wasn't perfect, but I couldn't think of any really bad thing I'd ever done. Maybe I was "blameless" enough to help. I asked God to help me get my rings back. It couldn't hurt to ask.

CHAPTER 19

Marty

I cruised past the building on the corner of the old town district and pulled out of traffic to park across the street. The storefront had that 1930s dust bowl look about it, with lots of dirty glass in the front and paint down to the primer. Its ripped awning dipped down like a fedora over one jaundiced eye.

I'd never really noticed the building before, even though I passed it every morning on the way to the elementary school, but it was perfect—on a main street with a neglected parking lot on the side, not really in a great part of town, but not so bad as to have break-ins every night. What if? What if one day I opened my own bakery there?

A fresh coat of paint in a pale shade of 1950s T-bird turquoise. Giant squares of black and white linoleum on the floor. A coffee bar along the wall with chrome and retro prints. A glass case filled with pastries, cookies, and decadent desserts, and the scent of bread rising. Round tables with chairs for two or three and a poodle-skirt pink awning with a crescent moon sign over it—*Blue Moon Bakery.*

Well, maybe I had thought about it more than I realized. I was made to bake, wasn't I? We didn't even have a bakery at Shop 'n Save. Every bit of bread and pastry we sold was trucked in already packaged. What a travesty.

What did it take to open a bakery, I dared to wonder as I waded at the edge of dangerous waters. Licenses, start-up money for equipment, supplies, staff, and utilities. Money and desire and more money. I'd never really done any research. It had seemed like a waste of time and an invitation for discouragement. I wasn't even sure I'd be good at the business side of it.

I eased the car back into traffic and headed to work. No need to start off the day this way, and arriving late to boot.

A weight lifted from my shoulders the night the Dodge pulled into the driveway and Dad unfolded himself from many hours in the driver's seat. Now I could cut back to my regular work hours. No more midnight baking to keep my sanity. No more going it alone with the girls. We had so much extra time now, with the opening of the farmers market still a month away, that we found ourselves sitting around watching reruns at night. One day I stopped by Walgreens on the way home and picked up a pack of Uno cards and the game of Clue.

It wasn't hard to interest the younger girls in the game, but Deja was a harder sell. We had some rowdy Uno sessions, and Win and I played partners with Clue until she caught on. Dad and Andie had an intense rivalry going on each night. It was apparent that Andie fancied herself a Clue expert. Dad finally beat her.

The laughter generated by our time together made me vaguely uncomfortable at first, and I couldn't put my finger on just why. It surfaced every time the girls lunged forward, yelling "Uno!" and slapping their cards on the table.

I remembered feeling that same way the time Dad tickled the girls at the dinner table, the first time I really heard Andie laugh. Late one night it came to me. Visions of Ginger in a seizure. In cataplexy, or struggling with suffocating congestion brought on by the excitement. We had to keep Ginger calm and avoid just such situations in order to manage it all. Fear was a learned response.

It wasn't easy, since she was a little jokester herself. Her favorite joke was about her feeding tube. The top flipped up on the feeding tube so the connector could be inserted, and she'd say "Fill . . . her . . . up . . . Mommy." That is, until she could no longer speak. The first time she said it, we laughed until she was choking.

On top of it, Ginger refused to wear headgear because she knew it set her apart from the other kids at school. She said it gave her "headgear hair." So the order of the day was to keep her life as uneventful as possible. I'm not sure it was best for Ginger, after all. Maybe it was just easier on us not to deal with the aftermath of distress.

But now we were laughing again. Full-on, tear-streaked, loud-mouthed laughter. Here we were, trying it on, and it fit fine. We'd been living with fear sitting in the darkened corner long after we'd needed to, daring us to let go and laugh. Andie had drawn swords with it without even knowing, and freed us, hesitant and gun-shy as we were. She brought laughter back to our home.

It made me want to hold her, to gather her up and feel her arms around my neck and her cheek against mine.

Would that time ever come?

Jo looked slimmer. The way she bent over refilling a Valentine candy display exposed angles in her hips where padding used to be. I told her so at lunch.

"Go figure— it'd take my husband's diabetes to make me slim down. Hey, I could be on *Oprah*. 'How my own weight loss saved my husband's life.' " She nibbled her rice cake thoughtfully, and said, "I should send that in."

"Dad's back."

"All safe and sound, is he?"

I nodded. "You know," I said as I paused to take a sip of my diet soda, "it really wasn't as bad as I expected." When I looked back over the weeks, I realized that God had helped us get through it unscathed and took care of Dad too.

"I'd like to see what he's got new to sell. Maybe I'll buy a painting for Walter's birthday. One of those Grand Canyon scenes."

"He hasn't shown us his new stuff from the trip. He's funny about his paintings. Probably has some touching up to do." I took another sip. "I heard from Andie's grandparents' attorney. They asked for an extension until June. I guess they're having trouble selling. I suspect their health is declining, too."

"That's good news for you. I mean . . . well, you know what I mean."

"Yeah, but it could be bad news for Andie. If it doesn't work out with us, the judge will probably send her to live with her uncle in Canada."

"How bad is that? Could be a great place to raise a kid."

"He has DUIs in two states."

"Holy moly." Jo picked at the shell on her hard-boiled egg. "Did Andie find her chain?"

"Not yet. If Deja took her rings, she's done a good job of hiding them. Or she's gotten rid of them, which is worse."

I smoothed out the foil from my sandwich and folded it over and over into a small square. How could a daughter of mine do such a thing? My Disneyland pin was missing too, the one from our last trip to Disneyland with Ginger. Could Deja have taken that too?

As I'd gotten dressed for work that morning, I'd dug into my change cup where I always kept the pin, and found it gone. I distinctly remembered pushing the back firmly onto it the night before because Andie had warned me that the old backs were faulty. And then I dropped it into the cup.

"You sure it was Deja who took the rings?" Jo asked.

"Well, who else? She had plenty of motive and opportunity."

Deja was so angry. She seemed genuinely hurt, the way she jealously watched Andie when we were together. Almost like she was looking for something. Favoritism, maybe? Betrayal? Maybe she was trying to even the score by taking things that were important to us.

"Could be she was set up."

I studied Jo. "Set up? By who, Andie?"

"Does she have any other enemies?"

"Deja pretty much alienates everyone."

Jo tipped her head down confidentially and hooked her eyebrows. "Well, if I were Andie and I wanted to get even with Deja for something, that would work. It got her in trouble and got you on Andie's side, didn't it?"

I grunted something to end the conversation and chewed on the possibility all afternoon. It left a sour taste in my mouth. If Andie was the sneaky one, it was possible that she could have taken my pin too. I never thought to go through *her* things. I wasn't sure it was even worth attempting. What if she noticed they'd been disturbed? She would just blame Deja, and the situation between them would worsen.

Visions of Andie in Walgreens squeezing that candy bar in her fist came to mind. And she liked pins. She'd noticed mine and even said she wouldn't trade any of hers. And there was that matter of money missing from the register at the drive-in. It had to be someone.

Was it worth the risk of making her suspicious to go through her things, and did I really want to find out that Jo was right? As a mother, I would prefer to remain ignorant if clearing the name of one child meant convicting another. In truth, though, I owed it to both girls to find out.

The next day, I took a long lunch while Andie was at school and went home to look through her boxes and suitcase. I felt like a sneak thief, but I didn't find the rings or the pin. I felt part relief, part disappointment.

I did find a Bible under her bed. I picked it up and looked over my shoulder to make sure Dad hadn't come in before I opened the cover. Words of endearment were written there. *From Gary to Noelle.* Words of love and commitment that I'd not heard in years. Her parents were obviously Christians, judging by the verse inscribed there. I flipped randomly through the Bible and found it well worn and colorful with marker.

So this was Andie's heritage. She was no stranger to church or to a Christian home. Her questions and doubts didn't come from a lack of knowledge. They must have come from a feeling of betrayal. "My heart-shape is plugged," she'd said. At least I knew she believed in God—why be angry with Someone she didn't believe in?

I went through Deja's stuff as well, with no luck, and carefully covered my tracks. I hurriedly ate a sandwich and went back to work, puzzling over the whole mystery, and dreading to know the outcome.

Report cards came in the mail that day, along with an envelope addressed to me in shaky handwriting and postmarked Pine Run.

The girls were distracted by their grades and didn't notice when I slipped the envelope into my pocket. Something told me I should read it in private.

Winnie and Andie both had B averages, which told me that Winnie was trying her best and Andie probably wasn't. I praised them both equally and kept my observations to myself. Deja had "no credit" in two classes, two Ds, and two Cs. Three of her teachers requested conferences. Her only comment was, "Hey, I passed PE."

She tried to get me to budge on her driver's ed, since I hadn't heard from her principal in several weeks, but I refused.

"This is your future we're talking about, Deja. Granted, we haven't heard from Mr. McNulty, and that's progress. But if your grades are this bad now, they'll only get worse if you're never around to do any homework. When your attitude improves we'll see a difference in your grades."

I went to my room and closed the door to read the letter. It was a good thing I'd waited. After a few pleasantries, her grandmother wrote that they would like one of Ginger's baby pictures, just to keep. I was stunned. They were finally accepting the fact that they'd had a granddaughter they never knew.

Jealousy churned within me. They could not have Ginger. I didn't have to share her. She was gone, and she'd always be mine alone. They didn't suffer her horrible illness. They didn't deal with unanswered questions, they didn't . . .

But hadn't they? Death can be a horrible illness in itself. They had plenty of unanswered questions—of course they did. Why were their children taken while they were young, with so much to give? Why were they left alone in their declining years with a precious burden instead of adult children to care for their needs?

In the end, I got out Ginger's baby book and selected a picture.

I knew that if they had to share their beautiful child with me, I had no choice but to share mine with them. It was the right and proper thing to do, no matter how much it hurt to hand her over to strangers.

Winnie had picked up a permission slip for the church snow trip. As I was filling it out, I dug through my top drawer for her immunization records, and something sharp stuck my finger. I looked in to find a tiny drop of blood and my Mickey pin. His happy little face smirked at me. It must have fallen into the opened drawer when I was getting ready for bed the night before, and, yes, the back had come off. So it was there all the time. I felt very low, having had doubts about Andie and Deja all day. I carried it out to the kitchen, sucking on my finger. The girls were doing their homework at the table.

"Andie," I asked, showing her my pin. "Could I have one of your extra pin backs?"

"Sure." She brightened and took off for her room. She returned with a red lanyard full of pins and a Mickey-shaped rubber pin back. She slipped the back onto my pin while Winnie ogled her lanyard.

"You've got quite a few pins there," I said.

She spread the lanyard out carefully over her homework, pressing each pin back tightly on. The words *Walt Disney Travel Co.* danced around the lanyard in white.

"This Sorcerer's Apprentice is my favorite. I picked out all the pieces at a pin store, and they glue it all together for you."

"Wow, it's big," Winnie said, reaching for the next colorful pin. "Oh, this one's cool. It's Alice in Wonderland."

"And look at this Winnie the Pooh," Andie said, wiggling

Tigger's tail. "It moves. And look—this is the Haunted Mansion, and you can open the . . . uh . . . box . . ."

"Casket," I said, reaching over to toggle the piece. The casket lid lifted to reveal Goofy trapped inside.

Winnie said, "You have a Mickey like Mom's."

"My Mickey's at the beach too, but it's different."

Mickey balanced himself on a surfboard with a giant wave about to break over him. The weight of my suspicions curled over me, threatening to drench me in guilt. How could I have suspected this kid of anything? Watching her animated face, and with her so close that I felt the heat of her and smelled the soap from her shower, made me feel foolish and ashamed.

I instinctively went over to the cookie jar, loaded up a plate of peanut butter blossoms and chocolate chips, and placed it in front of the girls.

"We need milk," I said, reaching for cups and the milk jug.

After we were settled with cookies on napkins and mugs of milk as my private peace offering, I said, "Tell me about all your pins. Start with Jiminy Cricket."

Andie not only told us about her pins, and which ones were unusual or collectible, but she knew things about the park only a seasoned traveler would know. It was as though we'd wound her key.

I'm not sure I could tell you what she said, because I was listening to the timbre of her voice and watching her eyes light with fire. It was more words than I'd heard her say in the whole sum of the time she'd been with us. She enchanted me.

Winnie slid onto my lap, even though she was getting too big for it, and I realized it was a habit that had begun back when Ginger was so needy. Winnie wanted reassurance, even as I focused on Andie, that she wasn't forgotten or replaced. I made room for her and smoothed her hair back behind her ears while I listened, my hands moving to braid out of habit. The feel of her cornsilk hair in my fingers couldn't have been more satisfying if I'd been weaving gold.

The thought occurred to me that the three of us together was a start. We were a beginning. I saw a glimpse of God's promise fulfilled—of our family reconciled—and I felt an unexpected ache. Could I risk loving this child of the snow?

CHAPTER 20

Andie

"Mrs. Bettencourt, I want to change my desk," Natalie said in homeroom one morning. She gave me a dirty look over her shoulder.

I didn't get it. Natalie and I always sat together.

"Why? What's the problem, Natalie?" Mrs. Bettencourt glanced from Natalie to me.

Natalie turned her head again and slashed me with her eyes. "I just don't want to sit there anymore."

"Well, I'll work on it, but I can't promise anything."

I backed up and goosed myself on my desk trying to sit down. What was up with Natalie? I couldn't remember saying anything that would hurt her feelings or make her mad.

Eating alone at lunch was not fun. I felt like I was on display. When I tried to talk to Natalie, she did an about-face and avoided me. So I tried to find out from Ashley what she was mad about. She wouldn't say, but her eyes withered like I should know.

I felt like the rug had been pulled out from under me. Natalie was my only friend in school and the only friend I'd had for a long time. How could I find out what was bothering her if she wouldn't even talk to me?

Once on the way to algebra, I saw Scott talking to Natalie, and they threw dirty looks my way. I couldn't even think of a reason for her to be talking to him. Whatever he was saying to her, I hoped she didn't believe it.

Mrs. Bettencourt asked me to stay behind after English. She told me to bring my notebook up to her desk, where she thumbed through my project folder. The girls hovered around Natalie and whispered on the way out the door.

She pointed out the doodles and scrolling that covered the front of my binder. "I see you're an artist, Andie."

"It's just scribbling."

"I hope that's not someone I know," she said, pointing at the slavering, horned demon.

"No." I turned my notebook facedown on the desk, but there was an even bigger, more detailed picture of demon child Deja on the back.

"An artist is something I'm not," she said. "I wanted to highlight some of our literature. Would you mind helping me out, maybe draw up some murals on butcher paper, if I provided the books?"

I didn't really want to draw for anyone but my mom and dad. The best they could do was to draw stick figures.

"I'm not really that good."

"You could come early before school, or stay after. Or you could work during lunch break, if you didn't mind missing it," she said.

Now, that was tempting. It would be better than sitting around by myself wondering what Natalie and the others were saying about me.

"Sure, that would be okay."

She pulled out a book on Egyptian art and history, and flipped open to a page of King Tut's tomb.

"This is what I had in mind. Large enough to cover that bulletin board. Do you think you could enlarge it?"

"Yeah. I did that for my dad's class."

She smiled, waiting for me to go on. Something about the way she looked at me made me talk.

"We . . . we went there, when I was in third grade."

"To Egypt? Andie, that's so exciting! What did you see?"

I pointed out some tourist spots in her book, mostly the pyramids, tombs, and museums.

"You'll have to share some of your experiences with the class." She must have read my face. "Well . . . of course, only if you feel like sharing. No pressure."

Closing the book, I asked, "When do I start?"

"Now, if you'd like. I'll get the paper."

I spent lunch there for two weeks working on the drawings of King Tut's tomb and scenery along the Nile. When I let myself remember our trip, I started looking forward to talking about it every day. I almost brought in some of my souvenirs, but then I worried about losing them and never seeing them again, so I left them in the box under my bed.

One day Mrs. Bettencourt said, "Maybe you should eat in the lunchroom today. Take a break."

"I'm almost done."

She folded her hands on her desk and looked at me intently. "Andie, what happened between you and Natalie? You two seemed to be hitting it off, and now you don't even speak."

I shrugged, like it wasn't important.

"Sometimes friends just need some time away from each other," she said. "Do you think that could be it?"

"Maybe."

I tried not to let it get to me. After all, it would be a waste of time to make friends here anyway, since I would be moving back in with Grandma and Grandpa. It was best to stay a loner.

Now I had even more reason to want to get away, and prayed even harder that the mobile home would sell. I wondered if God got tired of people whining all the time. I mean, the only time I talked to Him was when I wanted something. I imagined Him with a big Santa Claus beard sitting on a throne, giving a thumbs-up or thumbs-down. Lately, I'd pictured Him as a thumbs-down kind of guy.

I was glad that Carl had finally come home, because I worried about him. Not like I'd worry about my real grandpa, but he was nice and I knew the others would miss him if he died. When he got back one night he had a truckload of snow. We stayed up till eleven playing in it and making snowmen and throwing snowballs.

Marty's schedule went back to her normal hours after that, and Carl was home at night, so we had extra time. It was weird to have everybody in the house together. I mentioned that we used to play games at my house, and one day Marty came home with Clue and Uno. Every night we'd hurry up and get our homework done so we'd have time to play before bed. I insisted on being Mrs. Peacock, and I was the Clue Master until Carl got the hang of it. Even Deja came out and played once.

Winnie got excited about some snow trip from church, and she blabbered about it while we cleaned up the dishes one night.

"We stay overnight in a cabin, and we tube and play games. The church pays our way. Last year it was so cool. Bobbie, our counselor, broke her tailbone. Her tube hit a stick or something. Anyway, she shot off it like a bullet and landed on her butt."

I continued to put away dishes, listening to her spout off, not committing. I was ticked because it was Deja's turn to unload the dishwasher, and she'd gotten out of it by saying she was studying with Summer. I couldn't believe Marty fell for it.

"You wanna go, don't you?" Winnie asked. "I bet Natalie's going."

That would really convince me, after a month of not breathing in each other's direction.

"No, I don't want to go. Snow is so, you know, freezing cold. I'm not crazy about soaking all my clothes and being wet for the whole weekend."

"But there's a stove to dry your—"

"Winnie," Marty called. "If you're done, it's time for a bath."

Winnie padded down the hallway to the bathroom, and I took advantage of Deja's absence to search her drawers for my chain. I didn't find it, but a few other interesting things came up: a sock with a roll of money in the toe, and her journal—locked—covered with various forms of *Ridley* with hearts, *Mrs. Ridley Fox*, and *Foxy* intertwined with *Deja*. As pathetic as her attempts were to stake her claim on this guy, at least she had some artistic talent. I had never actually seen her boyfriend, but he must be pretty hard up.

And where did she get all that money?

Winnie had picked out valentines at Shop 'n Save, and when she showed them to me, I said, "Cute" in a fakey way that made her feel bad. Having a little sister was complicated, but did she really think I'd like dancing hippos in tutus?

Cyclops followed me into the bathroom when I got ready for bed that night. Sometimes he drank tub water. I tried to shoo him out without getting more cat hair on my pajamas, but something caught his attention in the floor vent, and he wouldn't budge. He reached his black paw deep into the vent on the floor, swiping and stabbing. Figuring I'd use whatever he played with to lure him out, I pushed him aside from the vent with my foot and looked in. My breath caught. There, on the dusty bottom of the vent, like a tiny coiled snake, lay my chain with the shiny wedding rings.

I got on my hands and knees and pulled the vent right up off the floor. I tried to be quiet while I did it. Cyclops had to be in the middle of what I was doing, and I pushed him away and reached in for my chain. A gigantic sneeze scared him off, and I gripped the chain in my fist so it wouldn't rocket out of my hands and down the vent into oblivion. Then I dusted off the rings and poured them into the pocket of my robe. I was so happy to have them back that I sent a little prayer up toward the ceiling. But I couldn't just walk out and tell Deja I'd found them. She was a walking time bomb right now, just waiting to blow.

How did it get in the vent? Deja could have unloaded it in there after we got suspicious of her. Or it could have fallen off the bathroom sink when I took a shower, or Cyclops could have knocked it off. I'd have to figure out whether I needed to apologize to her.

Yuck. The last thing I wanted to do was to apologize to Deja for anything. It made me want to go home even more.

I really avoided her after that. My chain was hidden in a box under my bed, and I was dying to wear it, but I could only take it out when Deja wasn't around, like when she bolted for control of the TV or for the phone.

Things were happening that made me want to go home, more

than ever. Like after my bath one night, I found a stack of clothes on my dresser that Marty had left there, and without thinking, I opened the drawer, tossed the clothes in, and slammed it shut.

I sank down onto the edge of my bed. Well, what was the big deal about putting my stuff away? It didn't mean anything. This wasn't about giving in; it was just easier to have them in my drawer. I could always repack when I was ready to leave.

I went out to watch TV. During a commercial, I went back and opened the drawer and slammed it. Get over it, for crying out loud, I told myself. I went back out and lasted through three more commercial breaks, but finally I couldn't stand it anymore. I took my clothes out of the drawer and repacked them in my suitcase.

It seemed like such a stupid, small thing, but it bugged me for days. I hadn't even thought twice before I dumped everything into that drawer.

I needed to call Grandma.

"Hey, Grandma. Have you heard anything about the house yet?"

"No, hon," she said. "People want a nice house, but they don't want to pay what it's worth. That's what your Grandpa says."

"But you said somebody looked at it." Was that me whining?

"Some people are just looky-loos. Don't worry. The right person will come along."

"Sure, I know," I said. "What about my case?"

"The lady lawyer said we can't do anything until we have a place where you can live with us."

"Grandma, I'm tired of being here. I want to come home."

There was silence at the other end. I started to think we'd been disconnected.

"They aren't mistreating you, are they?" she asked sharply.

"No, Grandma. It's just . . . I thought I'd be back home by

now. I didn't know it would take this long."

"Well, you can come for a visit soon, honey. Aren't you coming at Easter?"

"It's two months till Easter, Grandma."

"The time will go fast, you'll see. How long can you stay?"

"A whole week. It's spring break."

"We can't wait, sugar," she said.

I tested the waters. "Maybe by then I can move back home and just stay."

"We'll see, honey."

I didn't feel much better after I talked to her. Nothing was happening. I wasn't any closer to going home than before, and telling Mrs. Bettencourt about my parents had left me feeling as if I'd surrendered something I couldn't get back. Putting my clothes in the drawer without even thinking about it, playing games like I was one of the family. I was slipping away. I was assimilating like a Star Trek Borg.

On Valentine's Day I woke to find a small heart-shaped box filled with chocolate candies on my nightstand. Marty had one for each of us. I ate one piece, and then I remembered that my mom used to do that kind of stuff on holidays. Valentine chocolates, gold coins on St. Patrick's Day, candy corn on Halloween. The candy got kind of gloppy in my throat, so I spit it out.

All day in school, people sent Heart-O-Grams to each other for a dollar donation to the D.C. trip fund-raiser. I felt totally conspicuous being passed over and over. Natalie and her friends made a big show of opening theirs in front of me.

Deja was really moody that day. After school she set up a command post in our bedroom with the phone and told me to stay out.

I saw a stockpile of junk food just before she slammed the door in my face. I left her alone, except I knocked on the door and said I needed my backpack. A second later the door opened and out flew my backpack. Then the door slammed again.

I went out to the kitchen table to do my homework with Winnie. Marty still sat there, looking like a zombie surrounded by chocolate and dirty dishes. Winnie started needling me about snow camp again, and Marty shot her a look.

Why was everybody so touchy? Was I the only one in this family who wasn't screwed up?

In this family. Did I really say that?

CHAPTER 21

Marty

The empty building called to me, and I went past, imagining umbrella-ed tables out in front with people enjoying lattes and cinnamon rolls. I vowed not to drive down that street again. I might as well face the fact that I'd be working at Shop 'n Save until the girls were grown and gone, and save myself some disappointment.

After cruising by, I headed home to a pile of bills and the constant reminder that I was fighting a losing battle. Sometimes I felt like one of the two women before Solomon claiming the same child. Andie's mother reached beyond the grave and wouldn't release her. Just when I thought I was shaking loose her grip, I'd overheard Andie on the phone with her grandmother, practically begging to go home.

She seemed to be adjusting, maybe even beginning to *like* us. Perhaps, in some small way, she was, and it frightened her. Maybe that was why she sounded so bitter on the phone. I stood outside her door in the hallway with my feet glued to the carpet, stunned at this turnaround, knowing I should not be listening. Betrayal is what I felt. It was my own sweet illusion that Andie was finally coming around. And it didn't make me feel any better when she grew sullen and withdrawn after the call.

Could it be that years later the biological mother in Solomon's story tracked down that other woman and said, "I changed my mind; you can keep her"?

Every month the bills separated themselves into due, past-due, and seriously overdue. I pulled out the checkbook and tried to balance it against the bank statement. Andie's bankbook winked at me from the bill folder, and I wavered, ever so slightly.

If she was going to end up with her grandparents anyway, why not draw on her money for her living expenses? Allergy medicines, doctor's visits, school expenses, a winter coat—it all added up.

But if Russell knew we had access to Andie's money, his attorney would file for a reduction in child support in a snap. No, it was better if I could truthfully say I'd never touched it.

Valentine's Day was coming. I set aside a little from my own account to buy special treats for the girls and Dad.

The next day at work I picked out four little heart-shaped chocolate boxes, wrapped in red cellophane, and set them on Jo's check stand as I was leaving.

"Better throw one in there for yourself," she told me. "You don't want to be the only one without chocolate on Valentine's Day. We have to look out for ourselves, you know." She counted out the change from my twenty. "Leastways, I don't count on Walter to remember."

Early on Valentine's Day morning, I sneaked the candy into their rooms and placed them on their nightstands. Winnie squealed and hugged me at breakfast, downing her chocolates with milk. I reminded her to take her valentines for class, and we loaded up the car for school.

Deja was unusually quiet, and I noticed her eyes were puffy. I admit that initially I suspected drugs, but then I realized her nose was stuffy, and I knew she'd been crying.

Valentine's Day could be ruthless, like salt in a wound—even an old one—unless you slathered on a thick hide. And a thick hide will only keep you from loving again.

Two separate florists arrived at work with red roses in ceramic vases, and each time the younger checkers feigned disinterest when they were passed by.

Valentine's Day could be demoralizing, if you cared too much. I found the best way to deal with it was to keep busy.

I made a decadent chocolate mousse cake for dessert that night. Deja passed on it, which wasn't like her. When I found Andie trying to read on the couch with Dad watching basketball, I realized she'd been banished from their room, and that Deja had barricaded herself with the phone. It could mean only one thing—boy trouble.

My heart went out to her, but I wasn't altogether unhappy about her getting distance from the boy in the trench coat.

Valentine's Day was hard on singles in general. Even married, it'd been like any other day for us. Had Russell ever been romantic? It was hard to recall.

I sat back down at the empty kitchen table and served myself another slice of cake. I stuck the tines of my fork into the dense chocolate on my plate and lifted it to my mouth. Raspberry puree tingled my tongue. Maybe he had been romantic, in the beginning. I picked up the steaming Garfield mug and cradled it in my hands, feeling the warmth of it burning my palms. Yes, there'd been occasional flowers, and chocolates. And on the first Valentine's Day in our little apartment over the bakery, I had come home to find dinner all ready. Russell had set up the coffee table like a nice restaurant, with a tablecloth and candles and a red carnation in a vase. Dinner was only hamburger patties and canned vegetables, but I was touched that he would go to all that trouble for me. Who needed a dozen roses or a night out dancing? It was sweet.

But he didn't stay sweet. If our marriage was ill-fitting, it wasn't my fault.

I wondered whether he was still sweet on Starr, or if their marriage had been tried in some way, as ours had.

Something in me stirred, some dark nameless thing buried in a place where I tended the wound. I'd been wronged and hadn't deserved it. He owed me. I stared at my empty plate and pushed it away, the chocolate turning leaden in my stomach.

I knew the Bible verses that would prompt me to forgive Russell, but it was simply not possible as far as I could see. Perhaps if I'd ever witnessed some small sign of remorse. But he'd never flinched. Just walked away at the worst possible time and knocked the dust from his shoes. "I gotta go, Marty. I'm losin' it," was all he'd said, as though he'd rehearsed it. Or been prompted.

Later, he'd even accused me of wanting to get custody of Andie to prevent a reduction in his child support payments after Ginger died. As far as I knew, he'd never even been to Ginger's grave.

I traced the smooth lip of my coffee mug with my thumb. Ginger's anniversary was coming. March 5th. It was always in the back of my mind, and it was coming fast. In all fairness to Russell, maybe Valentine's Day, combined with the anniversary of Ginger's death, had ignited my ex-bashing. Or maybe it just lanced the wound.

No matter how busy I stayed, or how much I baked, I could

not overcome the sorrow that was beginning to build as March drew near. Was it better to face it head-on, run out to meet it? Maybe I'd pick up some coconut tomorrow.

I cleared the table as Winnie came out from her room with her backpack on her shoulder and let it slide heavily onto her chair. It hit the seat with a thud. She dug inside for papers and books. Then Andie joined her at the table with her own homework. Her backpack sounded just as heavy. They'd probably be visiting the chiropractor before they were sophomores.

Winnie tried to convince Andie again to go to snow camp, and I gave her a look that said *Drop it*. She grew sullen.

I forced myself into gear, unloaded the dishwasher, and filled it. I emptied the dryer and folded laundry. Keep busy, I told myself. Housework was mindless and plodding, and it didn't demand much concentration. It was perfect to keep my mind off things.

I kept myself occupied for a few days, but the thought was never very far away. There was always more laundry. I was shocked to find that Win's pockets were increasingly full of cookie crumbs, and I started noticing her buttons were straining at the waist.

One night when Andie was doing homework at the kitchen table and Deja was in the shower, I stepped into their room with their folded laundry and took time to hang up a few things in the closet. Scuffling noises came from beneath Andie's bed. I froze. What a time for mice, when Cyclops was banished from the house.

Then I heard a frustrated *meowrl*. Cyclops. Before Andie's arrival, he'd been used to sleeping under the bed, poor cat. I got down on my hands and knees and peered underneath. He'd pushed off the lid from a box and was trying to get inside. I grabbed the box and pulled it over to me, but Cyclops wouldn't give up. Whatever was inside must be good.

"Go, shoo!" I said, dragging him out. He had something clutched in the curl of his claw. It was silver and long and had rings threaded on it. Andie's chain.

Andie had the chain. It took a moment to sink in. I'd checked that box thoroughly before and found nothing. Had I overlooked the necklace, or had she found it later and put it there? And if she had found it, why didn't she tell us?

I gently pulled it from Cyclops's grasp. He didn't want to give it up, and I had the scratches to prove it. The rings were shiny gold, each worn thin in a spot.

Did she have them all along? If so, what would make her hate us so much that she'd make all of this up? Was she trying to get us to send her home?

I put the chain back into the box and shoved it under the bed. Cyclops didn't want to be gathered up, and I swatted him a little angrily. He struggled all the way to the garage door, where I deposited him for the night. Nursing my wounds, I took a cup of coffee to my bedroom and shut the door behind me. Anger and hurt and confusion gathered like the eye of a storm within me. I was tired of giving and giving and being taken for granted. How long should I try to make this family fit together?

On top of it all, I felt like a bad mother. Poor Deja. I'd been positive she was lying and guilty as sin. She still could be, but how could I know? She didn't help herself any.

Deep down, I wondered, was Andie really like her father?

CHAPTER 22

Andie

On the week after Valentine's Day, the big drive-in sign said FARMERS MARKET SAT. 8–4. The night before the big opening day, we helped Marty bake and wrap all kinds of goodies to sell. When I woke up about midnight to go to the bathroom, the light was still on in the kitchen and the radio was playing. She was still going at it.

On the first day, I helped Carl set up his booth with Winnie and Marty, and then I went to look around. There were stands selling vegetables and fruit from the coast that were pretty smelly, like garlic and broccoli and asparagus, but the other end of the parking lot smelled like kettle corn. There were booths with crafts, tamales, junk sales, T-shirts, pots and pans, toys, gadgets, and lots of other stuff. But nothing as good as Carl's art.

He had paintings of a little Native American boy in the snow, a pack of wolves in the forest, running horses, and the Grand Canyon. One picture was of a bunch of giant cactuses with their arms raised like they were being mugged. He was really good. Maybe one day I'd be that good too.

When we went to church the next day, all they talked about was the snow camp that Winnie was so hot to go to. Then the next Saturday, after we were done working at the market, the phone rang. I heard Marty say, "Hello, Pastor," and after a minute she looked over at me and said she'd call him back.

"Andie, do you want to go to snow camp?" she asked. "Pastor Jim says they're willing to pay for you and Winnie. You'd have a great time."

I glanced up from my book and shook my head. "No, thanks."

"Aw, Andie," Winnie complained. "Come on. Please. Pleeeeze. Just go with me."

I put my finger in my book to save my place. "Sorry, Winnie. I don't want to go."

"I have a picture. I'll get it." She bolted down the hall and came back with an opened scrapbook. Most of the pictures were out of focus and off-centered, but white with snow.

"See? You can go skiing and snowboarding. There's the cabin, and there's the hill where we tube." She pointed to a picture of her and Ginger. "See? Come on, Ginger. Pleeeze."

"Don't call me Ginger," I said. I could barely control my voice.

"I'm sorry. I meant Andie." She gave me a fakey, sweet look that usually worked on Marty and Carl. "Come on, Andie. I want you to go, 'cause you're my sis–"

I shot up from my chair. My book smacked the floor. "I'm not your sister! I am *not* Ginger. I don't want to be Ginger. I'm only staying here till Grandma and Grandpa sell the house and I'm going back home to Pine Run. So don't try to make me your sister!"

My voice rang off the walls.

Winnie backed up until she bumped against Marty. Then she grabbed her scrapbook and ran back to her room, slamming the door behind her.

Marty's lips were a thin line, and her nostrils flared. She turned her back to me. "Andie, just—go."

"But . . ."

"Go!"

I ran down the hall and slammed the door. I threw myself on my bed and lay there for a long time trying to figure out what happened. The words had exploded from my mouth like a shotgun blast, and I didn't even know my finger was on the trigger.

What was I supposed to do? Okay, so maybe I didn't say it in a nice way. I knew I'd have to apologize to Winnie, even if everything I said was true. She'd get over it. I felt worse about the way Marty looked at me, and I didn't know how or if I could apologize to her, or if it would do any good.

Deja was gone with Summer, and the house was really quiet. I fell asleep for a while, and when I woke up the room was shadowy. I listened at the door and figured the coast was clear, so I sneaked out the front door. Luckily, I didn't run into Marty or Winnie.

I wandered out into the parking lot where vendors at the farmers market were packing up for the day. A cast-off onion lay in the dirt, just begging to be kicked, but it burst on impact. Bad idea. I scraped off the toe of my shoe and avoided the produce area. It was a minefield of rotting veggies.

Over in the garage sale section, Carl was taking down his artwork. I leaned against the truck and watched him load up.

"Sold two today," he said.

"Which ones? I asked.

"Let's see. *Senora and Child* and *Spring at Slide Rock*."

He had a new picture up—two smiling blonde girls, about the ages of Winnie and me, standing barefoot in a mountain meadow. A chain hung on the taller girl's neck. It had two rings on it.

I whipped around to find Carl watching me. "Is that me and Winnie?" I asked.

"Why? Does it look like you?" He stepped closer and peered through the bottom of his glasses, then tilted his head to look at me over the tops. "So it does."

I wasn't sure how I felt being painted into a picture with Winnie. It was like another nail in my coffin.

"What, don't you like it?"

"Oh, yeah," I said, not really sure. But I had to admit it was good, and I didn't want to hurt his feelings. If I kept insulting people, I'd be sleeping on the street. "When did you paint us?"

"In Flagstaff. I was snowed in for a few days. Did it from memory, of course. Too early for wildflowers." He stepped back and cocked his head side to side. "I think it turned out pretty good myself."

I cocked my head to see it at a different angle. "Why didn't somebody buy it?"

"Oh, they will," he said, lifting down the painting. "Who could resist these beauties?" He gave a flirty whistle and laid it gently on a blanket on the truck bed.

I helped him take down the rest of the paintings and displays, and then I rode back on the opened truck gate. Inside the house it felt like somebody had died. Carl tried to make small talk at dinner, but I guess he saw the massive quantities of cookies and figured out there had been a meltdown.

That night sleep ran like a secret code I couldn't break. It was about midnight when I sneaked down the hall to Marty's room. Light was still shining under her door. I heard Carl sawing logs in the next room. I knocked.

"Come in."

I peeked in. Marty was reading in bed. She looked older with her hair down and no makeup on.

"Can I talk to you?" I asked.

She hesitated. "Close the door. Carl's asleep in his room."

I came in and closed the door quietly, even though I knew it would take a nuclear blast to wake him. I stopped at the foot of her bed.

She looked at me without saying anything, sitting propped up in bed like a queen with her subject, holding the power of life and death. She wasn't going to help me out on this. I reached up out of habit to grab my rings, but remembered they were still under my bed. I felt naked without them.

"Today, about snow camp . . . I just didn't want to go—"

"It's not about snow camp, Andie," she said.

I stopped for a minute, because I'd practiced what I wanted to say, and she'd thrown me a curveball. Dad used to say that—we were baseball people. So I started over. "I want to go home."

She closed her book without the bookmark. "Where did you find your chain?"

My mouth dropped open. She knew about the chain? I licked my lips, which made them sting. "In the bathroom. I mean, Cyclops found them when I was taking a shower. They were down in the bathroom vent."

"The vent." She studied me with her arms resting on the blanket covering her. "I see," she said, but I could tell she didn't. "So, when were you planning to tell us?"

I shrugged. "I don't know."

Her face suddenly looked hard.

"I mean, I was going to; I just didn't know how they got in there. I thought, what if Deja put them in the vent, you know, to get rid of them so she wouldn't get caught? But what if she didn't, and they just fell in? And if I had to apologize to her, well . . . I didn't want to do that unless I had to. Only if she was really innocent."

"But by keeping it a secret, you look guilty."

I shifted on my feet. "Like, how?"

"Well, how do we know you didn't make it all up? By hiding the fact that you found the chain, it looks like you had it all along."

It finally sank in. "You think I set her up?"

She relaxed back into her pillows. "It could look that way. To some people."

"Oh, my gosh. I didn't! I hate not wearing my chain. I reach for it all the time. It kills me to leave it under my bed." I reached up for it, and a thought occurred to me. "Wait—how did you find it? Did you go through my stuff?"

Marty looked down at her hands. "I went in to put some laundry on your dresser, and I heard Cyclops scratching at something under your bed. He'd pulled the chain out of a box."

We were both quiet, more like strangers than ever. I wondered if I was going to get punished or something. What was she allowed to do to me?

Finally she said, "Okay, let's just assume that it fell into the vent one night when you took a shower and that Deja never had it."

"Okay." I didn't want to say it. After all the rotten things Deja had done to me, I wanted her to be punished for something.

She cocked her head at me. "So do you want to tell her, or should I?"

It would be easier for her to do it, but she might make me look like the bad guy. Maybe I should handle it myself. "I'll do it. I'll figure out a way."

"Good enough. Now, getting back to what started this whole conversation." She cleared her throat. Maybe she'd rehearsed this part already. "I realize you'd rather be back with your grandparents. It hasn't been easy to move here and try to fit in—we know that."

I shifted on my feet, wondering what was coming.

"But this hasn't been easy for us, either, you know. You can imagine what a shock it was for all of us, losing Ginger and finding you." She stopped and seemed to have trouble talking for a second. "We want you to be you, Andie. We never wanted you to replace Ginger." Her voice caught, and she cleared her throat again. "But whether you want to believe it or not, there's a lot of Winslow in you."

She took her time, like she was translating from a foreign language.

"You don't seem to be happy here. I was hoping by this time you would be. I'm not sure it will get any better, and I want you to be happy. I feel like we've done our best to try to make you feel welcome." She grimaced. "Well, except for Deja. But maybe it would be best if you went to live with your Uncle Greg in Canada at the end of the school year. That is, if it doesn't work out with your grandparents."

I couldn't believe what I was hearing. She was giving me up! My heart inflated like a party balloon, and I tried to keep the smile off my face. "It will work out."

She looked at me sadly.

"If it doesn't, you might feel closer to your parents, living with your uncle," she said.

"Maybe."

Maybe? What was I saying? I did not want to live with Uncle Greg and Aunt Robin. They were probably the ones who'd sold my school picture to *Enquirer*. I'd be their indentured babysitter until the brats went to college. But . . . maybe they'd let me live with Grandma and Grandpa, instead of paying somebody to take care of them. I could save my Uncle Greg lots of money. Dad always said that Uncle Greg was all about money.

"Think about it, Andie. Now, go on to bed," she said.

I went back down the hall to my room. But there was no way I was going to think about Uncle Greg. It would be a colossal waste of time. I still had three months left before the end of school, and I'd be back with Grandma and Grandpa by summer, at least.

I stopped by the bathroom for a drink. I noticed my toothbrush leaned toward Winnie's in the holder, and I turned it away so the bristles didn't touch. You shouldn't touch a person's toothbrush. Deja kept hers in a cup, and soon Winnie could have the holder all to herself.

I felt that balloon inside me deflating, and my eyes looked back from the mirror like my other half was trying to ask what was going to happen to me.

Soon Marty was almost back to her old self, but Winnie wouldn't speak to me, even after I apologized for yelling at her. I didn't apologize for my words, though.

She left for camp the next weekend without saying good-bye. Maybe it would be easier if she stayed mad at me. Then she wouldn't be sorry to see me go.

Deja had kept to herself on her side of the room ever since Valentine's Day. I thought it was weird. She would jump for the phone every time it rang, but she never seemed happy when it was for her. Then one night I heard her sniffling after the lights were out. She got up and went to the bathroom. I could see through a crack in our door that her face was all blotchy and red. She was crying.

Whatever made her cry, she probably deserved it. Finally she was getting payback for something.

The next day in class, I overheard Scott saying Ridley had broken up with Deja. Since Scott was Summer's brother, I figured he would know. They were all laughing about how she cried and begged Ridley not to break up. Pathetic loser.

CHAPTER 23

Marty

Winnie boarded the church van Friday afternoon with all of her gear and put her window down to wave at me as they pulled away for snow camp. She seemed to have gotten over the whole episode with Andie, but I noticed she no longer spoke directly to her anymore. Who could blame her for self-preservation?

Andie seemed to alternate between barely controlled elation and withdrawal, which was probably her own plan for self-preservation. I knew she was in deep denial about her grandparents regaining custody, but there was nothing I could say to convince her of that.

I was elbow-deep in chocolate haystacks when the phone rang on Friday night. I picked up the cordless with two slick fingers, expecting it to be Winnie calling from a pay phone. "Hello?"

"Hey, babe."

The phone slid like a piece of peeled fruit, and I caught it just before it landed in the batter. Struggling to maintain my cool, I answered, "You don't get to call me that anymore."

Just hang up, I told myself. Self-preservation.

The sound of Russell's voice stirred the dust of countless nights spent mourning the poor fit of my life with his.

"Go away, Russell." Just hang up.

He swore.

I nestled the phone in the crook of my neck and turned on the faucet full blast to rinse my hands, one at a time—trying to wash away the soiled parts of me.

"Look, Marty. I don't want to start nothin'."

"Then why did you call?"

"Just checkin' in to see how my girls are doing."

"Your girls?" I wrenched the water off, and the pipe squeaked.

"Deja and Winnie, they there?"

"Leave them alone. It's too late for you, if that's what you think."

"Can't we have a normal conversation for once?"

"You lost that privilege years ago."

Silence on his end. Maybe he'll hang up and go away. My heart echoed, *Maybe he won't call for another two years.*

I hated the way he could still make me feel.

"How's Carl?"

"He hates you more than ever."

More silence. What was stopping me from hanging up?

"You still baking? Starr, she makes a pretty good rhubarb pie, but between you and me, she can't make apple for the life of her."

I felt my shoulders align naturally. "What do you want, Russell?"

"All right, Marty. You don't want to talk? Fine. You know, I *could* pick up the girls for spring break, if I wanted to. They haven't seen our place yet. Maybe stop by Sugar Pine Point. Camping. Jet skiing. Bet they'd like that."

I licked my lips, tasting chocolate. It was a power play, and it had drawn the response he wanted.

"That's going to be pretty hard to do when Sugar Pine doesn't open until after Memorial Day. Don't you remember?"

"You're harpin' on that again."

"Yeah, well it stands out in my memory."

"It worked out, didn't it? We found a campground."

"In Forest Grove. Down the road from our house. It took all day, just to find a place to pitch a tent in the dark. We were twenty miles from the girls' beds."

What was wrong with me? Why was I arguing with him about things that happened years before? I wiped sticky chocolate from my cheek. "It's not important anymore."

"So maybe I'll pick them up and take them to Bodega Bay instead. Starr hasn't seen it. When's spring break?"

Was he deliberately choosing these places to bait me? Before Ginger had gotten sick we'd spent a miserably wet weekend there because he hadn't checked the weather forecast ahead of time. We had to buy clothes at Salvation Army just to keep the girls dry.

"Dress warm. And take ponchos."

He swore. "Yeah, yeah."

I felt wicked. "It could be a good thing, you never know. Maybe Starr and Deja will really hit it off."

"Starr's fine with it. Anything I want to do is just fine with her. Now listen, Marty, I get visitation, and if I want them for the summer, I can have that too. The judge said so."

Why now? I stifled a sharp retort, knowing that the girls would become pawns between us. Was it possible that he simply regretted all the time spent away from them? Could he be missing them?

"So . . . this Andrea," he said, feigning nonchalance. "She workin' out all right?"

"AnDRAYa," I corrected him, without thinking.

"Whatever."

Amazing, how much Deja sounded just like him.

"She look like the others, or what?"

A desire to protect Andie injected my veins. My own failures with her were fresh in my heart. "Leave her out of this, Russell."

"She's my kid. If I want to see her—"

"The courts won't let you take her."

"What do you mean? I'm the father." He paused. "You tellin' me I'm not the father?"

I could lie and say Andie wasn't his, just to protect her, but the truth would come out, and he would only use it to make me look bad to the girls. I couldn't stand to lose any more daughters. I glanced toward the door and lowered my voice so Dad wouldn't hear if he came through from the garage. "No, of course you're the father," I said. "The court's just being very . . . cautious, that's all." I moved the phone to my other ear and leaned into it.

"Yeah? How?"

"They send out a worker once in a while."

"A worker? What kinda worker?"

"You know, a court worker. A social worker."

"Why's that?"

I really didn't want to tell him that Andie wasn't completely mine yet, that she may be up for grabs. I already regretted that I had more or less given her up already.

"They have to go by the book. Until it's all settled."

"I thought it was all settled."

"It is, pretty much," I lied. "It's just court procedure."

There was silence on his end. I heard the screen door slam in the distance beyond him, and he lowered his voice. "She look like the girls? You know, more than, than . . ."

He couldn't even say her name.

"More than Ginger?" I finished.

"Well, yeah."

I thought of Andie's silvery blonde hair, and her blue eyes with the same hazel flecks as his. How she moved like a young colt off the halter on the rare occasions when she felt truly at ease. "She looks like Winnie."

"That right? Blonde hair?"

"Lots of it."

"Shoot, Win didn't have no hair for so long, I thought she was going to be a baldie. She still roly-poly?"

I smiled in spite of myself. "I guess you could say that."

He chuckled. "Little Butter Baby."

A memory played out, bittersweet. Russell, shirtless, carrying bald Winnie in the crook of his arm like he was cradling a bowling ball. Her skin white against his farmer tan.

"Russell," I said, leaning back against the counter. "Why did you call? Really?"

He cleared his throat. "Well, I've been thinking. I don't know where . . . you know, it's comin' up on March and that." He paused. He must have been gathering courage. "I don't know where her grave is."

When I didn't—couldn't—answer right away, he took it for refusal, and his voice pitched. "I got a right to know, that's all. She's my kid."

The moment of familiarity between us dispersed like mist, and we were back on the same footing.

"There aren't that many cemeteries in town. Get Starr to help you."

He swore. "For cryin' out loud, Marty, she's my kid! I got a right to know."

"No, Russell," I said before hanging up. "I thought you might, but you don't."

Mercifully, Russell's call came at the beginning of the weekend of Winnie's absence, and I could lick my wounds in private without her around. I had nothing to give anyone at that point, not even my sweet, needy baby girl.

It's amazing to me that you can be away from someone for years, and within seconds you're back at the same place like it's bookmarked, no matter how hard you try to be strong. Your thought processes have built-in memory, triggers so predictable that the mere mention of a name can kick them into gear. That could be the only explanation for why I sank into depression after my conversation with Russell. Toward the end of our marriage, nothing I did was good enough. I wasn't good enough. Being reminded of that only served to magnify my failure with Andie.

I tried not to think about his threat to use his visitation rights. In a twisted way, Starr and I were silent allies, making sure he never had contact with the girls. It was disconcerting to realize that we were both in it for selfish reasons.

Ginger's anniversary loomed, and I bent mentally to meet it. Sunday afternoon, I opened the freezer for a package of hamburger, and frozen baked goods spilled out into my arms. I scrambled to catch baggies and loaves, shocked that the freezer was so tightly packed. I turned to set them down on the table, only to find it was already stacked with plates and pans of goodies. Chocolate chips, peanut butter blossoms, brownies, oatmeal bars, scones, nut bread, biscotti—food was everywhere.

I sagged into a kitchen chair, not even mindful of the frozen baggies burning through my sleeves. When had I made all this stuff? I struggled to remember my activities over the past few days.

A thought sickened me. Winnie was gone. Was I overdosing on baking, or was it that ordinarily Winnie's constant grazing kept the table clean?

Winnie got back Sunday night with her face sunburned, full of stories about her weekend at camp. We always forgot to pack the suntan lotion. Every other sentence was about her new friend, Rae. I suspected that she was trying to make Andie jealous, but it didn't seem to be working.

I guess I started sleeping a lot, and I came in late to work one morning, which rarely ever happens. I had to ask Robert to make three overrides on my register in the first hour I was there. I could tell he was irritated. He gave me a look after the third time, and told me to "get it together."

I saw Jo step away from her register, march over to Robert, and back him into a corner. She grilled him, leaning in with her arms folded across her chest and her chin in the air. She nodded over to me, and he looked down at my feet. Whatever she said next took him by surprise. He threw his hands in the air and stomped off toward the manager's office.

Jo came over and put my CLOSED sign on the belt, announcing to the rest of my customers that Stephanie could help them on aisle three. Then she shooed me back toward the employees' lockers.

"Listen, you need to go home." She opened my locker and pulled out my purse, threading the strap over my shoulder. When did she learn my locker combination?

"I'm okay," I protested, pulling the strap off my shoulder.

"You're okay? Look at your feet."

I looked down. I was wearing two different shoes.

"You plan to wear the other pair tomorrow?" She put my purse strap back on my shoulder and unzipped my bag. She dug around in it and came up with my keys. "Now, I'm guessing you've hit overload, because this isn't the first crazy thing you've done lately. You've got too much on your plate, is all. Take the rest of the day off—Doctor Jo's orders."

"But Robert . . ."

"Don't you worry about Robert. His wife would love to know he always schedules Candy to close on the nights he works late."

I stood for a moment, but my feet wouldn't move. I sagged onto the bench. "Russell called."

Jo stopped fussing, obviously caught off guard. "Oh, you poor lamb." She sank down beside me, sitting shoulder to shoulder on the narrow bench, and threaded her arm through mine.

I filled her in briefly on my conversation with Russell and ended with a confession of how I'd basically burned my bridge with Andie.

She listened quietly without offering a quick fix. "Do you think you can make it home okay?"

Home. The place I least wanted to be at that moment. I nodded.

She patted my knee and announced that she needed a smoke.

I got up, and she hugged me the way my own mom would've done. I had to fight back the tears.

I took her advice and left work, but I couldn't make myself go home. I took the interstate and went east, ending up in a little gold rush town in the foothills. I wandered into antique shops, quiet and reminiscent of gentler times when court visitations and DNA were unheard of. Old buildings that smelled like the ranch house in Elko, with the blue-and-white dishes from my childhood stacked alongside printed tablecloths and tin tumblers with fading colors where little fingers had gripped the sweating cups on hot summer days.

My brother, Charles, always drank my Kool-Aid concoctions, no matter how bitter or how sweet. I licked my lips, mildly surprised to find no traces of grape or cherry lingering there.

It occurred to me that I hadn't eaten, and I pulled in at Starbucks. When I got out of the car I realized I was still wearing my orange apron and yanked it off. I ordered plain coffee and had every intention of curling up in a cozy armchair with a newspaper from some faraway city to lounge for as long as I wanted. But listening to the chatter of the young professionals in line ordering one-pump-light-chai-passion-tea-whatevers, with room, made me feel self-conscious with my plain-Jane tastes, and I took my coffee back to the car to drink alone.

Sitting in the car with the silence throbbing all around me, I did an impulsive thing. I put on my seat belt, turned on the ignition, pointed the car north toward the interstate, and took off. I just drove. I didn't care where I was going. I had no idea, and that was the point. I drove very fast for hours.

I rolled the window down so the cold air slapped my cheeks, and rested my arm on the door, driving one-handed. I pushed down the voices flailing at me to turn around and go home and do laundry or bake, or be there for the girls, for heaven's sake. Tuning the radio to a heavy metal station drowned the voices out. I turned it up loud and focused on the landscape, how it changed from foothill to flat to a bowl ringed with mountains.

I suppose every woman has contemplated leaving at some point in her life, just with the clothes on her back and her purse, with her stress following her, driving her on. I wasn't so different.

Hours later I ended up in Redding. I sat nursing another coffee at a McDonald's by the freeway, shaken to the core. The longer

I sat watching the little families come into the enclosed playground, and the old men eating alone, the more I knew the choice was right there, laid out before me.

For a while I actually contemplated leaving it all behind, and the thought frightened me. I was a balloon untethered, rising above all my problems. How easy it would be. Then a child caught me by the string.

That child was me.

I became my brother's shadow from the time I was old enough to keep up. There were seven years between Charles and me, and I confidently rode his coattails to adventure. Exploring the boundaries of our ranch, escaping imaginary bandits, he kept my secrets and kept me safe. I idolized him.

But even at my young age, I knew that Dad was hard on Charles. Nothing my brother did ever pleased Dad. Something happened between them the week Charles turned eighteen. I covered my ears and hid in the bathroom, too young to understand why they argued, but knowing it was bad. When I realized he was leaving, I chased Charles down to the end of the dirt lane, my bare feet sending up tufts of fine powder to grit in my teeth, and my tears running hot fingers down my face and neck. He stopped and hugged me roughly. Then he held me away from him and told me to go back. That was the last time I ever saw him.

I was that child all over again. Those feelings of abandonment and bereavement were resurrected the moment I saw the Redding exit sign and realized how far I'd gone.

I really didn't want to cause my family any more pain than they'd already gone through. When it came right down to it, we were all in it together. It's hard to explain, except that I knew God was telling me that the choice was really more about *me* than about staying or leaving. I would be the same person, with or without them.

I couldn't change Deja or Andie or Russell. I couldn't change the fact that I was a divorced woman whose pulse still skipped at her husband's voice, living with her widowed dad and kids, with a precious child buried in a crummy district cemetery without even a proper headstone to mark her grave. I couldn't change my mistakes from the past, my regrets about lost loved ones, or my personal failures. I could only go on from there.

Was it possible that the change could happen inside of me? Would I be the same person when I returned? There were things I needed to let go of. I had to find a way to let go of Russell and my bitterness toward him. I had to abandon the dream of a perfectly functional family. My family was just right. Quirky, yes, but perfect in its own brand of dysfunction. I had to relinquish my need for Andie to replace Ginger, and I had to admit that maybe—just maybe—I had suspected I had the wrong child from the very beginning.

And at the same time, I had to take steps toward the future, even if it involved taking risks. I could make long-range plans to open a bakery after the girls were grown, couldn't I? And I could love Andie even if she never loved me back.

I had to turn around. I guess most women do. I chewed on it the whole way home, oddly touched that the God of the universe saw me as worth the trouble to flag down on my way out of state. Maybe I didn't fit in my skin exactly, but knowing that I'd made the choice to return home made it better drape my contours, ever so slightly.

The hand I'd been dealt was what it was. In the next few weeks, I'd have to fasten my seat belt and brace for impact. Ginger's anniversary loomed ahead in the shadows.

It was dark when I pulled in and parked beside the truck. Dad looked up from his basketball game when I came in and said gruffly, "Where you been, girl?" like I was sixteen again.

"Driving," I said, plopping down beside him on the couch. I threaded my arm through his, not allowing his worry to come between us. He looked a mixture of irritation and relief.

"Driving." It was something he understood. "Where'd you end up?"

I rested my head on his shoulder. "Redding."

"Surprised the car made it that far."

"Is everyone in?"

"I fed 'em and set them to doing their homework. You might want to call Jo. She called twice."

I kissed him on the cheek. "I didn't mean to scare you, Dad. I just needed to think."

He patted my knee, nodding silently. "Supper's on the table, if you're hungry."

I went into the kitchen and ate my cold plate of hash while standing by the sink. Afterwards, I went to the girls' rooms.

Winnie hugged my waist and scolded me for being late. When I checked in Andie's room, she looked up without speaking, blinking like a little owl. Deja asked, "Where did you go, Mom? We had to eat Grandpa's hash for dinner. It was so gross. I need to take some junk food for English tomorrow to suck up to Mr. Gotsch. Cookies or brownies or something."

"Don't worry. We have tons in the freezer," I said, closing their door. "Good night, girls."

CHAPTER 24

Andie

Marty sent us to school loaded with muffins, biscotti, and cinnamon rolls for the teachers, double chocolate chip cookies for our friends, and braided egg bread for the custodian. She stayed up late every night now to bake. For some reason her key had broken off in her ignition. Could it be because of me?

"Winnie, what's up with Marty?" I asked.

She racewalked ahead of me, but I double-timed and grabbed her arm.

"Wait," I said.

She stopped and gave me a Deja look. She'd been rude to me ever since camp. She couldn't stop talking about this new girl she'd met. Rae's so cool and perfect and she walks on water. Junk like that.

"What's bothering Marty?" I asked. "She still mad, or what?"

"I think it's almost the day when Ginger died."

"Oh." We continued on to the custodian's room with our goodies. "You mean, the anniversary of her death?"

"Yeah. She died before Deja's birthday."

"When's that?" I asked.

"March eleventh."

The next day I made things worse, even though it wasn't my fault. I came out to the kitchen minding my own business, and Marty was there, surrounded by the usual eggshells, flour explosions, and gooey beaters. I asked her what she was making.

"Coconut dandies," she said. She scooped some dough into a spoon and presented it to me like a trophy. "Try some."

Little pieces of coconut stuck out like stiff white worms. I looked at the empty coconut bag on the counter; I could imagine its sickening sweet smell and the way it would slick my tongue with oil. I took a step backward. "No, thanks. Coconut makes me sick."

She lowered the spoon, looking as if I'd slapped her. "What?"

"I mean, I used to like it. But once when I was little, Mom bought a giant bag of coconut, and I hid in the closet and ate half of it and I was sick for two days."

She stared at me for a long time. Dough dripped from the spoon onto the floor. She grabbed a paper towel and swiped at the floor. "No problem," she said, really perky. Jekyll and Hyde. "I can make something else. Chocolate chips or molasses joes."

I slid my eyes over to the table stacked with goodies.

She turned on the garbage disposal and dumped the whole bowl of dough into the sink.

"Marty! They're probably really good. It's just that—"

"No, there's something off about them." She let it run until I thought it would eat the sink too. She finally flipped the switch and turned off the water.

"Will you clean up for me?" she asked. Before I had time to answer, she had turned the corner. She headed down the hall to her room and quietly shut the door behind her.

Whatever. It gagged me to handle the coconut mess, but I wanted to clean up the scene of the crime. When I was done, I went to Winnie's room, knocked, and slipped inside without waiting for an answer, closing the door behind me. She was on the phone.

"What?" she asked, trying to be the ice queen.

"Something weird's going on," I said. "Hang up."

"No way," she said, doing her best Deja impression. "I'm talking to Rae."

I told Winnie it was about her mom, and she told Rae she'd call her back. I filled her in about what happened with Marty, except that I left out the fact that I wouldn't taste the dough.

"Mom was making coconut dandies?" She sank down to the edge of her bed. "And she just threw them away?"

"Yeah. Why?" I asked.

"Mom hasn't made them forever. Ginger was addicted to them."

So that's why she was so hot for me to try them.

"I begged her to make them. 'They're too much trouble,'" Winnie said, imitating a snooty Marty. She jumped up and took two steps to the door.

I jumped up and barred the way. "Where are you going?"

"Why can't she make them for us? She woulda made them for Ginger. Perfect little Ginger."

I'd never heard Winnie bad-mouth Ginger before.

"Easy, turbo," I said. "Can't you see something's going on?"

"Like what?"

I chewed the inside of my cheek, thinking. "You said Ginger's anniversary is soon. It's gotta have something to do with that."

Winnie's face smoothed out and sagged. "Oh, yeah. Like she was making them because of Ginger—"

"And couldn't finish them," I ended. Because she wanted *me* to be Ginger, and I wouldn't even taste them.

We both sat down on the edge of her bed.

"Wow," Winnie said. "I guess that's why she doesn't make them anymore."

It stung a little, thinking that Marty wanted me to be someone else, but I still felt sorry for her. "We need to be really nice to your mom till this is over."

"Yeah. No arguing. Or whining."

I think our pact made her forget to be mad.

"Andie, when did your other mom and dad die?" she asked shyly.

Other. When would she ever get it? "When I was ten."

"What makes you remember them?" she asked, not really looking at me. "I mean, like coconut dandies. You know, stuff you can't eat anymore, or something?"

I thought for a minute. "Broadway musicals."

Her head tilted to the side like a kitten charmed by a dangling string.

"Like *Phantom. Les Misérables. Cats.*"

She still looked lost.

"Annie? The Sound of Music?" I said, for the musically impaired.

"Oh, yeah. I know what you mean," she said. "Your parents listened to that?"

I nodded. "We knew them by heart."

"Do you still listen to them?" she asked.

"Sharing a room with Deja? Get real." I got up from the bed and opened the door. "Do you think Deja remembers about Ginger's anniversary? Maybe you should warn her. She might make it a little easier on Marty."

She frowned. "I guess so. Would you do it?"

I snorted. "Yeah, right. Go tell her now. She'll probably listen to you."

After a minute, Winnie came back to say that Deja's response was, "Like it's not going to ruin my birthday every year."

At night, I talked to God about Marty. None of this was her fault, but she was paying for it anyway. And I figured she'd had more than her share of hurt, since she'd taken care of a sick kid that wasn't even hers to begin with. Except for Grandma and Grandpa, it was the first time I'd prayed for someone else since I'd prayed for my parents to be safe on their trip.

That Sunday, Marty cried all through church. I was blindsided. People huddled around her after the sermon, hugging her, crying. Watching them, I had this guilty feeling, like a kid might feel who talked to a stranger and got stolen. Even though I'd been a baby and couldn't have done anything about it, I felt like it was my fault.

I knew it didn't make sense. But I had a sickening feeling that if only I'd been in the right crib where I belonged, Marty wouldn't be suffering right now. She really was my mom. My biological mom. She carried me in her body and gave birth to me. Suddenly I had this bad urge, and I had to get out of there.

Pushing the door open, I ran around the side of the building to the back parking lot. I bent over double and threw up by the curb. I don't know why. I don't even know how long I was there. I was crying against the building when Carl found me. He never said a word. He just gave me his handkerchief and put his arm around my shoulder and led me back to the car.

Marty and Carl left the house later in the afternoon. Winnie said they went to Ginger's grave. When they came back, Marty had some dirt on her knees. That stirred up even more memories for me. Going with Grandma and Grandpa to take plastic flowers to Mom and Dad's graves. It was hard to believe that they were there, under the ground, but their names were on the headstones with the same date. It just didn't seem real.

Everybody except me slept the afternoon away. Even Deja. I tried to be quiet, not because I was afraid of her, but because I felt a little sorry for her. Because of everything that happened with the Ridley breakup, and the kids laughing at her in school, and Ginger.

I finished my homework, and when I threw away some old papers from my notebook, I saw Deja's empty vanilla musk perfume bottle in our trash. That gave me a crazy idea. Her birthday was coming soon, and I had a little money stashed away that Grandma had sent. Was it worth it? Would she appreciate it? Probably not.

I went out to the TV to watch old movies and made myself some hot chocolate. I felt lonely and weird, being the only one awake all afternoon. The gutters chugged rain. At about five o'clock I turned on some lights, and the others finally started waking up from the spell. I guess they were waiting for the day to be over.

The next time we picked up Marty from work I had my money with me. I sneaked away to the cosmetics aisle and found a small bottle of Deja's spray cologne. After Marty left her check stand to get her purse, I got in the express line and paid for it, and hid it under my coat.

I wrapped it in the Sunday comics, but I didn't put my name on it. After her birthday dinner at a spaghetti place we came back for cake, which looked like Sleeping Beauty's castle. Marty had definitely pulled herself together. It was pink with turrets, and I was afraid Deja would toss it across the room, but she actually liked it. Go figure.

Deja opened her gifts, almost like a normal person. She actually sounded shy when she thanked everyone. Then she came to my gift.

"That's from me," I said.

She picked it up like it was an incendiary device and glanced at her mom. Marty nodded at her to go ahead, and Deja cautiously pulled open the paper. Her jaw dropped a little, and she didn't exactly look me in the face.

"Thanks," she said. She inspected the seal on it to be sure I hadn't tampered with it.

Marty smiled at me. "That was nice, Andie."

Later, when I was reading in bed, Deja brought in her gifts and put them away. I saw her spray some of the vanilla musk on her arm and rub her wrists together.

She looked over at me. "What's up with this?"

I hesitated. It was my moment of truth. I dug into a box under my bed and pulled out the chain with the rings.

"I found these in the bathroom vent. I mean, Cyclops found them."

I wouldn't say things were friendly between us after that, but at least I could wear the chain again. We had a tentative cease-fire for a while, until Cyclops came up missing.

My allergies hadn't gotten any better, and some days I was miserable. I missed more school and cost Marty more money at the clinic.

Cyclops prowled around my side of the room at the window early one morning, knocking over my stuff, crying to get out. Deja had left our bedroom door open so he could sneak in the night before. I was so tired of it all that I whacked at him when he jumped on my bed, and this time I connected. I must have been half asleep, because I hit him pretty hard with my fist. He clawed me and jumped down. I heard him crying at the front door, so I got up to let him out, and he hissed at me when he left. He didn't come in that night.

They called and called him for days. Even though I didn't tell anyone what happened the morning he left, Deja considered me the prime suspect and accused me every chance she got. I don't think she woke up when I slugged him, or she would have told. Unfortunately, I had the jagged scar, the motive, and the murder weapon. The only thing missing was the body.

The court lady with the bird name came back one day, sneaking around and asking questions, trying to sound casual. I didn't buy that casual part, because when she asked to come in, I don't think she was really waiting for an answer. Marty let her in, standing there with her arms crossed wearing her "on the edge" face.

Ms. Crow, or Sparrow, or whatever, was looking for something. She pretended to be polite, asking to open things and then doing it anyway. When she came to an opened bag of cat food in the cupboard, she stopped.

"Where's kitty?" she asked.

Then I knew she was really looking for signs of Cyclops. Marty sort of deflated in front of us, and I remembered that I'd told the lady about my allergies the last time she came. I slipped my arm behind me to hide the ugly red scratch Cyclops had given me.

I finally put two and two together. Here was that kid power I'd been looking for. One word about Deja, one complaint about Cyclops or how sick I'd been, and I could really screw things up for Marty.

Marty was trying to explain about the cat food and looking like she just wanted to give up. The lady wasn't being mean, just doing her job, pecking at Marty with questions, making little bloody spots on her.

I don't know why, but I didn't use it. The power, I mean. Maybe I felt sorry for Marty after Ginger's anniversary and then losing a pet on top of it. But this lady made me mad, the way she was treating Marty. Anyway, if I made trouble for her, they couldn't send me back to Grandma and Grandpa because the house hadn't sold yet. If they took me away from Marty, they'd send me straight to Uncle Greg.

"Cyclops ran away," I said.

They both stopped talking and looked at me. I could tell the lady didn't really believe me, so I kept going. "A couple weeks ago. We put up signs, but I guess he's gone for good this time."

The lady looked disappointed. I think she was hoping he'd pop out from somewhere and rub against her leg. I got the feeling she liked being right.

She gave up on Cyclops and checked out the other rooms. I don't know what she expected to find there. Guns, pipe bombs, a meth lab? Maybe she's found that stuff in other houses—who knows? She asked Marty if she could speak to me alone. I looked at Marty, but she just lifted her eyebrows in surrender. I guess I didn't have a choice.

Marty left, and the lady turned to me. "Why don't you show me your room again?"

Luckily, Deja was gone. "Andrea . . ."

"AnDRAYa."

She came into my room acting like she's on my side, and she couldn't even say my name right.

"Of course. Andrea. How're things since our last visit?"

I shrugged. "Fine."

"Have you been well? Getting enough to eat?" She scoped out the room as she talked. What was she looking for this time?

"I guess."

"So how are you and . . ." She looked down at her notes. ". . . Deja getting along?"

Boy, I was tempted, but I just answered, "Peachy."

She nodded like she didn't completely believe me. Things got really weird after that.

"Deja's what, seventeen?"

"Sixteen."

"Does she ever have any friends over to the house?"

"Sometimes her friend Summer."

"Does she have any boyfriends?"

"Only Ridley, but they broke up."

"Did he ever come over?"

I snorted, feeling kind of snotty. "No-o."

"What about Marty and Carl? Do they ever have anyone over?"

That's when I realized that not one single grown-up had come over since I'd been here. And somehow I knew that it didn't look good, either, that Marty and Carl didn't have friends. This nosy lady reminded me of those reporters.

"Marty has a friend at work named Jo. They're really good friends. I think they went to the same high school, but Jo doesn't ever come over." I remembered Winnie saying Carl had a girlfriend, but I didn't want to mention it.

"I see. Does she have any boyfriends? Does anyone ever spend the night?"

Spend the night? As in "sleep together"? What kind of people did she think we were? "No way." Then I said, like that explained everything, "We go to church."

She smiled and clicked her pen. "Yes, but that doesn't always mean that . . . well . . . even people who . . ."

I waited, not wanting to make it any easier on her, but she cleared her throat instead. "How're you doing in school?"

My grades were okay. I never got sent to the principal's office, except when I melted down on the first day. She asked me if I'd made any friends and I said yes, because of Natalie. She didn't ask if I'd lost any friends, so I didn't feel like I had to tell her that part of it.

After she finally left, I wondered what she would have done if I'd said yes to any of the above. Yes, Cyclops sleeps in my bed. Yes, strange men stay here every night. Yes, Deja hates me and is planning a drive-by.

Marty stuck her head in the door after the lady left, looking almost shy. "I guess we'd better put up some signs around the neighborhood," she said, and I remembered the lie I'd told about Cyclops.

"Yeah, I guess so." I didn't want Marty to read more into what I'd done than I meant. "Just in case she comes back."

It's funny, I had kid power in my hands like a fluttering bird, and I'd let it go. Chucked it up toward the sky. Maybe I'd subconsciously decided it was okay to be nice to her because she'd admitted defeat. Mercy on the battlefield. Or maybe I didn't feel like I belonged anywhere now that she'd given me up, and I wasn't quite ready to let go.

We put up signs around the neighborhood and asked the neighbors if they'd seen Cyclops, but nobody had. Secretly I was happy, even though I had to pretend I wasn't. I was beginning to feel normal again. I could smell things just like normal people whose heads weren't underwater all the time.

✦ ✦ ✦

When Cyclops had been gone for a month, Carl painted a picture of him in the garden from a photograph so they'd have something to remember him by. At church, Winnie raised her hand and asked them to pray for Cyclops to come home.

I had never been raised around pets, and I thought they were overdoing it a little. There were so many good things about not having one. The laundry room didn't smell like cat pee because Deja hadn't changed the litter in a week. Marty didn't have to spend money on litter, or for cat food that Cyclops would cry for and then ignore. The furniture didn't get any worse because he wasn't there to claw at it. I didn't have to take so much medicine and feel like a walking zombie at school. Life was easier.

I wondered if Cyclops ran away because of me. You know, bad vibes and all. I felt better now that he was gone, but the family didn't. So I prayed. I never asked God to make Cyclops come back. I just asked Him to take care of Cyclops and make the family get over missing him. Maybe that was selfish, but I think God understood where I was coming from.

CHAPTER 25

Marty

All that time spent baking and running away from thoughts of Ginger's anniversary did absolutely no good. I really didn't expect it to. I just hoped to take the edge off of it, or maybe dull the blade a little. As a final resort, I brought home coconut. I decided to call it out—face it down as part of my new outlook. But the ghosts that materialized with the scent of coconut disoriented me and drove me to my bed.

Standing at Ginger's grave on the anniversary of her death, I felt the loss anew. The day was gray and the clouds swirled overhead, threatening. The wind whipped my hair, and I dropped to my knees in my skirt on the damp ground to replace the spent daffodils in the vase with bearded irises, hoping they wouldn't blow away. Through my tears I noticed that the weeds had grown back, thick and green, obscuring her sweet name on the simple square of flat granite, and I yanked at them until Dad took me by the elbow and said there was a better time for that.

He held me, shivering. There were no words left to say.

The first heavy raindrops fell, and we made our way back toward the car. I noticed the other plots. So many flowers and teddy bears and balloons, you could trip over them if you weren't careful. All signs of love and remembrance. Her grave was so bare by comparison. Watching through the car window as we pulled away, I knew what was missing. Ginger would have had a father's bouquet, if only my bitterness toward him hadn't gotten in the way.

I took to my bed when we got home, unable to deal with anyone else's needs. Rain drove against the windows in sheets, and I pulled my comforter up to my neck. I would give over that day to grieving and then move on. Deja's birthday was only a week away, and I had to pull myself together to make it special for her.

Just on the edge of sleep, I recalled seeing Julian Barrett at the back of the church that morning, standing with his hands in his pockets, looking grim.

The next morning I woke up feeling like I had a hangover, but I went in to work anyway. Life went on, ready or not.

Easter had blossomed at Shop 'n Save. When I walked in, Robert stood at the foot of a ladder helping one of the new baggers suspend a giant inflated rabbit from the ceiling over the candy aisle. Jo stood beside him complaining that the potted lilies had to be moved to the opposite end of the store or her sinuses would burst. On my lunch hour, I picked up candy for the girls and an extra Easter basket for Andie.

Life got back to normal. Well, normal for our family. Deja and Winnie fought, and Andie pulled back into her shell. Something was up with Andie, and I hadn't yet seen any evidence that she'd told Deja about finding her chain. Perhaps she was trying to think of a way to apologize. I felt for her. After the way Deja had treated her, it wouldn't be easy.

The farmers market added two more growers and an antique dealer. When I helped Dad set up his paintings, I asked him to set aside the one of Winnie and Andie in the meadow, and not to sell it just yet.

At the rate Cyclops was shedding his winter coat, he'd soon be naked. I vacuumed huge clumps as soon as I spotted them, but either Andie needed a change in dosage or she wasn't taking her meds properly, because she ended up with another sinus infection. Or I suppose it could have been just a run-of-the-mill virus.

I made another appointment for her at the clinic. To my surprise, after the doctor checked Andie out and wrote the prescription, he asked her to have a seat in the waiting room and stepped out into the hall to ask a nurse to bring my chart. He motioned for me to hop up on the table.

"How are things at your house?" he asked, stretching out the blood pressure cuff and wrapping it around my upper arm.

"It's been kind of hectic. Just . . . a lot of things going on."

He pumped the cuff on my arm to the strangling point. I was quiet while he listened. Then he loosened the valve and stripped off the cuff, looking thoughtful.

"What kind of things? Anything out of the ordinary?"

Where should I start, I wondered. I gave him a very brief rundown of our life at home, skimming the fact of Ginger's anniversary. He "hmmed" and pursed his lips together.

There was a brief knock, and someone reached in to hand him my file. He opened it, flipped through the pages, and made a notation. "It sounds like you have your hands full. We don't have you on any medications, do we?"

"No."

"Your blood pressure is a little high. One fifty-four over ninety. We like that bottom number to be lower." He pulled an instrument from his pocket and checked my eyes with his light, one at a time. "Any high blood pressure or strokes in your family?"

"Not to my knowledge. My dad's pretty healthy. But he hasn't had a checkup in a long time."

He checked my ankles and asked if I had any problems with my digestion. Did I smoke, or drink more than a glass of alcohol a day? No, no, no. When he asked if I had trouble sleeping, I said no, but that I often felt tired, even so.

He poked and prodded a little more, and then he pulled out a form and completed it in doctor scrawl. "Get this blood panel done. I want to see you back here in two weeks. With everything you're dealing with right now, I'm thinking you might benefit from an antidepressant. I need that blood panel before I prescribe anything."

I trudged out to the front desk to set up another appointment, suddenly feeling old. High blood pressure, swollen ankles, bad digestion—those were old-lady illnesses he was talking about. The fact that he even *asked* suggested that they were already possibilities. Next I'd be looking at bifocals. But the fact that he thought I showed signs of depression depressed me.

I found Andie fighting sleep in a chair in the waiting room, and I told her I'd drop her off at the house before I went to pick up her prescription. On the way home, she glanced at my authorization for blood work, and then studied me sidelong.

Finally she asked, "Is that for me?"

"No. It's mine, don't worry. No more blood tests for you."

She relaxed for only a moment. "Are you sick?"

I shrugged. "Don't think so. I don't feel sick."

She studied me solemnly for a minute, looking like she had

something on her mind, but curled up toward the passenger window without saying anything.

Maybe she just felt lousy, or maybe she was worried about me. I indulged myself to believe the latter.

I found the perfect card for Deja's birthday. It had a teenager on the front dressed in black with piercings and tattoos, but on the inside the same girl was smiling and dressed like a princess, but with her crown on at a jaunty angle. I bought it and wrote inside, "You're still my princess."

It gave me an idea for her cake, and I hoped it wasn't more than I could handle. On the afternoon before Deja's birthday, Summer took her to the mall to let her pick out a gift, giving me lots of time. It took effort to get myself motivated to start such a big project, but once in, my creative juices began to flow. I spread out a picture of Sleeping Beauty's castle and considered the possibilities. It could work, I decided. At least, it would *suggest* that it was the same castle. Winnie and Andie came through once or twice during the afternoon, admiring my creative genius. I only hoped Deja would feel the same way.

Deja chose an expensive restaurant for her birthday, which we had to veto, darkening her mood. Everything with her was a test of our love; it couldn't simply be a matter of finances. Everyone else got to go where they wanted for their birthdays. She didn't actually finish the thought that we must love everyone else more, but it was implied. And so it went until we negotiated a cheaper place.

Winnie wanted to bring her new best friend, Rae, but I nixed that before Deja even started. It was enough that we brought Andie along, according to Deja, who said she was just a "barnacle on the family" and not a real member. I almost cancelled all our plans at that point. I would have if Andie had been around to hear it.

After dinner at the Spaghetti House, we came back home to open presents. Deja was truly impressed with the cake. We gave her a new portable CD player with some edited CDs, and Winnie got her a subscription to a magazine that she wanted. I made a mental note to peruse each issue when it arrived in the mail, in case I needed to pull out anything offensive.

Andie placed a package wrapped in the Sunday funnies on the table and pushed it over to Deja. To our surprise, Andie had gotten her a bottle of her favorite cologne. So that was what she'd been so secretive about.

The two briefly exchanged awkward looks, not really smiling, but with their countenances brightening slightly. They hadn't exactly taken a step toward each other. But they had at least stopped moving away and were looking back over their shoulders in each other's direction.

As the week went by, I realized that the doctor was right about my blood pressure. At times, my pulse pounded in my ears. I had plenty of opportunities to notice.

Apparently, someone left Cyclops in one night, and when Andie let him out in the morning, he never returned. So of course to Deja she was the prime suspect, having been the last one to see him alive. She also had a nasty jagged scratch on her arm, which she said was "nothing."

When Ms. Wren showed up at the house again, I noticed Andie pulled her sleeves down over her scratch and kept her arm behind her back. Initially, I took heart. She gave up a perfect opportunity to make us look bad to the caseworker. But the way she tried to cover for Cyclops made me suspicious. Maybe she had more to do with his disappearance than she let on.

CHAPTER 26

Andie

Carl drove me up to Pine Run on the Friday night before spring break. I took everything that was important to me because I didn't trust Deja. Even though we were getting along better since I gave her the birthday gift, I knew she still blamed me for Cyclops's disappearance.

I called ahead so Grandma would wait up until I got there. For a split second on the phone, she sounded like she didn't remember I was coming.

Grandma and Grandpa seemed about the same, only shorter. Grandpa didn't say much, and Grandma repeated everything she'd told me on the phone, just like it was news. She gave my clothes the once-over when I unpacked, and took me to K-Mart on Saturday to get a new Easter outfit. I could tell she was disappointed at the selection. She probably expected frills and lace in yellow and lavender, but I picked out a flippy black skirt and a hooded shirt with a front pocket. Not exactly fancy. She sighed and said whatever made me happy.

She tried to steer me down the aisle with the white plastic purses and flowered hats, but I detoured through the video section.

The next day we stunk up the house with vinegar and boiled eggs and food coloring. I think Grandma was enjoying it as much as I was. We were dipping eggs in mugs of color when the phone rang.

"Hello," Grandma answered. "Yes, it is. . . . Today? . . . No, not today, I'm afraid. My granddaughter is here for a visit. . . . No, no, it wouldn't be convenient tomorrow, either. Maybe next week. . . . Okay, you call back now. Thank you. . . . Bye-bye."

"Who was that, Grandma?" I balanced a bright fuchsia egg on a wire wand. My name, written in waxy crayon, was just beginning to materialize.

"Oh, no one. Some pesky real estate agent. They always call at the worst times."

The egg slipped off the wire back into the cup, splashing pink on the newspaper.

"Grandma, someone wanted to look at the house, and you said no?"

Her mouth pulled together like her old drawstring purse, and her cheeks pinked. "No, no, the place is a mess. And it smells like vinegar. Nobody wants a home that smells like vinegar. They'll call back after the holidays."

"But I'll help you clean up. Call them back. Please!"

"No, no. There's plenty of time for that later," she said crossly. "Besides, there are some things that need work before we can sell, and we can't afford to do them right now. We've got water damage from a leak in the roof, and the air conditioner needs to be replaced."

I was stunned. How long had this kind of thing gone on—realtors calling and Grandma stalling?

I dipped my fuchsia egg over and over into the color, but my name appeared as disconnected dashes and curls. I retraced with the wax crayon until a spider crack sprinted across the surface, and I added more vinegar and food coloring until the color came out dull and muddy.

We colored the last eggs in silence and cleaned up the mess. Grandpa called from the living room, and Grandma asked me to get his sweater from the bedroom.

That's when I saw the picture on the dresser. It was a school picture of Ginger when she was in about first grade. I knew it was her. I had this sickening feeling in my stomach. I sank down onto the bed and stared at her. How did they get it? Did Marty send it, maybe to convince them that Ginger really belonged to them, and that I was hers? Or . . . or did they ask for it?

Why didn't they throw it away?

I pulled on my sweatshirt and went for a walk, letting the door slam behind me, because I couldn't stay inside with them anymore.

My old route to the bus called to me from behind Grandma's house, and I followed. It was almost unrecognizable. The secret path I'd taken to school to hide from the park manager and could have walked blindfolded was now so overgrown that it took me a completely different way. Cold, damp air sliced through the pines, still smelling like winter. There was no sign of spring anywhere.

Deep in the brush, in a clearing where I used to play, I found a campsite. I froze. A fire ring sat ashen cold, and empty food cans and rags lay scattered around like they'd rolled off a trash truck. A shelter of cardboard and wood leaned against a tree. I expected transients or gypsies to come out of the bushes and claim me for one of their own. I backed up and hurried back along the trail toward the house, feeling a stab of panic because nothing looked the same as it had, and angry that wackos had claimed my spot.

But what did I care about the path? When I came back to Pine

Run to live, we'd be in a different house and I wouldn't have to sneak out to catch the bus anymore. Then I remembered about the realtor's call, and for the first time I realized that I might not be here a year from now as I'd planned.

Finally I got back to the yard. I took a critical look at everything, like someone who was coming to buy the mobile home. The yard was in pretty bad shape. Weeds had taken over Grandma's flower bed, and pine needles covered everything. Bilbo's color had faded in the sun and the rain, and some creeping vine reached up tendrils to choke the realtor's sign. I paused to rip the vine away and give Bilbo a spit-shine with my sleeve as I passed by.

I sank down onto the top porch step, and was startled to overhear Grandma and Grandpa discussing me. It wasn't hard, even through the storm door, since Grandpa was practically deaf now that he wouldn't wear his hearing aid anymore.

"Well, of course that's what they want," she said. "Seven hundred dollars is a nice check to get every month. And how much of that do you think goes to Andie?"

Money? To me? Grandma must be losing it.

Grandpa mumbled something I couldn't hear.

"Orville James, are you saying Greg would take advantage of Andie?" Grandma snapped.

I snorted. He already had. Somebody had to have sent that school picture to the tabloids.

"They could fly her back down at Christmas. Maybe for the summer. At least she'd be in a family. Not stuck with a couple of old people."

My lungs deflated like a flat tire.

Grandpa mumbled again, and I crept under the living room window to hear better.

"I know she won't. I just don't see how it can be any different.

Andie's not happy down there with those people, and the lawyer said the court would consider Greg and Robin, if they were willing."

Grandpa said something else, and Grandma yelled back, "Well, why wouldn't they? Andie's his sister's child, isn't she?"

Grandma and Grandpa were thinking about sending me away. My stomach felt twisted and wrung out like a washcloth. They were going to give me up. They were lying to me. I brushed tears from my eyes. All this time, they'd made me think they really wanted me, and now they were trying to get rid of me.

There was another hurt buried deeper in her words. She was so sure Marty wanted me for the money, not for myself—that wasn't even an option.

Well, I *had* been a pain to Marty at times, and I didn't try very hard to fit into their family, but Grandma didn't know that. She just *assumed* the only reason they would want me was because they thought I had money.

Marty was always so nice to me. Seeing how I treated her sometimes, I don't think it would be humanly possible to be that nice unless she really did love me. Living with a person every day, it seems like she would slip up once in a while if it was fake. Unless you were convinced you were loving someone else, like with the coconut dandies.

I quietly slipped off the porch and stumbled down the bank of the stream that ran behind Mrs. DeMarco's. At the edge of the water, I sat on a flat rock and buried my face in my arms. What was wrong with me? Why did I have this strange life where people fought over me, but no one really wanted me?

Suddenly I felt that I wasn't alone. I wiped my eyes with my sleeve and looked around, but no one was there. Still, I felt a presence—but not in a bad way. More like a warmth. Peacefulness. It was unreal. At first I thought I was just worn out from crying, but it was more than that. For a second, I wondered if it was Mom.

Maybe heaven isn't that far away. It could be in some parallel universe where she could see and hear me, but couldn't break through. But that wouldn't be Paradise, would it? Watching your kid suffer and not able to do anything about it? I remembered Mom telling me that Jesus said there would be no crying in heaven. No—she'd be crying, if she could see me now.

I tipped my head back to look at the sky, to look for God. I looked up for a long time, until dark clouds gathered into thunderheads. The chill burned my nose and throat as I sucked in evening air, trying to get a grip on myself. The Union Pacific whistled as it crossed through town. If this calm came from God, He was keeping it a big secret.

I had a vision of Carl bringing me that fake tree at Christmas. I smiled a little, remembering how he looked kind of shy when he brought it inside. My throat got tight and started to ache. That tree had made me feel so special. Loved.

He didn't seem like the type to try to trick me, but how well did I really know him? After all, I'd thought I knew Grandma pretty well.

Water swirled around the pebbles on the stream bottom, making little blips on the surface. It tumbled and splashed, trapping debris that fell in its way. A birch leaf spun around and around in the same tiny whirlpool, until I fished it out with a stick and flicked it into the free-flowing portion of the stream. It was only a leaf, but I couldn't sit there and watch it fight the current with no hope of freedom.

I pitched stones until it was too dark to see my breath. Grandma called me once, but she didn't know where I was, so I ignored her. Let her worry a little. Maybe she would realize her luck and stop calling.

The next time she called, her voice sounded kind of hysterical, so I got up and went back to the house. She rubbed my cold hands with her warm ones and made me put on her flannel robe. We had clam chowder and tuna sandwiches. Comfort food. I felt bad for making her worry.

The rest of spring break was a blur. Whenever Grandma asked what was wrong, I made up something. I wondered what Winnie was doing. I started working on a book report that I didn't have to hand in for two weeks, but I couldn't finish it because I didn't have the paper that explained how the teacher wanted us to do it. So I called Winnie to see if she could find it in my room and read it to me. Carl answered, and he said Winnie was at Rae's and wouldn't be back for two days. He said I could call Rae's house if I wanted to talk to Winnie, but I said no. It wasn't important.

She probably didn't even notice I was gone.

The day before Easter, I got a box in the mail from Marty. In big letters on the outside of the box it said DON'T OPEN UNTIL EASTER. Grandma frowned when she saw it, but I didn't care. Maybe Marty bought it with some of that money I was supposed to be getting.

On Easter morning I woke up early and ripped into the box. Inside was an Easter basket covered in purple cellophane. It was so cool. In my opinion, you never outgrow an Easter basket. Inside sat a stuffed purple rabbit and a solid chocolate rabbit, yellow Peeps, and millions of jelly beans. I was so stuffed, I had to force down Grandma's blueberry muffins at breakfast, just to be nice.

She acted like Marty's basket was nothing.

"Don't eat too much," she warned. "That stuff will make you sick."

Maybe she wished she had gotten me a basket herself.

I started praying before we even got to church, right after Grandma cut off a bus that was exiting the freeway. We had a few other close calls, mostly merging into traffic and making turns without signaling. It rattled Grandma when people blew their horns at her, and I felt a little bit sorry for her.

I got into it with God during the sermon. In my head, I told Him how I felt about Grandma and Grandpa, and Marty's family, and Uncle Greg. I asked Him, could He please fix it? Prayer had worked to find my chain, and I figured that maybe He would answer this prayer too. If He could move a giant stone from a grave, He could move some of the roadblocks out of my way—plow through them with a monster truck. Couldn't He? Like selling the house—sell it right out from under them and force them to buy another one.

I wondered how far free choice went with God. Nobody would ever love me as much as Mom and Dad had. But couldn't He make someone come close?

My bag was packed and sitting by the door when Carl came to pick me up that afternoon. I wondered if my grandparents were glad I was leaving, but then Grandma hugged me extra hard, and I knew she still loved me.

I didn't talk much on the way back. Finally I asked Carl if he'd sold any paintings.

"Just one. *The Bucking Bronco.* Business has been slow. Too much rain."

"I saw that picture in your room. And the one of Marty and Tipper," I said. "Didn't you get a blue ribbon for that one?"

"Yup. The Elko County Fair. My first and only award."

"I won a ribbon for a picture once," I said shyly. "A carousel horse with streamers. I was little then."

"Do you still have it?" he asked.

"It's rolled up, under my bed."

"I'd like to see it sometime. Have you taken any art classes?" he asked.

"Yeah, at the parks and rec. That's where I won the ribbon. But I never sold anything. I'm not that good."

"Selling doesn't mean you're a good artist. People mostly buy because the art triggers some memory, or makes them feel good," he said. "You can't always tell which ones will sell. And sometimes you're sorry you sold 'em at all."

"Did that happen to you?" I asked.

He nodded. "Sold one of our old ranch house near Elko. A few years later I went back to paint it again, but it was gone—leveled for a golf course."

"That's too bad. What happened to Tipper?" I asked.

"Tipper? He was put down years ago. He was old when Marty was a little girl."

"Why'd you move to Newberry, if you liked your ranch so much?" I asked.

He hesitated, and looked out the driver's window, pretending to be watching traffic. Something told me he wasn't. He cleared his throat. "Betty got cancer. Marty's mom. She needed to be near the special treatment hospital."

The one that died before Winnie was born. I felt like an idiot.

"The old place was getting to be too much anyway," he reasoned. "We couldn't keep up with it. And Marty was already married and gone. It was time."

He didn't convince me.

I knew I should stop asking dumb questions, but something inside me wouldn't shut up.

"Does Marty's husband live there? I mean, ex-husband."

He kept his eyes fixed on the empty road ahead and said evenly, "Yup. Far as I know."

A Dairy Queen loomed ahead.

"I think it's time for a Blizzard," he announced, drifting into the exit lane.

I knew that trick, but I let him buy my silence with food anyway.

The other times, when I came back from Pine Run, I'd felt like a bird being caged up again. But when I saw the house this time, I felt like a homing pigeon flying back home.

There had to be something wrong with that.

CHAPTER 27

Marty

Easter weekend was big at the farmers market. People came looking for fresh vegetables and fruits for their holiday dinners and went away with asparagus, artichokes, and strawberries.

I didn't officially have a booth. Dad's permit for the market didn't include my baked goods. But I knew that the health inspector was miles away. I'd overheard Julian telling the pastor that he'd be out of town on Easter and regretted missing the service.

Dad looked over at my table, set up in front of the truck with the overflow on the opened truck gate. I'd covered the table with a festive plastic tablecloth printed with bunnies in top hats. In addition to my usual biscotti and cinnamon rolls, I'd brought egg bread, bunny cookies with pastel sugars, muffins, caramel delights, and a coconut cake.

Dad passed his hand over the stubble on his chin. "Girl, I hope you know what you're doing."

"It'll be fine, Dad," I said, setting out a plate of samples that just begged customers to jump in. I had to start somewhere.

An hour after opening, sales were brisk and things were going pretty well. The smell of hot caramel corn enticed me to take long, deep breaths, and the sound of wind chimes in the light breeze put magic in the air. Dad even sold a Grand Canyon picture. In between customers, we talked about the reopening of the drive-in on Memorial Day weekend. Dad said he needed a part for the projector, one that was expensive and difficult to find. I suggested eBay. He said there was a shop in Oakland that he would try first.

Fleta, of Fleta's Flowers in the next booth, stepped away between customers to buy a cinnamon roll from me. She jingled like a gypsy when she walked. Her hair was plaited into a long gray braid, and she wore a red bandanna over what I suspected was a thinning scalp. Her bohemian ways were a throwback straight from the sixties. Her eyes slid over to Dad while we talked.

In addition to flowers, Fleta sold wind chimes and whirli-bobs. She had a talent for capturing beautiful tones with different mediums, and I'd filled our porch with her artwork. Dad never responded to her attentions. He told me to keep a lookout for funny smells or roach clips. I was shocked that he even knew what they were.

As she turned to go, I saw a familiar form weaving through the organic vegetables, headed my way. Julian. Apparently his travel plans had changed. Suddenly, the smell of caramel corn nauseated me.

He smiled and nodded to vendors as he passed by, making a beeline for me. There wasn't a thing I could do about it. Illogically, part of me was thrilled to see him. But the part that involved my brain realized I was in deep trouble. Whatever happened, it would be bad.

Fleta said "The fuzz" under her breath, and quickstepped back to her table.

He sauntered straight to me, a man on a mission, metal clipboard in hand.

"Good morning," he said, briefly smiling before scanning my table setup. "Nice morning for the market. Sales going well?"

His smile set off a small thrill like a sparkler inside me. Mentally, I tried to douse it with fear and bad thoughts.

My mouth went dry when I saw the badge pinned below his left shoulder bearing the official logo of Whitcomb County. He was definitely on duty. I tried to smile naturally, but it twisted my face like a grimace.

"You have some wonderful-looking goodies here, Mrs. Winslow. Would you mind showing me what's in that box under the table?"

A box—under the table? Mechanically I reached beneath the table to show him the contents of the box. Bags of bunny cookies waited silently for their turn on the table. Was he buying or setting me up?

People walked by my table, glanced at the goodies, and then moved on in response to the obvious stress levels I emitted.

"Mrs. Winslow, you're not listed as a temporary vendor under Mr. McAlister's permit, so I'm assuming you're operating without one."

"Without what?"

"A permit."

I actually felt my blood pressure rise. This would be a good time for a stroke. It would have kept me from saying the dumbest thing you can say to a health inspector when you don't have a permit.

"Have a caramel delight."

He got a quirky, incredulous little smile on his face. "Are you trying to bribe me, Mrs. Winslow?"

I flinched. "No, I . . ."

"Because you've already broken several health code regulations."

I felt the color drain from my face. I glanced over at Dad. His fists were plunged into his pockets, and he was eyeing Julian like he wanted to punch him.

"You're selling food from the tailgate of a vehicle. You're storing food in a container less than six inches from the ground, and your baked goods aren't properly packaged and labeled. Your artificial nails require that you wear gloves when handling samples. I need to see a health permit covering the kitchen in which they were prepared, and a seller's permit for Whitcomb County."

I blanched. How could I have been so stupid? Fighting tears, I silently cursed those happy bunnies in top hats dancing around plates of biscotti and that ridiculous green coconut cake. They mocked me.

"You're right. I don't have a permit." I looked up, trying to maintain my composure. "This is the first time I've ever set up a table like this. I've sold a few things to the vendors before the markets opened—"

"Mrs. Winslow." He lowered his voice, leaning in slightly. "Do us both a favor and don't tell me how many times you've broken the law."

"Broken the law?"

"It's a misdemeanor. You should know that."

What an idiot I was. I knew that the health inspector visited the market. And even if Julian had been out of town, he wasn't the only inspector in the county. Did I think I was so good that I'd be an exception to the rule? Had I expected him to be lenient, just because he liked my baking or . . . well, maybe even me?

"I'm closing you down."

Suddenly, I was angry. Unreasonably angry. I felt set up. What if he'd led me to believe he'd be gone, just to catch me?

"Fine," I said, yanking the box from under the table and throwing the leftover food into it. "It was a bad idea, anyway."

"Operating without a license—yes. But this would be an excellent way to build clientele, if you follow the legal guidelines."

I shoved the box of goodies onto the truck bed.

I turned my back to him, wadding up the tablecloth and stuffing it into the box. Saying things under my breath I didn't dare say to his face.

The only thing I couldn't put in the box was the cake. I'd put so much work into making it look like a backyard egg hunt. I wanted someone to enjoy it.

I turned back to him, holding the cake. "Can't I just *give* this away?"

He shook his head. "Sorry. It all has to go."

I could feel myself start to unravel. A twitch developed in my jaw, and I clenched my teeth against it. I held the cake balanced on one hand, hefting the weight of it. Considering. This wild visual came to me of Julian picking green buttercream frosting out of his eyes and nostrils. Slicking his perfectly groomed hair. Was it worth it?

It could be incredibly satisfying. I ran a finger across the base of the cake and stuck the icing in my mouth, sucking it off my finger. Faintly lemon. Perfect. I put my hand on my hip and looked him in the eye as an evil smile blossomed on my face. It was the primal urge of every baker to throw a pie in the face of the county health official. Lifting my chin slightly, I mentally took aim.

He looked from me to the cake and back again. His eyebrows lifted, and his mouth slacked. For one perfect moment in time, I had him at a sweet disadvantage.

I'll give him credit. He didn't step back. He just casually shifted his feet to a defensive stance and cocked his head with a knowing smile.

"That's assault on a county official, Mrs. Winslow. It would be a shame to have you arrested in front of all these patrons."

For a long moment I stared him down, just to let him know I wasn't intimidated. Then I lowered the cake without breaking eye contact, sweetly saying, "What on earth are you talking about?"

I really should have been more careful. It was a heavy three-layer cake on a cardboard cutout, and I was so busy trying to stare him down that I didn't notice the tremble in my wrist until it was too late. My arm gave way from the weight.

In excruciating slow motion, the whole thing tipped toward him, flipped over, and splattered at his feet on the blacktop.

He jumped back and looked at me in shock. I covered my mouth with my hand, horrified at the culinary Picasso of yellow cake, green icing, coconut, and jelly beans. He lifted one pant leg, turning his foot to the side. Bright green icing flecked the bottom of his khakis up to his knees and covered the toes of his suede mocs.

I shook my head. "Julian, I am so sorry."

He looked taken aback by my use of his first name. I couldn't believe I'd used it, myself.

I don't know how to explain what happened next, except that I just lost it. *It* being sanity—that thing that differentiates us from blithering idiots. And I started to laugh. I covered my mouth with my hand to keep it in, but emotion oozed out of every pore and became a giggling, snorting, nervous laugh that I couldn't contain. It grew into a hysterical half laughing, half crying kind of uncontrollable noise that rose up and claimed me. I raised my hands in surrender, trying desperately to gain control.

I couldn't even help him clean off his shoes and pant legs.

Fleta reached over and handed him wads of paper towel. I ducked around to the cab of the truck to get some tissues to blow my nose and to get away from the green splatter on the blacktop. I sagged against the door of the Dodge Ram, gulping air. Facing reality.

What had I done? He would never believe it was an accident after that stupid implied threat. I pressed the tissue to my mouth. What would happen to me now?

I looked back at Julian. He glanced up at me and took a few last swipes at his pant legs. He stood up tall, stepped delicately around the mess on the blacktop, and marched over. Anger colored his face and tensed all the handsome lines. He gestured over his shoulder and demanded in a barely controlled voice, "What on earth were you thinking? Do you know how many people witnessed that?"

My face crumpled, and my chin wobbled. Moaning like a wounded cow, I sobbed into my tissue. I turned to face the truck. "Don't look at me," I said, like a petulant child, wishing I could climb into the engine where it was safe and dark.

I cried until I could finally sniff back the sobs. With my back to him, I said, "I am s-so sorry. It was an accident. I'm not the kind of person who . . . who . . . I've n-never even had a ticket."

I cried some more into my tissue and wiped my nose, thinking how my face must be ugly and blotchy. Stupid. Why should I care how I looked?

"Please, stop," he said, sounding tired.

I sniffed and pressed my lips together, turning to face him, hugging my arms across my chest. I took a shuddering breath.

His anger had scaled down to mild irritation. "You've put me in a difficult situation."

I stood very still. "But I didn't—"

"It doesn't matter what I think or you think. It matters what those vendors out there think. I have no history with these people, and if they believe you deliberately threw that cake, I'll lose all credibility. And I take my job very seriously."

"I'm sorry. I'll make sure they know it was an accident."

"It would be better if they saw you take legal steps to correct the situation." He looked at me arrogantly. "You know, having talent doesn't put you above the law."

A verbal slap with a velvet glove. I bit my tongue to keep from making things worse.

"If I find you operating without a permit again, I'll issue you a misdemeanor citation. The law allows a fine of three times the cost of the permit up to one thousand dollars and/or imprisonment in the county jail for up to six months." He straightened and took a breath. Then he took a business card from his pocket and handed it to me. "Call me when you're serious about opening a bakery."

I took the card, and he made his way over to Dad and handed him a card too. From the way Dad nodded without comment, I knew he was being reminded that he could lose his permit. Then Julian wove his way through the vendors and left.

I caught Dad's eye over the tailgate and winced at the position in which I'd placed him. I mouthed the word *sorry*.

I looked at the card in my hand. His name stood out in bold font against the white cardstock. JULIAN R. BARRETT, R.E.H.S. COUNTY OF WHITCOMB DEPARTMENT OF HEALTH AND HUMAN SERVICES.

I shoved it in my pocket, not really sure why I was keeping it. There was no way I could ever face him again.

CHAPTER 28

Andie

When I got back from Grandma's on Sunday, I found Winnie enthroned at the kitchen table surrounded by her subjects: biscotti, egg bread nested with real Easter eggs, caramel delights, and bunny cookies. Her Easter basket was already dismantled.

Marty must have short-circuited.

"What happened?" I asked, figuring it had something to do with Deja.

"The 'spector shut Mom down."

"Swallow," I said crossly.

She gulped down milk, and explained. "The inspector came to the market yesterday and told Mom to stop selling her stuff. So she had to bring it all back home. He was so snotty." Her hands on her hips, she mimicked, 'So open a bakery.' That's what Fleta said."

"Fleta."

"The flower child. Grandpa calls her that."

"Oh, yeah. The hippie lady. With the braid." Two ripped halves of a crumpled business card lay smoothed out on the table.

Together they read, JULIAN R. BARRETT, R.E.H.S. Blah, blah, blah.

"I guess he never had one of her cookies. He would have changed his mind about closing her down."

"Mom tried that. He got real mad and 'cused her of bribing him. Whatever that means. She threw a cake at him." She drowned a bunny in milk. "He made Mom cry. I hate him."

"She threw a cake?"

"Yeah. It was really fancy. Too good to throw at *him*."

I laughed, still not convinced, because Winnie exaggerated too, just like me. "She hit him in the face?"

She shook her head. "She says she dropped it by accident and it got all over his shoes, but I think she threw it." She licked sugar from the corner of her mouth and scrunched up her forehead. "I 'member one time when I was little, she spiked a big blob of hamburger at Dad's feet. Like a football."

It sounded so Deja-like. It gave me more respect for Marty. Deja was a jerk, but she didn't let people push her around.

Deja walked through the kitchen and grabbed a handful of cookies without acknowledging that either of us existed. This huge zit-thing was hanging on the side of her nose, looking all irritated and sore. She was waiting for us to say something about it, but Winnie and I just beamed silent messages to each other with our eyes.

After Deja slammed the bedroom door, we burst into muffled giggles.

"When did she get her nose pierced?" I asked.

"Yesterday," she said, spraying crumbs. "It looks like a big booger."

"A big sore booger." We laughed again, and I shushed Winnie to keep Deja from coming out.

"She can't wear it to school," I said. "Won't the hole close up if she takes it out?"

Winnie shrugged. "Maybe. I bet Summer dared her."

I put a bunny cookie in my mouth, snapping off the head and chewing. Enormous sugar crystals flaked off like diamonds. "Did Summer get her nose pierced too?"

"Naw. Summer gets people to do stuff she's scared to do. So they get into trouble and not her."

I studied her as she licked her finger and pressed it onto the table, collecting stray sugar crystals.

"Did you figure that out by yourself?"

She shook her head. "Deja told me."

"What did Marty say?"

"She yelled a lot. Mostly about infection and AIDS and junk. She calmed down when Deja said at first Kendra was going to do it at her house because she's some kind of expert pierce-person. But she wasn't home, so they went to the mall instead."

"Omigosh. That happened yesterday, after the inspector came? Marty must have been wearing a target."

"Yeah. Poor Mom." Winnie chewed slowly. She glanced over at me covertly and fingered her right earlobe. "Rae got her ears pierced for her birthday. I wanna get mine pierced too, so we can wear the same earrings."

"That's swell." I got up from the table and rinsed my glass in the sink. Then I went into the living room and plopped down on the sofa with the remote.

I remembered to thank Marty for the Easter basket. I told her when she was sitting at the table at dinner, so she wouldn't try to hug me. She just smiled and wiped her eyes. Gosh, I didn't mean to start her up again.

✦ ✦ ✦

Spring break was officially over, and we had a hard time getting up for school the next morning. Kids were wearing shorts and sandals to school like summer had magically appeared the day after Easter. They thought they were cool, but I knew they were really cold.

On Wednesday there was a short message all garbled on the answering machine. We could only make out a few words before the hang-up. Marty checked the area code in the phone directory.

"Canada." She blinked and looked over at me, and I could tell she was thinking the same thing I was.

Could it be Uncle Greg? Maybe he'd figured out about my money too. Or maybe Marty had started the ball rolling herself, to give me back.

The phone rang again during dinner that night, and Deja bolted. She came back looking thoroughly disgusted, wordlessly handed the phone to Marty, and sat back down. Marty glanced at the caller ID and left the table to talk in her bedroom.

She was gone long enough for her spaghetti to get cold and her Parmesan to congeal. She came back chewing her lip.

Winnie asked, "Mommy, what's wrong?"

"It's Andie's grandpa."

I sat up, stung.

"That was your Aunt Robin on the phone. Your grandpa fell and broke his hip. He's doing okay, but he'll be in the hospital for a while."

I felt the world telescoping away from me. I should have been there. Maybe if I had been, this wouldn't have happened.

"He broke his hip? How did he do it?"

"He fell on the front porch. Your grandmother called them

from the hospital. Her neighbor's staying with her," she said. "Mrs. DeMarco, I think. She's driving your grandmother back and forth to the hospital."

Why didn't they call me first, instead of Greg? He never visited or even called them.

"Can I call Grandma?"

"Give her a chance to get home first. Visiting hours are probably over by eight."

Grandma's phone rang busy until my bedtime, and Marty said maybe her phone was off the hook. She was probably staying overnight in the room with Grandpa anyway. Or maybe with Mrs. DeMarco.

I secretly called the hospital at nine, nestled in the bathroom with the phone and hoping my voice didn't ricochet off the walls. There was only one hospital in Pine Run, so it wasn't hard to get the number. As I dialed, I wondered how I would get Grandpa to hear me without yelling at him. But I worried for nothing.

The phone picked up. "Room 231."

"Grandma?" I asked.

"No, it's not."

"Who is this?" I asked. Who would be in his room, if it wasn't Grandma?

"I'm an RN," she said.

"A what?" I asked.

"A nurse, honey." She hesitated for a second. "Who did you want to speak to?"

"My grandpa. Mr. James."

"He's resting right now. Why don't you call back tomorrow, when family members are here?"

Family members? "But that's me," I said, stupidly. "Is he okay?"

"I'm not allowed to give out any patient information. Call back tomorrow, please." She hung up.

Marty peeked around the door and startled me. "So, how's your grandpa?"

I dug into the floor with my toe, feeling five years old. "He's resting."

She leaned against the door in her bathrobe with her hair hanging down on her shoulders and her eyes bald without makeup. "We can drive up to visit him this weekend, if you want," she said.

"Can we?"

"Just a day trip. You'll have to come back home with me."

"That's okay. Just so I can see him," I said. "Thanks, Marty."

She smiled tiredly and told me to get ready for bed.

We drove up on Saturday. It wasn't hard to find the hospital. There were big signs on the freeway.

We parked and got out. It was still cold up there, and I was glad I'd remembered to grab my hoodie.

We went in to check his room number at the front desk. Room 231 was on the second floor. I stopped at the water fountain outside his room to get a drink because my mouth was dry from worrying.

It was hot in his room. If Grandma hadn't been there, I'd have thought we were in the wrong room. The skin on Grandpa's face sagged against his bones in sleep. Almost like a skeleton. His veins showed blue under his skin, thin, stained, and watery, the color of used tea bags. Grandma perched, humpbacked, by his bed, smoothing his covers nervously.

The room had that kindergarten bathroom smell. I wrinkled my nose, but no one else seemed to notice.

Grandma told us that he'd tripped on the steps in front of their house. He was doing fine, but he would be in the hospital for a few weeks. They had to sit him up every couple of hours to prevent pneumonia, and he didn't like that. It hurt his hip to bend in the middle.

He never woke up while we were there, but Grandma said she'd tell him we came by. He was pretty doped up. Marty asked if there was anything we could do for her, but she said no, her neighbor was coming by to take her home later.

I didn't want to leave Grandpa. He looked so much older in that bed with the kiddie rails. But it was a relief to get outside. I breathed in the fresh pine when we walked to our car.

"Andie, do you have a key to your grandma's house with you?" Marty asked.

"Yeah. It's in my pocket. Why?"

"Let's swing by and see if they need anything. She probably hasn't had time to do any shopping."

Pine Run is small, so it was easy to find the mobile home park from the direction of the hospital. There were only a couple of turns. We pulled in behind Grandma's Lincoln.

"Look," Marty said, wiggling a broken step on the porch with her shoe. "That must be where he fell. That should be fixed."

We didn't even need a key—Grandma had forgotten to lock the door. The house smelled stale, so we opened some windows to air it out. The fridge was empty, except for a jug of expired skim milk and a carton of egg substitute. Marty sniffed the egg stuff, wrinkled her nose, and ran it all down the garbage disposal.

We scrubbed the bathroom and mopped the floor, which wasn't easy, considering Marty was wearing a nice outfit, and a new full set of fake nails. Then we gathered up their dirty clothes and filled the washer. We made a run to Safeway and stocked the fridge with fresh milk, egg substitute, and juice, and the freezer with frozen dinners. The sun had heated up the place, and I peeled off my hoodie. Lastly, I dug out a hammer and nails from Grandpa's toolbox, and we did the best we could to fix the step.

On the ride back to Newberry, I felt pretty good about helping Grandma. I glanced over at Marty. She was singing along with the radio and driving one-handed, and her sunglasses reflected the road ahead in a weird, sideways angle. She'd chewed off the pink lipstick she had carefully applied in the rearview mirror before we went into the hospital. She sensed me watching, and looked over.

"What?" she asked.

"That was nice, what you did for Grandma."

"Well, you did it too, kiddo." She gave me a playful shove. "That bathroom was a two-woman job."

I grimaced.

"Not just the bathroom. Everything. Washing their clothes, and buying her food. You didn't have to do that."

She shrugged, cocking her head. Some of her hair came out of her clip.

"She's your grandma, and she needed it." She tucked the lock of hair behind her ear.

"Grandma hasn't been exactly . . . nice to you."

She thought it over for a second.

"No, Andie, she hasn't. But you don't win people over by giving back hurt for hurt. I don't hold anything against your grandparents. Under the circumstances, I would probably be the same way."

Win people over. Like Grandma accused Carl of doing with the Christmas tree? Did Marty do that stuff to be nice, or was she trying to win me over? Her nails clicked on the steering wheel. Things must be looking up, if she could afford her twice-a-month visits to Nail Palace again.

"I heard Grandma say that I had some money. From my parents' insurance. And from the settlement."

She glanced over at me and back to the road. I couldn't see her eyes through her reflective lenses. Finally she nodded. "It's in a savings account in your name for living expenses. We could draw on it, but we never have. And we won't. It's for your college when you're eighteen."

"Oh." I felt crummy, like I'd accused her of stealing.

"Did they tell you we wanted your money?" she asked.

"No. I just heard them talking once."

"I bet you have," she said under her breath. "Well, they're wrong about this. Andie, sometimes older folks can get confused about things. The world is changing so fast, they don't always trust people. Your grandparents are worried about you, and they don't want you to get hurt. I think they overdid it just a bit there. We are *not* after your money."

Considering how tight money had been since Christmas, and how hard Marty worked, I knew she was telling the truth. "I know."

She reached over and squeezed my hand. "Since we started going back to church, I realized that I need to forgive them for the way they act toward us sometimes. I know they're just worried about you. Still, it's not always easy to forgive, believe me. But God gives me the strength to do hard things."

I'd heard that before. I blurted out, "But why can't God just take away hard things?" I turned my head toward my window. I hadn't meant to say it out loud.

"Well, He could. But my problem is your grandparents, and I know you wouldn't want Him to take them away."

My head whipped around.

"He wouldn't do that, Andie. But do you see what I mean? He's helping me to deal with my problem instead of taking it away or letting it make me bitter. And He's making me a better person because of it. Who knows? Maybe their attitude toward me will change a little too." She shrugged. "We'll see."

I tried to think about something else. It was too much, right after seeing Grandpa in the hospital. We stopped for hamburgers on the way back because it was late. When we got home, Winnie saw our milkshake cups and whined, like she thought we were having fun without her.

I gave Marty Uncle Greg's number to give him an update on Grandpa's condition. Then I sneaked down the hall to her bedroom door to eavesdrop on the call.

I heard her say, "Andie and I went up to the hospital today to see your father."

She paused.

"He's resting, but the doctors are concerned about pneumonia. They're getting him up and around every so often to prevent that. Otherwise, he's pretty drugged with pain medication, which is understandable."

Silence again.

"She's holding up pretty well, under the circumstances. Actually, I wanted to talk to you about their situation. I think it would be a good idea for you to visit soon."

Silence, then her voice was shrill.

"Andie and I went over to the house after we left the hospital. It needs some upkeep. Your father fell on a broken step on the porch, and your mother or a neighbor might be next. We cleaned up some, but there was no food in the house—"

She waited, then her voice was strained, like a wild horse that might break loose and kick a hole in the fence.

"I'm suggesting they need some kind of adult caregiver to stop by once a week or so. Somebody to do their shopping and some housecleaning, and monitor your father's health."

Whatever he said next really made her mad. Her voice kicked up a notch.

"This isn't about Andie." Silence.

"I am not . . . I am *not* trying to prove they are incapable of taking care of her—"

Dead air, then she spoke so softly I could barely hear. "And for your information, we do not need her money."

Her voice rose again. "I'm saying that you don't realize the seriousness of their situation."

Silence again.

"How long has it been since you last saw them?" she asked, then a split second later, "Well, it may not be any of my business, but I think you'll be shocked the next time you do. You know, I only called because I wanted to help."

A brief silence, then, "You bet it's your responsibility, and you'd better take it more seriously, for your parents' sake."

Ding! She must've slammed the phone down. I heard her get up from the bed, and I ran light-footed down the hall back to my room.

In my bed, I thought about how I could be that person, the one who did their housecleaning and shopping. Okay, maybe not the shopping. Not yet. But Pine Run was a small town, and I could get around on my bike if I had to. And in a year I'd have my learner's permit, so Grandma wouldn't even have to drive. They needed me now more than ever.

So Uncle Greg had accused Marty of trying to prove Grandma was unfit to have custody. She had already given me up, but I guess she hadn't contacted him yet about handing me over when school was out.

The thought of living with Uncle Greg and Aunt Robin almost made me hyperventilate. I'd be a free babysitter for my obnoxious cousins, Brent and Kyle. Slave labor, like Cinderella. And I'd have to move to Canada. I saw a travel brochure about their town once. It was way up in the northwest—some kind of winter resort—and the scenery was beautiful. The brochure said there were sixty-five frost-free days every year. Like that was a good thing.

Dad told Mom once that Greg would be rich if he banked his money instead of drinking it away. Mom had shushed him. I was too young to understand then, picturing a cup stuffed with dollar bills and Uncle Greg trying to drink it. I was so fixated on the idea, I swallowed a dime, just to see if I could do it. Mom had to look for it later, which was gross.

But then Uncle Greg caused a big argument during a July Fourth barbecue, and Dad took away his car keys, so then he took a swing at Dad. There were beer cans everywhere, and Uncle Greg wanted to make a run to 7-11. That's when it all added up.

Uncle Greg didn't really want to pay someone to help Grandma and Grandpa, so if he got custody of me, and I handed over my money, maybe he'd let me stay in Pine Run.

I was lying on my bed, trying to figure it all out and swallowing hard at how old Grandpa looked in the hospital. Even Grandma seemed different over Easter. She moved slower and lost things and got snippy with me over nothing. Sometimes it would hurt my feelings, but I knew she didn't mean it.

Had they always been that way, and it had seemed normal because I lived with them? I tried to remember, but it was fuzzing over, just like Grandma's handwriting. I could hardly understand the last letter she wrote to me.

They were getting older and older, and I couldn't stop it.

It wasn't fair, all this stuff that was happening. I dug under my bed for Mom's Bible, frantically flipping pages, hungry for highlighter. I stopped at Philippians. It was a rainbow of color. Near the end of the book, in hot pink, with a star in the margin, was the promise *I can do everything through him who gives me strength.*

It was just like Marty said when we went to see Grandpa. She'd gone through a lot too, and seemed to think it worked.

I asked God to give me strength to do whatever I needed to, and it's a good thing I did. It seemed like nothing could be harder than everything I'd gone through already.

CHAPTER 29

Marty

The car chugged and sputtered to a stop in the middle of traffic in front of the elementary school, exhaling with a sigh. The girls hopped out with a quick *Bye* and ran. I cranked the key, but the engine refused to turn over. Switching on my flashers, I waved people around, enduring the looks of angry parents who were trying to get to work on time.

Dad arrived five minutes later to find me sitting alone in front of the school blocking the fire lane. Together we pushed the car into an empty parking space. He was pretty sure it was the battery, but when he hooked up the jumper cables, it wouldn't hold a charge.

The secretary in the school office said we could leave the car there for a few hours while he got a new battery. She wasn't particularly agreeable about it, and made sure we understood that it would be towed if not moved by the end of the school day.

I couldn't report to work until it was taken care of. The added expense of a battery put a real dent in my grocery budget, which was already crunched by getting to work late that day.

I wondered if my express trip to Redding had shortened its life.

Dad had spotted a leak of some kind while he worked on the car. I spent the evening in a lawn chair handing him tools as he fooled with the transmission. He finally got around to the subject of Julian's visit to the market.

"What kind of trouble you in with the health inspector?" he asked, his words muffled from his position under the hood.

I picked at a loose thumbnail. "I'm not in trouble. Not unless I do it again. I'm so stupid. I knew better." My acrylic nail flicked off onto the garage floor. "I don't know what made me think I could make a go of it."

"You were making a go of it. That's the problem, far as I can see. Hand me that filter."

I handed it over. "Dropping that cake was a complete accident. Believe me, I was tempted to throw it. But that thing took me two days to decorate."

"'Course you wouldn't throw it. County official and all. You were just upset."

I crossed my arms and my legs and jiggled my foot. "He was so . . . smug. Telling me I'm breaking the law selling my little goodies, like I was some mafia boss."

He came out from under the hood and stretched. "You know you need permits, girl." He dug around in his toolbox for a funnel and dove back inside the hood.

"Gosh, Dad. Couldn't you just say 'he done me wrong'?"

"Man's just doing his job protecting the public. Can't say as I've seen him before. Must be new." He reached a hand toward me. "Hand me that tranny fluid."

I handed it over carefully so that it didn't drip onto my clothes.

"It was just a few cookies and cinnamon rolls and biscotti. I mean, it's been years since the health department showed up at the drive-in."

Dad poured transmission fluid like cherry cough syrup into the funnel.

"Farmers market's a different kettle of fish. We've just been lucky. Or maybe the old health inspector got comfortable. We'll have to cowboy up before we open the drive-in. In case this new fella takes notice."

"It's my fault if he does." I stood up and wrapped my arms across my chest against the chill.

Dad emerged from under the hood and wiped his hands on a rag he kept stuffed in his pocket. "You know him? I recall you using his given name."

"I don't *know* him. I met him at the school carnival," I said while folding up my lawn chair and leaning it against the garage wall. "And I've seen him at church a couple times."

He got in the car and turned on the ignition, letting it idle. Then he got out of the car and reached back under the hood, pulling out the dipstick. "If you want help gettin' your bakery set up, call the man. He seems willing." He wiped the dipstick with a rag and reinserted it to check the fluid level. He frowned at the results. "May need a flush."

"I'm not up for more humiliation, Dad."

He looked over the top of his bifocals at me and lifted his eyebrows. "I don't think humiliation's what he's got in mind."

I blushed. "Oh, Dad."

He opened the trunk and put an extra bottle of transmission fluid and the funnel into the box with the garden gloves and the spade.

"Baby her along," he said, closing the hood. "We got to get a few more miles out of her."

I called Dr. Shafer's office about the results from my blood work, and the nurse told me to come in. I refused the antidepressant he wanted to prescribe. After taking my blood pressure, he insisted that I take a little red pill once a day to stabilize it, and I knew it would be foolish to refuse. I'd need to control my blood pressure if I ever faced Julian again.

I'd rehashed the scene a million times, wondering what rumors would now circulate at the farmers market, knowing I couldn't face those vendors so soon after my crime. The following Saturday, I dragged Deja out of bed and sent her down in my place to help Dad set up. Forcing her to help on a Saturday morning before daylight was an ugly scene. She dragged herself back to bed when she was done, complaining that people kept hassling her for cinnamon rolls during setup.

I even avoided church, just in case Julian was there, and that did me and the girls no good.

So many doubts clouded my judgment and undermined my confidence. Where in the world could I find the money to start a business, or find a kitchen that the health department would approve? What made me think my baking was anything special?

What if my stupid antics did call attention to the drive-in? We did our best to keep it clean and rodent-free, but you never knew what a zealous health inspector would find, especially if he'd been embarrassed at the farmers market and had a bone to pick. And if the drive-in closed, or if the repairs were extensive, we'd never be able to make ends meet.

Suddenly it dawned on me. The kitchen. We had a kitchen at

the drive-in. We had a sink and an oven and a freezer. And a permit. Right on our own property. Right under my nose.

It would have to pass inspection. Did I dare show it to Julian? He would either allow me to use it to bake, or find major issues with it and close us down completely.

Snagging the keys from the hook in the kitchen, I crossed the parking lot to check the condition of the snack shack. The lock gave a little resistance after so many months of disuse, but finally relented. Silence met me as I opened the door—a good sign that mice were absent. The cement block building didn't allow many points of entry for creepy crawlies except the drains, but the stale, funereal air made their presence seem likely all the same.

I stepped inside. The deep double sink was scrubbed clean. The drain in the floor lent a leisurely tilt toward the center of the room and never backed up with icky water. The behemoth oven, an original part of the drive-in, could still simulate the surface of the sun and cook the interior of the building on a hot summer night. Although Dad needed to tinker with it occasionally, it was dependable.

It would do. That evening, I checked with Dad about my plan so he would be aware of the risk I was taking, in case he thought we had something to worry about. He shrugged and said it was better to find out if there were any problems before summer.

It still took two weeks to gather the nerve to call Julian's office. I smoothed out his business card, which I'd dug from the trash and taped together the night of the offense. I left a brief, awkward message on his voice mail, but no phone number. Another few days passed before I gathered the nerve to try again. This time he answered, sounding pleasantly businesslike.

"Mrs. Winslow, I can't return your calls if you don't leave a number."

My cheeks grew hot. Had I taken my blood pressure pill that morning?

"I was afraid you might still be angry about the cake."

"Well, I am still picking green icing from my shoes."

"It was a stupid accident. I apologize."

"All right, officially I'll call it an accident. It's never smart to lose your temper with a county official—"

"I agree."

"But if you *had* lost your temper, I think, in your case, there may have been extenuating circumstances."

I blinked. Was he toying with me? "What do you mean?"

"Well, the last time I saw you at church, I believe you were having a difficult time."

This was so out of context that I had to stop and think what he meant. On his end, I heard creaking, like he was shifting in his office chair. When I didn't answer, he continued.

"I gather it had something to do with a recent loss in your family. A child, I believe."

Ginger's anniversary.

"I guess, under the circumstances, you might have been feeling extremely emotional. It's understandable."

I considered hanging up. "I have been under a great deal of stress lately."

"I wasn't trying to discourage you from opening a bakery. But you do have to go about it the right way." He paused. "Is that something you want?"

My moment of truth. I stood poised on a high dive, the smooth, unbroken surface far below reflecting my fear and posing a glassy barrier to my dreams. But here was a man who wanted to help me. Someone who knew what he was doing. I couldn't let this moment pass.

I arched and took the plunge.

"Yes, it is," I said. "What do I need to do first?"

During the next twenty minutes I gave Julian a brief rundown of my experience as a baker for Ursula and Guy back in Elko.

He explained the application process and gave me a list of forms and permits to download. He also made an appointment for me to stop by his office one afternoon after my shift to make sure the paperwork was completed properly. If things went well, I would show him the drive-in kitchen and hope for the best.

I decided to take one step at a time, and not worry about money or a kitchen or failure in general. I sent up a prayer. If God wanted it to happen, it would.

CHAPTER 30

Andie

I don't know what was wrong with Deja. Maybe she saw her portrait on my binder, or maybe she still blamed me because Cyclops was too stupid to find his way home. Whatever it was, she had me in her sights.

She was there when we got the call that Grandpa had pneumonia.

"Too bad you weren't there to help Grampy," she droned from her bed, intently painting her nails. "I bet your grammy's afraid he'll die."

"It's not my fault he's in the hospital," I said, jamming my pillow into a clean pillowcase. "Nobody said he was going to die."

"Sure." She held up a nail and blew on it. "Who's looking after your grammy? You know, old people don't eat much when they're alone."

Punching the pillow with my fist, I said, "My grandma can take care of herself."

I didn't really believe that. I hadn't heard from Uncle Greg since Grandpa checked into the hospital. I wondered if he'd taken Marty's advice and hired someone to help.

Deja gave me little digs whenever we were alone. I tried to ignore her, but it was working on me. I found myself staring into space during homework, or in the library, or watching TV. I chewed off my nails until the cuticles were sore and bleeding.

Grandma's phone rang busy for days, and the one time it really rang, no one picked up. I pestered Marty until she was sorry to see me coming.

"Marty, will you call the hospital again for me?"

She sighed. "We'll try again after supper. Get plates out of the dishwasher, please, Ging—Andie," she said, then went on without looking at me, "and the forks."

She had never called me Ginger before. I wondered, why now? I caught sight of myself in the hall mirror when I went to call Carl for dinner. Marty had only called attention to the obvious—what everyone else could see except me. I was morphing into Ginger. I sat in Ginger's chair at dinner. I slept in Ginger's bed, in Ginger's room. I was assimilating.

That night I sat in Winnie's chair at dinner instead, just to be different. When Winnie started to complain, Marty shushed her and changed the subject. After dinner Marty called the hospital without even looking up the number.

She had connected with Pat, one of the night nurses, when we'd visited the hospital. So when we were lucky enough to reach Pat at the nurses' station, she filled us in on Grandpa's condition, even though it was against regulations. She said his condition was "guarded." Whatever that meant. Marty gave her our phone number in case there was any major change, and she promised to call us. Marty tried to reassure me, but worry creased her forehead.

"When can we go see him again?" I asked.

Marty pinched the bridge of her nose and squeezed her eyes shut for a second. "We'll try to go this weekend. I'll ask for another day off."

Winnie brought in the mail while I was doing homework at the kitchen table, and dumped it in the middle of my social studies book. In the stack of mail was an official-looking envelope addressed to Matilda Winslow from an attorney's office in Canada. I picked it out of the stack and took it to Marty in the laundry room.

She stopped sorting when she saw the return address, and looked up at me. Ripping off the end, she puffed it open with a breath, then snapped open the document. Speed-reading, she shook her head.

"Your Uncle Greg has petitioned for custody. There's a hearing set for June fourth in the judge's chambers." She folded it slowly and stuffed it back into the envelope.

I looked down at the pile of dirty sheets and towels on the floor, feeling soiled and crumpled myself. This wasn't what I wanted, but if the judge made it official, I'd have to go. No one cared at all what I wanted.

"I know we talked about going to your uncle's after school is out. But he's doing this on his own. I never contacted him about it." She smiled shyly. "I guess I was hoping you'd change your mind and stay with us." She reached out and took my hand, squeezing it gently. "We can fight this, if you want to."

It felt good to know she wasn't trying to get rid of me. And I didn't want to hurt her feelings. But she asked me.

"Grandma and Grandpa really need me now. I could clean their house, and . . ."

And that was about it. I couldn't drive them to Safeway, or pick up their medicine at the drugstore, or take them to the doctor.

Marty let go of my hand. The tired look on her face said she doubted it would happen.

"Well," she said, picking up her sorting where she'd left off. "We have no choice but to appear. It's in the judge's hands."

At about that time Cyclops came home. He was pretty beaten up with a torn ear and scabs all over his body, so Marty took him to the vet. As it turned out, Cyclops was pregnant.

I didn't know how they could have been so wrong about Cyclops being female. I'd never actually picked him—her—up, so I didn't feel so stupid. The only one happy about it was Winnie. She started thinking up names for the kittens. Marty just looked really, really tired, and Deja's comment was, "He better not have those kittens on my bed."

I squinted at her. "Then don't let *her* in."

I wondered what kittens would do to my dosage.

I tried to call Grandma again, but got no answer. I wished I had Mrs. DeMarco's phone number. It was Tuesday. The weekend was four days away.

CHAPTER 31

Marty

I drifted to a stop across the street from the abandoned building. The ripped awning had been stripped away. A man in paint-stained coveralls chipped at bubbled and flaked paint on the front of the building. A door on the side opened to the alley, and another man dragged out refuse, tossing it into a Dumpster. A realtor's sign rested in the now-sparkling front window.

I stared at their progress until I knew I'd be late for work. Then I numbly signaled, wrestled the car into drive, and pulled into traffic. Losing the building was my payment for so stupidly breaking the law. I didn't deserve a bakery if I couldn't even take care of the basics. At that point, I seriously needed those antidepressants.

There was no way I could afford to buy that building. I thought of Andie's money, just sitting there in a bank account, of no use to anyone.

Was it reason enough to want to change my mind about letting her leave at the end of the school year? And did that make me a bad mother, even to wonder about it?

Yes, because then her grandparents would be right about me.

So many bills, so little money. The car had a new noise I couldn't identify, and it fought me whenever I tried to put it into gear. Dad needed an expensive part for the drive-in projector. And so it went.

On top of everything else, when I'd gotten around to tallying up the resale totals from the snack shack for our tax return, I unearthed some disturbing news. I was now certain that Deja had been skimming money from the register. For that much money to disappear in the short time that Andie worked there would have been obvious. Now I'd have to confront Deja about the thefts.

But money was only one of the disloyal reasons to keep Andie, I realized then. If I was honest deep in my gut, the other reason was my need for her to fill a void in our family. I'd even called her Ginger one night at dinner. It tripped over my tongue and slapped her in the face. The coldness had curled from her like dry ice, and I knew I'd never convince her it was a simple, stupid mistake.

Her uncle wanted her now. I could tell she didn't like him very much. I suspected he wanted her as a live-in housekeeper for her grandparents, just as she wanted also. But if he got custody of her, and I discovered that she was caring for her grandparents alone, I would be the supreme witch for turning him in and destroying her hopes. She would never love me then.

Perhaps it was time to let her go. Give her up and let her be happy with her grandparents, if it was possible. Just go on with my life and try to forget. But what was all of this about, if not to love her and keep her?

A knock on the driver's side window made me jump. Jo stood outside the car, bent over slightly, looking in.

"You going to stay in there all day, or go to work?" she asked, her voice muffled through the glass.

Looking around, I realized I had made my way to work from the old building and was parked in the employee parking area with no memory of how I'd gotten there. Funny how your body runs on instinct when you're stressed.

I gathered my purse and got out. "Jo, you scared me to death."

"What in the world are you doin' in there? Daydreaming about Mr. Right?" she teased as we headed inside.

"I'm just thinking about everything I need to do, that's all." We nodded at coworkers as we passed. "Remind me to tell Dad I need the truck on Saturday to take Andie to see her grandparents."

"Her grandpa still in ICU?"

"No, he's slowly improving. But they're worried about pneumonia."

"I'm not feeling so hot myself."

I glanced at Jo. She did look pale. I selfishly hoped she wouldn't get worse over the weekend and ask me to fill in for her. No matter how inconvenient another trip to Pine Run would be, I had no choice but to arrange to get the truck and go. The Toyota would never make it.

I hoped her grandfather would.

Our computer was acting buggy, so we went to the library to download the application information. My dream was only a fragmented black-and-white outline at that point, like a kid's dot-to-dot. Getting help from the librarian meant sharing my hopes with one more person, coloring in the steps with progress or setting myself up for more public failure.

Winnie used her library card to check out several books about kitten care. I almost reminded her that we couldn't keep Cyclops's kittens. But then I realized it might not matter.

When the librarian asked Andie if she wanted a card, she said she already had a card for Pine Run, and declined. I didn't say a word.

By June Andie could be gone from our lives. With a mixture of guilt and relief, I realized how much easier our lives would be, and how much emptier.

CHAPTER 32

Andie

Deja got a ride with Summer's mom after school on Wednesday and beat us home. Marty picked us up instead of Carl and dropped Winnie off at Rae's house before she took me home. Perfect Rae. Whatever. Then Marty went back to work to fill in for Jo, who had the flu.

"You got a call," Deja said to me, like it was barely worth her attention. "Some guy in Pine Run."

My heart pounded in my throat. "Who was it?" I asked.

"Don't know. Your uncle, maybe." She pointed the remote at the TV like a gun and punched channels.

"What did he say? Deja, this is really important."

She ignored me. I stood between her and the TV.

"He said your grandpa might die. Now, move!"

I ripped the remote out of her hand and gritted my teeth, willing myself not to cry. "Are you lying, Deja?"

She glanced at my other hand, which had balled into a fist. I'd never hit anyone before, but I was on the edge. A flicker of fear spasmed her face as she jumped up from the couch. "Get away from me," she said. "Go look for yourself."

I threw down the remote and ran to check the caller ID.

She called after me, "You're dead when Grandpa gets back."

The area code on one call was for Pine Run. I called the number back. The hospital operator answered, and I said, "I need the room of Mr. Orville James, please."

There was elevator music. Then someone picked up.

"Hello? Hello, Greg? Is that you?" Grandma's voice shrilled against noises in the background.

"No, Grandma, it's Andie!" I shouted back. It sounded like there was a seal barking in the room. A sick one. "What's happening? Is Grandpa okay?"

"I can't talk now, Andie. Bye."

She didn't exactly hang up the phone, but must have set the receiver down in the cradle wrong. I guessed that was why her home phone was always busy.

The voices were garbled. It sounded like a ton of people were in the room. I figured out that the barking seal was Grandpa. He coughed so hard, I thought he would split open, then—a dial tone, just like an Alfred Hitchcock movie. Somebody must have hung up.

Slowly, I hung up the phone, biting my lower lip and feeling tears sting my nose.

I should've been there; then maybe bad things wouldn't have happened.

Please, I reminded myself. I was nobody. Just being there wouldn't change anything in the world.

I took a couple of cleansing breaths, but I couldn't shake it. The feeling probed into deep, secret places. *It wasn't my fault,* I wanted to shout. *I'm only a kid.*

When I thought of Grandpa looking small in that bed, in a jungle of tubes, I couldn't see his face clearly. That's when I realized it wasn't about him. Well, maybe a little, but mostly it was about Mom and Dad. They were the ones I couldn't help. They were the ones I couldn't see clearly anymore.

A wave of sadness pulled me under. I felt tangled in it, held down, squeezing the breath out of me. I whimpered, and covered my mouth with my hands. In my head, I knew that being with Mom and Dad wouldn't have changed a thing either. I would have died too. But nothing makes sense when you feel that way.

I couldn't change what would happen to Grandpa. But I couldn't live with the doubt and guilt if he died and I wasn't with him. I couldn't stand to get another postcard from the beyond that said, *Why weren't you here?*

I had to see for myself.

I had to go now. I was standing by the checkout in Walgreens again with that candy bar warming in my fist, watching the door of opportunity flutter open right in front of me, ready to close shut.

I looked at the clock. It was getting late, and soon Marty would be home. I couldn't wait any longer.

I went to my room and dumped out my backpack. I threw in some clean clothes, my toothbrush, my book, and Mom's Bible. I found my Mickey pin and slipped it into my pocket for luck. Shrugging on my jacket, I hesitated. How would I get there? I'd spent my last dollar on Deja's birthday, and the drive-in hadn't opened yet. I couldn't get to Pine Run without money.

Deja's money sock. I checked the living room to be sure she was watching TV. Then I dug through her top drawer. The sock with the roll of bills in the toe was gone. I checked her other drawers, but no luck. I almost gave up, but she couldn't have spent all that money so fast with nothing to show for it. Then I saw Ridley's old jacket hanging in her closet. She'd never returned it, and on a hunch, I slipped my hand into the pocket. Bingo.

Where in the world did she get all that money? I took out seventy-five dollars. It barely made a dent in the roll. When I stuck the rest back into the pocket, I felt something hard and pulled it out. Her old school ID card.

It was kind of a shock looking at her picture, because it was like I was looking at myself, only older. Her hair was still blonde then. Freaky. A lock of hair had fallen across her right eye, and she looked totally disgusted.

Maybe it was a sign. What if I got carded at the bus station? I didn't know the rules about kids traveling alone. I looked up in the mirror above her dresser and pulled loose a lock of hair, letting it fall across my eye. Then I practiced looking snotty. I could pass for fifteen. Deja and I could be twins. Ew.

I recognized the pink T-shirt she was wearing in the picture, the old one with a heart-shaped skull on the front. I quietly dug around for it in her drawers. I might have to stuff the front to look older. I grabbed one of her dark lipsticks and her eyeliner too.

At a theater class I took when I was ten, I'd learned that getting people to believe you is more in your attitude and body language than in makeup or costumes. I shoved the shirt in my backpack along with the money. This could be the performance of my life.

It was crazy, and possibly dangerous to leave like this. But I didn't see any choice. Carl was gone, and Winnie was at Rae's, and Marty wasn't due back for a while. At least I'd have a head start.

Marty. Oh, man. If I left now, she'd never want me back.

I tiptoed into her room, took the Mickey pin out of my pocket, and left it on her dresser as kind of a peace offering. Maybe he would bring her luck. I didn't want to hurt her feelings. I looked around at the fluffy pillows and the pictures of Ginger on her nightstand one last time. Ginger and I suddenly had more in common. We both hurt Marty, and we didn't even mean to.

I was running out of time. I stuck my head into the living room as I headed to the kitchen.

"Where's Carl?"

"Dunno. Gone. Lucky for you." Deja answered without looking up from *Ferris Bueller's Day Off*. Ferris was speaking to the camera, explaining how to fake clammy hands. I saw her lick one of her palms and gag.

Carl's absence would definitely make my escape easier. Things were falling into place. I scoped out the food situation. It would be dark when I got to Pine Run. I checked the cookie jar and found oatmeal cookies and chocolate chips, so I scooped up a handful and tossed them into my backpack, along with a banana and a drink box.

I looked up the address of the bus station in the phone book. The street sounded familiar, but I'd have to call for directions, and I couldn't do that from the house. I dug in the junk drawer for quarters.

I grabbed my sweatshirt and slipped out the back door, keeping to the bushes until I was out of sight of the house and parking lot. Weaving my way behind stores and strip malls, I found a pay phone and called the bus station. A ticket to Pine Run was forty-five dollars.

I went into a bathroom at the mini-mart, changed into Deja's shirt, messed up my hair for effect, and pulled some hair down over one eye. I draped lots of paper towels on the sink so I could get closer to the mirror without getting icky yuck on my shirt when I put on the eyeliner. Boy, that stuff takes practice. I put on lipstick and stood back to take a look. Perfect. I looked like a slut.

I peeled enough money off the roll for the ticket, put that money in my front pocket, and put the rest in my backpack. I posed a couple of times in front of the mirror until I had it down.

Thirty minutes later I was at the bus station, shaking inside and wanting to hurl. At the last minute I took out Deja's ID and memorized her birthday, just in case. Mentally, I got into character. I slouched, let my backpack hang carelessly from one shoulder, and looked totally bored. Taking a deep breath, I went up to the window and got in line to buy my ticket.

"One ticket to Pine Run." I slapped the money down on the counter and added "please," like I really didn't mean it.

He glanced up at me and spoke in a monotone. "No one fourteen or under without a guardian for night arrivals."

"Duh." I tossed the ID at him.

He scanned it, lifting an eyebrow. "This ID's old."

"No kidding. My mom melted my new one when she threw my jeans in the dryer instead of hanging them up like I told her to. *She* melted it, not me, and I'm not paying ten bucks for another one. I don't need one anyway; the principal's office knows me."

Was I talking too much? I rolled my eyes for effect. "My birthday's right there. I turned sixteen March eleventh."

He studied the picture. I could tell I was losing him. I exhaled in disgust and gave him my best "Deja." Then I hooked my thumbs in my shirt and said, like he was impaired, spitting out the last word, "I'm wearing the same *shirt*."

Slowly he took the money and gave me the ticket for the six-thirty bus. I gave a fakey smile and another insincere "thanks" and turned away. I don't know how Deja could stand to treat people like this all the time.

I sat down away from the windows in case Marty cruised by,

praying the guy wouldn't come to his senses. I tried to breathe normally.

Boy, some really scuzzy people hung around there. And a lot of crying babies with tired, angry parents, and homeless people.

"Hey, you. Stop jigglin' the seat," a woman shouted.

I looked down to the end of the row, wondering who was being yelled at, and realized it was me. But who was doing the yelling? A giant pile of dirty laundry with arms and legs sat there. I didn't know where the sound was coming from until I saw a face peeking out of a little window of material, like it had been swallowed. The woman was wearing a ton of clothes at once—scarves, shirts, pants, hats, coats, a nightgown, blankets. Layers and layers. Beside her on the floor were bags of junk. She was either homeless or on her way to the dump. She looked like a giant yarn ball that had rolled around picking up pricklies and trash.

"Stop jigglin' the seat, or I'm coming down there!" she shouted, baring her teeth and spitting.

The clerk yelled at us. "Do I have to call the cops?"

My head jerked in his direction. Why did this wacko woman have to call attention to me? The man's red face inflated. He sat wedged so tightly in the small window, I knew that if I bolted it would take him time to back out of his cubicle and come after me. But the crazy lady had his full attention. He knew her, all right. It must be part of his job to watch for crazies. And runaways.

She jerked her head in my direction. "She'll have the whole place down around our heads if she don't stop that shakin'!" she yelled, spiking it with words I hadn't heard since that time Uncle Greg argued with Dad over the car keys. I forgot to stay in character.

The ticket man waved the phone receiver in the air and pointed it toward the woman. "Sylvia, you settle or I'm calling the sheriff again." To me, he said, "You. Stop shaking the seat."

Then I realized my legs were bouncing on their own like a windup toy, and all the plastic chairs were connected and shaking. I got up and walked out of his line of sight, clutching my backpack to my chest to keep from brushing against anybody weird. I leaned back against the dirty wall and slid down to a crouching position to get hold of myself.

At that point, I'd pretty much blown my cover, and seriously considered going back to Marty's. I could put Deja's money back in her drawer and wait for the weekend to go see Grandpa. Maybe Marty wasn't even home yet, and I could sneak in before they realized I was gone. She'd be mad if she caught me coming back, but not nearly as mad as if I went through with it.

The noises in Grandpa's room kept playing in my head. Did the call from Pine Run really say he was bad off? I didn't trust Deja, but if the news was bad, she'd enjoy telling me about it. I should have been in Pine Run all along.

I wavered in limbo and chewed the raw skin around my nails until it stung. The speaker announced my bus number. Time to decide.

Marty had already given me up. I didn't belong to Grandma and Grandpa anymore, and I didn't yet belong to Uncle Greg. Winnie had Rae now, and Natalie had ditched me a long time ago. I was nobody's, so why should it matter to anyone what I did?

Last call for the bus to Pine Run and all points east.

Leaving the bus station would mean more than just getting on a bus with strangers—okay, with scary strangers. It would mean slamming the door on the little bit of security I'd found at Marty's. Was it really so bad there? And could I live there if Grandpa died and I'd been too scared to do anything about it?

The door to freedom was slamming shut. I forced myself to remember how I'd felt in Walgreens when I'd first been tempted to do what I wanted, instead of what everyone else wanted.

I nosed a sliver of courage buried deep inside me and pushed aside all the what-ifs. I wasn't chicken. I'd already faced more stuff than a lot of grown-ups. I could do this.

Shouldering my backpack, I put one foot in front of the other, left the safety of the station, wove my way through creepy strangers, and boarded the bus.

I chose a seat up front near the bus driver, but not so close that he might make conversation. They probably got runaways all the time. Technically, I wasn't running away. I knew where I was going, and had someone at the other end of the line. So what if they weren't expecting me.

I kept my nose buried in *The Fellowship of the Ring,* even though it was hard to stay focused with my stomach queasy from the bus jerking to a stop at every corner between the bus station and the freeway. Once we were on the freeway, my stomach settled down and I ate some of my snack.

I used the bottom of Deja's shirt to wipe off the crumbs and dark lipstick. Maybe I'd mail it back to her that way. Boy, would she be ticked. The lipstick smeared bloodred into the heart shape. What was happening to me? It had never felt good to be mean before.

I turned to the window and pretended to sleep, but I was really listening, feeling that old need to will the driver to stay awake. The light got soft and purpley outside, and the lights came on in the bus. The windows mirrored the people I was trying to avoid. I kept a tight grip on my backpack.

I kept up the Deja persona because that way, people left me alone. Or maybe they left me alone because Someone was watching out for me.

It took about two and a half hours to reach Pine Run, with all the stops we made. It gave me a lot of time to think. For the most part, I felt numb, free-falling without knowing where or when I'd land.

It felt like I'd been working without a safety net ever since I found out Grandma and Grandpa were thinking about giving me up. This was the closing act, and I really needed to know the net was there to catch me if I fell.

I imagined that Grandma, Grandpa, Marty, Carl—they each held a corner, and God pulled it taut. I pictured Him like the ring-master in my circus, making sure there was just enough cushion to break my fall without breaking my neck.

Well, like I said, I had a lot of time to think, and I was feeling kind of whacked out.

It seemed to take forever, but we finally passed the exit for the hospital. My heart started pumping, and I tried to keep my bearings so I'd know how to get there from the bus stop when I got off. We passed my old middle school. The lighted sign said JUNE 3 LAST DAY OF SCHOOL and JUNE 4 GRADUATION, and I watched it until it was out of sight. It was only a month away. I should be there, graduating with my friends.

We got to Pine Run fifteen minutes ahead of schedule. It was nine o'clock when I stepped off the bus alone onto the dark, empty street. The bus pulled away, and I could hardly put two words together in my head to ask God to keep me safe.

CHAPTER 33

Marty

Dad called me at work early in the afternoon to say he'd found the part for the projector in Oakland, but he wouldn't be back in time to pick up the girls from school. I told him I'd take them home, and reminded him that I needed the truck on Saturday to take Andie to Pine Run.

For two days Jo had put up a good fight against whatever bug she had, but she'd turned almost transparent by lunch and Robert let her go home. I took a break to pick up the girls from school, drop Winnie at Rae's, and take Andie home. Then I raced back to finish both my shift and Jo's, even though it meant cutting it close for my appointment with Julian. I considered leaving him a message on his voice mail that I might be a few minutes late, but changed my mind. What if he answered?

After work I hurried home with just enough time to get cleaned up for my appointment. I yanked slacks and sweaters, skirts and jackets from their hangers, trying to find something businesslike, yet attractive. I felt nervous about facing him for the first time since the incident. My manila folder was all ready with the completed application. But if I was honest, I had to admit it was more than just the incident or the permit process that twisted a knot in my belly. I felt an undeniable attraction for him.

Keep focused on the business aspect of the meeting, I told myself.

After slipping on black slacks and a pale blue sweater, the next step was to smooth my hair into a french braid. I stood before my mirror with a hairclip in my teeth, trying to make my fingers cooperate.

That's when I noticed a Mickey pin on the dresser. He rode a surfboard, and it wasn't one of mine. I turned it over and examined the black rubber Mickey ears on the back. It was Andie's. Why was it in my room?

I stuck my head into her bedroom to ask about it, but she wasn't reading on her bed as usual. I found Deja in the living room.

"Deja, where's Andie?"

"Dunno," she said without looking up from the TV.

The house lay quiet, except for the background noise of the movie. I peered through the kitchen window into the backyard, expecting to see Andie huddled under her favorite reading tree, even though the sky was clouding up.

I went back into the living room and looked out the screen door. "When was the last time you saw her?"

"Um . . . maybe when the movie started."

"How far is the movie?"

"Almost over."

Almost over. Two hours had gone by, at least.

"Did she say anything?"

"Hm?"

"Deja!"

She looked up in surprise.

"Pay attention to me. Did she leave? Where is she?"

"I don't know," she said, looking back to the TV. "I'm not her babysitter."

Her body language said she knew more than she let on. I took the remote and turned off the TV. She glanced up to protest, but when she saw my expression, her complaint died on her lips.

"Talk," I commanded. "What happened when she came home?"

She stared at the floor and hugged the couch cushion to her chest. "Andie's uncle called from Pine Run before she got home, and when I told her, she flipped out."

"Her uncle? What did he want?"

"I don't know. He said he'd call back later."

"And she flipped out? Just because he called?"

She shook her head. "She's wacko."

I looked at the Mickey pin again, the wheels turning in my head. Andie kept close tabs on her pins. One wouldn't fall carelessly and end up on my dresser. She had to have put it there herself. But why?

I glanced at my watch. She was probably around somewhere. I'd need to leave in a minute to make my appointment with Julian on time, but I checked out her room once more. Nothing seemed out of place.

Call it mother's intuition, but something wasn't right. The room was too perfect, the bedspread too neat. Her backpack wasn't tossed in a heap in the corner. In fact, it wasn't there at all. Her copy of *The Fellowship of the Ring* was missing from her nightstand.

A sour taste of foreboding began in the back of my throat. I dropped to my hands and knees and dug beneath her bed.

Her mother's Bible was gone.

Andie had run away.

CHAPTER 34

Andie

This was crazy. I got completely turned around when we left the freeway. Pine Run looked like a ghost town, with all the stores closed and trash blowing across the street. The old-fashioned streetlamps glowed like alien orbs hanging in the darkness.

I found a pay phone by the bus stop and called the hospital. I tried to sound older and more sure of myself, and the operator gave me directions without any problems. She sounded too tired to notice anything out of the ordinary. She said it was only about a mile or so to the hospital from downtown.

It was really creepy, walking in the dark to the hospital, but I didn't have a choice. I finally found my head voice and prayed the whole way like a mantra, hoping that I hadn't maxed out my number of prayers allowed for the year, and that God wouldn't think I was too stupid to help.

At the end of the street, the sidewalk ended, and I stepped off into nothing until my foot finally hit dirt and jammed my head onto my neck. I left the weird orb-lamps behind me, and gradually my eyes adjusted to the faint light of a full moon. I walked along the road, way off to the right, so when cars came by I could jump into the bushes. The crunch of my feet on gravel sounded so loud, I could have been dragging cans. Dogs barked from almost every house I passed. Where there was a fenced yard close to the road, the dog would lunge at me and I'd freeze, afraid I'd wet my pants, until I realized it couldn't get to me. Then I'd hurry on so the dog would shut up and the owners wouldn't look out the window.

The good thing about the gravel crunching was that I'd know if someone was following me. About halfway there, a car pulled off the road and the driver got out. I ran under the trees and squatted in the bushes where I could watch him. He was only checking his mailbox. He kept banging it to get it to stay shut. His car door slammed, and he pulled away.

I had to pee in the bushes after that. Things scurried in the leaves. Strange squeaks and calls spooked me; I knew they were probably nice, furry animals in the daylight. I promised God that if only He kept me safe, I would never do this again. Then I prayed for Grandpa.

"Please God, keep him safe. More than me."

I started back along the road where the street was dark again, and finally saw the faraway glow of parking lot lights across a field. I couldn't risk being seen on the driveway up to the hospital, though. It was lit up like a prison yard.

I cut through an open meadow, hoping I wouldn't run into any skunks or coyotes. A couple of times I stumbled, hearing rustling in the bushes nearby. I stepped into water and got muddy up to my ankles. It turned out to be some kind of swamp, and I had to find my way around it without getting into deeper water. Once I stumbled and got my hands muddy when I put them out to catch myself. Luckily, the moon reflected on patches of pond water, and I finally made it around. I had to keep going—I was too close to give up now.

I sneaked around to the front of the building, but there were too many people around to go in yet. I hid out in the meadow until the parking lot was empty. Then I discovered they locked the front doors at nine o'clock, and I had to go around to the emergency entrance. That entrance had automatic doors, like Walgreens, and I took it for a good sign. It was mostly deserted. I could see a person sitting at a desk inside, but it was a slow night for emergencies. I needed a small distraction to sneak in unnoticed.

The sprinklers came on in front of the building and scared me, hissing and spitting in the dark. It was nine thirty before a car pulled up and people got out. It looked like a pregnant woman, and I figured she would keep the nurses busy. I got the courage to walk in like any other visitor, but just before the automatic doors slid open, I saw my reflection. I was so dirty, I should've been pushing a shopping cart with Sylvia. My hair was wild, and my hands and legs were muddy almost to my knees. I stepped aside to wash my muddy hands in the sprinklers and tighten my hair in a scrunchie I found in my pocket. I rubbed my legs with cold, wet leaves and scrubbed my shoes on the wet grass. I kept glancing at the parking lot, feeling exposed the whole time with the path lighting shining on me. But it would be pretty stupid to leave a trail of footprints all the way to Grandpa's room.

Looking through the glass doors again, I waited until the nurse at the desk logged on to her computer, her head dipped down and the light from the screen glowing on her face. Gathering my courage, I slipped in and racewalked around the corner, keeping low.

I went into the first bathroom I could find and locked myself in, not breathing until I sagged onto the floor. This was harder than I thought, sneaking around, especially without a plan. When my heart stopped hammering, I washed off the dirt and the eyeliner, and wiped the mud from the sink with paper towels. I listened at the door for a long time, and looked underneath for feet, hoping no one was waiting outside to ask questions.

I looked at my watch. Nine forty-five. It was now or never. I couldn't stay there. The janitors probably cleaned at night, and they'd have keys to everything. Opening the door a crack, I saw the coast was clear. I slipped out and down the hall.

The long hallway had a portrait of the hospital's founder and some bizarre modern art, but no elevator sign. When I came to an intersection of four corridors, a big silver dome on the ceiling over my head took in my presence, like I was under a giant microscope. I crouched down out of view. Then I realized I could see into the other hallways in it. How convenient. I guess it's helpful to see oncoming traffic when you're wheeling gurneys around corners. No one was coming, so I took a right.

There, dead ahead, stood the elevator doors. Bingo.

CHAPTER 35

Marty

"Deja, this is serious. Andie is gone," I said, sliding my arms into my jacket. I slipped the Mickey pin into my pocket. "Tell me right now what really happened between the two of you. No more lies."

She sank into the corner of the couch, pulling her knees up to her chest.

"Why was she upset that her uncle called?" I demanded. "Is her grandpa worse?"

"I don't know. He only said he would call later."

"Is that what you told her? Nothing else?"

Silence.

"What did you tell her?"

"I was just teasing. Omigosh."

I crossed my arms and waited.

"I said her grandpa was really . . . bad. But I didn't tell her to run away. That's *so* not my fault!"

"You mean you said he was dying? Deja, how could you do that to someone?"

She lifted her eyes to mine—defiant. "All you care about is her," she spat. "You always take her side. 'Deja, don't upset her.' 'Be quiet in your room, Deja.' 'Don't be mean, Deja.' She's your perfect little doll. Just like Ginger."

If she had physically slapped me, it wouldn't have shocked me more. Pressing her advantage, she continued to scratch her claws across my heart.

"Winnie and I didn't exist after Ginger got sick. You never came to school, or cared if we got in trouble. You never took us anywhere. Dad couldn't even stand to be here. I thought after she died, it would be different. But nothing's different. Andie is Ginger now."

My hand went to my throat. "That's not true, Deja."

"I hate her. I hope she never comes back."

I gripped the back of the chair beside me for support, feeling pierced and bloody. Mortally wounded. That my own daughter could have stored up so much hatred without my even knowing. It was unfathomable.

Could she be right?

I couldn't deal with that now. I pushed it to the back of my mind, in the same place where I kept the knowledge that Deja had actually stolen from the family.

I groped for my purse, cell phone, keys. "When Dad gets home, tell him I've gone to look for Andie." I stopped at the door with my back to her. "I would do the same if it were you."

I stumbled out to the Toyota, got in, and turned the key in the ignition. It sputtered and coughed and shuddered, but I pumped the gas pedal and the engine caught. Feeling numb and wretched, I struggled to put the car into drive and pulled away from the house. Dusk was settling in, and I had the presence of mind to switch on the headlights as I pulled out into the street.

I knew where she was headed. But did she have the means to get to Pine Run on her own? Please, God, don't let her be hitchhiking.

I cruised the streets in town for twenty minutes before it occurred to me to check the bus station. I parked there and went in, scanning the faces. No luck. I cut in line to ask the ticket agent whether a girl of her description had gotten on a bus. His cubbie smelled like an ashtray. He squirmed a little when I asked the question.

"Lady, we don't let minors fourteen and under travel without permission."

"I know, but she could pass for older than she really is. Her name is Andie Lockhart. Winslow." I showed him a school picture. I saw recognition in his face.

"I'll check it out." He punched into his database. "Winslow?" He paused. He looked up at me. "No *Andie* Winslow."

"You have another Winslow?"

"Sorry, lady, no-can-do."

I was a woman on the edge. I practically climbed into his window, jabbing a long fingernail an inch from his nose. "Look," I snarled, "if you let my fourteen-year-old daughter get on a bus alone, you're in it up to your—"

"All right, all right, lady. Back off." He motioned for me to keep my voice down and looked furtively to the other passengers. "Name of Deja," he said, confidentially.

"Deja?" I straightened up and gave him his space back. "Deja's at home."

"Showed me her school ID. It was old, but her birth date was on it. Even had on the same shirt in the picture." He looked at me disapprovingly and tsked. "Really nasty attitude on that one."

I ignored him. "Which bus?"

"Six thirty to Pine Run. Arrives 9:15."

I raced back to the car and drove to a gas station to fill the tank before hitting the freeway. The gallons ticked by as the tank filled, like the seconds passing before she was safe again. Lights were coming on all over town, and I thought of her, alone in the dark and vulnerable and worried for her grandfather. I had to find her.

I took the on-ramp for the interstate, buckling my seat belt one-handed as I slammed my foot on the accelerator. I got the Toyota up to fifty. It was as fast as the car would go before shuddering violently. A strange noise gurgled in the engine.

It wasn't until I passed from the lights of town into the growing dark of the countryside that I realized I should call the police. Why hadn't I thought of that back at the gas station? I grabbed my cell phone, but it bleeped. BATTERY LOW. I didn't have the charger with me. I'd have to pull over and call at the next town. I dug in the change tray, searching out quarters. I had enough change for maybe one call.

I knew it would look bad, her running away like this. What would the judge say? That she obviously wasn't happy. That I was an unfit mother. That Deja was right, giving ammunition to her uncle's petition. We might lose custody of her completely.

The Mickey pin rested in my pocket. Andie had left it on my dresser for a reason. Was she sorry for leaving? Was she saying good-bye or "come and find me"?

I glanced at the clock, and deflated inside. Thirty minutes past my scheduled appointment with Julian. There was nothing to do about it. I didn't even have his number with me.

He'd probably waited in his office for fifteen or twenty minutes, then gone home. I was a flake who couldn't even show up for an appointment. He was wasting his time on me. My one chance to realize my dream, and I'd sailed away from it at fifty miles an hour in the opposite direction. All because a headstrong, rash, hurting young girl hadn't trusted me enough to wait until I got home.

CHAPTER 36

Andie

It was a nerve-racking elevator ride up to the second floor. Not because I was afraid of elevators, but what would I do if the doors opened and someone was standing there? Visiting hours were over. How would I explain being there at night without an adult? Maybe an unsuspecting candy striper would come along, and I could jump her for her uniform.

I flattened myself like a chameleon against the elevator interior. When the doors opened, I was still alone. I peeked out and down the hallway. The elevator dinged, and I jumped out of it so it would close and shut up.

I tiptoed along the hallway and froze when I heard voices. There was absolutely no cover in the hall, so I stepped into a patient's room. Some guy was snoring like there was a monster inside him trying to escape. When the footsteps passed, I peeked out and into the hall again. Grandpa's room was the third on the left. I crouched low, hurried down the hall, and sneaked into his room. Shrugging out of my backpack, I let it slip to the floor and went to his bed.

Well, not his bed. It wasn't Grandpa. Not unless he had found a fountain of youth and grown a dark mustache since I'd last seen him. The other bed in the room was empty.

This was the right room, I *knew* it. The one by the water fountain in the hall.

Why wasn't he here? Could it be . . . maybe . . . wait. I rubbed my eye with a gritty knuckle. Maybe they just moved him to another room. Yeah, just a different room. Maybe all the noise on the phone was, you know, from moving the bed and all that equipment. Maybe to a room with life support or something.

Voices came down the hallway. I hid behind the curtain by the empty bed and pressed into the shadowy corner. A nurse came into the room. I could see her outline through the curtain. I held my breath and prayed. She checked the patient and started to leave, then reached down for something.

"What's this? Somebody left a backpack," she said to someone in the hall.

Shoot me now. I'm such a geek.

"Too bad. Send it down to lost and found, I guess," said another voice.

As their voices receded, the nurse added, "Check it for ID first."

I whacked my palm against my forehead and sagged against the wall. There went the rest of my money. Then I remembered that my school ID was on a lanyard inside. I had to get out of there.

I had some change in my pocket. If I could get to a pay phone, I could call and ask the operator which room Grandpa had been moved to.

It was risky, but I had to find my way back along the corridor and get to a phone. Voices came and went. I stepped out from behind the curtain. The patient's heavy breathing kept time with the soft *beep* of the machine beside him. I slipped out, got back into the elevator, and punched the button for the ground floor, bouncing on the balls of my feet to make it hurry.

The elevator opened, and I took it down to the first floor. It opened to another deserted hallway, and I could smell food. I slinked along until I came to a cafeteria. The scent of popcorn and pizza made my stomach growl. I peeked around the corner where people in lab coats and green scrubs were snacking at plastic tables. There was a pay phone on the outside wall by the entrance. If I was quiet, no one would even notice me.

I curled into the phone with my back to the entrance and dug in my pocket for change. Thirty-five cents. Don't screw this up, I told myself. That's all you've got. I looked up the hospital's number again and held my finger on it while I dialed. The operator answered.

"Orville James?" she said in answer to my question. "There's no Orville James registered, ma'am."

"But . . . but he was here. The other day. He broke his hip, and then he had pneumonia."

"One moment, please." There was silence; then she came back. "The patient checked out today."

"Checked out?" Was that code for *permanently*? "But where did he go?"

"I don't have that information, ma'am. Perhaps you could check with his doctor tomorrow," she said in an irritated voice.

I hung up the phone and tried not to cry. He couldn't have gone back home. Grandma couldn't take care of him. Now I couldn't even call her to find out. I was so tired. There was no way I could walk all the way out to their house tonight. What could I do? Where would I stay? I had no plan B.

CHAPTER 37

Marty

I plowed ahead, trying to guess where the bus would pull off to pick up more passengers on its way to Pine Run, and trying to catch it. Maybe they would radio the bus driver to keep her from getting off. But if Andie suspected that she was being watched, she might slip off the bus before it even got to Pine Run to avoid being caught, leaving her miles from safety.

She would never come home willingly unless I promised to take her straight to the hospital first. I would have taken her there anyway. Part of me was angry and didn't want to reward her for her reckless behavior. The other part of me was prepared to give her anything if only I could find her safe.

A light came up in the lane behind, illuminating the interior of the car. I glanced in the rearview mirror, and the car's headlights flashed in my eyes. It changed lanes without signaling and zoomed around on the left as though I were standing still.

This is what I was reduced to. Realizing what was important too late, then chasing it, just out of reach.

The past days and weeks and months of walking on eggshells and denying my longing to be loved by Andie had changed me. It had taken my simple, motherly love for her and made it into an extension of my love for the child I'd lost, until a rejection by Andie was the same as being rebuffed by Ginger.

Deja's accusations played in my head, clinging to me like a heavy mantle of betrayal. I tried to think of times when I'd been unfair to the girls or showed favoritism to Andie. She'd never let me get close, never left herself open to affection. But perhaps I had shielded her from family responsibilities. Made excuses for her cool attitude. Treated her more like a guest than a member of the family. Maybe that alone had placed her on a pedestal in the girls' eyes.

Sure, I told her we wanted her to be herself, but deep down, did I really mean it? If I had, I never would have taken it so personally that she hated coconut. Perhaps I was afraid that if I truly saw her faults and her own uniqueness, I'd have to face the truth that she was nothing like Ginger at all.

Tears kept at bay by sheer determination now clouded my vision, and I brushed them aside to keep focused on the road ahead. I reached into my pocket and clutched the Mickey pin. The cool hardness and glossy surface were softened by the fact that she'd left it for me to find. This child—grieving and vulnerable—had given me something precious to keep us connected.

Maybe it would be best if you went to live with your Uncle Greg at the end of the school year. I was a bad mother.

Plodding along at only fifty miles an hour left plenty of time for self-condemnation. I couldn't even listen to the radio. Every song reminded me of my shortcomings or the futility of loving someone. Listening to the radio was too normal a thing to do.

After a long, gradual climb in elevation, my headlights flashed on a freeway exit sign, and I took the off-ramp. A lone gas station cast a pool of light, and I coasted to a stop beside a pay phone. It was only nine o'clock, but the station was closed and I was alone in the middle of nowhere.

I collected change from the ashtray and called home. Dad answered in the voice he reserved for chastening and worry.

"Where're you at, girl? Don't you turn on your cell phone?"

It was good to hear a familiar voice other than the one in my head telling me I was worthless.

"Sorry, Dad. My cell's dead, but there's probably no signal up here anyway. I'm at a gas station on the freeway, about an hour outside of Pine Run. Did Deja tell you what happened?"

"I cruised in about eight. Deja and Winnie were crying on the couch. Finally got it pieced together. So Andie ran off?"

Deja—crying on the couch?

"Deja told her that her grandfather was dying. I think Andie used Deja's old school ID and bought a bus ticket to Pine Run."

"Well, I'll be. You gassing up?"

I glanced over my shoulder at the empty station. "No, it's closed. I filled up before I left town. Dad, I need you to call the sheriff in Pine Run and tell them to meet the bus. It gets in about fifteen minutes from now. And tell them to check the hospital. I'm pretty sure that's where she's headed."

"Will do. You be careful. Let us know when you find her."

CHAPTER 38

Andie

The thought of spending a cold night outside in that scary meadow freaked me out. I almost missed the "something" about the voices in the lunchroom, but "female minor" put me on alert. I peeked far enough into the lunchroom again to see two uniformed officers showing something to some of the lounging staff, who were shaking their heads. Maybe it was my ID.

I bolted. Walking double-time down the hallway, I darted back under cover when two nurses left their station. I ended up back at the hallway intersection. Which way to the emergency exit? Hiding in the meadow was better than spending the night at juvenile hall. Then my brain kicked in. There was an exit sign on the wall, pointing to the right corridor. Duh.

I cruised through the intersection and down toward the exit. The closer I got, the louder the voices got at the end of the hall. I plastered myself against the wall and peeked around the corner. There, talking to police, between me and the exit, was my Uncle Greg.

He didn't look too happy. I don't think I'd ever seen him looking so uncool, except when he'd been drinking. He must have jumped out of bed. I didn't even know he was in town.

Grandma never told me he was coming. Maybe Marty's little lecture had worked, or maybe he'd come for me. If that was the case, we were starting off totally on the wrong foot.

I strained to hear what they were saying. The words made no sense, but I could tell how they felt about the whole thing. This sick feeling came over me, and I broke out in a sweat.

I backtracked to find the bathroom where I'd first cleaned up. I went in without turning on the light and quietly locked the door. Panting and sweating, with my stomach doing triple axels, I slumped to the floor and put my head between my knees. I could get through this. I had no choice.

The whole idea had been pretty stupid. I wasn't any closer to finding Grandpa, but I was a whole lot closer to doing time. The nurse had called the police, or maybe Marty had.

Was Marty mad, or worried about me, or both? I wondered when she'd finally realized I was gone. I felt like a rat, scaring her like that. She didn't deserve it. She had always been nice to me.

The nausea passed. I felt completely alone in the world—a black hole where a person used to be. I curled up on the floor in a fetal position. The floor tile was cut into a million little squares, all in rows, still sandy from people's shoes. The grit of it dug into my cheek. The toilet gurgled and stopped, knocking far away down the pipes inside the walls.

Reaching up, I locked my finger in the wedding rings and wished Mom and Dad were with me. Lying on the cold tile in the dark, I knew they weren't there and would never be again. Would Marty?

When I left this bathroom and got out of the hospital, I might as well keep on going. Who would want me now? Who wanted a stupid kid who was trouble? I wondered what they did with runaways in Pine Run.

I prayed harder than I'd ever prayed in my life. I told God that I had really, really screwed up this time. I asked Him to help me, because the police were out there. And Uncle Greg. My stomach ached when I remembered his angry face. *And I don't . . . I don't think M-Marty wants me anymore.* I stifled a sob with my arm and pushed my mouth against it until I felt teeth marks breaking the skin. I didn't care. I deserved it. I deserved bad things.

I pulled on the chain so hard, it snapped and stung the back of my neck. Then I remembered the verse Mom had highlighted about me being the "good thing" that God had given her. If she could see me right then, she might rip that page out and light it with a match.

No. No, she wouldn't. It was like a voice spoke those words inside me. No, never. She would never.

Mom loved me, no matter what. No matter what.

I remembered Marty in that silly Halloween costume with the cat ears and the whiskers that wrinkled when she smiled. How she was always taking pictures with her fingernails in front of the lens. That funny, dreamy look on her face when I told her about my Disney pins, and how she cried as though we hadn't only broken Ginger's ornament, but also her heart. How something stupid like a thank-you could make her cry. The times I'd stepped away from her touch so I wouldn't feel the heat of her hand.

But as many times as I stepped away, she'd kept right on tucking a stray hair behind my ear or squeezing my shoulder or patting my arm. What if she never wanted to touch me again?

Suddenly, I knew I didn't want that to happen. "Please, God," I said. "Help me. Send Marty."

Voices went by outside and paused. Someone knocked on the door, and I jumped away. A few seconds later, they moved on. Silence.

I wiped my eyes on my sleeve and took some toilet paper off the roll to blow my nose. It's almost impossible to blow your nose without making any noise whatsoever.

I stared at the door. It could be a trap. Maybe they just made it sound like they were leaving. I pressed my face to the floor, looking for feet in the hallway. There were none as far as I could see in either direction. This was my chance. The bathroom was no longer safe. The janitor would come to clean and find me. It was now or never.

I noiselessly unlocked the door and turned the handle, opening it so just a sliver of light showed. I peeked outside. It was clear.

Look natural, I told myself. I forced myself to stand up straight so I wouldn't attract attention. Who was I fooling? A kid in the hospital at this time of night? I might as well wear a neon sign.

The emergency exit was the fastest way out. It was also the only way I knew. Stopping at the end of the hall, I peeked around to check it out. The floor was strangely quiet. Maybe something was up, or it was just a lucky break for me. Maybe Wednesdays were slow nights. Emergency looked empty. A radio played smooth jazz somewhere.

There was so much open space between me and the exit doors. But if I could get to them, they would automatically open, and I would be outside before they knew it. They'd never catch me in that meadow.

Voices came behind me down the hall. I turned the corner and ran for it. I heard my name and running feet. I was almost free.

I slammed on the black matting in front of the sliding doors that triggered them to open. I lunged at the glass. Bam! I hit the glass like a bug on a windshield and bounced off hard onto my bottom.

They didn't open. The stupid doors didn't open. I pressed my palm onto my forehead. That really hurt. Little shooting stars. Ow.

CHAPTER 39

Marty

I left the pay phone and glanced at a slowly passing pickup, acutely aware of how vulnerable I was in that lone station under a spotlight. I quickly got into the Toyota, locked the doors, and turned the key in the ignition. But when I tried to put the car in reverse, it shivered and jerked.

I killed the motor to keep from making it worse, and watched the pickup move down the road. I tried to think. "Baby it along," Dad had said. The car was clearly on the verge of collapse. If I pushed it to the point of no return, I might never get there. I could lose Andie, or worse. This couldn't be happening.

I sent up a fervent prayer for help and cautiously unlocked the car door to get out. Not knowing what else to do, I opened the hood. If that didn't send a distress signal, nothing did. I closed the hood and called Dad collect.

When I explained the problems I was having, Dad thought for a moment. I could almost hear the gears turning in his head. He asked if I saw any leaks. I told him to hold on, and left the phone dangling while I popped the trunk for a flashlight. The batteries in the flashlight wouldn't connect, and I banged it against my palm, triggering a dim beam of light.

I had to get down on my hands and knees to see beneath the car. My dress slacks and blue sweater would never be the same. Dad was right. A slow drip was leaking onto the blacktop. I reached far underneath and smeared some onto my finger. Then I backed out from beneath the car and shined the flashlight on my finger. I went back to the phone and told him about the pinkish-brown smear on my fingertip.

"Transmission fluid," he said. "I was afraid of that. That's why you're having trouble getting it into gear. You'll have to add fluid."

"Wha—how? The gas station is closed, Dad."

"There's a bottle and a funnel in the trunk."

I sighed deeply, on the verge of tears. The night was passing, and I didn't know where Andie was, and I didn't want to do this. "Did you get the sheriff?"

"Yeah. They're out looking for her." He cleared his throat. "You want me to come up, or can you add the fluid by yourself? You've watched me do it often enough."

I felt relieved that the sheriff would be watching for her, but it wasn't enough. "No, Dad. I can't wait that long. Just tell me what to do."

"All right. First make sure the car is sittin' level. Put it in park and let the engine idle for a while."

Minutes later, I was back with Dad. "Okay, now what?"

"Now, shut it off. You got the tranny fluid and the funnel?"

"Got it."

"The dipstick is situated between the battery and the engine. Got an orange top on it."

"Okay, so I put the fluid in there?"

"You got to check the level first. Wipe the dipstick off with a rag and stick it back in. Then pull it out and check the level at the *hot* mark. If it's low, add a little bit. *Don't* overfill it. And be careful you don't burn yourself."

"Okay. Don't hang up."

"There's a rag under the seat," I heard him say before I left the phone dangling by the cord.

The fluid level looked like bad news to my untrained eye. I removed the cap from the bottle and positioned the funnel in the pipe, letting a small amount of the cherry-syrup fluid trickle down. Then I paused to let it settle in. Juggling the flashlight, the funnel, and the fluid at the same time made it a messy affair. Shining the flashlight into the pipe, and seeing no evidence of fluid, I added a little more. Then I went back to Dad.

"I added about a cup," I guessed. "A cup and a half. Maybe two." I must be losing my touch. I rarely needed to measure. "Do you think that's enough?"

"Don't know. Start her up and check the level again."

I wiped the oily fluid from my hands with the rag, and without thinking swiped at a spot on my sweater, smearing it into an ugly dash. It didn't smell at all like cherry cough syrup.

The fluid level wasn't yet in range. Carefully I dribbled in more fluid, guessing at the amount, while trying to keep my clothes from getting more grease from the car.

The next time I checked, I was good to go.

"I think it's okay now, Dad. The level is between the two hot notches."

"That's my girl. Check it again after you get there. If it keeps leaking, you'll have to add more."

"Pray for me, Dad."

"I will, punkin."

This time I was able to put the car more easily into reverse, back up, and pull out onto the highway. Slipping my seat belt on one-handed, I glanced at the clock. Nine thirty. Did the sheriff have Andie, or was she alone in the night?

Don't think about it, I told myself. For crying out loud, just drive.

I gunned the motor to fifty-five. Fifty minutes later I passed the bright lights of the hospital just off the freeway to my right. I considered taking the exit to the hospital, but drove a half mile farther to the exit for Pine Run. She may not have made it to the hospital yet.

The exit emptied onto a quiet street of closed businesses and a bus stop, which was just a covered bench in full view of any creep lurking nearby. There was no sign of Andie or of patrol cars.

She probably knew the fastest route to the hospital, but I had to keep to the streets. I cruised along in the direction I felt she might have gone, slowing to peek down alleys and into yards, feeling a little like a creep myself.

Outside the town limits, the road funneled down and the sidewalk vanished into scrubby bushes. A full moon cast an eerie glow on the unfamiliar street. Scattered houses with dented, leaning mailboxes backed up to the road, and long driveways crept away from it into gloom. Where the houses ended, tall trees stepped in. The deep spaces beneath their boughs allowed no moonlight through. Across the road, open fields reached out to the distant mirage of parking lot lights. The thought of Andie alone on this stretch of road made me sick.

Please let her be at the hospital, I prayed. Keeping an eye on the shoulder for any sign of her, I made my way down the road and into the hospital parking lot. The front was dark, so I went around to the emergency entrance. Of course, visiting hours were over. It was ten thirty.

A sheriff's vehicle was parked in the emergency driveway. I pulled up behind, forced the car into park, killed the engine, and jumped out. Let them tow it, if they could get it into gear. I ran to the glass doors, ignoring the fear that she might not want me.

That no longer mattered. I had to know where she was.

CHAPTER 40

Andie

Angry hands grabbed me.

"Andie, are you hurt?" Uncle Greg said.

"Don't move her," an officer said, pushing him aside. "Just lie still for a minute," he said to me.

"Andie, what do you think you're doing here?" Uncle Greg demanded.

The policeman told him to back off, in a firm, polite way that Greg didn't argue with. Once they decided I wasn't hurt very badly, they got me an ice pack and sat me in a chair away from the door. The nurse with the ice pack said she had to unlock the emergency doors now. So it was a trap after all.

The officer took out a little notebook. He asked me what my name was.

"Andrea Lockhart. Winslow." I pointed to the backpack the other cop was holding. "That's mine. My school ID is in it." Deja's ID was safely in my back pocket.

He radioed in that I was found and safe and wrote it into his book. I wondered what a rap sheet looked like, and how long mine was going to be.

"Well, Andrea, I'm Officer Dunn. You've got some people mighty worried about you, young lady. You mind telling me why you ran away?" He looked really big in his uniform, with his leather holster squeaking every time he moved.

"I wasn't running away. I just wanted to see my grandpa."

"Is he a patient here?" he asked.

"He was. But he's gone."

"Andie, we moved him to another care facility today," Uncle Greg interrupted.

The policeman gave him a look.

"Well, we did!" Uncle Greg said to the cop, turning away with his hands on his hips.

Officer Dunn gestured to another policeman, who took Uncle Greg across the room. Then he asked me why I left the way I did, and when I explained, it sounded really lame. I could tell he wasn't happy with me. Maybe his shift was supposed to be over, but he had to hang around looking for this crazy runaway. Maybe I interrupted his dinner.

God, what will happen to me now?

The emergency door opened, but I was crying, and all I saw was a blur.

"Andie!"

I rubbed my eyes. Marty. She took a step forward and covered her mouth with her hand. I jumped up and ran to her. She reached out for me, gathering me in. I buried my face in her neck, and she hugged me so tight. It felt so good, like falling into a soft vanilla cloud.

She pulled back my hair and took my face in her hands, examining my forehead.

"Baby, what happened to you?" Her eyes were brimming with tears.

I told her how I hit the door. Officer Dunn came up, and she didn't look too happy with him.

"Are you her mother, ma'am?"

"Yeah, she's my mom," I said.

Marty looked me in the eye, and her face crumpled up. No words came out, but her head bobbled frantically like the hula dancer on the dash of the Dodge.

He wanted to see her ID, just to make sure she wasn't trying to steal me or something. Whatever.

We sat in the waiting room, and Marty kept her arm around me the whole time. I noticed her hair was messed up and her clothes were dirty, so I asked her what happened.

"Just a little car trouble," she said, like it was no big deal.

It took awhile to get everything straightened out at the hospital, but the officer said they didn't need to fingerprint me or take mug shots. I think he just said that to scare me. It was eleven thirty before they said we could go. Uncle Greg said we could spend the night at Grandma's, since it was so late. Marty looked worried at first, not letting go of my hand. But I said I wanted to, and she said okay.

We didn't talk the whole way over to Grandma's in the Toyota. I didn't know what to say. Marty kept looking over at me and squeezing my hand, sniffling and smiling at the same time.

She asked to use Grandma's phone to call Carl so they would know I was safe. I felt really guilty then, because I'd made them all worry about me. Well, maybe not Deja.

The next morning at Grandma's breakfast table, we talked. Uncle Greg had arranged for Grandpa to move to a convalescent hospital, since his hip was healing and Grandma couldn't take care of him alone. I guess Marty had done some good when she told him off on the phone.

I apologized for scaring everybody and promised to never, ever do anything like that again. Marty said Deja felt really bad about the things she'd said. Uncle Greg had called from the hospital to tell me that Grandpa had been moved, and she'd lied about it to scare me.

"Andie," Grandma said, "I have some news. We've sold our house—"

"Oh, Grandma!"

"But I'm afraid we won't be buying another one." Her hand, thin and creased like an old folded map, covered mine on the table. "Honey, we love you very much, your grandpa and I. But we're old, and we can't get around like we used to. It's not the place for a young girl to grow up." She patted my hand. "We're moving to an apartment with people who can help out with things, like doctor visits and meals."

Uncle Greg spoke up. "It's a modern assisted-living facility. It's a great place for Mom and Dad. They won't have to worry about anything. And they'll be with other people. Someone will look in on them every day. I've checked it out. It comes highly recommended. Top of the line."

If it was top of the line, it probably cost him a lot. Maybe Dad was wrong about Uncle Greg being all about money, or maybe Uncle Greg was trying to make up for the times he hadn't been a very good son. Either way, it was a relief to know it wasn't all up to me anymore.

"Now, I need to ask you a question," he said. He glanced at Marty, then back at me. "Robin and I have discussed it, and we're willing to have you come and live with us, Andie, if you want to.

We've already contacted an attorney about it. You probably got the notice about the hearing."

Marty barely breathed.

"We heard that you weren't happy in Newberry with . . . your present family. Now, I'm going to leave it up to you. We don't want to force you into anything. I loved your mom and dad, and I know they'd want you to be happy. So." He put both elbows on the table and steepled his fingers. "What's it going to be? Do you want time to think about it?"

I looked at Marty until she looked back. Her mascara smudged her eyes into shadows, and her hair was clipped all messy on the back of her head. She'd been through a lot for me.

"No. I want to stay where I am," I said to her. "Can I, Marty?"

She squeaked a little gasp, then reached over and squeezed me tight. She was crying, and laughing too. I guess that was a yes.

"Can I still visit Grandma and Grandpa?" I asked.

"As long as you don't pull another stunt like you did last night," she said, trying for serious, but she couldn't help smiling. "As often as we can."

Uncle Greg looked relieved. Maybe he didn't want my money, after all.

"If you want to visit your cousins some time, we'll fly you up," Uncle Greg offered.

"Sure, thanks," I said. I'd file that one away.

After breakfast, we said good-bye to Grandma and Uncle Greg, but before we left, Uncle Greg pulled Marty aside and they talked on the front porch. I could see them through the window. She wiped her eyes with a tissue and put her hand on his arm. Whatever he said must've been a real downer. I wondered if he was straight up about Grandpa's condition.

Marty took me to see Grandpa at the care home before we left.

He was sitting up in bed and still coughing, but he was talking, and Marty said his color was good. I told her how badly he had scared me, barking like a sick seal over the phone, but she explained that it meant his congestion was breaking up. It was a good thing after all.

Neither of us told Grandpa what happened the night before. I didn't want him to feel like he was responsible for my mess.

In the car, I asked her what Uncle Greg was talking to her about on the porch. She said my cousin Kyle had been diagnosed with Niemann-Pick. They'd thought he might get lucky, but he got it late like his brother. They didn't want to tell Grandma and Grandpa, and that's why he and Aunt Robin hadn't been around much. Marty told him to be honest with them.

And then she got serious with me.

"Everybody's glad you're okay and that you're coming back. But, Andie, you can never do something like this to us again, especially not after what we've gone through in the last couple years." She kept her eyes on the road ahead. "If you're going to be part of the family, we have to be able to trust you. And you have to trust us. Do you understand what I'm saying?"

I felt crummy. "Yeah. I'm sorry." My voice sounded hoarse.

She reached across the car seat and cupped my chin in her hand, giving me a tearful smile. "I was afraid of losing another daughter last night."

"I prayed that you would come, Marty. I guess God heard me."

"He heard me too, baby. He always hears us." She wiped her eye with a knuckle. "You know, when you first came to us, I wanted so badly to be a normal family again. Like we were before Ginger died. I probably wasn't fair to you."

I looked up at her, waiting.

"Well, I tried to move on, without really considering everything you were dealing with. I mean, about your parents. Maybe I rushed you a little."

My eyes dropped to a candy wrapper on the floor.

"Is that why you felt you couldn't wait to see your grandpa, because of what happened to your parents?"

I nodded.

"You poor kid. Can you talk to me next time? Tell me how you feel?"

"Okay."

Carl was home when we got there, and he hugged me tight. I think he was surprised that I hugged back. Winnie was glad to see me, and Deja even came out of our room when she heard us come in. She said hi and went back inside.

That night I unpacked my suitcase into my drawers.

I wouldn't say things were great between me and Deja, but the whole episode had released some steam from her jets.

"You okay?" she asked, not looking up from her magazine.

"Yeah."

"Good, 'cause you owe me seventy-five dollars," she said, in her old voice.

"I have some of it in my backpack," I said.

I was handing over thirty dollars when Marty came in and snatched it from my hand.

"Where did you get all this money, Deja?" she said as she counted it.

Deja buried herself in her magazine. "I saved it last summer," she answered.

"And how much was your bus ticket, Andie?" Marty asked.

"Forty-five."

"Seventy-five dollars," she said to Deja. "Where did you get it?"

Deja was silent. Marty turned to me.

"Where did you find the money, Andie?" she asked me.

I looked up in dread. There was a whole roll of money in that jacket pocket. Stuck between Marty and Deja again. This was becoming a habit.

I didn't say anything, but my eyes automatically darted to her closet.

I saw a satisfied look on Deja's face behind the magazine when Marty went through her closet, even checking Ridley's coat pockets. It wasn't surprising that Marty came up empty.

"You and I will be having a discussion before the drive-in opens," she told Deja. "Andie, you will be manning the register all summer."

I may be slow, but by the time Marty left us, I had it all figured out.

"I'm not paying you back that money, after all," I said, grabbing my book and finding my place, propped on my pillow.

Her voice was poisonous. "You what?"

"You stole that money from the drive-in."

She shrugged. "I didn't steal it. I just borrowed it."

That sounded familiar.

"It's the same thing. I'm paying my forty-five dollars back to Marty, not you," I said. "Just remember, I saw that roll of money in your pocket."

"Whatever." She put down her magazine and rolled over on her side facing me. She had a devilish look on her face. "So what's it like, running away? Were you scared?"

I thought about Sylvia in the bus depot and walking to the hospital in the dark and hiding with people chasing me. But I knew that the really scary part was almost losing my way with Marty.

"Yeah. It was scary," I said. "But not like you think." I rolled over with my back to her and buried my nose in my book.

Monday was a school day like any other, just like nothing had happened over the weekend. I wondered if Deja spread the word that I was now a runaway.

Natalie and her friends closed in on me at recess.

"I want to talk to you," she said, hugging her notebook to her chest like a shield of armor.

Her friends turned toward one another, pretending to be talking about something else.

"Okay." We stepped away from them for privacy. I chewed my cuticles, waiting for her to start.

"I heard something, and I want to know if it's true." She looked taller. And really mad. Maybe she was powering up to pound me.

"What?" I asked, trying to sound normal.

"I heard you said my family was a bunch of pathetic losers, and there was no way you would ever come to my house. That we probably had fleas, or lice, or some flesh-eating bacteria."

"What!"

"And that you drew a picture of me on the back of your binder. With horns and junk." She was so in my face, I had to take a step back.

"No, that's Deja! Look." I flipped over my binder and showed her the drawing. "See the heart on her shirt? It says Ridley. And she has a nose ring. She got her nose pierced over spring break."

Natalie backed down a little, but still wasn't convinced.

"Well, maybe you added that so I wouldn't know it was me."

The huddle of girls watched us with hooded snake eyes, and I shifted to move them out of my direct line of sight.

"Who told you this stuff?" I asked.

She hesitated. "Scott."

"Scott Worley? And you believed him?"

She looked over her shoulder at the huddle of girls. "Well, he didn't exactly tell me. But I heard him laughing about it."

Suddenly, it hit me. Deja. Deja must have put him up to it.

"Wait. This all started back when I lost my chain."

I filled her in on the battles that had gone on while Marty was working overtime.

"Why would Scott care about that?" she asked.

"You know his sister, Summer? Well, she's Deja's best friend. They're joined at the hip. She was probably helping Deja get payback. You know, for making it look like she had my chain." It had worked too, I thought to myself.

Natalie thought about it for a long time. I could see it playing on her face.

"Natalie, why would I say that stuff about you?" I asked. "You're the only friend I have here."

Her grip on her notebook loosened, and she rested it on her hip. She chewed her bottom lip. I could almost hear the wheels grinding in her head.

"But that day I asked you to go to the mall after church, you guys weren't doing anything. Why didn't you come?" she asked.

That was a tough one. I wasn't sure myself, but I had to make it good.

"I was scared," I said.

"Scared?" She sounded offended. "Of what?"

"It wasn't you, or your family, or anything. I don't know." I stared at the ground, trying to conjure courage from the asphalt.

"It's just that I haven't had a friend in a long time. And . . ."

She waited. I shifted on my feet.

"And I didn't want to be sorry when it was time to go back home to Pine Run."

"Oh." Her shoulders sagged. "We could still write. I mean, if you want."

The bell rang, and I smiled. "I'm not going anywhere. I'll tell you at lunch."

The bird lady came by again. This time she seemed nicer, and she smiled when I went to stand next to Marty and put my arm around her waist. I convinced her that Cyclops never came into the house anymore, which was true because she had six kittens in the garage and never left them alone. I even tried to give the lady a kitten, but she sneezed when I held one up to her face.

I asked Marty if the lady would come back, and what about court. The court date was in June. She said her attorney, Mr. Walker, said there wouldn't be any problem that he could see. Since I wanted to stay there, and Grandma and Grandpa didn't have a place for me to live with them, and Uncle Greg had decided not to fight for me, the judge would probably let me stay. But I could visit Grandma and Grandpa any time I wanted. And Ms. Wren wouldn't be coming back very often.

Marty wasn't baking so much anymore. You could open the freezer without triggering an avalanche of cookies and bread. She could even make coconut dandies without shorting out.

The first day I dug out shorts from my dresser, the windows were open in the house and you could smell the mowed grass.

Somebody in the neighborhood fired up a barbecue. It was the middle of May, and Marty's little tire-boats in the yard were blooming with flowers, and the birds were singing like crazy.

I passed barefoot by the kitchen in the afternoon and saw this strange guy sitting at the table. Not strange, like a skinhead with pentagrams around his neck, just different. He was dressed nice, like a dad.

Marty and Winnie stood by the sink with Winnie's arms wrapped around her waist. Marty smiled kind of embarrassed, because the man was eating one of her cookies and his eyes were rolling back in his head.

Marty looked really pretty. Happy. Her hair was up in a ponytail with little wispies hanging down, and her cheeks were pink, and she was biting her lip. He said something about her bakery, and she laughed and said it was the Blue Moon Bakery. Then she saw me. She introduced me as her daughter, and that felt weird, in a nice way. I remembered seeing him at church.

He said, "Hey, kiddo," and smiled.

He seemed like the kind of person that it was okay if he acted like he already knew you.

CHAPTER 41

Marty

The phone rang what sounded like years away, and I fought the urge to hang up before anyone answered. Please don't let Starr answer, I sent heavenward. Part of me hoped for an answering machine to pick up instead of a human being. The other part knew that a message, if I left one, would probably just get erased.

Russell answered. "Y'ello."

My mouth went dry, but my heart didn't do cartwheels this time. "Russell, it's me. Marty."

"Marty. So . . ." He paused. I imagined him glancing over his shoulder or curling into the phone to discourage Starr from overhearing. "What's up? Starr put the check in the mail last week; I know that."

"It's not about the child support." I plunged in. "You got a pencil?" I paused. "Newberry District Cemetery. Row ten. About halfway down. Hers is a flat granite marker on the ground. There's a big, rose-colored monument to the right of it that always has teddy bears and balloons around it."

"Wait."

I heard rummaging.

"Okay." He repeated slowly, "Newberry District Cemetery. Ten, halfway down."

"I thought you should know.

"Thanks, Marty."

"Good-bye, Russell."

I went out to the garage. The Sons of the Pioneers were singing about cool, clear water on Dad's old cassette player. I decided to upgrade him to a CD player for his birthday before the cassette player died and he had no music to work by. Of course, that meant replacing all his cowboy music.

He was cleaning out and washing the vehicles. I folded his maps to store away for next winter, along with the tire chains and horse blankets. A map of the Southeast was in the mix. Florida figured prominently on the cover.

I held it up questioningly. "Dad?"

He paused in his work and wiped suds from his cheek. "Thought I might take an extra week or two next winter."

"Tell Charles hello for us."

The white sheet was draped over a still form against the wall of the garage. Taking a corner of the sheet, I pulled it off, revealing a standard wheelchair without any fancy bells or whistles or motors. It was dusty and cobwebby, but otherwise intact. It was only a wheelchair, after all. Nothing more.

Dad came over to stand by me. After a moment I said, "I guess it's time to pass it along."

"You sure?"

I nodded. "Yeah. I'm sure."

Dad bundled the sheet and used it to swipe at the biggest webs. "I'll get it cleaned up. Any idea who could use it?"

"I know someone who might."

Dad unfolded the wheelchair and started to clean it up while I went to my bedroom.

Ginger's special box occupied the right half of the top shelf of my bedroom closet. Dislodging it was tricky, and involved reorganizing other things jammed in around it. I wrestled it down amid falling hats and high school yearbooks, and set it on my bed. Opening it could be like a Christmas gift or Pandora's box.

I lifted the lid and set it aside. It contained the normal baby stuff, just like Winnie's and Deja's boxes. Soon I would have Andie's keepsake box too. Her grandmother had promised we could take it when we went up next month to help them pack for their move. They couldn't take much with them to the assisted-living facility. Andie had told me she wanted the Christmas decorations from her old house on Evergreen. I'd promised to drive by her old house so she could see it again.

Under Ginger's infant dresses and yellowing satin baby shoes, and the old immunization records and her birth certificate, were cards of condolence. I shuffled through until I found the one I was looking for. It was from a family we'd met through the hospital who had two children with Niemann-Pick, and two younger kids healthy at the time. I hoped they still were. I tore off the return address on the envelope. If they didn't need the wheelchair, they could probably put me in touch with someone who did.

As I was putting the lid back on the box, I saw Ginger's hospital identification bracelet lying beneath her stuffed bunny, and fished it out. It was a piece of plastic with a snippet of paper inside, the ink on the name staining the paper blurry. *Winslow, Matilda female #19356 10/31/93.*

Funny, seeing my name there on the bracelet that started it all, so small and tight and hardly looking as if it had ever fit a human wrist.

In some ways, I guess we all start out fitting snugly into who we are. We come into the world with our days laid out before us. God's name stamped on us. Then we strain against it—break free. Lose our identities. We end up belonging only to ourselves, or worse, to some dark, unnameable guilt or self-hatred or bitterness. Then, miraculously, like a jealous parent, God comes to reclaim us. He fits us with a life that once again has Himself written all over it. *She's My child,* I imagine Him saying. *I reclaim her.*

When you look at it that way, I guess you could say we're all switched at birth.

CHAPTER 42

Andie

The drive-in reopened on Memorial Day weekend. We restocked the snack shack with junk food, paper cups and straws, paper towels, toilet paper, and pizza.

There was one new addition—the meadow picture of Winnie and me that Carl mounted on the wall behind the cash register.

Marty asked me to record the phone message for the season. The end of the recording meant something special to me: "Tuesday night is only four dollars a car, because it's family night at the Blue Moon."

That's because it's my family now. Even though I don't understand everything that happened, I think God knew what He was doing. He heard me when I was in trouble, just like Marty said. And when I lost my parents, He had another family waiting to love me. Marty said I have to trust Him to work things out for me. When I compare it to my way of working things out, I think it's way better to let Him do it.